THE CAPTAIN OF HER HEART

"What the hell are you doin' out here, woman?"

Dominique froze. "I-I was looking for you, Captain Hawkins. I just wanted to th-thank you for saving us today." She turned to leave. Cole felt a long-forgotten sensation tear at his chest; a resurrection of feelings he did not want to bring to the surface again. "Wait," he called out.

Her steps halted at once.

Cole cursed himself for speaking before he had a chance to think about his actions. She turned around to face him. He noticed how, even in the near-darkness, her eyes glistened like jewels.

"Monsieur?" she asked in a whisper.

Cole reached out and slid one hand around her neck, his other hand wrapped around her slender waist. He pulled her up against his taut body with one forceful motion, and his lips descended until they connected with hers.

A kiss was the last thing Dominique expected from this man. She gasped for breath when the captain's lips released her throbbing mouth. He leaned ba̶̶ ̶ ̶t̶ill held tight to her waist. Fleetingl̶ ̶ ̶ ̶ ̶ ̶ to pull away—to ̶ ̶ ̶ ̶ ̶ ̶e didn't want to ̶ ̶ ̶ ̶ ̶d him to keep h̶ ̶ ̶ ̶ ̶ ̶ain and again . . .

VERONICA BLAKE

YUKON LOVE SONG

ZEBRA BOOKS
KENSINGTON PUBLISHING CORP.

ZEBRA BOOKS are published by

Kensington Publishing Corp.
475 Park Avenue South
New York, NY 10016

First Printing: November, 1993

Printed in the United States of America

DEDICATION

Throughout the years—all the good times, bad times, and the craziness of my life—I have always been able to count on two very special friends. This book is dedicated to Carol Lewis and Marie Riley . . . thank you for being there, and, most of all, for understanding.

Prologue

San Francisco, June 1898

"Top dollar paid for suitable mail-order brides for lonely gold miners in the Yukon territory." Brigitte Laval read the newspaper heading out loud. There was little enthusiasm—or interest—in her voice. Her gaze leveled on her daughter's face. Beneath the flimsy silk material of her dressing gown, Brigitte's shoulders gave a careless shrug. A cynical laugh echoed through the small room as she narrowed her heavily made-up lashes, adding, "There's plenty of lonely men right here in San Francisco, ma petite, and a woman doesn't have to freeze her fanny off or marry any of 'em either."

Still chuckling, Brigitte glanced down at the newspaper again. Then her head jerked up, her eyes widening as she looked towards her daughter. "Surely you're not considering doing this?"

Dominique Laval gave a defiant toss of her head and coolly met her mother's gaze. Dominique could remember when both of them had eyes the same shade of azure blue, and her mother's hair had been as black as her own. Now Brigitte's vibrant-hued eyes were faded. They lacked the luster that had once lit their jeweled depths, and her hairline showed streaks of gray. Dominique knew they had nothing else in common, either.

"That's why I'm here," Dominique said. Her gaze flitted around the shabby room and an expression of compassion clouded her expression. In the twenty years of her life—from Paris to San Francisco, she had seen dozens of brothels and each one had seemed worse than the last. "I am doing more than just considering it. My bags are already packed and waiting for me down on the wharf."

Brigitte's lips, heavy with red lipstick, parted as a stunned gasp escaped. She shook her head from side to side, and didn't appear to notice when her pearl-studded comb slid from her hair and dropped silently on the worn red carpet. A cascade of dark tangled hair fell around her shoulders as she spoke. "I knew you would hate being a maid. How you could scrub other people's floors for these past couple of years I'll never understand, especially after I spent all that hard-earned money to see to it that you attended the best schools wherever we went."

"I didn't hate being a maid," Dominique

8

said in defense. "It's just that I don't want to be a maid for the rest of my life." She dropped her hands to her sides defeatedly. Her mother always managed to remind her of the sacrifices she felt she had made in order to send her to private schools. Dominique knew she had been lucky, too. If her mother had not sent her to those schools, she would have grown up in the different bawdy houses where her mother worked. "I really do appreciate all that you've done for me, Maman. But my schooling didn't teach me how to earn a livelihood, and being a maid did bring in a decent wage." She refrained from adding that she would rather scrub floors and wash dished forever if it meant she would not have to resort to the type of life her mother lived.

"But, this is foolishness," Brigitte said. She waved the newspaper in front of Dominique's face. A worried frown creased a deep line between her eyes. "Have you thought of the hardships a woman would suffer on a journey such as this? Even if you do make it to this God-forsaken Yukon place alive, then you're stuck with some disgusting old miner who is so desperate for a woman that he has to pay—" Brigitte's words stopped abruptly. She felt a heated blush began to work its way through her pale cheeks. Her gaze locked with Dominique's.

"Haven't you always wanted me to follow in your footsteps, Maman?" As the words slipped past her lips, Dominique's body stiffened with guilt.

Brigitte tossed the newspaper down on the red bedspread, walked to the window and pulled back the heavy tapestry drapes; she avoided looking at Dominique. Sunlight flooded the dark room, the brightness making the gold and red decor seem tawdry.

Dominique studied the small form standing at the window. Framed in the harsh rays of sunlight the lines of age were evident in Brigitte's face. She looked old—haggard—and she wasn't even forty! Her clinging dressing gown revealed the outline of a body that had known the touch of far too many men. Dominique closed her eyes, then turned away from the pitiful sight of her mother. She cleared her throat, loudly. "Well, I'd better go. I just wanted to bid you adieu."

Brigitte dropped the curtain, shutting out the sunshine. She swung around abruptly, her gaze seeking Dominique's face in the dim light. They stared at one another until Brigitte could no longer stand the silence. "This could be the last time we'll see each other, ma pauvre petite," she said. Her voice was barely more than a whisper.

"We'll see one another again—someday, Maman." A heavy lump settled in the pit of Dominique's stomach.

The hint of a smile curved Brigitte's lips. "Someday? Well, maybe your rich gold miner husband will bring you back to San Francisco . . . someday."

Dominique gave a shrug, but her eyes revealed the pain she wanted to deny. A fleeting image of her mother's life passed through Dominique's mind; dirty barrooms, drunken men with groping hands, slobbery kisses. Dominique cringed inwardly. She lived with never-ending fear that she would end up just like her mother. Since she had graduated from finishing school at sixteen, she had worked as a maid here in the bay city. Her employment for the rich and elite had only intensified her determination to find a life of respectability for herself. But here, on San Francisco's Barbary Coast, there was no opportunity for the daughter of a well-known prostitute. As a stranger in the Yukon, Dominique hoped there would be a chance for her.

"Adieu, ma chere Maman," Dominique said. "I'll never forget all that you've done to help me." Her voice was hoarse, her eyes misted with tears she would not allow to fall. There was nothing left to say. She took a step toward the door, but something compelled her to turn around toward her mother again. She returned to Brigitte and embraced her, breathing the familiar smells of whiskey, sweat, and even the smell of stale sex that emanated from the older woman. But a deep sense of sorrow filled her heart. She wanted to remember her mother in a different way . . . wanted to remember everything good about this woman who had given birth to her twenty years ago.

"Adieu, and bonne chance" Brigitte whispered as she pulled back. There were tears sliding down her face, leaving grimy rivulets in her makeup. Brigitte's mouth opened slightly as if there was something else she wanted to say. But, in spite of her emotional display, she remained silent.

Dominique made no attempt to speak either. She wished she could explain her feelings to her mother, but they had never talked much. Brigitte did not know that while her daughter was growing up she would fill her empty hours roaming through the affluent parts of town. Dominique would try to imagine the interiors of those beautiful homes, and the lives of the families who lived in them. She vowed to herself that someday she would find that kind of home and respectability for herself.

Dominique stared at her mother for an instant as they embraced. A wave of forgiveness washed through Dominique, but at the same time the need to escape beckoned. A poignant smile curved her lips as she released her hold on her mother and again turned to leave.

The sense of release stayed with Dominique as she left the brothel and headed down the boardwalk towards the dock. In her coat pocket she carried a ship's ticket, and more money than she had ever imagined she would possess; a total of five hundred dollars. The money and the ticket were part of her dowry. Jack Scroggins—her future husband—had sent them to her after she had responded to the newspaper advertisement.

Jack Scroggins.

His mere name conjured up images in Dominique's mind of a hard-working, God-fearing man; an adventurer who had headed off to the untamed Yukon in search of his fortune.

Jack Scroggins.

An excited shiver raced through Dominique. Jack Scroggins had found his fortune on the frozen northern shores. Dominique sensed that in the distant Yukon Territory all of her dreams would come true, too.

One

Cole Hawkins had awakened in a foul mood, and his temperament was not improved by the time his passengers boarded the riverboat at noon. "There they are," he said sarcastically, with an abrupt wave of his arm toward his passengers. "Gold-diggin' whores— all of 'em."

Luther Allen grunted in reply. His gaze scanned the women who were crowding the steamer's deck. He had to agree with his captain. More than likely, most of the women who had signed on for this journey were prostitutes who saw this as an opportunity to become the wife of a wealthy gold miner. "There's some might pretty ones among the lot," Luther said. He heard the captain give an indignant huff.

Cole crossed his arms over his chest. "A beautiful woman is a man's destruction, Luther."

Luther smirked. He'd known Cole Hawkins

for close to fifteen years. Not once could he remember the captain taking up with an ugly woman. "Guess you'd be speakin' from experience then," Luther said. Another snide grin curled his lips when he noticed the dark scowl Cole cast in his direction.

"I'd best be gettin' down there," Cole said, ignoring Luther's insinuation. "By the time I'm through with those hussies they'll be wishin' they could crawl back to whatever alley they came from." With a smug toss of his head, Cole walked toward the stairway leading to the lower deck.

As he followed, Luther had the urge to laugh, but he refrained. With a whole boat full of 'fallen angels,' Luther figured Cole would be like a little boy in a candy store.

The activity on the lower deck was chaotic. The constant chatter of female voices and giddy laughter filled the air. Distinctive scents of cheap perfumes mingled with the smells of the river. Cole gave another disgusted grunt as he and Luther stopped before the group of women.

Within seconds of the men's appearance the noise began to die down. Dominique ignored the muffled giggles that still echoed through the crowd as she focused her attention on the scowling captain and his first mate. The taller man, she noticed, took a casual stance, with long, muscled legs spread slightly, hands clasped behind him. His expression, however, was not so relaxed. Beneath thick, dark brown lashes, his gray eyes glittered with impatience. Locks of hair in a rich, deep shade of chestnut brown—tousled from the wind—tumbled over Cole's forehead and past the collar of his navy-blue pea coat. Framed by the thick hair was a face tanned dark and, Dominique thought, ruggedly handsome, with an aura of mystery enhanced by a scar that drew a straight line beside his left eye and ended just below his cheekbone.

Before Cole spoke, he let his gaze wander over the entire crowd again. His piercing stare silenced the last of the women's giggles and whispers. A barely-noticeable grin lifted the left side of his mouth when he realized he had every woman's complete attention. He allowed the silence to hang over the crowd for a few more seconds. His crooked grin became more visible.

"Good day, *ladies*," Cole said. He put an emphasis on the last word, which suggested he was making a crude joke. "Welcome aboard The Lady Susanah." Cole glanced around the deck of the large riverboat, then his eyes narrowed as his gaze swept over the women once more.

He motioned toward Luther, "This is First Mate Allen." The two men nodded their heads at one another in a gesture of respect. "And I'm Captain Hawkins," Cole announced when he turned back to face his passengers. He leaned forward slightly. "This means I make all the rules." With one long stride,

Cole closed the distance between himself and the women. His gaze did not focus on any one face as he continued to speak. "And while you're passengers on my boat you will abide by all my rules."

Cole's chin tilted upward and his shoulders squared. He lowered his intimidating stare toward the woman who stood closest to him. Unintentionally, he allowed himself to gaze into her blue eyes, the bluest eyes, Cole was sure, he'd ever glimpsed. He stared at her for a moment longer. A mild sense of surprise filtered through him when he noticed that her face was free of the heavy face paint most of the other women wore on their cheeks and lips. He tried to divert his attention, but he couldn't look away from her. His gaze traveled lower until he had studied her from head to toe. Again, he was surprised. The style of her dress, and even her hair, was sensible and conservative. For a whore, he told himself, she was unusual. He blinked, then cleared his throat, loudly. He forced himself to look away from the dark-haired beauty.

"Uh—I'm th-the captain," Cole stammered. A nudge from Luther's elbow snapped Cole back to his senses. "As I already stated," Cole added. His voice regained its tone of authority. He did not have to look at Luther to know the expression his first mate would be wearing. Nor did he have any doubts what Luther was thinking right now, either. But this time Luther was wrong. Cole had sworn to himself

18

that he was not going to sample one morsel from this smorgasbord of femme fatales—no matter how tempting she might be.

"My rules are simple," Cole continued. He began to stalk back and forth in front of the women. "No fighting, no whining, and no complaining, 'cause it won't do you any good. You sleep where you're assigned, eat what is served, and keep my boat clean. Above all, you stay out of my way." Cole stopped pacing, glanced down at the blonde harlot in front of him. There was nothing about this one that tempted him as he added, "And I'll stay outta your way."

He resumed his pacing. "The men who hired you to come to the Yukon Territory have paid handsomely for your safe passage." Cole's voice assumed a patronizing tone. "But, money can't buy everything."

The captain halted beside Luther again. A brisk breeze flitted across the deck. The strong odor of fish from the fishing boats in the harbor dominated the air when the wind blew. Most of St. Michael's dock was lined with steamers that were preparing to transport anxious passengers up the Yukon. The wide expanse of the river was black with what seemed like an endless line of steamboats. Their route was the most expensive one to Dawson City—the gateway to the rich gold fields of the Yukon Territory. But the river was somewhat easier than the alternatives, which included long, treacherous treks over snow-laden mountain passes that were already overcrowded with gold-seeking stampeders from all parts of America and Canada.

"Money means nothing to this river," Cole continued. He looked upstream of the mighty Yukon. Soon, her murky waters would be afloat with riverboats and the rough-hewn rafts that were being built by eager miners on the banks of the river. Cole swept his arm through the air, motioning at the river. "The Yukon has her own set of rules. In places, she is as serene and content as a sleepin' babe. In other places, her white-water rapids and deep undercurrents are vicious and deadly."

Cole's tone of voice and his serious expression left no invitation for comments. "For the next one thousand and seven hundred miles, all of us are at this river's mercy."

An oppressive silence reigned. Then, a softly accented voice broke into the quiet.

"Monsieur? Captain?"

Cole knew—even before he turned around—that the woman who had just spoken was the blue-eyed beauty he had noticed earlier. His vow to stay away from his female passengers was pushed to the back of his mind the moment he heard her speak. Her accent—and manner of addressing him—was proof of her nationality, and Cole had a real weakness for Frenchwomen. As he turned to look in her direction, he caught a glimpse of Luther's smirking countenance. A threatening scowl consumed Cole's face, but it did nothing to intimidate his first mate. Luther's dark blonde beard and mustache separated as his sly grin widened. He met Cole's narrowed gaze, but only for an instant before Cole's attention was turned to the woman.

Dominique took a step forward, stopping several feet away from the captain. With difficulty, she swallowed the heavy lump in her throat. "I just wish to correct something you said, Monsieur."

Cole's penetrating gray eyes focused with Dominique's blue gaze. He'd always loved the way those Frenchwomen said, "Monsieur." He especially liked it if they called him that in the most heated moments of passion. The thought gave rise to a slow ache in Cole's loins. He felt a rush of heat blanket his face as he tried to remind himself of his vow—and of his reasons for making that vow. Cole knew from his own experience that there wasn't a whore alive who couldn't be bought for a dollar or two. The idea of hard-working gold miners giving up the biggest portion of their fortunes for this bunch of so-called "mail-order brides" disgusted him.

As the seconds passed, and their gazes continued to drill into one another, Dominique was overcome by uneasiness. The captain's cold stare almost seemed to strip away all of her defenses. But she refused to allow her insecurities to show as she continued to stare up at him.

"Was I mistaken about something?" Cole

asked. His attention was drawn to the way her lower lip curved outward into a slight pout, and his male senses were once again alerted. One thick brow cocked slightly above the eye narrowly missed by a deep scar.

"Yes, Monsieur. You insinuated that we are merely property, and that we are for hire." Dominique was grateful her voice did not reveal the shaking she felt inside. Her bravery began to gain strength and she gave her head a haughty toss. "Myself, along with these other women, are betrothed to the men who paid for our passage from San Francisco to Dawson City." The twenty-two women who stood on the deck shook their heads in agreement. An assortment of indignant mutters echoed across the deck.

The left corner of Cole's mouth quivered slightly as he resisted the urge to laugh. Beside him, he heard Luther chuckle. "Well, I reckon I might've been mistaken." He leaned down until his face was only inches away from the woman's as he added, "But you'd have to prove to me that I was wrong." His voice was slow, and filled with indecent innuendo. He noticed a reddened blush flare through her cheeks—and once again he noticed how lovely she was, especially now that her lower lip was draped into such a tempting and kissable pout. Then, as if he was doused with a splash of freezing water, Cole's mind flashed back to memories he had not recalled for a long time; recollections of emotions that went far deeper than his disgust for the plight of these women, and much, much deeper than the desire this woman's presence evoked. The scar on the side of his face began to burn.

"Take over," he said to Luther as he swung around and stalked past him.

Cole's sudden departure induced a wave of murmuring among the women. His unexpected retreat left Luther speechless for a minute, although he was sure he knew what was eating at the captain's insides. Frenchwomen always affected Cole in a strange way. His passion for females of French descent was Cole's curse, and he had been cursed ever since that messy affair in France a few years ago. Luther cleared his mind of those unpleasant memories, and tried to concentrate on the business at hand. He leveled his gaze on the pretty brunette. She was staring at the closed door where the captain had disappeared. Her narrowed eyes and tight mouth made her anger obvious.

"We'll set sail immediately," Luther announced. "Get settled in, and if you have any problems see me." Luther made a point of emphasizing his last statement by hitting his hand against his chest.

With an aggravated toss of her dark head, Dominique gathered up her skirt. She hesitated as she glanced back toward the captain's cabin. Instinctively, she looked at the first mate. He met her gaze, then gave his head a negative shake. His expression contained an unspoken warning. A feeling of defeat crept through Dominique as they stared at one another. Something told her that she would not get past the first mate if she attempted to go to the captain's cabin. Before they docked in Dawson City, though, Dominique was determined to have Captain Hawkins' apology. At this time, however, it appeared she had no choice but to retreat to the crowded cabin she would share with three other women during this last leg of her journey.

From San Francisco to St. Michael, in the Yukon Territory, Dominique had travelled on a huge ship called the Excelsior. Seasickness had haunted her for the first few days. Once her queasiness had passed, the last week of the ocean voyage was uneventful—with the exception of an occasional outburst from one or more of the women. A feeling of despair closed around Dominique as she glanced at her three cabin mates. One woman—a buxom blonde who went by the name of Silver Belle—was settling down on her bunk. Oblivious to anyone else, Silver Belle took a swig from the flask of whiskey she always carried, and which to Dominique's amazement, never seemed to run dry.

The other two women, Lulu and Eva Marie, looked like they could be from the same mold as Dominique's mother. Their faces were coated with gaudy make-up. Elaborate hairstyles topped their heads, and their flamboyant garments were not proper attire for traveling. Dominique sighed as she plopped down on her own bunk. It was no wonder Captain Hawkins had insinuated they were all harlots.

"Our captain sure seems to have a helluva big chip on his shoulder," Lulu said. Her bright red lips curved into a taunting grin as she glanced at Dominique.

"Even with that scar, he's a handsome devil," Silver added. Several loud hiccups escaped from her mouth as she twisted the cap back on her flask, then slipped it into the pocket at the side of her fuchsia satin dress.

"He's hateful and rude." Dominique rose up from her bunk. The lurching of the steamer pulling away from the dock made her grab for the nearest wall.

Lulu giggled. She glanced at her companions, and winked. "I wonder how he got that nasty scar?"

Silver and Eva Marie joined Lulu in a round of giggling and speculation over the possibilities of the captain's injury.

A disgruntled snort was Dominique's reply to their comments. The thought of spending the next week cooped up with these three trollops made Dominique feel as if her seasickness was returning. She thought it ironic that she had embarked on her journey to escape from this type of influence and she was headed for the desolate Yukon Territory with a riverboat full of women who were just like her mother.

The boat took a sharp turn. Its timbers shuddered. The sound of water lapped against the sides of the steamer. To Dominique's dismay, the noise did not drown out the women's high-pitched giggling.

"I bet he got that scar fighting over a woman's honor," Eva said.

"Or battling pirates on the high seas," Lulu added.

Silver belched loudly. "Naw. He probably got in a drunken brawl in some whorehouse and—"

Dominique's head grew light. Her stomach did another flip-flop. "I need some air," she said. She jumped to her feet and wasted no time escaping from the tiny berth. The upper deck offered little relief. Some of the other women milled around on the deck, a couple of others leaned over the rail and peered down into the murky river water. Dominique made her way to the end of the ship and found an empty stretch of rail.

Another cool breeze whipped across the deck and several long strands of her hair tossed around Dominique's face. The bulk of her ebony hair was secured in a tight bun at the nape of her neck. Unconsciously, she brushed back the loose tendrils with her fingers. As her gaze rose to the stern, a funny sensation gripped her.

The captain was standing at the bow. Below him, on the front of the bow, were elegantly painted black letters spelling out the name of the steamer, The Lady Susanah. Captain Hawkins seemed oblivious to everyone and everything around him. Not able to help herself, Dominique stared at him. His tall form was unmoving as he looked straight ahead. His well-built body sloped forward in a casual manner as his hands gripped the rail. The tension he had shown when he had addressed her earlier seemed gone; now, he exuded power and confidence that induced a feeling of security in Dominique.

As if he felt her presence, Cole turned around. Their eyes locked for a moment. Then, he pivoted briskly, and walked out of Dominique's line of vision.

She continued to stare at the empty space where he had been. The sense of comfort she had previously felt fled with him. Dominique shivered, and wrapped her arms around herself protectively. She looked at the other women who stood along the rail. No matter how hard she tried to deny it she had to admit they were all alike in certain ways. Their destination provided all of them with a new start—and common goals—which included the respectability of marriage. But none of them had any way of knowing what really awaited them in Dawson City.

Dominique realized the captain's negative attitude was beginning to affect her enthusiasm for this journey. She was determined not to allow him this satisfaction. Uninvited, his taunting image remained in her mind, his belittling words still burning in her ears. What had he meant when he said she would have to prove to him that he was wrong about her?

When she reached Dawson City—she told herself—she would never have to prove anything to anyone again. Jack Scroggins would be a good husband; her wedding would be beautiful . . . and she would be perfectly respectable—in spite of people like that hateful Captain Hawkins.

Two

Dominique raised her fist to the closed door. The weather had been horrible ever since they had departed from St. Michael, and she had not seen Captain Hawkins the entire time. Rain, sleet, and icy winds had forced many of the smaller steamers to stay in the port of St. Michael. The Lady Susanah, along with several others, had pushed on to Dawson. The wisdom of this decision was questionable now. Visibility was obscured because of the rain and dense fog. Other than trekking to the Grand Cabin three times a day for their meals, the passengers had hardly left their staterooms. But, a short time ago, the rain had decreased. Dominique took this opportunity to try to talk to the captain.

The long, boring days left her with little to do but think about her reasons for coming to the Yukon Territory. The captain's degrading remarks were still lodged in her memory, and she tried to convince herself that her reason for coming to see him now was simply to clear the air—to make him understand that not all the women who were going to Dawson City were whores. One woman Dominique had met was a schoolmarm from Nevada who was afraid she would be an old maid if she didn't seize this opportunity. And there was another woman who used to be married to a rancher down in Texas. Her husband had died three years earlier, so now the widow was looking for adventure without compromising her morality.

Dominique had overheard a comment from one of the crewmen at breakfast this morning, too. The man's remark had been similar to the captain's insinuation, and it had fueled Dominique's determination to change the attitude of all the men on this boat.

Dominique had an ulterior motive, too. For her own self-respect, it was important for her to keep reaffirming the reason she had taken Jack Scroggins' money and embarked on this mission.

Standing in front of Captain Hawkins' cabin—prepared to knock on his door—Dominique sensed she was wasting her time. She kept remembering the way he had stared at her the other day, when he had been standing at the bow. A cold chill raced through her at the memory.

Dominique pulled her hand back from his cabin door. She clutched the front of her raincoat together as another downpour assaulted the steamer. An unexplained sense of panic washed through her. She knew she had to get away from here before Captain Hawkins discovered her lurking outside his door. She turned around, desperate to make a rapid retreat, and a startled gasp caught in her throat.

"Are you lookin' for me?" Cole said. There was a note of impatience in his voice. A black beret sat crookedly on his wet curls. Raindrops hung from the short stubble of whiskers that darkened his jaw. The tiny lines that added character to his face were creased with dirt as if he had been doing hard labor. His wet clothes—black wool trousers and the navy-blue pea coat—were also coated with mud. Dominique had an impulsive urge to wipe the grime away from his scar with her fingertips. In spite of his rude behavior she found herself wondering when and how he had gotten this injury.

When she made no attempt to reply to his question, he grunted with impatience. "I'm in a hurry," he said as he pushed past her. He shoved open his cabin door. It thudded against the interior wall with a loud bang.

Foreboding inched through Dominique as she stared at the captain's dishevelled state. "Has something happened, Monsieur?" she asked.

Cole didn't glance in her direction. He dug through a small tool box that sat in the corner. When he located the tool he was searching for, he turned around. For a second he allowed his gaze to rest on Dominique's worried face. He blinked as though he was trying to clear away her image. Then, he gave his head a negative shake. "The river's been low this summer. Now with all this rain fallin' all at once, the water's been swallowed up by muddy tidal flats."

When he made no further attempt to explain the seriousness of the problem, Dominique's sense of doom abounded. "Mon Dieu! Are we sinking then?" she asked in a worried tone of voice. A dozen terrified thoughts pounded through her head. She'd thought this last portion of her journey would be the least eventful, and she was completely unprepared to encounter this impending disaster.

Though it was his intention to push past her without hesitation, Cole halted his brisk stride. He stared down at her as he wondered if all Frenchwomen's accents became more pronounced when they became excited or nervous. He recalled how difficult it was to understand Susanah when she was anxious about something. Cole's brief journey into the past was interrupted by a sudden gust of icy wind that whipped across the deck like a cutting edge. The ship lurched violently to its side and Cole stumbled forward. Instinctively, he reached out to Dominique.

The sudden tilt of the ship left Dominique grasping for something to hold onto. She grabbed Cole's arm, and clung to him like she was drowning. Cole saw the panic in her face. Briefly, compassion overwhelmed his stony heart. But just as quickly, his armor was once again in place. He pulled his arm away from Dominique's clinging fingers. She wavered as though she was going to fall down. He made no attempt to help her this time.

"I've gotta go." he said. "You'd best get back to your cabin and stay there," he added as he turned to leave.

Dominique leaned against the outer wall of the captain's stateroom until her shaky legs felt strong enough to support her weight. The cold wind left her shivering; the rain that fell in pounding droplets soaked through her clothes, and the vicious rocking of the ship left her head spinning. But the urgency in the captain's voice chilled her to the bone. She turned to call out to him. Only the foggy rain-drenched corridor greeted her frightened gaze. The iron stairway that descended to the bowels of the steamer looked almost ominous as the increasing fog started to settle around the dark opening.

The wind and rain began to build in velocity. With each of its brutal swipes, Dominique's fear also increased. She gasped in panic and the freezing wind whipped the breath from her open mouth. As much as she despised sharing a cabin with Silver, Eva Marie, and Lulu, there was nothing she wanted more at this moment than the sanctuary of their tiny crowded quarters. Even with this thought in her mind, something stronger compelled her to make her way toward the stairway where the captain had descended.

As her cautious steps drew her closer to the stairs, Dominique glanced over the rail that ran along the edge of the deck. Fog was slowly swallowing up the boat, but the heavy veil did not descend all the way down to the water, yet. Ever since leaving St. Michael, Dominique had noticed how grey and murky the waters of the Yukon always appeared. Now, the river was so laden with muck it seemed as though there was no water flowing at all. The boat rocked to its side again. The strange sound of the paddlewheel digging into the thick mud reached Dominique's ears. A shiver raked through her entire body.

The steamer jerked forward, then slammed to a sudden halt. The violent action threw Dominique down on the deck. She cried out, although she did not realize she had made a sound. She was aware, though, of other noises; the vicious howling of the wind, an unnatural sound like something being sucked down into the mud, and the banging and clanging of barrels and tools rolling across the tilted deck. In an effort to keep herself from tumbling toward the edge of the deck, Dominique grabbed frantically for the railing at the top of the stairs. Her hands were wet, and the railing was slippery. She felt her fingers losing their grip. She was consumed by terror as she realized that the steamer must have bogged down in the devouring mud. If she lost her hold on this railing and tumbled over the side, she would be sucked down into the black murk, too.

Dominique's tangled skirt and layers of petticoats encumbered her movements. Her high-heeled boots scraped against the wooden planks as she fought to retain her hold on the wet rail. She could feel the rail growing more slippery, and her fingers growing more limp. The rain pelted down without mercy. Dominique realized her fight was in vain. Her fingers could not hold on to the rail forever. She lurched forward again when she felt the iron slip away from her fingertips. Once more, the rail slid from her hands. Although she was not ready to be defeated, her spinning mind could not grasp another course of action. She felt herself rolling away from the rail—and towards the edge of the deck.

She was not aware of Cole Hawkins' presence until his strong hands clasped her arms, and he began to drag her away from the edge. A sense of relief and strength surged through her as he pulled her down the stairs with him. After he stood her on the floor, he continued to hold her for a few seconds longer. When Dominique's head started to clear, she gazed up at him. Words of gratitude surfaced, but Cole Hawkins cut her off.

He released her, but did not wait for her to reply. Nor did he allow his gaze to lock with hers as he spoke, "I've got to get to the upper deck." He spun around and started up the stairs,

"Monsieur! Please, tell me what's happening!"

The panic in the woman's voice caused Cole's steps to falter. Her grasp on his coat sleeve halted his retreat. In spite of his determination to leave, Cole glanced down. Wide, terrified blue eyes stared up at him.

"Please, Monsieur?"

Cole's countenance drew into a mask of conflicting emotions. He made no further attempt to leave. "The steamer can't push through the mud flats."

"Will we be able to get out?"

Cole shrugged. He tried to will himself to look away from her pleading gaze. His eyes would not do his mind's bidding. He felt as if something inside him had snapped. He wanted to sweep her into his arms and protect her from all harm.

The boat twisted farther to the side. Cole did not stop to reconsider his actions. He knew he could not leave this woman alone in the bowels of the sinking boat. "You'd best come with me," he said. He clasped her hand as she gripped his coat sleeve.

Dominique did not question his sudden change of mind. Her fingers wrapped tightly around his hand. The heels of her boots slipped on the wet rungs of the iron stairway, but the captain dragged her up behind him with little regard to her clumsiness. On the upper deck, they were greeted once again by the strong gusts of wind and rain. Dominique gasped as she tried to catch her breath—and retain her balance. Her main concern, though, was to keep up with the captain. His long strides made it difficult for her to stay with him, but determination gave her energy. They stumbled along the deck, clinging to anything that kept them away from the edge of the tilted boat.

Panic ruled the Lady Susanah. Men shouting, and the terrified screams of the women, were accompanied by the endless howls of the wind. All of the passengers, it appeared, had come up to the foredeck. Every stationary object had at least one or more women clinging to its frail sanctuary. The male passengers—along with the crew members—were frantically trying to toss long ropes to the branches of the trees that bordered the riverbank. Their task was made nearly impossible because of the distance between the steamer and the land. The heavy fog complicated their desperate attempts; it was possible to see only several feet in either direction. Even when one of the ropes did appear to catch a branch, there was no way to see if the noose was wrapped around a strong limb, or was merely dangling from the edge of a frail twig.

Cole continued to drag Dominique behind him even though he could have left her with any of the other passengers. Dominique, however, did not give him the opportunity to leave her behind. Sheer determination kept her at the captain's heels, no matter how difficult it was for her to keep up with him or to hang onto his hand. The entire time Dominique was struggling to remain with him, she was also painfully aware of the seriousness of their situation. The attempts to lasso the trees on the riverbank was to provide an escape from the sinking steamer, but how long did any of them have until the whole boat was sucked down into the black mud?

Dominique cringed when she thought of trying to cling to the slippery rope while inching along towards the riverbank. As they approached the bow where the men were already preparing to test the shaky escape route, Dominique's terror increased. A man— an extremely brave man—Dominique thought, was climbing up on the rail. Another man was tying a rope around the man's waist and securing it to the rope that disappeared into the heavy fog. Dominique's body shuddered as she watched the man step off the rail. Within seconds he was swallowed up by the fog. Dominique's gaze immediately riveted to the rope that was wrapped around a heavy pole on the deck. Through the haze, she could see the strain on the rope from the man's weight.

Miraculously, the rope held. After several unbearably long minutes, the rope grew slack again. Everyone watched in worried anticipation until the rope was tugged on several times from the shore—a signal from the man that he was safe. A cheer rang out from the men aboard the sinking steamer. The joyous sound, however, was quickly drowned out by the relentless howling of the wind. Their spirits undaunted, the men waited patiently until each of the ropes received a signal from the land. A sense of urgency gripped the entire ship. Above the roar of the wind and rain, the voice of the captain called out, "The women go first!"

Dominique did not have time to disagree with the captain's command. Nor did she realize what was happening when he pushed her forward and began to wrap a rope around her waist. Numb, Dominique did not allow her thoughts to dwell on what would happen if the rope broke before she reached the riverbank. She did, however, permit herself to look at the captain's face while he concentrated on securing the rope. Dominique was sure the worried expression on his face was not because he cared about her safety. In the brief time since they met, his opinion of her was more than obvious.

When Cole finished knotting the rope around her waist, his gaze was automatically drawn up to her face. The wind and rain had loosened the severe bun she wore at the nape of her neck. Her raven hair was plastered against her head, along the sides of her face, and hung over her shoulders in water-laded strands. Wide blue eyes stared at him from beneath long, wet lashes. Her lips were trembling as if she was crying. But, if her tears mingled with the rain, Cole could not tell. She seemed so vulnerable that once again, he was overcome with the urge to protect her— hold her . . . and more.

"We're ready to let 'er go, Captain."

Luther's voice broke into Cole's thoughts. Reality returned. Cole placed his hands around Dominique's waist and lifted her up. His gaze remained locked with hers for a brief second longer.

The narrow railing offered no support for the smooth leather soles of Dominique's boots. She held tight to the top of the captain's broad shoulders, afraid that if she turned loose of him she would topple over the side and disappear forever in the mud.

"Hold onto the rope—never let go!" Cole said as he pried her hands from his shoulders and forced her to grasp onto the rope. He drew in a deep, trembling breath, which made him aware of how much he was affected by her fear. He cleared his throat, and tried to ignore the rapid pounding of his heartbeat.

"You're on your own until you reach land," Cole shouted as his gaze raised to her face. For one fleeting moment, all the mayhem seemed to fade away. He sensed something, maybe it was something he glimpsed in her face. It was something he could not explain in this moment of madness. But, whatever it was, Cole knew that once they were safe again, he would have to know what it was about this woman that aroused feelings he thought he would never experience again.

"She's ready," Luther called out after he had double-checked the ropes Cole had just tied. He backed away from the rail, and turned to signal for Cole to let her go. Fleetingly, Luther saw the way Cole was looking at the woman. He didn't have time to worry, or wonder about the emotions he was sure he'd seen in Cole's expression, because at that instant the Lady Susanah took another plunge farther into the mud.

Screams from the women filled the air, rising even above the pounding rain and wind. Dominique felt herself being flung away from the rail. She swung, helplessly from the rope overhead. Captain Hawkins' words kept echoing through her mind. "Never let go . . ."

Three

The two years Dominique spent scrubbing floors and doing other menial chores proved to be a crucial asset. Her arms and upper body muscles were strong, as was her endurance. Inching along the rope, though, was still the most difficult task she had ever tackled. The cold fog encased her in its eerie mist, and was so dense she could not see more than a few inches of rope at a time. She did not allow herself to look down. Neither her gaze, nor her concentration, wandered as she dragged one hand over the other one to move herself along the taut rope.

After a few minutes nothing seemed to exist outside of Dominique's foggy world. She could no longer hear the cries of the other passengers coming from the steamer, nor was she aware of the sloshing sounds of the churning mud and water below her. Hanging onto the rope was her only concern. The cold kept her from realizing the pain of her rope-burned hands as she focused on reaching land. Dominique had no idea how long she had clung to the rope, but it felt like an eternity. Just as she thought she could not hold on one second longer, a pair of hands grasped her, and pulled her down to the ground. Dominique's body stiffened with fear for the first instant she felt strange hands on her body. But almost at once, an overpowering sense of relief replaced her fear.

"You made it, Missy."

"I—I thought I never would," she said in a hoarse voice. For a moment, her legs felt too wobbly to walk. She leaned against the man for support as he untied the rope from her waist.

"You'd better get outta the way now. We've got another one comin' from the boat."

Dominique stumbled away from the edge of the muddy river. A rush of pain drew her attention down to her hands. She felt as though a million pins were poking into her hands where bits of rope were slivered into her raw, exposed palms. Blood mingled with the raindrops when she forced herself to uncurl her hands and look at her injuries. The rope had rubbed the skin from her palms, and the movement caused more acute pain to shoot from her hands and up through her arms. A light-headed feeling overcame her, but she knew she couldn't give into the luxury of fainting, or even crying.

On land, the fog was not as heavy as it was

over the river. Dominique glanced around until she spotted a grove of cottonwoods a short distance from the riverbank. Their wide-spreading branches offered some meager protection from the endless downpour so she forced her heavy legs to begin the agonizing climb up the sloping bank that led from the river. Even though the mud on the riverbank was over the tops of her boots, knowing she was on land eased some of her discomfort. Still, her wet clothes seemed to grow tighter, colder, with every step she took. Chills shook her body and her teeth started to chatter. By the time she completed the short climb to the top of the riverbank she was shaking so hard she could barely move. She clutched her arms around herself tightly, feeling as though she was about to freeze to death. There was one minor benefit however—the cold made her hands too numb to feel any more pain.

From the top of the small incline, Dominique could see the activity down at the river. The fog was starting to lift, and the outline of the steamer was visible. The sight of the big ship tilted almost completely on its side, and bogged down so firmly in the dark mire, made the situation seem even more bleak. Dominique glanced at the ropes that were strung from the ship to the trees along the riverbank. She trembled when she tried to imagine herself hanging from one of those ropes. She decided she had been lucky that she could not see through the fog as she made her way to the shore. Her shipmates who were struggling across now were not so lucky.

Four ropes were secured from the steamer to the trunks of the trees. Three more men made their way from the Lady Susanah to the land. They joined the first man in his efforts to keep the ropes taut as the other passengers started the treacherous journey. Even as she watched, Dominique felt a stunned sense of disbelief. Each of the ropes supported one of the women. They dangled from the swaying ropes just inches above the mud. An inch or two at a time, the women crawled along the ropes. Many times one of them would lose her grip for an instant or two. In the tension-filled seconds that followed, arms and legs would flail through the air until they regained their hold on the overhead rope again. Only the ropes tied around their waists prevented them from plummeting into the dark muck.

The escape from the Lady Susanah was a slow process, hindered by the abominable weather. The fear that the ship would sink farther into the mud flats was foremost in everyone's mind. As time passed—and more people made it to safety on the riverbank—this became less of a threat. Late in the day the rains finally ceased to fall. The temperature was no longer so chilling. Even the fog was almost gone by the time the last of the women were unloaded on the riverbank.

Dominique was oblivious to the other women as they joined her in the shelter of the trees. In spite of the women's crying about their rope-burned hands, the cold, and all their other discomforts, Dominique's attention never wavered from the Lady Susanah. Captain Hawkins had diligently helped all of his passengers and crew depart from his wrecked ship. She watched in nervous anticipation as the captain heaved himself over the rail, then began to make his way along the rope without bothering to tie the security rope around his waist. He was a tall man—over six feet by at least one or two inches. As he climbed toward the land his feet dragged through the mud. But since he was also in excellent physical condition it was not difficult for him to move hand-over-hand along the rope. In no time at all, he was standing with the other men on the muddy riverbank.

Dominique exhaled and realized she had been holding her breath. She tried to convince herself her interest in Captain Hawkins' well-being was merely because they would all need his help if they had any hopes of making it back to civilization alive. Her gaze riveted on the steamer again. She knew they would not be continuing their journey on the Lady Susanah. Her attention shifted to the countryside. The untamed Yukon Territory was blanketed with dark, seemingly impassable forests that climbed the slopes of the rugged snow-capped mountains. A feeling of doom settled in Dominique's heart.

"Guess it ain't true," Silver Belle said. She

gave Dominique a nudge as she motioned towards the men. In her hand was her empty whiskey flask. Before climbing the rope, she had downed half of the contents, the remainder she gulped down as soon as she reached the riverbank.

"What?" Dominique asked, absently. Her eyes immediately sought out the captain standing among his crew. They appeared to be in deep conversation about the fate of the ship.

"I'd always heard a captain goes down with his ship." A rude chuckle followed, but Silver fell into a solemn silence when Dominique glared in her direction. "It was only a joke. What's eatin' at you, anyway? You and the captain got somethin' goin' on between the sheets?"

"Mon Dieu! Is that all you ever think about?" Dominique retorted. Her indignant reply was as chilling as the icy glare she cast at the other woman.

Silver shrugged. A serious expression tugged at her grimy, make-up smeared face. "What else is there?"

"Staying alive for one thing," Dominique spat back. She opened her mouth again to add her opinion of Silver's intelligence, but decided to keep quiet. Pity shot through Dominique when she looked at Silver again. The image of her mother passed through her mind. Silver honestly did not know there was more to life beyond her boudoir door.

Dominique knew that before this journey was over, they all would be a lot wiser than they had been when they had left San Francisco. That is, if they were still alive when this was all over.

Dominique's attention was diverted from Silver when she glimpsed the captain walking towards them. He was not looking at her at first, but as he approached the top of the ridge his gaze moved from one woman's face to another. When he saw Dominique his footsteps halted for an instant. The fire his brief gaze ignited spread through Dominique and melted away all the coldness she had previously felt. She returned his intent stare, but their brief eye contact was interrupted when he was bombarded by questions and complaints from the other women.

Cole tore his attention away from Dominique. His head shook from side to side as he listened briefly to the hysterical cries coming from several of the women. The dangerous expression on his mud-caked face induced their silence at once. "It won't do you any good to cry about your miseries. Be glad you're standing here now, and not sucked down in the mud like . . ." his voice dropped. He glanced over his shoulder toward the riverboat. With a pang of regret, he realized how much he had lost today. This steamer was his last hope to escape from this country—and the life—he had grown to hate. When he continued to speak his voice was even more harsh.

"There's nothing to be done for the Lady Susanah. As soon as we've dried out we'll be movin' on."

"How?" was murmured by several women.

"On foot." Cole ignored the women's groans and protests. He looked up towards the sky. The sky overhead was still gloomy and grey, but the clouds were beginning to lift. "It's clearing up. Once we get us some fires burning it won't take long to warm up." His narrowed gaze swept over the women. A deep sense of frustration overcame him. When the steamer bogged down in the mud, most of them had rushed out of their cabins wearing nothing more than their dressing gowns and a shawl. Several had the good sense to throw on a coat, but none was wearing clothes that were suitable for hiking through the rugged Yukon country. Cole doubted any of them even owned clothes that would protect them against the unpredictable elements here.

"We'll camp here tonight and head out first thing in the morning. There's a fort not far up the river from here. I'm gonna retrieve all that I'm able to from the steamer before it sinks down any more."

"What about the things we left in our cabins?" Lulu asked. Her voice quivered as a visible shiver shook her body. Her hair hung in wet tangles around her shoulders, and the silk robe she wore clung to her. She wrapped her arms around herself in an effort to control the shivers that shook her body.

"Food and blankets are the things we need most." Cole's voice lacked sympathy. "For now, you can busy yourselves looking for firewood." He motioned toward the cottonwood grove that was spread out behind them. "You should be able to find some drier wood in the forest." When he turned around to leave, he glanced at Dominique briefly as he added, "Don't get lost." Cole continued down the embankment without further comment.

"He probably hopes we'll all get lost, and then he can be rid of us," sobbed a redhead who looked as if she had been crying for hours.

The sound of the redhead's trembling voice dragged Dominique's attention away from the sight of the departing captain. With all the whining and crying going on she knew Captain Hawkins probably figured they were all a bunch of spineless creatures who were never going to survive out in the Alaskan wilderness. This thought refueled her strength. She forced her aching body to straighten to its full height.

"We've got to toughen up or we're never going to make it to Dawson City alive," Dominique said. She tried to make her voice sound strong. Inwardly, she was every bit as scared as the rest of them. They were a pitiful looking bunch with their wet hair hanging down over their eyes, their wet clothes clinging to their bodies, and a layer of mud caked over all of them. Instinctively, Dominique reached up to touch her own dirty face. She wondered how they would ever wash all this mud off themselves.

"The captain's supposed to take care of us, but he's not even trying to help us," a woman named Janie said in a whimpering voice. She shivered visibly under the wet silk robe that clung to her body like a second skin.

The other women's weakness seemed to increase Dominique's desire to survive. She tossed her head back and swept her gaze over her companions. When she spoke again her voice contained a note of sarcasm. "I don't know about the rest of you, but I've been fending for myself all my life. I don't need the captain to take care of me now." After only a few seconds of hesitation, Dominique's words began to infect the rest of the women.

"I can take care of myself, too," spat one woman. A chorus of the same sentiments echoed from everyone else.

Addie McFadden—the widow from Texas— stepped forward, a determined expression on her muddy face. She was a tall, stout woman in her early thirties. Dominique—who was not overly short at five feet four inches—had to tilt her head back to look up at Addie's face when she stood beside her. Their gazes met with a sense of camaraderie.

"The first thing we need to do is follow the captain's orders," Addie said with a tone of authority. "We'll split up into groups of four or five and go into the forest to gather wood.

Mark your trails, and be back within a half an hour." Addie didn't wait for comments or protests. She pointed at Dominique, then towards three other women. "Let's get goin' before it gets dark. Then we can clean ourselves up and settle in for the night."

Darkness was already on the heels of the afternoon, and would fall even earlier because of the stormy weather. As Dominique trekked through the mud beside Addie and the others, she could not resist the urge to glance over her shoulder to the area where the captain stood. Her heartbeat accelerated. A rush of adrenaline surged through her veins. He was watching her—or at least looking in her direction. Unless it was her imagination, he appeared to have the traces of a proud smile on his mouth. Dominique quickly looked away. Her steps picked up, in spite of the mud that sloshed in the soles of her boots. The last of her weariness evaporated like the last traces of the fog. She was rejuvenated, filled with hope again. She knew—somehow—that they would survive this disaster. Her determination to prove to the captain that she was a strong woman—and mostly that she was a good woman—fueled her on. Her reason for being here in the first place, her intended bridegroom, Jack Scroggins, never even entered her mind.

Four

"I have to admit it," Luther said thoughtfully. He chewed on a piece of dried beef as he spoke. Above his thick beard, his freshly scrubbed face was a reddened hue, matching the chapped skin of all the other passengers of the ill-fated Lady Susanah. He wore a knitted cap pulled down low on his forehead, which concealed the curls of his dark blonde hair. "I didn't think those little gals would be able to handle all this trouble. But they was real troupers 'bout climbin' those ropes. Yep, sure surprised me."

Cole shrugged his shoulders. Since he had expected them to do nothing to help themselves, he was more than a little surprised about the way the women had rallied together. Not only had they gathered wood and started their own campfires, they had managed to tend to all their own needs. Once they had the fires burning, they had migrated to a spot up the river where the mud flats had not devoured the water. After they had cleaned themselves up as much as was possible under such adverse conditions, they'd dined on strips of jerky and coffee. Now, they were all bedded down on branches that had been dried out by the fires, then spread out to lay on to keep them off the wet, muddy ground.

Cole had seen—and heard—the way the French girl and the big woman with the southern accent had taken charge of the other women earlier. The French girl's courage surprised him. But he wasn't surprised by her admission that she had been taking care of herself all her life. He'd sensed something extraordinary in her right from the beginning, when he had first gazed into her mesmerizing blue eyes on the day they had set out from St. Michael's. She seemed to possess an inner strength that most women in her profession lacked. It was Cole's opinion that the majority of women who entered into a life of prostitution did so because they were lazy. Marriage promised women respectability, but it was a life-long labor of hard work. Cole reminded himself there were women who were exceptions to the rules. He figured there were probably a few women around who felt they had no other way to survive, or were just too weak to resist a life of sin. The French girl, however, didn't seem to fit into either of these categories. Since Cole's stubborn nature had already determined that she must be categorized, the idea he could be wrong never entered his mind.

Regardless of her reasons for becoming a "fallen woman," Cole found that he was still impressed by her bravery. When he had tied her to the rope, then pushed her off the ship's rail into the heavy fog, she could have collapsed with fear, or cried and begged for him to carry her across as most of the other women had. Instead, she hung onto the rope and fought her way through the fog until she reached the riverbank. The more he thought about her, the more he was intrigued by her.

Dominique, his mind taunted. He had heard the other women call her by that name. Cole thought it was a beautiful name, befitting a woman with her beauty. A strong and beautiful woman . . . his curiosity about her was even more aroused. Why would a young woman with her obvious assets have sold herself to some old coot she'd never even met, and doom herself to a miserable life in the frozen Yukon, he wondered.

Cole leaned forward and rubbed his hands together over the flames of the campfire. The encampment had grown quiet. Only the crackling sounds of the fires broke through the silence. He was bone-tired—too tired to even sleep. Cole, along with several of his crew, had made a couple more trips back to the Lady Susanah to haul supplies from the steamer to the land. There had been some stock—horses, cattle, and a few goats—stabled on the foredeck. The animals had been set free to fend for themselves. None of them had been seen on land, so it was believed they had not been able to swim through the mud. The men had been forced to abandon the Lady Susanah when it had taken another deep plunge in the mud. The steamer was now tilted completely on its side, buried in the mud all the way past the fantail. Any hopes of rescuing the ship and its remaining contents were dashed when it became apparent how deep the mud had become in the bog. With the exception of the few supplies they had salvaged, the rest of the cargo was lost, too. The inhabitants of Dawson City would suffer this loss; the Lady Susanah—along with the other large riverboats that had left the port at St. Michael—was loaded with commodities for the boomtown. There were no signs of the other riverboats. They, too, could be stranded somewhere along the muddy Yukon. If the winter snows caught Dawson City without a good stock of food and necessities, the entire population could be in for a long, cold winter of starvation.

Luther's remark about the women's achievements did little to ease Cole's sorrow over losing another Lady Susanah. This was the third Lady Susanah he had lost, though the first two were not riverboats. The last one—an ocean liner—had clashed with an iceberg in the Bering Sea two years ago. The ship had been his pride and joy; a sleek beauty that had taken him around the world. When she'd been marooned in the frozen Northlands, a part of him had also been destroyed. He'd salvaged part of the wreckage to buy the riverboat. The purchase of the riverboat had been for one purpose only; to make enough money to buy another ship. A feeling of despair settled in the pit of Cole's stomach. He wondered if his last chance to return to the sea as the captain of his own ship was as lost to him as the steamer that was buried in the mud of the river. Unconsciously, he rubbed at the scar on the side of his face, thinking of the woman whose name he had given to his vessels. Lady Susanah Rowland. His scar began to throb as if it had ripped open again, and it had been over a decade since the wound had been inflicted.

Luther noticed Cole's gesture. He knew the thoughts that were probably going through his old friend's head right now. It had been close to fifteen years since they had befriended one another. At twenty-four years old, Luther was a seasoned old seaman. Cole, at eighteen, was just beginning his love affair with the high seas. Even though he was the younger of the two, Cole proved himself to be an exceptional sailor. His outstanding abilities landed him in positions of authority, but Cole always made sure his sidekick shared in his bounties. During the years they had been sailing together, there was hardly an adventure they had not experienced. They'd fought wars while cresting the highest waves, engaged in battles with ruthless pirates, loved different women in a dozen or more ports, and watched the sun set on nearly every foreign shore. Luther smiled to himself as he recalled those bygone days. Uninvited, the image of Susanah Rowland taunted his happy memories. He glanced at Cole again, his attention focused on the scar Cole was still rubbing.

"Maybe we outta pick a different name for our next ship," Luther said. "Susanah's always meant bad luck, if you ask m—"

"Well, nobody asked you," Cole cut in with a surly growl. In one abrupt movement he rose to his feet. He reached down and scooped up one of the blankets that was spread out beside the fire before he stalked away without another word. He knew what Luther was up to, and he wasn't in the mood to have his past mistakes rubbed in his face again.

"Ah, hell," Cole grumbled as he wandered along the edge of the dark forest. Luther's right. Everything—and everybody—who bears that name is cursed. Against his will, Cole's thoughts traveled to a faraway land, and back to a time he tried not to dwell upon often. Twinkling green eyes, flaxen curls and silken skin taunted his memory . . . Susanah. So beautiful. So wicked.

"Hell!" he said again, louder and more intensely. He didn't want to remember, or long for the intimacies he had once shared with Susanah. But just her memory had aroused those feelings again. He reminded himself of how much he hated her for her deceptions and lies. So why couldn't he stop thinking of her?

A noise from behind him made Cole stop dead in his tracks. Susanah's image fled, along with the lascivious thoughts she always induced. He dropped his blanket on the ground. From his wide leather belt hung a knife sheath, which contained a bone-handled hunting knife, the one weapon he always carried. His hand was positioned on the handle when he spun around to confront the source of the noise. It was almost too dark to make out her features, but Cole knew her at once. His foul mood did not disappear, but it was shadowed by other feelings which surfaced the moment he realized it was her. The combination of these conflicting emotions did nothing to ease his deep frustration.

"What the hell are you doin' out here, woman?"

Dominique froze. She hadn't meant to startle him. It had been her plan to call out to him just as he had turned on her. "I-I was looking for you, Monsieur."

"You found me."

His brisk tone left Dominique unsure of her reasons for following him. She had not been able to sleep, and when she had seen him leaving the campsite, she had left her common sense behind, and chased after him.

"Well, what do you want?"

"I-I just wanted to th-thank you for saving us today."

"Not necessary."

She was unable to make out his expression in the faded light, but Dominique noticed his tense stance relax. There were other things she wanted to say, but the words seemed to stick in her throat. An uneasy silence hung in the air.

"I guess I'll get back then," she said in a low voice. The look of tenderness she thought she had glimpsed on his face earlier today—the emotions she thought she could see in his gaze—they must have been in her imagination. "I'm sorry I disturbed you."

She turned to leave. Cole felt a long-forgotten sensation of tenderness; a resurrection of feelings he did not want to bring to the surface again. "Wait," he called out.

Her steps halted at once.

Cole cursed inwardly at himself for speaking before he had a chance to think about his actions. She turned around to face him. He noticed now, even in the near-darkness, her eyes glistened like jewels. The outline of her angelic face tilted to the side as she stepped closer. Each step she took toward him made her image clearer. Cole could not look away. His eyes drank in the shadowy sight of her as if they had never glimpsed such a beautiful image. Even after all she had been through that day, her beauty was undeniable. Her black hair—loose and tumbling over her shoulders—blended in with the black background of the forest. The raven tendrils created a dramatic frame for her pale skin. Cole's fingers ached to touch her soft cheek, her hair, her lips . . .

"Monsieur?"

Cole swallowed hard. Her voice was so soft. Monsieur. Susanah used to call him Monsieur. Cole reminded himself that this woman was just a whore. A beautiful French whore. And he needed her tonight; because of what had happened today, because his memory had reconstructed forgotten longings, because this woman was here now, and because she was so damned beautiful. With these thoughts controlling him, Cole reached out and slid one hand around her neck, his other hand wrapped around her slender waist. He pulled her up against his taut body with one forceful motion. His show of strength was unnecessary. She came to him without resistance. His lips instinctively descended until they connected with hers. His natural urges were ruling him now. Nothing could stop him.

A kiss was the last thing Dominique expected from this man. This impulsive action confused her, even frightened her somewhat. Fleetingly, she thought about trying to pull away—to run away. The feel of his lips, however, affected her in a way that left her defenseless against his advances. She realized she didn't want to get away from him. She wanted him to keep holding her, to kiss her again and again, and make the wondrous feeling that was flowing through her body last forever.

His mouth demanded a response that edged on desperation. Dominique understood. After all they had been through today, all the hardships and uncertainty awaiting them, she also felt a sense of urgency to know what it meant to love and be loved. She returned his kiss without hesitation. Her arms automatically rose up to encircle his neck. Their lips, and their bodies, melded together. Dominique felt engulfed in a blanket of security and warmth. All her fears and pain evaporated. She pressed closer to him, her heart pounding. Could he hear the deafening sound of her heart, she wondered? Was her kiss producing the same type of undeniable and wonderful feelings in him?

Regardless of the years he had pined for Susanah, Cole had never denied himself the comforts of a woman. On more occasions than he cared to remember, he had sought out women who served his needs, and who didn't require any emotional entanglements—women who were just like Dominique Laval. All he looked for in his bedmates was that they were French, and that they were whores. As he continued to ravish this one's lips with kisses, Cole realized there was more than just a sexual urge ruling his actions; he wanted the comfort of being close—of being held—by this woman. These were feelings that could lead to complications Cole did not want to encourage.

Dominique gasped for breath when the captain's lips released her throbbing mouth. He leaned back, but still held tight to her waist. His other hand twisted in the long hair at the nape of her neck, pulling her head back slightly. He pushed away the worrisome thoughts that had plagued him an instant ago. Instead, he reminded himself of this woman's status; she was accustomed to giving a man pleasure without further involvement. Why shouldn't he be the recipient of her pleasures tonight? Again, his lips descended, the exposed line of her neck their target. A soft moan escaped from Dominique as his mouth traced a fiery trail along her throat.

She had been kissed before, but no man had gotten any farther than an uninvited kiss before Dominique had set him straight. Since she had been working as a maid there had been other kisses, too. Amorous employers had tried to seduce her in their lavish mansions when their wives were gone. They met with the same reaction as the rest of the lecherous men who had tried to lure her into bed. But, never, never, had she been kissed like this before.

She'd always told herself she would know when the time was right—when the man was right. As Captain Hawkins continued the delicious assault on her neck, Dominique convinced herself that nothing had ever been more right.

She relaxed, and let her head tilt back as his kisses torched her skin. Every conscious thought fled from her mind. She felt as though she was soaring like a bird . . . higher and higher. A slow burn ignited in the pit of her stomach, and worked its way through her entire body. Her knees buckled. She clung to Cole like metal to a magnet.

Her complete surrender was obvious. Cole felt her go limp in his embrace. He pulled her into his arms as his lips sought hers again. Their brief separation had left her moist lips cold, but his kisses quickly warmed them again. He felt her shiver. Reality broke into their heated passion. The night air was cold and damp, they would probably freeze to death if they didn't stay close to the camp-fires. She snuggled up against him and Cole pushed reality to the back of his mind. They could keep one another warm. Besides, he had a blanket . . . laying somewhere in the mud at his feet.

With an impatient groan Cole pulled away from Dominique's soft lips. "Woman," he said in a husky voice, "I'd like to do a helluva lot more than kiss you, but right now we've got to try to be sensible." She continued to relax in his arms, her breathing still heavy with un-requited passion. Cole's loins ached with de-sire. "To hell with being sensible," he muttered.

Driven by his building urges, Cole began to carry Dominique farther into the black forest. He stopped when it became too dark to make out the trunks of the trees.

"Monsieur? There is something I must tell you," Dominique said when he paused. Her voice was raspy. She shivered again. Because of the brothels she had inhabited with her mother, she had grown up knowing almost all there was to know about sex. Now that she was finally ready to submit to a man, she realized she was terrified. More than anything, though, she wanted Cole to know that he was going to be her first lover.

A grunt was Cole's reply as he placed her on the cold ground. Here in the trees, fallen leaves provided them with a natural mattress. Cole felt her shiver again. It was only common sense to make a fire. But this woman had produced such a desperate need in him, nothing made sense anymore. How long had it been since he'd had a woman? He tried to think back. He'd found a pretty little French whore in Seattle just a couple of weeks before.

"I-I just wanted you to know," Dominique whispered. She knelt down on the ground beside him as he pulled her down with him. Here in the forest the ground was hard and cold. The darkness was blinding. She could not even make out the captain's face, and he was only inches away. Another shiver racked her body.

"I'll keep you warm," he said in a hoarse

voice. His arms reached out in the darkness until they located her again.

"No, that's not it." Her voice was shaking, but it wasn't from the cold. "It's just so important for you to know that I'm not what you think I am." She grasped for a way to tell him what she wanted to say. But there were so many conflicting thoughts flashing through her mind—and all these wonderful new sensations eating away at her body. "I not a-a wh . . ."

He cut off her words. The darkness did not prevent him from finding her lips again as he claimed her mouth with a demanding kiss. Her words were meaningless to him. Almost every whore he had ever been with seemed to feel a need to justify herself. He'd heard all the excuses and sob-stories. Besides, her actions proved more than her words. He wondered if there wasn't a woman alive who didn't attempt to defend her virtue at the same time she was raising her skirts for some man. But—he reminded himself—none of those things mattered. All that was important now was forgetting the heartbreak of today's tragedy, even if only for a short time. This woman was making him forget.

His hand pushed past her raincoat, then travelled down over the swell of her bosom. He felt her body tense. The tip of her breast swelled against the material of her dress. Something wild and primitive exploded in Cole. He knew how strong Dominique could be, but the passive and timid way she was behaving at this moment was driving him to the point of no return. He pushed her back until she was flat against the cold ground. His hand slid down until he was able to grasp the hem of her dress. Her skin was frigid to his touch as he ran his hand up along her legs. Not waiting to be detoured from their destination, his hands skimmed over her undergarments. His proficient fingers tugged at the waistband of her pantaloons. The entire length of her body was still tense and stiff, but she didn't protest as he shoved her pantaloons down from her hips, then tugged them from her legs and feet.

Cole's hand dove under her dress again, then traipsed over her smooth, flat stomach. Expertly, his fingers worked their way in between her tightly clamped legs to an island of warmth. Undaunted by her refusal to part her legs for him, Cole thrust two of his fingers into her. He heard her give a startled gasp. A vague sense of uncertainty entered his mind but his own needs were too demanding for him to ponder her strange behavior.

Conflicting thoughts continued to rage through Dominique's mind but they were overpowered by the other sensations she was experiencing. She felt as if liquid silver raced through her body. The cold no longer penetrated her skin. The fire of his touch brought her to the boiling point. Only a small part of her wanted to tell him to stop. She wondered if she would be as bad as her mother if she let him continue, but she told herself this was different. She was nothing like her mother. Besides, she didn't want him to stop. The intrusion of his fingers into her most private domain had shocked her at first. But now he was gently massaging her, and working his fingers inside her in ways that made her want to cry out in delight. She never wanted him to stop. Without a conscious thought, she allowed her tense legs to relax.

Cole wasted no time positioning himself between her thighs. On top of her, he continued to kiss her lips and tantalize her with the sensuous motions of his exploring fingers. Her response aroused his curiosity again. Unlike other whores he had been with, she seemed uncertain of how to reciprocate his advances. Cole wasn't in the mood to analyze her actions, however. Relieving the throbbing pain in his own loins was his first priority. He pulled his fingers from her moist crevice long enough to undo the belt that held his knife sheath, and unfasten his pants. As he shoved his pants down past his hips, he realized Dominique was lying so still he could not even hear her breathing. The blackness of the night stole away her image, but Cole almost wished he could see her face. He reminded himself it didn't matter if he couldn't look into those dreamy blue eyes, or if his gaze couldn't explore her firm, luscious curves. The solace they were providing one another was all that mattered. If he told himself this enough times, Cole knew he would be convinced. Then, all the other strange emotions that kept trying to intrude past the armor around his heart would be overpowered.

Dominique wasn't aware she was holding her breath. She was, however, vitally aware of the rock-hard shaft of Captain Hawkins' manhood pressing against her abdomen. She could no longer deny the fact that they were actually going to make love—here and now in this cold, dark forest—a realization that made her wonder what madness had stolen their minds. There wasn't time to regain her sanity, because Cole continued to chip away all her defenses. His knees nudged her legs farther apart. A bolt of shock shot through her she realized her clothes were no longer a barrier. The hardness she had felt against her abdomen a moment ago was now beginning to push inside her with a slow, pulsating pressure. Despite the cold temperature, his bare skin felt like fire against her own heated flesh.

A strangling sense of panic claimed Dominique. She knew time was running out. Nothing seemed to make sense to her. She wanted this man to make love to her, but the circumstances no longer seemed right. Lying here on the ground, with her dress and raincoat hiked up around her waist and his pants tangled down around his knees, made her feel like an animal. No . . . this wasn't right. She opened her mouth to explain all of these things—to try to make him understand why she couldn't go through with this. But only a loud startled cry escaped from her mouth when his next move drove him down into her without any warning.

He had felt her tightness when he first started to enter her, but nothing could have surprised him more than when he felt himself tear through the barrier of her innocence. The sound of her pain-racked sob, and the knowledge of what he had just taken from her, pulled at his heartstrings. There were a dozen questions crowding his thoughts, but he could not find a way to ask them. He remained on top of her—buried deep within her moist depths—unmoving for several minutes. That she was a virgin was beyond his comprehension. He had been so sure she was just another whore. The realization that he had judged her wrongly made Cole's guilt mount, and created a deep need in him that went far past his previous needs. Words still eluded him, but he knew he had to find a way to make up for his cruel assumption of her character. He would tell her he was sorry later. First he would prove something to her . . . he'd prove how he would never hurt her again.

With slow movements Cole began to move inside her. He felt her body relax as each of his gentle actions began to awaken her slumbering desires. His lips sought hers once more. She kissed him without hesitation, but he felt a dampness on her cheeks. He raised his hand to her face, and traced the hot trail of her tears with his fingertips. An avalanche of tender feelings tumbled through Cole. He'd never had a woman cry when he made love to her, and never before had he known such a powerful sense of bonding with another person. Unable to control himself any longer, Cole drove himself deeper. He heard her moan softly—not in pain, in ecstasy. And, he thought he heard her murmur, "Monsieur . . .", but he wasn't sure if he'd only imagined it.

After she realized there was no turning back, and once she had experienced the first spear of pain, Dominique could not help but give in to the pleasure of her body. Not even the pain in her rope-burned hands was noticeable any more. Each of his movements caused her to soar higher and higher. She began to imitate each of his actions until they were moving together like one indivisible being. Nothing could compare to the magnificent sensations that were surging through her body. Each time he plunged into her, the wondrous feelings increased until she felt as though something was about to shatter inside her. As this powerful sensation escalated Dominique was oblivious to anything other than this moment—this man—and her own feelings of passion.

Cole felt himself being driven to a point where he was forced to give into the natural release of his pent-up desire. He clutched Dominique tightly against him, and pushed himself deeper, harder. Her soft moans reached his ears, and as his movements grew more intense, Cole's own impassioned noises created a chorus with hers. He plunged down for a final time, shuddered with an engulfing sense of fulfillment, then took a deep, gasping breath.

Afterward, Cole and Dominique clung to one another—exhausted and satisfied. Not until the sensual joy began to fade, and the chill of the night air began to penetrate past the ecstasy, did their thoughts start to turn to the consequences of their behavior.

Five

The first night they spent in the Yukon wilderness was the most miserable night Dominique had ever endured. After they had made love, the captain acted anxious to get away from her. He told her they needed to get back to the camp so that they could stay close to the fires and get some sleep. Dominique knew this was necessary, but what she didn't understand was his silent withdrawal. As they made their way back to the campsite, he didn't say a word. Once they reached the encampment, he had only mumbled a quick "good night," before he retreated to the opposite side of the camp.

Sleep eluded Dominique. The chill in the night air penetrated the blanket she wrapped around her, and the cold seeped clear through to her bones. Several times during the night Dominique stoked the fire that was nearest to her make-shift bed, but nothing warmed her frozen limbs. Even more wearying than the cold was her overwhelming urge to cry. She was determined not to give in to the threat of tears, even when they hovered like vultures in the corners of her eyes.

Throughout the long night she kept telling herself that the captain's behavior was exactly what she should have expected after their sordid rendezvous in the wilderness. She had seen how the men treated her mother after they satisfied their own needs. When a woman no longer served a purpose, the man was ready to move on. The thought torturing Dominique the most was that she had been so determined to prove to the captain that she was not the wanton woman he perceived her to be. Instead, she had only managed to prove him right. The strong morals she was certain she possessed had disintegrated the moment he had touched her. She was no better than her mother—except her mother received money for her favors. Dominique had received nothing more than Captain Hawkins' silence and cold indifference. How could she have been so stupid? Her stomach constricted into a sickened knot. Mon seigneur! She didn't even know his first name.

Sitting next to the fire, Dominique constantly gazed over to the area where the men slept. The captain appeared to be having a restless night, too. Dominique noticed he did more than a normal amount of tossing and turning. Just as the sun was beginning to break faintly through the lingering clouds, he

74

kicked his blanket away, gave an aggravated grunt, and rose to his feet. Then, as if he sensed he was being watched, he swung around. There were traces of surprise in his expression when their eyes met.

Cole wanted to look away, but where this female was concerned, it seemed he could never obey his own commands. Nor could he help but notice how helpless she looked sitting there in the glow of the early morning fire. Even in this faint light he could tell that she had not slept at all. Her eyes were rimmed by dark smudges, and the puffiness hinted she had spent a good share of the night crying. Cole felt a weakness in his limbs. He tried to shake off the feelings that surged through him; a wasted effort. "Ah, hell," he muttered.

Dominique heard his aggravated tone. She cringed as he stalked towards her. When he stopped in front of her and extended his hand, she was not certain what to expect from him.

"We've gotta talk," he said. He glared down at her. In spite of the feelings he was determined not to acknowledge, he could not control the thoughts that continued to push their way into his mind. She looked so afraid of him. He wanted to sweep her into his arms again—just like he did last night. And, he wanted to do all the other things to her that he had done last night. Next time, though, he wanted it to be completely different. He wanted to make love to her in a soft, warm bed . . . wanted to touch and kiss every inch of her silken skin, and wanted their naked bodies to unite without any barriers. He wanted to make love in the daylight, where he could see her firm, young body and watch the way her beautiful face looked when she was in the throes of passion. He wanted everything to be perfect next time. Next time! Hell! Why did she affect him like this? A gruff grunt escaped from his mouth.

Dominique did not argue with him, although she could not imagine what they had to talk about. When she gingerly placed her hand in his, he yanked her roughly to her feet. Her determination not to show him any of her weaknesses kept her from crying out in pain when he clutched hold of her injured hand. Her mind contrived a dozen things he was probably going to say to her. Undoubtedly, he was relishing the fact that he had proven himself right about her character.

She stumbled along beside him until they were once again out of the campsite. He headed to the area where they had made love the night before. A grey light was filtering through the dense trees, lending an eerie aura to the grove. The branches of the cottonwoods, still heavy with the previous day's rainwater, hung almost to the ground in some places. A thin layer of frost coated areas of the ground where the dim sunlight had not been able to reach. Dominique's gaze scanned the damp ground for evidence of what had happened here last night. To her relief, there were no traces of their foolish escapade.

"Why didn't you tell me?"

Cole's demanding voice broke into Dominique's self-condemning thoughts. She stared at him. His question left her confused. He still held her hand. She could no longer ignore the burning pain his tight grip induced. "My hand, Monsieur, you're hurting me," she said.

A confused expression washed over Cole's face. He glanced down, then loosened his hold as he turned her hand over in his. The sight made him groan inwardly. He did not have to ask her what had happened to her hands. Since none of the women was wearing gloves when they escaped from the steamer, all of them had rope-burns on their hands. Luther had given them salve for the burns last night. Cole and most of the men had worn gloves when they climbed the rope, so he'd had no idea of the severity of the women's injuries.

"It's not really so bad," Dominique said when Cole's observation of her hand extended into a long silence. "Compared to everything else, it doesn't hurt much at all."

Her meaning was clear. Cole's gaze snapped back to her face. "Why didn't you tell me you'd never had a man before?"

She looked down at the ground. A heated sensation soared through her cheeks. He had not turned loose of her hand. He cradled it carefully. The flames that soared through her face did not compare to the fire in her soul that was created by his tender touch. "Would it have made any difference?" she whispered. Her face tilted upward again. She looked into the grey depths of his eyes.

"Yes," he said softly. His mind was once again creating the image of how badly he wanted to make love to her again. "Everything would have been different if I'd known." He released her hand and began to rub her cheek with his fingertips. "I would've taken things a lot slower, been gentler with you. A woman's first time should be special."

The tone of his voice, and most of all, his words stunned Dominique. "You were so convinced that I was a . . ." she faltered, unsure of what she wanted to say.

Cole shrugged, attempting to appear nonchalant. "I was mistaken."

"I forgive you, Monsieur."

Monsieur. He loved to hear her call him that, but he also wanted to hear her soft voice say his name. "Cole," he said.

"Cole?"

"My name—that's my name."

"Cole," she repeated more firmly. Inwardly, her hopes soared.

He wasn't disappointed. The way her accented voice spoke his name was almost like a caress to his ears.

"But I doubt if I'll ever forgive myself, Cole," she added. The urge to cry began to swell up in her breast again. A stinging sensation burned at the corners of her eyes.

"Why? For being a woman and having normal desires?" Her obvious torment filled him with a sense of protectiveness. He could not ignore the flood of emotions that washed through him. He vaguely remembered these feelings . . . of falling in love. His heartbeat began to thud erratically in his chest. It was beyond his comprehension that he was capable of experiencing these tender emotions again.

Dominique took a deep breath. She closed her eyes for a moment. How could she make him understand what she did not understand herself? "Until last night," she began, "I had always believed that my first time would be on my wedding night. I've been saving myself for the man who would be my husband."

Her statement was followed by an engulfing silence. For the first time since they had been drawn into one another's arms, they were both reminded of the reason they had met one another, and of the man Dominique was traveling to Dawson City to marry.

Cole's fingers stopped fondling her cheek. He dropped his arm down to his side. His eyes—misted with desire an instant ago—were now void of all visible emotions. A chill rushed through Dominique as she watched his transformation. His steely gaze narrowed and he looked away from her.

"I reckon everybody's startin' to wake up by

now," he said in a gruff tone of voice. "We probably should get back to the camp." He turned around, but then paused. He didn't know how to handle the feelings that were consuming him now. He'd just admitted to himself he was falling in love with her—this was already more than he was prepared to handle. Now, he must also deal with the anger and jealousy that were devouring him.

As she stared at his back, Dominique was torn with conflicting emotions. She knew the mention of her wedding undoubtedly was why his attitude had taken such a drastic turn. She wanted to reach out to him—to tell him that maybe fate had been saving her for him. Because now, she could not imagine being with Jack Scroggins, or any other man except Cole ever again. Instead, she stood mute. Unless he told her what he felt, she could only draw her own conclusions. From what she'd always been subjected to, she believed he would want nothing more to do with her after last night.

Unexpectedly, Cole swung back around. Dominique drew in a sharp breath. Her gaze rose up to his face. His expression was unreadable, but in the depths of his grey eyes she thought she glimpsed a strange mixture of desire, and, something else . . . something explosive. Fury? She couldn't tell, but staring into his eyes aroused in her a longing like she'd never known. Her entire body trembled—her legs felt like they had just turned to liquid. An ache, a sweet tortuous ache, swelled up in her loins and spread throughout her body.

Her innermost feelings were so evident in her expression that Cole couldn't stop himself. He reached out and pulled her into his embrace. As she moved closer, Cole noticed her eyes close, and her lips part slightly in anticipation of his kiss. Yearnings he could not deny surfaced once again. Like pieces of a puzzle, their lips fit together. His tongue flowed easily into her mouth, tantalizing hers until their tongues entwined like erotic dancers.

For a time that seemed an eternity, while also ending much too soon, Dominique savored Cole's impetuous kiss. No amount of reasoning could convince her that they shouldn't be doing this again. She wrapped her arms around his neck, pulling herself up on the tips of her toes. His arms tightened around her waist. She wondered how she had survived for the past twenty years without knowing this man. There was nothing about him that didn't tempt all her female senses; his manly scent, his towering muscled body, the crooked smile that curved his lips. His eyes, so gray they looked like smoldering silver, and even the long, straight scar that ran down the side of his face excited her. Dominique let her fingers inch up his neck until they raked through the long tendrils of dark brown hair that curled over the collar of his coat. His thick hair entangled her fingers. She was aware of the rope-burns on her palms, but no amount of pain could tear her away from him.

Cole forced himself to pull back, to catch his breath. The sun was breaking through the scattered rain clouds that lingered from the previous day, the rays were peeking timidly through the branches of the tall pines. In the brighter light Cole tenderly observed Dominique's face. He was not disappointed. From last night's kisses, and from the one he had just claimed, her lips were swollen and slightly red. A barely noticeable tremor shook her bottom lip. Her eyelids hung heavily over her misty blue eyes. The tips of her long raven lashes fanned down, almost covering her eyes with their heavy veil. Her breaths were short gasps, and a rosy blush colored her ivory cheeks. Cole's loins tightened. He wanted to make love to her again—here and now.

"Cole? Oh! I didn't k-know you were with-with anyone," Luther stammered. His gaze flitted back and forth between Cole and Dominique. For an instant, his expression contained a look of surprise, replaced almost at once with a sly grin as his attention focused solely on Dominique's flustered state. Cole's taste in women never varied, Luther thought. And, it seemed that no matter where they were—or no matter how adverse the situation—there was always a French whore around to suit Cole's desires. Luther glanced at Cole. The sly grin that separated Luther's lips curved wider. Cole appeared to be even more disconcerted than the woman.

"I just wanted to let you know that the women are awake. We can break camp as soon as you're ready." Luther's smile reclaimed his lips. He added, "Sorry, if I broke up somethin' here." He met Cole's gaze as his eyebrows raised up in a speculative gesture.

Cole stepped away from Dominique. He wondered if his face was as flushed as hers. Luther's interruption had only intensified his yearning to make love to her again. He opened his mouth to speak to Luther, but words eluded him. What Luther had just said completely escaped his mind.

"I-I will go back to camp," Dominique muttered to Cole. She could not bring herself to look at the First Mate. As she walked away she felt as if she was in a daze. The passions Cole's kisses had created devoured all her senses. Although she dared not look at either of the men, she could feel both sets of eyes on her as she walked away. Her self-consciousness made her stumble through the grove. Only one thought raged through her mind; if the First Mate hadn't shown up, a repeat of last night would have occurred. This thought did not induce feelings of disgrace—only a wanton desire she could not shake off.

"You devil," Luther chuckled. "Have you been out here with her all night?"

Cole turned his discriminating gaze toward Luther. Though they had been friends for a long time, there was nothing friendly in Cole's attitude at this moment. Since he didn't feel Luther's questions deserved an answer, he chose to ignore it. "I've decided it would be foolish for all of us to walk to Fort Yukon."

A careless shrug shook Luther's shoulders. "It'd be faster—that's for sure," he said. "This mornin', all them women is whinin' and complaining. Half of 'em caught cold. I don't think they'd be able to make the trip anyway, with what the way they're dressed and all. If I took off by myself, I could—"

"No," Cole interrupted. "You're better at handling the women." He wondered if his voice sounded convincing. Inwardly, his mind was contriving an outlandish plan, and even when he said the words aloud, Cole couldn't believe what he was saying. "I thought I'd go—and maybe I'll take the-the French girl with me."

A surprised gasp emitted from Luther. "You sure about that, Cole?" He stepped closer. His gaze studied Cole's face. As usual, an unreadable mask greeted his inquiring eyes. "I mean, last night was, well, just one night. You'd be alone with her several days—and nights—if you took her to the fort with you." Luther paused. He continued to stare at Cole. The silence from his old friend told him more than words. "I'm startin' to get the feelin' this is more than your usual infatuation."

"No," Cole snapped, almost too quickly. "I

enjoy her company, but that's all there is to it." His face felt warm, almost fevered.

"Well, she's promised to a man in Dawson City already," Luther said in a patronizing tone.

"I know."

"He's paid for—"

"I know!" Cole growled. He threw his hands up, then let them drop at his sides in an aggravated gesture. His gaze leveled on Luther. "I know, damnit! And I've thought about all that, and I don't care." Cole shook his head, and glanced down at the ground. When he looked up at Luther again, his turmoil was written clearly on his troubled face. He met his friend's eyes. Neither of them spoke for a long moment.

"I don't reckon it's any of my business, anyway," Luther said, then added as he started to turn around to leave. "I just don't want to see you get hurt again."

"It's not like that," Cole said. When Luther turned back to face him with an incredulous expression on his face, Cole continued. "This time I know what I'm gettin' into. It's different than it was with Susanah. When we get to Dawson City, it's over."

"Just like that?"

"Yep!" Cole started forward, stopping when he was abreast with Luther. "I'd best get on my way as soon as possible." He glanced up at the sky. The clouds were slowly devouring the sun again. "This weather gonna make travelling real slow."

Luther gave a grunt, but refrained from voicing his opinions. It wasn't the weather that was gonna slow Cole down. But Luther knew he couldn't talk sense into Cole's hard head once he made up his mind about something. He also knew Cole was lying to himself if he believed his own words. The fact that he had even mentioned Susanah told Luther that Cole was comparing his feelings for Dominique Laval to the feelings he had once felt for Susanah Rowland. Luther groaned inwardly as he fell in step with Cole. He knew Cole was headed for trouble if he was falling in love with the Frenchwoman.

As he kept astride of his friend, Luther debated whether or not he should attempt to talk Cole out of this foolish notion of taking the woman with him. From the corner of his eye, he glanced at Cole. A mask of determination was set on his face. He glanced to the side as if he could feel Luther's stare. They both looked away quickly. Luther remained silent. Nothing he said would make a difference, but Luther sensed Cole's excursion to Fort Yukon might make a big difference in the outcome of the rest of his life.

Six

Dominique did not question Cole's motives for asking her to accompany him to the post at Fort Yukon. The idea of being in his presence—alone—for even a few more days was too exciting to allow herself to worry about what would happen when they reached the settlement. The reaction from the other women—and even worse, from Cole's crew—was not favorable. Although everyone agreed it made sense for the women to remain at the campsite while someone went to the post to get help, the captain's choice of traveling companion was questionable.

"Wouldn't it make more sense for you to take a couple of the men along?" or "What good would a woman do if you ran into trouble along the way?" were the most asked questions. Cole answered them all with icy stares that left his intentions clear—and unyielding. Within an hour, Cole and Dominique were headed out of the camp.

Dominique wore an assortment of warm clothes that Cole had gathered for her, all of which were almost identical to the clothes he wore; a floppy brimmed hat covered her head, and a sheep-lined coat, wool trousers, long-johns, socks and tall boots that were large, but definitely more suitable than her laced-up high-heeled boots, completed her ensemble. The clothes she wore were men's garments, all too big, and even though she felt ready to tackle the long trek to the post, she had never felt more unattractive. To be with Cole, though, Dominique would gladly wear a bur-lap sack.

"How long will it take us to get to Fort Yu-kon?" Dominique said as she struggled to keep up with Cole's long strides. Her boots felt as if they would fall off if she raised her feet too high.

A shrug raised Cole's broad shoulders. He glanced at Dominique, and immediately slowed his steps when he noticed she was hav-ing trouble keeping up with him. "It all de-pends on the weather, and what we encounter along the way."

"W-W-What we encounter?" she stam-mered. Her head filled with images of wild animals. His next words confirmed her thoughts.

"Bears, wolves, who know?" Cole shrugged again, adding, "This is wild country, woman. The wildest you'll ever know." His voice took on a tone of respect.

"Worse than the river?"

The hint of a smile curled his lips. He glanced at her again. For an instant, he let their eyes meet. "That river is a winding, vengeful serpent." He drew in a deep breath, and his voice became almost wistful as he added, "Too bad the river's not more like the ocean."

Dominique recalled the ocean voyages she had been on in her life; from Paris to America, then from San Francisco to St. Michael. Because of the seasickness she always suffered, neither of those trips were among her favorite memories. "Have you ever sailed on the ocean?" she asked. The look of disbelief he cast in her direction made her feel as if she had said something horrendous. He stopped and turned to stare down at her.

"I've sailed more oceans than you've ever even heard of," he said indignantly. With an aggravated gesture, he motioned in the direction of the muddy Yukon. "Do you think I've spent my whole life steering a paddlewheel steamer through this hell-hole of a river?"

His reaction to her question surprised Dominique—and attracted her full attention. "Why are you here if you hate it so much?"

"Money," Cole stated flatly. "Haulin' supplies and passengers to boomtowns is where the money is these days." He resumed walking at a fast pace again.

To catch up, Dominique practically had to run. She stumbled repeatedly in the over-sized boots. When she was in step with him again, she glanced up. The glowering expression on his face did not prevent her from attempting to satisfy her curiosity. "Is that the only reason you're here?"

Cole's gaze remained straight ahead. He wondered if she was always so nosy. "That's the main reason. Isn't that the reason you're going to Dawson City?" The instant the words were out, Cole wanted to kick himself. He wasn't sure what he expected from this trip. He only knew he had an unexplainable compulsion to be with this woman, and he did not want to spend the entire trip exchanging barbs with her.

"My reason for going to Dawson City has nothing to do with mo—" Dominique's words were cut off when Cole stopped abruptly and put his arm out to the side to block her next step. She gave an indignant huff, but fell silent when she heard the serious tone of his voice.

"Look . . . over there." He pointed toward the trunk of a large spruce tree.

Dominique's gaze scanned the area. They had been walking beside the river ever since they had left camp. The river's route was leading them farther inland—closer to the pine forests and the snowy mountains. Dominique stared at the tree Cole was still pointing at, but could not understand why he was so interested in the scratched-up trunk. She shrugged, then turned her attention back to

Cole with the intention of finishing the conversation he had started about her motives for traveling to the Yukon. He didn't give her a chance to speak about the subject again.

"See those marks?" He stepped closer to the tree. The trunk was big—at least a foot in diameter. The branches had been torn away and the bark shredded along the trunk for seven or eight feet from the ground. Cole gave a low whistle as he studied the marks.

"What made them?" Dominique asked, moving to his side. Her gaze travelled up the length of the trunk. On closer observation she noticed deep scratches on the tree.

"Grizzly," Cole answered. "One hell of a big one, too." Instinctively, he glanced around, then looked down toward the ground. He gave another low whistle, and shook his head from side to side. "Look here," he said, pointing down at the large paw prints in the soft ground. "Those are fresh—real fresh."

A sense of foreboding claimed Dominique when she studied the huge tracks that surrounded her own smaller feet. "How can you tell?"

"They were made after the rain." He straightened up, and looked over his shoulder again as if he almost expected to see the grizzly standing behind them. Along with the rest of the gear Cole had packed before they left camp this morning, he had brought along a shotgun that had been salvaged from the steamer. Unconsciously, he clutched the gun

91

tighter, and let his forefinger rest on the trigger.

Cole's nervous actions were observed by Dominique, which served as fuel for her own fear. Since she'd never been in the wilderness before, the thought of encountering any sort of wild animal made her leery. But something as fierce as a grizzly bear was the most terrifying thing she could imagine. She imitated Cole's actions and glanced around anxiously. Once again, the sky was covered by stormy, black clouds. The dense forest appeared dark and gloomy. Dominique could almost imagine a snarling beast charging out from beneath the branches of the trees. An involuntary shiver raced through her body.

"We'd be wise to keep moving," Cole said. "This territory belongs to that fella," he motioned toward the tracks, adding, "At least, I hope it's a fella, and not a female with cubs."

"Would that make a difference?" Dominique asked. She noticed he was gripping the shotgun so tightly that his knuckles were starting to turn white. Nervously, she began to clench her own hands into tight fists.

Cole shrugged, and avoided looking at Dominique. Aboard a ship, there were few situations he could not handle with expertise. But out here in the middle of the untamed Yukon, he knew his own inadequacies when it came to dealing with land-related emergencies. He wasn't completely ignorant, though.

"A sow will be more protective—and more likely to attack without being provoked."

Dominique broke out in a cold sweat. She looked around again as she clutched her arms around her waist and shivered. The image of being attacked by a monstrous bear was more vivid in her mind now. For reassurance, she looked back to Cole. His expression offered her little comfort. He was still glancing around with a worried frown on his face, too.

When Cole noticed that he was being observed, a sense of shame overcame him. He reminded himself that it was not his habit to shrink from danger. He wondered when he'd changed from a man who feared nothing into one who constantly looked over his shoulder, worried about the threat of unseen foes. He braced his shoulders and loosened his hold on the shotgun. "I don't see any reason to start worrying about something that probably won't happen."

The obvious change in Cole's attitude eased a bit of Dominique's fear. She nodded her head in agreement, and forced a weak smile. "That old bear probably doesn't want to mess with us any more than we want to mess with him."

An easy smile came to Cole's mouth. Her innocence was so evident. He wondered how he'd ever thought she was just another whore. This thought reminded him of the main reason he had brought her with him. He had a lot to learn about this beautiful woman, and the sooner they made camp for the night, the sooner he could begin his quest. "We're wastin' valuable daylight," he said hurriedly. From his past trips up the Yukon he remembered a deserted cabin a few miles from where they were now. It was his plan to make this cabin their destination for the night.

Without further comment about the bear, Dominique resumed her place at Cole's side. Although she did not voice her fears, they remained with her as she tromped through the muddy terrain. The storm clouds still hung heavily in the air, but fortunately the rain did not fall. Occasionally the cry of a loon, or the distant howl of a wolf would shatter the quiet. Every sound terrified Dominique, and even the harmless animals they encountered, such as porcupines and caribou, did not diminish her fear of meeting up with the bear.

"Does it always rain here in the Yukon?" Dominique asked when she noticed Cole staring up at the sky.

"No. Usually it snows." He glanced at her, adding "Just a few weeks ago there was still ice on the river." He grunted. "Now, that damn river's nothin' more than a giant mud hole. There's no sense to nothin' in this country."

Dominique avoided asking him more questions about the Yukon Territory since it was obvious the subject was not his favorite. Besides, she was learning first-hand about this country, and so far she had had to agree with

Cole's opinion. She tried to push her fears to the back of her mind as she concentrated on keeping up with Cole once more. The last thing she needed right now was for him to regret his decision to bring her along.

"We can keep going. I'm not tired, Monsieur— I mean Cole," she said when he stopped for the third time during the afternoon.

A suggestive smile curled one side of his mouth and his left brow lifted slightly, while his mind travelled ahead to the activities he had planned when they reached the cabin. "You can tell me whatever you like, but I'll make the decisions about how often we stop." Truth was, he didn't want to tire her out before tonight. Teasingly, he reached over and pulled on the brim of her floppy hat. The smile that instantly lit up her luminous blue eyes made his heart skip a beat. His grin transformed from one of lustful anticipation to one of tenderness. "I reckon we can keep goin' for a while longer," he said in a husky voice.

Dominique eagerly nodded in agreement for though naive, she recognized the look of desire that flashed in the depths of his gray eyes. She had no trouble matching his long strides as the idea of the impending night dominated her thoughts. Shivers of anticipation raced through her, along with a sweet ache that recalled what it was like to be intimate with him.

Luck was with them as they travelled, and

only an occasional sprinkle fell from the black clouds—barely noticeable compared to the rain storms they had endured in the past few days. Cole continued to lead her along an invisible trail that followed the course of the water. For short distances they would lose sight of the Yukon River when it was necessary for them to climb around large rock quarries, or detour around deep gorges. As soon as possible, however, Cole would head back toward the river. He knew without the lead of the river there was a good likelihood that he would get them lost in the wilds of the Yukon Territory.

"That might be a good place to make camp for the night," Dominique said as they passed a low overhang that was encased by shrubbery and a couple of craggy pines. Day was fading into dusk and the impending darkness only added to her fears of encountering the grizzly. The small crevice would hardly protect them from the bear, but at least they would not be out in the open. It would also provide a meager shelter if it should start to rain again.

Cole barely glanced toward the overhang. "I know of a better place." His voice exuded a confidence he didn't feel inwardly. He thought they would reach the cabin long before nightfall. The farther they walked, the more worried he became that he had somehow bypassed the cabin on one of their detours. As the daylight diminished, Cole's uncertainty increased. If they didn't come to the cabin soon, they would have to stop some-where else. He only hoped they wouldn't re-gret not stopping in the spot Dominique had suggested.

Since Dominique felt certain that Cole knew this area well she began to relax slightly. "Are we close to a settlement or homestead?" she asked. She looked up in expectation, but the dim light did not allow her a clear view of Cole's face.

"We're not even close to civilization yet." Cole's step faltered. He stopped and squinted his eyes at something in the distance. A re-lieved sigh escaped from him. "But look up there," he said in a triumphant tone.

Dominique's gaze followed his. She turned around to face him again. "Is that a cabin?"

His head gave an eager nod. He hoped it still had some of the comforts of home inside its rugged log walls. Images of a warm, soft bed—and Dominique lying in the middle of that bed—flooded his mind. "We'd better grab some firewood, and burrow in for the night," he said. His quickened gait accentuated the enthusiasm in his voice. He took several long strides, then bent down to scoop up an armful of wood from the broken spruce branches that littered the ground.

His excitement infected Dominique. She giggled as she rushed to catch up with him. As she grabbed a couple of pieces of wood, her thoughts became consumed with visions that were similar to Cole's lascivious ones.

"How long have you known about this cabin?" she asked as they headed toward the structure.

"I've passed it every time I've traveled to Dawson City." He dropped his load of wood when they reached the cabin, and pushed the door open. Although he hadn't expected the door to be locked, he still experienced an instant relief to know they would not have to break into the cabin. A musty odor greeted their nostrils, but compared to the dampness in the air outside, the cabin seemed like a haven.

"How long has it been since somebody lived here?" Dominique asked as she entered. She blinked several times while her eyes adjusted to the darkness.

"It's been deserted for almost a year, but it seems to be holdin' up good." Cole knew that logs rotted fast in this wet climate. They were lucky this one was built out of large logs that would withstand more rain than most. He paused for a moment until his vision adjusted to the black interior of the cabin. There were two small windows, with glass panes, but they were too grimy to allow much outside light in. When he could see the layout of the inside, he stood his shotgun against the wall by the door and made his way to the wall with a rock fireplace. A small pile of dry wood was stacked beside the hearth. Cole added the wood he had brought to the pile, then tossed his pack to Dominique. "There's bedding in there," he said. His voice sounded high and shaky to his own ears. He tried to ignore the pounding of his heart as he knelt down and began to make a fire.

Dominique stumbled forward and retrieved his pack. She did not speak. Her head was buzzing with thoughts that left her mute. She glanced around, forcing her eyes to focus on the sparse furnishings in the cabin. A table with no chairs stood in the center—and against the far wall she could make out the distinct shape of a bed. Her feet moved toward the bed on their own accord. Once she reached the bed, she placed Cole's pack at her feet and blindly dug out the blankets he had packed for this trip. With trembling hands, she smoothed a blanket down over the lumpy mattress. The rope burns on her palms throbbed slightly. She thought about looking for the salve in Cole's bag, but then her mind filled with visions of lying with Cole on this bed. Her only pain now was the agony of having to wait until her images became a reality.

Cole heard her approach. It had taken nearly all his willpower to keep away from her while she made the bed. Her presence at his side created such a distraction that Cole found it almost impossible to concentrate on making a fire. The knowledge that she was watching every move made him feel awkward. He was aware of her soft breathing as she knelt beside him. It took him several attempts before he had a small blaze trailing up from the twigs he was using for kindling.

"Well, that should burn," he said. His voice was raspy, his breathing heavy. As he rose to his feet, he reached down and pulled Dominique up with him. Their bodies rubbed together, then pressed together as if they were one. He sought her lips without hesitation. The flame that shot through him was more ablaze than any fire he could ever start in the fireplace. He had planned to cook supper first, but food seemed unnecessary now.

Dominique was not surprised by his actions. She'd noticed the way his hands were trembling as he built the fire. She was aware of the way his breathing had become heavy, and she couldn't deny the underlying current of desire that had been with them all day. The instant he touched her to help her to her feet, there was no holding back the inevitable. Dominique's arms encircled his neck, her body responded to his nearness. Her lips parted to make way for his eager tongue. Every fiber of her being yearned for more as her hands massaged his neck, and the rock-hard muscles along his shoulders and back. Their lips and tongues fused together. She felt his hands slip inside her coat and begin to caress the swell of her breasts. His fingers lingered long enough to bring the tips of her breasts to taut attention. The sensations that surged through her made her legs quake like a new-born colt.

Cole felt the shudder shake her body. His own body began to shake. He thought of all the things he had planned for the night. The emotion this thought evoked, along with the anticipation, was overwhelming. Cole tore his lips away from hers, but their bodies remained molded together as if they were one. With aid of the dim light from the fire he could see her face when he gazed down. From under the brim of her hat, she stared up at him. They spoke silently with their eyes; words of love that neither of them could admit out loud, and words of passion that they could never resist.

"I'm going to do it right this time," Cole whispered. He reached out, pushed her hat off and pulled the pins from the bun that restrained her long hair. The heavy mass tumbled down her back. Cole captured the raven cascade in one hand, and gently drew it over the front of her shoulder. He smoothed the thick tresses, drawing his hand over her breast in a slow, tantalizing motion.

Dominique drew in a small gasp. Her tongue slid out of her mouth, and moistened her parched lips. "Did we do something wrong last time?" she asked. Her voice was breathless—barely audible.

The sight of her moist lips was Cole's undoing. He sighed deeply and nodded his head. His gray eyes were shot with silver bolts that resembled lightning. "I'm afraid so." He pulled his gaze away from her and glanced around the small cabin. His attention settled on the bed and a smile curved his lips. "But tonight, I'll make up for all the wrongs."

He turned back to the fire and tossed several large logs in the middle of the flames. They would burn for a long time, and he didn't want to worry about anything except for the promise he had just made to this woman. When he returned his attention to Dominique, the expression she wore made his heartbeat race. He recognized her look; it echoed his own feelings, and it drove him to hold her closer.

Once again, his mouth descended on Dominique's. Their kisses were demanding now, almost beyond reason. Without losing the enslaving hold on her lips, Cole began to move her toward the bed. This was an easy task, because she was mindless to anything other than his kisses—and the other things she knew were soon to come. When they reached the edge of the bed, Dominique felt herself being lowered down onto the mattress. The weight of his hard body pressed her down farther. She was aware of the hard leather of his knife sheath pressing into her thigh. Then, a coldness washed over her as he suddenly pulled away and stood up.

A sense of panic rushed through Dominique as she pushed herself up. Her head was spinning, leaving her dizzy and weak. She stared up at him, her thoughts raging between confusion and fear as she tried to decipher his strange behavior. "Did I do something wrong?" she asked in a trembling voice.

Cole looked down at her. His head shook slowly from side to side. "No—it's me." He reached down and held his hand out toward her.

Dominique's gaze moved to his hand, then back up to his face. Her hand shook as she placed it in his waiting palm. She let him pull her up from the bed. A dozen thoughts flew through her mind, but only one was coherent. She was certain she had done something wrong! On wobbly legs she stood up, her gaze lowered. She was afraid—and ashamed—to gaze into his face again.

Inwardly, Cole cursed at himself. He was about to make the same mistake he made the first time he had made love to her. But, luckily, he had been able to stop himself in time before he had lost all control. Now, he intended to proceed in the manner he had been planning all day. Her gaze shot up to his face again. Surprise clouded her expression. "I promise I'll get it right this time," he said with a crooked grin curving his lips. "We have all night, and I want to savor every single minute of it." His smile widened as he slowly started to undo the buttons of her flannel shirt.

Although she was still confused, Dominique began to understand what he meant when his hands lingered on each button. As he undid a button, his fingertips drew taunting lines along the skin that had just been exposed. Her awareness increased as he gingerly removed her shirt, then he bent down to shower slow, teasing kisses on her neck. His hot, moist kisses slid lower as his lips continued to nip and kiss every inch of her neck and chest until he reached the tip of one of her breasts, where his proficient mouth latched hold of the hard kernel and began to suck in a slow motion that made Dominique cry out in ecstasy.

While his tongue and lips lavished attention on one breast, his hand kneaded and caressed the other, drowning Dominique's senses in pleasure. She understood now that there was much more to making love than just the final act, and she was eager to learn all that he could teach her. She embraced him and let her hands slide down his muscled back, desperate to know the feel of his bare skin, and to fondle his hard body in the same manner he was doing to her.

Her hands slid around until she was able to grab hold of his coat. Cole became aware of her efforts, and forced himself to straighten up. He helped her strip off his coat, and when her fingers fumbled with the buttons on his shirt, he impatiently undid them himself.

The feel of his bare chest beneath her hands sent Dominique's sense reeling. His rock-like muscles, and a scattering of soft, downy curls, were more soothing to her hands than any ointments or salve. Her fingers traced circles around his nipples, and slid up and down his firm chest with a devouring devotion. She felt like swooning, but did not want to miss one second of this wondrous new experience. Imitating Cole's previous actions, she leaned forward and began to kiss, lick and nibble at his bare chest.

Her teasing kisses broke the last of Cole's patience. He groaned with pleasure as he playfully pushed her down on the mattress. His lips found her mouth again as his hand undid the buttons on her trousers and slipped easily inside. Her flat stomach felt hot to his touch and, as his hand slid lower, the heat increased. Unlike the first time, her legs offered no resistance when his hand inched into the moistness of her pulsating womanhood.

Dominique felt a cry rise up within her. He was doing such a simple thing with his finger—merely massaging working it in minute circles—but the effect made Dominique insane. What he was doing was exquisite, but after a few minutes, it was not enough. Her fingers began to fumble with the buckle of his belt; she tugged frantically on the clasp.

Cole's kisses halted for a second when he realized what she was trying to do. He rose up slightly, undid his belt, and carefully placed the belt that held his treasured knife beside the bed, then allowed her to unfasten his pants. His body shook with rapture when her hand closed around his hard shaft. "Oh,

Monsieur," he heard her gasp. His emotions exploded. There would be no more holding back.

Dominique was uncertain how to proceed now that her curiosity led her to touch Cole in the same way he was touching her. She knew she must invent a different way to return the delight he was evoking in her. Her inventive mind commanded her sweating hand to tighten around his manhood, but she was not granted more time for exploring. Cole's groan reached her ears as he pulled away from her. She had no more than one second to worry about his withdrawal, because almost instantly, Cole pulled her pants down and in one swift movement, yanked her boots off as he discarded her pants.

Inch by inch, his gaze moved up to her face without missing one hollow or curve of her body. The soft light of the fire cast a golden sheen on her firm young body. Cole found himself in awe of her beauty when his eyes finished their close observation. He gazed into her misty blue eyes. For a moment that seemed endless, he remained motionless. Tonight had only just begun, but already he knew he had achieved far more than he had planned.

He wasted no time in doing away with the rest of his own clothes. For a moment, he stood above her, letting her inquisitive gaze travel over him. The shimmer in her vibrant-hued eyes grew incandescent. Her moist lips parted slightly as her breathing grew labored. The short breaths made her bosom rise and fall in rapid succession. Cole felt his chest tighten, and his loins swell even heavier. Gently, he nudged her legs apart with his knees as he lowered himself down to the bed.

Still reeling from the magnificent sight of him, Dominique was vitally aware of the way their heated flesh melded together when he joined her on the bed. He kissed her again—starting with her lips, then moving lower and lower, until he had kissed every inch of her—even the tips of her toes. Then, he began a sensual ascent with his mouth stopping to kiss her in the secret place she had never imagined he would want to kiss. His hands clasped her hips, raising her up until his lips and tongue could sear a wildly torturous trail in the center of her womanhood.

Dominique held his head firmly in her hands, her fingers dug into his thick hair. She writhed beneath him, whimpered, then cried out his name. His tongue's exploring invasion transported her to a heaven she had never dreamed existed. When she thought her body was about to shatter into a million fragments, he pulled away and began to kiss his way back up to her lips again. She felt him position his hips so that his hard shaft was pressing against the same area he had just lavished with such undivided attention. Her hands instinctively grabbed his shoulders as she braced herself for his first plunge.

Although he was aware of her readiness, there were still places Cole wanted to awaken before they journeyed farther. He let his iron-hard shank taunt her, while his lips and tongue charted another course to her ear and the tender skin surrounding it. She squirmed beneath him, murmuring words in French that he could not understand, but that fanned the fire in his soul. He felt her hands sliding down to clasp his hips, and he felt her legs spread farther apart. The waning control he still possessed fled. His mouth sought hers again as she started to draw in a deep breath. His kiss claimed her gasp, the air she breathed belonged to both of them at the same instant as he drove himself downward.

The night became a kaleidoscope of sensual experiences for each of them. Cole made love to her over and over again. His endurance and constant arousal surprised even Cole, for never had he been with a woman who gave him so much strength. The knowledge that he was the first man to teach her the language of love added to his stamina. Her eagerness to learn, and to use what she was taught to give pleasure back to him, left Cole crazy with desire.

The soft hazy glow of dawn was upon the cabin before they were forced to give in to their complete exhaustion. Together they reached the ultimate summit their bodies could conquer. Then, locked in one another's arms, they slowly descended back from the magical land they had discovered in the darkness of the night. Cole knew his existence in the real world would never be the same again.

Seven

Even before she opened her eyes, Dominique knew this was going to be a wonderful day. What else could follow such a perfect night? The smile that rested on her kiss-drenched lips was a natural accompaniment to the happiness she felt in her heart. For a few more minutes, she kept her eyes closed and revealed in the memories of the love she had shared with Cole. The cabin felt warm, and in her mind, she could imagine soft flames dancing in the fireplace. Instinctively, her arm slid across the mattress. Her fingers reached out with the intention of satisfying their desperate need to touch Cole again. They met with nothing more than the barren bed.

Dominique's eyes opened with a jolt. She stared at the empty bed until her sleepy mind cleared enough for her to focus her attention elsewhere. "Cole?" she called as she sat up. The cabin was illuminated by a golden glow from the sunlight filtering through the two small, dirty windows. The fireplace held only smoldering orange embers. An uneasiness crept through Dominique. "Cole?" she cried once more. She kicked the blanket away from her legs and sat up.

A coffee pot sat on the hearth, and the rich aroma of fresh-brewed coffee dominated the air. Dominique slid out of the bed, taking a blanket with her to drape around her unclothed body. Her hand trembled when she reached out to touch the tin coffee pot. It was still warm, so she knew Cole had not been gone long. Her heart began to pound like a hammer in her breast as she turned to grab for her clothes. The only thought in her mind was to go looking for Cole. Just as the blanket she held around her fell to the floor into a heap at her feet, the door swung open.

A low whistle emitted from Cole. His mouth curved into a suggestive smile, while his gaze slowly caressed her body. "Now that's a hell of a lot better than the breakfast I had planned."

Dominique felt a hot blush rush through her entire body, but she made no attempt to cover herself. His eyes seemed to touch her, even from across the room. Every inch of her skin where his gaze skimmed was left ablaze until she felt as though she was being consumed by the heat. She swallowed hard, and tried to catch her breath. Only a weak—and pleading—moan escaped from her parted lips.

The effect she had on Cole was immediate. To his eyes and mind, nothing existed beyond these cabin walls. Unconsciously, he leaned his shotgun against the wall, and shoved the door shut again. He did not try to deny his feelings, or argue with himself as he walked toward her. If he didn't take her in his arms again and quench the throbbing desire she aroused, Cole knew he would be aching all day long. As he approached her, his gaze drank in the breathtaking vision she created: her eyes, it seemed, were even more blue. Their twinkling spheres reminded him of diamonds mixed with sapphires. The passion in the their jeweled depths enticed his own hunger. The tangled strands of her long ebony hair hung in wild profusion around her bare shoulders and down past the middle of her back. Cole remembered how his lips and his hands had caressed and fondled her satiny-smooth skin. His yearning for her became overpowering.

"I was wor . . ." Dominique's words faded away. His intentions were obvious as he walked toward her. Before he even touched her she was lost to an eddy of desire. She drew in a deep breath in anticipation of his kiss. Her body grew fevered, and a primitive need arose in her soul that controlled all of her senses. Her face was tilted back when he reached her, and her lips were parted.

Cole wrapped her in his embrace. He let his savage kiss command the moment. This morning he felt no need to go slowly. Last night he had taken the time to explore every aspect of her sensuous body, and even more time to cater to her inexperience. He'd wanted to tutor her on every aspect of love-making; to take her to the highest peaks, and leave her a memory of a night she would never forget for the rest of her life. He felt confident he had fulfilled his goal. But this morning he was driven by a furious need. Perhaps this urgency was aroused by the disturbing things he had just seen outside the cabin. Whatever it was that controlled him, it left him aware of only one thing; he had to make love to Dominique once more before they left this cabin.

Spiraling sensations of delight engulfed Dominique when she felt Cole's arms lift her from the floor. Their lips continued to bestow potent kisses. His tongue—abrasive and devouring—entered her mouth. Dominique expected to be carried to the bed. Instead, he sat her down on the table top. His mouth never left hers, but Dominique was aware of his other actions. With one hand he was hastily unfastening his trousers. His other hand was wrapped snugly in the depths of her thick hair at the nape of her neck.

Dominique's spinning mind tried to concentrate on returning his kisses, but her attention was being drawn elsewhere. She thought she had learned all there was to know about making love last night. It seemed they had been in every position that was humanly possible. She realized now, she was mistaken.

Cole broke away from her lips to catch his breath. His longings for this temptress stole away more than just his breath—all of his senses were controlled by her alluring presence. His gaze sought her, his loins throbbed for her, and his heart was lost to her.

When he'd been outside the cabin this morning, his thoughts had dwelled on things he had once promised himself he would never think about; he had wondered if it was possible for him to have a future with Dominique. The thought of the man in Dawson City who had bought and paid for her tore at him. For one crazy minute, Cole had even thought of paying the man back the money himself. Then, Dominique would be free of her bridal obligations. But reality had soon claimed Cole's mind. He reminded himself that he had no money, and now with the riverboat gone, he had no means of earning any. He was sure Dominique had probably spent most of the money the gold miner had sent to pay for her passage to Dawson City. He reminded himself of one other important thing; she had given him no indication that she wanted to be freed from her impending marriage.

The agony of this realization had sent Cole into an even deeper explosion of jealousy. He'd tried to calm himself down before he returned to the cabin. He knew what he was capable of doing when jealous fury commanded him. The mere memory had made the scar on the side of his face throb relentlessly. Then, he had noticed the bear tracks leading up to the cabin. All other problems seemed minor. Like the tracks they'd seen yesterday, these had also been made after the heavy rains. And like the other tracks, the ones around the cabin were made by an exceptionally large bear. He retraced the bear's steps on shaky legs. They emerged from the forest, led straight to the cabin, and encircled the entire structure. Below the cabin's two small windows, Cole could tell where the bear had raised up on his hind legs. A clammy sweat broke out on Cole's body.

He had knelt down and studied the tracks more closely. He didn't know much about wildlife, but he was sure there weren't too many grizzlies as enormous as the one who had left these tracks. Had the grizzly from yesterday followed them to this cabin? He traced the tracks to the riverbank, about a quarter of a mile away from the cabin. There, he'd been consumed by a desperate need to get back to Dominique. Although he did not plan to tell her about the tracks, her fear of the bear had been obvious the previous day. His plan was to eat a quick breakfast, and then put as many miles between them and the bear as possible. When he'd opened the door and seen her standing there—fevered and unclothed—every other thought fled from his mind.

Dominique pushed his coat back from his broad shoulders, and undid the buttons of his shirt. This was becoming a habit, it seemed, and each time it became easier. She slid her hands beneath his shirt and clasped her arms around his hard body. His hands lifted her buttocks up slightly from the tabletop and he entered her with one powerful lunge. Her gasp was stolen away as his mouth claimed hers in an imprisoning kiss. For a moment she was engulfed in agony for last night's endless passion had left her sore and tender. Before long, however, she became caught up in the savage passion he unleashed . . .

Her pain became a raging ache as he drove deeper. His hands held her tightly against him, and her legs instinctively wrapped around his hips. Each of Cole's movements took her with him; they were bonded together. Dominique felt as though she was on the ocean, cresting the highest waves over and over again, until they finally rocketed her high above the water. She heard a deep, animal-like moan escape from Cole at the same instant she thought her own body had soared beyond the realm of sanity. She clung to him like a dying woman might cling to her last breath.

For several minutes neither of them moved. Cole attempted to catch his breath, and corral his run-away emotions. He knew he had made love to her as brutally as a rutting bull, yet he sensed she had felt the same type of fevered need. With a quivering sigh, he leaned back to gaze into her face. Their eyes met, and almost seemed to embrace. Cole thought of the things he had been pondering when he was outside. The words he wanted to say—the questions he wanted to ask—lay heavy in his throat. If she had not reached up and touched the scar on the side of his face, he might have said what he yearned to say.

Dominique's finger gently traced the scarred tissue from its beginning at the corner of his eye, to its ending a little below his cheekbone. She thought she noticed him flinch slightly, but she didn't remove her hand. "How did you get this?" Her voice was soft, inquiring. The tip of her finger still touched the end of the scar. The guarded expression that closed down over his face, the flickering silver bolts reflecting in his eyes, made Dominique cringe inwardly.

"In a sword fight," he said in a gruff voice. He pulled back, cleared his throat, and began to fasten his pants. "The sun is out; looks like the stormy weather has finally blown over."

For a time Dominique did not reply. She watched his withdrawal, and envisioned the violent sword fight in his past. She recalled how in France men fought duels to win the hand of the woman they loved. Her gaze continued to study Cole's unreadable expression and brisk actions. It was not difficult for her to imagine a proud man like him fighting to

117

claim a woman's love. What surprised her, though, was that he apparently had lost the fight—and the woman.

"I got me a real hankerin' for some food. Even the mess we got served on the boat would be welcome right about now." Cole's words rushed over one another. He stalked to the fireplace, grabbed a long twig and stirred the dying embers. "Might be the last warm meal we'll have before we reach Fort Yukon," he added. He thought of the bear tracks. They wouldn't be killing or cooking any game that might entice the old grizzly's appetite.

Awkwardly, Dominique slid off the table. Her clothes—and the blanket—were across the room. She had no choice but to parade past him. A fiery sensation cloaked her entire body in a thin sheen of perspiration. Although he had felt, caressed, and kissed every portion of her, Dominique was still overcome with a strangling sense of modesty as she began to inch toward her clothes. Cole turned from the fire just as she walked past him. Her footsteps faltered—she swallowed hard. Before she was able to take another step, he was drawing her into his arms again.

Cole buried his face in the dark profusion of her hair. He drew in a burdened breath, and held her naked body tightly in his embrace. "I got the wound fighting over a woman on the French Riviera," he said unexpectedly. He was surprised by his own admission. He had never spoken to anyone but

Luther about Susanah, and that was only because Luther had been there when he had made such a fool of himself.

Dominique remained silent for a moment. His pain was undeniable, and for reasons she could not decipher, his words sent her heart plummeting into a pit of despair. "You must have loved her very much," she whispered. Unconsciously, her fingers clutched the back of his shirt.

Another heavy sigh left Cole's lips. "I did love her, but it was a long time ago. Those feelings are dead now." He felt Dominique nervously twisting her hands against his back. He didn't know what he was trying to convey to her by discussing the subject. "I-I . . ." he leaned back to gaze into Dominique's face, his thoughts a tangled web.

A sharp pain seared through Dominique's heart. She could see the turmoil in his gaze, but she had her own uncertainties to deal with right now. Was he trying to tell her his ability to fall in love again was dead, too? What would he do if she told him that she didn't want to go to Dawson City . . . that she was in love with him, and she could never be with another man for as long as she lived? "I must tell you," she began. Her voice was shaky, just like her knees. "About Dawson Ci—"

He pressed his fingertips to her lips to silence her. "I don't want to talk about that." He could not control the rapid thudding in his chest. It felt as if his rib cage was about to explode. "I just want to concentrate on the time we have now." His voice assumed a tone of desperation as he added, "I don't want to think about what tomorrow might bring, and . . ." his words halted abruptly. Most of all, he didn't want to think about Dawson City and the man Dominique was supposed to marry. All of his common sense told him their future could not turn out as he wished. If only he had something to offer her. He sighed again, then leaned down to kiss her trembling lips. He caught a glimpse of shimmering tears in her eyes, and his own eyes began to sting too. He told himself it was caused by the unfurling smoke from the fireplace.

Cole's kiss was so tender, barely more than a brushing of their lips. It was a complete contrast to the way he had kissed her when he first entered the cabin. Everything he did continued to confuse Dominique. She still had a burning desire to tell him how she felt about him—and about the future. But the words he had just spoken made her unsure of how much she should say. Maybe he was right, she told herself, maybe they should just concentrate on now, on today. When, and if, they made it to Fort Yukon, she would tell him all the things she longed to say.

"Hungry now?" he asked again when he pulled away. His gaze instinctively lowered. He noticed a reddish blush work its way from her cheekbones and down the entire length of her curvaceous body. He also noticed the way he was affected again. He had no doubt he could make love to this woman nonstop for twenty-four hours a day. And he would, too, if he didn't have Luther, his crew, and all the other passengers from the riverboat depending on him.

Dominique gave her head a brisk nod as she scurried to her clothes. She knew it would be useless to try to speak; there was a huge lump in her throat. The embarrassment she felt, though, was secondary to the torment in her heart. Maybe, even when they did reach Fort Yukon, she still would not be able to tell Cole how much she loved him. Maybe he would only want to be rid of her by that time.

She let her mind draw an imaginary picture of the woman Cole had loved so passionately. Dominique had never been to the French Riviera, but she had heard her mother talk about the beaches of endless white sand, the fabulous villas clinging to the vine-colored hillsides, and the abundance of wealth among the Riviera's exclusive inhabitants. To the image of a beautiful woman, Dominique's imagination added money, prestige . . . and unquestionable respectability. Dominique's spirits plummeted. How could she—the daughter of a whore—ever hope to win a man who had known such high breeding and substantial wealth? Dominique could not deny that Cole had brought her along for one purpose only; to fulfill his own lustful urges. Nor

121

could she deny that she had been a willing partner to his disgraceful plan.

Dominique silently cursed herself as she pulled on her clothes. Chastising herself did little to relieve the throbbing pain in her breast. She was overcome with the urge to run from this cabin, and keep running until she had escaped from the pain, and from Cole. She couldn't bear the idea of not being with him, though, so she did nothing.

"Can I-I h-help with breakfast?" she asked. Her voice was weak and it cracked when she spoke. She approached Cole with slow steps. He was digging supplies out of his pack and handed her a small black frying pan. Dominique noticed he avoided meeting her gaze.

"Luther packed us some biscuits," he said as he handed her the pan. "And there's some eggs in here that survived the trip from the Lady Susanah." He tried to make his voice sound light and cheerful. It was a wasted effort. The unhappiness that was echoed in the tone of her voice affected him in a profound way. Cole straightened up and let his pack drop at his feet. He gazed down at her, noting the sorrowful expression on her lovely face. Words eluded him as his thoughts continued to dwell on his own short-comings. He feigned a grin, and tried to think clearly as he asked, "Can you cook?"

His question brought a smile to Dominique's mouth. She reached out and took the two eggs he held out to her. "Monsieur, I might have been nothing more than a maid in San Francisco, but I did manage to pick up a few cooking hints from the chefs." She turned toward the fireplace swiftly before he noticed how hard it was for her to keep from crying.

A flash of surprise claimed Cole for a moment. A maid? He grew furious with himself as he recalled how grossly he had misjudged her. Maybe he had been hanging around with unsavory women for so many years he no longer knew a decent one when he met her. He watched Dominique in silence as she busied herself with the breakfast. Questions taunted him: Her accent was proof she had once lived in France, so how did she end up in California? Why would such a beautiful—and resourceful—woman feel the need to go to an awful place like Dawson City and marry a man she'd never met? Cole's curiosity continued to grow as he dug eating utensils out of his pack.

"How long have you been in America?" he ventured as he held out a tin plate for the eggs she had just cooked. She shrugged, and turned away from him again as soon as she had scooped the eggs out of the pan.

"Since I was a child."

"You came directly to San Francisco from France?"

Her head shook from side to side. She still

did not turn to look at him. "No. We left Paris and sailed to New Orleans first."

"We—you mean you and your family?" Cole noticed a tenseness in her stance. He wished he could see her face, but she kept her back to him as she gave her head a quick nod. When she remained still and silent, he decided to attempt another approach. "I traveled to France with my parents when I was a child. We also sailed to England." He knew the last thing she probably wanted to hear was the details of his childhood, but for reasons he did not understand, he felt a need to tell her about his past. "They wanted me to have culture, so they spent their entire life savings to take me to Europe the summer I turned thirteen." He chuckled, remembering how horrified his bible-toting parents had been when he declined to follow in his father's footsteps and take over the family business—a general store in midwestern Ohio. "From the first day I set foot on that ship, I knew I was meant to be a sailor. And, the day I turned eighteen, I headed back to the sea."

Dominique turned slowly, wiping away a lone teardrop as she gazed up at him. His love and passion for the sea was evident in the way his gray eyes shone with excitement. She remembered his reaction when she had asked him why he was no longer sailing the ocean. Her gaze settled on the scar at the side of his face. She sensed his sword fight and his reasons for being in this desolate country might somehow be related but before she could ask him the questions that plagued her, Cole changed the subject again.

"We'd best eat up, and get on the move as soon as we can," he said quickly. He'd noticed the way she was staring at his scar, and he wasn't ready to talk to her about Susanah. Hell! He didn't want to talk about Susanah ever again. But the scar she'd left him with went far deeper than the ugly cut down the side of his face . . . and it left him with a memory from which he could never escape.

Eight

The morning was not progressing as Dominique had thought. After eating breakfast quickly, with little conversation, they packed up their gear and left the cabin. Tears stung Dominique's eyes once more as she glanced back at the cabin for the last time. She was certain she would never have another night as special and wondrous as the night she and Cole had spent here. In her last glance, she tried to memorize the rustic log-walls of the cabin, and the towering Arctic spruce trees that rose up behind its sloped roof. The cabin and its surroundings seemed picture-perfect to her. She knew she would never forget one tiny detail of this magical place, or of the night of passion she had shared with Cole Hawkins.

"Dominique?" Cole called when he noticed she had stopped. "Did you forget something back there?" He still hadn't told her about the bear tracks around the cabin. He figured he could worry enough for the both of them. The faster they moved out of this area, the safer he would feel. Surely, he told himself, they would be out of the grizzly's territory soon.

Blinking back the tears, Dominique shook her head. "No, I didn't forget anything." She tried to force a smile as she tore her gaze away from the cabin. She moved forward and caught up with Cole as he glanced up at the sky.

Only a few wispy clouds still lingered, but the damp chill clung to the air for most of the morning. The ground was muddy only in spots, so walking was easier today. As the morning eased into afternoon the sun's rays began to warm up the temperature. Cole knew the Yukon's idea of a summer day meant one of two things: relentless rain or muggy heat that drew hordes of blood-thirsty mosquitos who preyed on anything that moved or breathed. By midday, it was obvious the latter was true.

"What is that?" Dominique asked as they climbed a small ridge and glanced down into a narrow ravine that was devoid of trees.

Cole paused, and squinted his eyes. "Ah hell!" he spat. He drew in a sharp breath, adding, "That, woman, is more vicious than any grizzly we'll ever encounter."

Full of foreboding, Dominique stared down at the black cloud that hung in the air in the clearing. "But, what—"

"Arctic mosquitos," Cole retorted. He patted the pack he carried. "I brought along some of the repellent we kept on the steamer. Whenever the sun is out you can expect swarms of these little demons."

A gasp escaped from Dominique as she watched the swarm swell in size right before her eyes. She wiped a band of sweat from her forehead, realizing it was becoming too hot for all the layers of clothes she was wearing. The heavy clothes were sticking to her perspiring body. She reached up with the intent to remove her wide-brimmed hat.

"Don't take anything off," Cole commanded as he started to dig in the pack. "You'll need every bit of clothing you have on, and maybe more."

"But it's getting hot," she complained. He cut her off sharply.

"Better to suffer a little heat than the bite of those sharp stingers sinkin' into your flesh." His gray gaze narrowed with a silent warning when Dominique opened her moth to disagree. Her mouth closed without further comment.

"Here," Cole said when he found what he was looking for. He produced a tin lard container. "Smear this all over—on your clothes and especially on any skin that's exposed." He glanced down in the hollow and added, "Hurry."

His sudden urgency caused a cold shiver to race down Dominique's spine, in spite of the warm temperature. Her hands shook as she pulled the lid off of the lard can. An overpowering scent assaulted her nostrils. She coughed, and shoved the lid back down on the container.

"It's got creolin in it," Cole said, yanking the container out of her hand. He pulled the lid off, wrinkled his nose at the strong smell, but forced himself to dig into the lard mixture and scoop out a heaping handful. Without hesitation he reached out and smeared the greasy glob down the front of Dominique's coat. She started to back away—he stepped forward, adding, "I've heard of animals going insane from the bites of these insects." She halted her retreat. She peered up at him from beneath the brim of her hat. Knowing he had her attention, and knowing the seriousness of their predicament, he continued in a forceful tone. "Even grizzlies are afraid of those," he motioned with his head toward the heavy swarm.

Dominique's gaze followed the direction of his nod. A startled cry flew from her mouth. The mosquitos were moving toward them like an angry storm cloud. She reached into the lard can and began to smear the rest of her clothes, face and hands with the horrible smelling concoction.

As Cole rubbed himself down with the repellent, he pondered over their options. He was still reluctant to hike too far away from the river. From experience on the riverboat, however, he knew the mosquitos thrived in the lower elevations, and especially where there were wetlands. His thoughts were interrupted when the first of the hungry insects engulfed them. They hit like a violent gust of wind, and even though Cole knew what to expect, he gasped when he felt their powerful force. He quickly clamped his mouth shut, but too late. In his gasp he inhaled a mouthful of the insects. He spit out as many as possible, but fear of entrapping more in his mouth made him swallow the rest. He fought back the urge to gag, and forced his attention to focus on Dominique.

The shock of the mosquitos' attack left her too stunned to move for a second. When her sense of survival kicked in, though, she began to swing her arms wildly through the air in a wasted effort to drive away the suffocating throng. Like Cole—and to her horror—she immediately discovered her cries of surprise attracted the pests into her mouth. Gasping and spitting, she attempted to expel the insects at the same time she uselessly flailed her arms.

Cole's decision about leaving the lowlands was made without further thought. He grabbed one of Dominique's arms in mid-air, and dragged her with him as he headed away from the river. Even though she tripped and stumbled frequently, she recovered her balance quickly, and stayed at his side. They walked at a fast pace, but never broke into a run. The heat of the day, and the heavy layers of clothing they wore, sapped their energy. They pushed on without communicating in any way. The insects moved with them, hovering over their heads, in front of their faces, and fluttering against their lips whenever they were forced to take a breath. In spite of the lard and creolin repellent, layers of the pesky mosquitos covered their clothing. Frequently, the sharp prongs of their needle-sharp lancets would burrow past the thick padding of Cole's or Dominique's clothes, piercing and biting until they were gorged with blood.

After a while, Dominique was no longer aware of the stinging bites. She knew she could not allow coherent thoughts to enter her mind for fear that she would discover she had gone mad—just as Cole had said animals did when they were tormented by these horrible insects.

As they entered the pine forest that blanketed the foothills, Cole halted their swift retreat. He produced the lard can again. Without words, they both doused themselves again with the meager protection. For a few minutes of welcome peace, the mosquitos backed off. But, as soon as Cole began to lead Dominique deeper into the shrouded woods, the insects swarmed around them again. Cole followed a non-existent trail, which climbed steadily through the dense forest of pines. He had no destination, other than to find escape from the blood-stealing insects. He had heard at higher elevations, where the wind frequently blew, the mosquitos were seldom present. He hoped this proved to more fact than fiction.

Dominique was sure she couldn't take another step. Whenever they would pause for a moment or two, however, the mosquitos would completely engulf them. The hope that they would eventually escape was the only goal she sought as she pushed herself on. Finally, after a seemingly endless time, the sun began to fade; the temperature grew cooler, and miraculously, the mosquitos ceased to follow.

"We'll camp here tonight," Cole announced as soon as he felt they were free of the mosquitos. He glanced around nervously. They were surrounded by the tall Arctic white spruce trees. Being the only breed of their species to survive at the higher elevations, these spruce were small trunked and sparsely branched. Cole didn't care if they had no branches at all, he was just relieved to find peace.

"I will never understand why anybody would want to live in this damn country," he growled while he pulled his hat off his head. Rivulets of sweat ran down his face. In an angry gesture he wiped them away with his gloved hand. He dropped his pack on the ground, then rested the shotgun against the side of the large pack. His arm and shoulder ached from the weight of the pack, but he knew they needed everything it contained.

Dominique followed his lead, and yanked her hat off. A cool, gentle breeze touched her sweating face. She was sure they must have climbed all the way to heaven. Her clothes felt glued to her body. The wool pants and flannel shirt were scratchy, and her skin was raw. Her mind echoed Cole's opinions about this place, but she was too tired to voice them out loud.

"Are you all right?" Cole put his own discomfort aside to help Dominique remove her heavy coat. Her face was swollen and red from mosquito bites. He told himself he would rub salve on them before they fell asleep.

Dominique only had enough energy to nod her head. She knew she was alive because death probably wouldn't be so miserable. The recurring thought of a tub filled with scented water, clean clothes, and a soft bed filled her mind. She moaned softly. Cole's arms immediately encircled her from behind. She leaned back against him, letting his strong embrace be her sole support. His chin resting on the top of her head felt almost too heavy a burden. It created a throbbing pressure in her head that bolted down through her body and left her legs shaky.

"We'd better get some rest," Cole said in a low voice. He'd noticed how weak she seemed to be. He worried she would get sick, and up here in the middle of nowhere, there would be nothing he could do to help her. Reluctantly, he released her and retrieved his pack. He dug out their bedrolls and spread them out beneath a nearby spruce.

Dominique had not moved the entire time

he had prepared their beds. She was staring in his direction, but her gaze did not seem to be focused on him. Her expression was blank, almost as if she was in a trance.

"How 'bout some supper?" he asked. She replied with a slow negative shake of her head. Cole's worry abounded. "You have to eat something to keep up your strength." She shook her head again.

"I'm too tired to eat," she replied. Her voice echoed the exhaustion she felt in her body. In her weary state, her mind was jumbled with rational and irrational thoughts. She was overcome with the urge to tell Cole how she felt about him. Every moment they spent together seemed to expand her feelings for him. In just the short time they had been together they had shared everything from tragedy to passion. These experiences instilled emotions she knew would never leave her for as long as she lived. She wanted to know what Cole was feeling, and she needed to ask him if they were still going to be together after this ordeal was over. The one sensible thought in her head, though, kept telling her that this was not the right time to bombard Cole with these emotional questions.

"Come over here, woman," Cole said in the forceful tone he used when he commanded his crew. "I'm not goin' to argue with you. I'm goin' to rub salve on your face, and then you're goin' to eat something." Her head jerked up at the sound of his deep voice. Cole thought he saw a flicker of anger flash through her blue gaze. Anything was better than the forlorn look her face had carried a moment ago.

"I beg your pardon, Monsieur?" Dominique retorted. She was too tired, and too much on edge from the emotions she was trying to cope with, to let him talk to her as if she was a child. The anger his tone of voice aroused in her was invigorating. She tossed her head back, and placed her hands on her hips. Her gaze drilled into his with a narrowed look of defiance.

A smile came easily to Cole's mouth. "I guess you're not ready to give up. You had me worried for a minute there." He started to step forward, but the sound of a lone wolf howling off in the distance stopped him in his tracks as a cold shiver whipped through his body.

Dominique clutched her arms around herself and shivered visibly. "That's such a lonesome sound."

Cole dismissed the wolf from his thoughts as he stepped toward Dominique. "Now, about supper? You have a choice between canned beans or no canned beans, and biscuits." He stepped in front of her—almost close enough to lean down and kiss her.

Dominique raised her gaze to his face. Her intention was to resume their conversation. When she noticed the swollen, red mosquito bites on Cole's face, however, every other thought fled from her mind. Instinctively, her hand rose up to her own face. Her eyes widened, and a surprised gasp escaped from her mouth. Until the instant she became aware of the mass of bites they had not bothered her. Now, her face erupted with a hot, stinging sensation. "Mon Dieu!" she said in a raspy voice as she began to rub vigorously at her cheeks.

"A little of Luther's special salve will take care of those," Cole said. "Don't scratch at 'em, or they'll leave scars." He noticed her gaze touch briefly on the area where the old scar ran down the side of his face. She glanced away, then offered no resistance when he reached out and pulled her hand away from her face. A rush of fire shot through the side of Cole's face. He'd never cared much about how this scar looked, but now he wondered if it looked ugly or hideous to Dominique. He reminded himself that it didn't matter; once they reached Dawson City she wouldn't be looking at him again anyway. This thought only increased the pain that emanated from the scar and the sadness that tore at his heart.

"I'll rub some of the salve on you first," Dominique said. The look of acute pain that had just crossed his swollen face made her own discomfort seem minor.

Cole felt a fevered flush overtake his body. He wondered why he couldn't seem to control or hide his emotions anymore. He shrugged, released his hold on her hand, and turned away. "I'll get the salve," he said hoarsely. From the pack, he dug out the medicine and their food for supper. He had taken enough for three days, the length of time he figured it would take them to hike to Fort Yukon. They'd been out for two days, and now that they were up on the mountain with no river in sight, Cole was not sure if they would reach the post before they ran out of supplies. Without the river as his guide, Cole was not sure they would *ever* find Fort Yukon. A cool mountain breeze whipped through the trees, but it did nothing to soothe the defeated feeling in Cole's body.

"I'll take that," Dominique said as she took the salve from his hand. She noticed that after he had dropped the pack back down on the ground, he seemed to freeze, staring off into the darkening forest with a far-away expression on his face. He blinked when she spoke, and shifted his gaze to her face.

"Sit down here," she ordered. She motioned to the bedrolls he had spread out under the tree. She thought she detected a sheepish expression wash over Cole's face.

"How 'bout we do each other—at the same time?" he suggested. He forced himself to put his worry about being lost to the back of his mind. Tomorrow, he could start to worry again.

They sat cross-legged opposite each other and gently rubbed the medicine on their faces. The shadows of night embraced them, making it impossible for Dominique to see the look in Cole's gray gaze. She could feel the tenderness in his touch as he cared for her mosquito bites. With equal devotion, she tended to his bites. The lower portion of his face had sprouted a coarse sprinkling of whiskers. Using her fingertips, Dominique was careful not to let the sharp whiskers poke the newly-healed skin on the palms of her hands.

"Are you ready to eat now?" Cole asked when they were finished doctoring their bites. He heard Dominique sigh, then she surprised him by scooting up to him and wrapping her arms around his mid-section. His arm automatically encircled her. He leaned back against the tree, stretching his legs out so he could hold her close.

"I want to talk," Dominique said. She could feel the pounding of his heart against her cheek. His heart's rhythm had a comforting effect, and almost instantly, she felt her eyelids grow heavy.

"About what?" Cole's voice was steady, but his thoughts were raging through his head. There were things he wanted to talk to her about, too.

"You . . . and me."

Her words were barely audible, but Cole heard. The knowledge that she was thinking along the same lines as he was induced a sense of panic in him. He felt a trembling sensation in the pit of his stomach. "W-What about u-us?" he mumbled.

Dominique's exhaustion was quickly overcoming her waning resistance to stay awake. She desperately wanted to talk to him, but she could feel herself slipping farther into an engulfing darkness. "About Dawson . . ." the words clung to her thick tongue as they faded away.

Cole felt her grow limp against him. He heard her breathing grow even and steady. Her last words still hung heavy in his mind. What had she wanted to tell him about Dawson City? Cole exhaled hard. The quaking knot in his stomach tightened. He had the urge to shake her awake, and demand to know what she was about to say. But then, he started to think about all the other worries that plagued him. His thoughts traveled back to the days when he had been captain of his own ship. Then, he'd had money, power, and self-respect. He could have offered Dominique the world. Now, he had nothing to offer. Until he regained some of what he had lost, how could he talk to her about anything? At least she had a future awaiting her in Dawson City.

Cole's eyes closed, yet sleep eluded him. He stroked Dominique's back as he held her close to him. She smelled like lard and creolin, but Cole didn't notice. Throughout the long night, he was aware of only two things; the way he felt about her, and the pain he knew he would suffer when he was forced to say goodbye.

Nine

Cole did not sleep much that night. In fact, he had hardly slept since he had met Dominique. Most of the night he held her close while he wallowed in his self-pity. Towards dawn he dozed for a while, but a sound woke him with a start. He leaned forward and listened for the noise again. Something was moving through the trees close by. Carefully, he eased his arm out from under Dominique's sleeping form. She stirred slightly when he laid her head down on her bedroll. A soft sigh rolled from her parted lips, but she did not wake up. In the grey light of the breaking dawn, Cole studied her face for a second. Her mosquito bites were barely more than small red dots this morning, and the lines of exhaustion he had seen in her face last night were gone. To Cole, she looked like a sleeping angel. He started to reach down to touch her cheek, but his hand froze in mid-air when he heard another noise. He recognized the sound as a low growl.

With cautious movements, Cole rose to his feet. As he stood, he grabbed the shotgun with one hand. With his other hand, he clasped the top of his knife handle. He was more skilled with a knife than he was with the gun. To use the knife, though, he would have to get a lot closer to a wild animal than he wanted to be. Cole paused to listen for the noise again. It came only a second later, along with a rustling sound as something moved closer to the campsite. Cole glanced down at Dominique. She had not moved again. Cole's grip on the weapons tightened as he started to move away from the campsite. Several times, he stopped to look back over his shoulder at Dominique. Each time he stopped, the rustling sounds drew his attention back toward the forest.

The campsite was out of Cole's line of vision when he was able to glimpse through the tangle of spruce woods the source of the noise. He halted, and stared at the silver-grey timber wolf that watched him from only several yards away. The upper lip of the wolf curled up in a snarl as he leveled his glittering yellow gaze on Cole. Neither the wolf or the man moved, each hypnotized by the sight of the other. Cole held his breath. He was aware of the faint wild smell of the large wolf as a mild breeze whispered through the trees. The wolf was in an alert stance with his tail raised, his ears standing straight up as he growled menacingly. The bristly hairs along his back stood on edge. He began to turn his thick neck in a slow movement and his hind legs bent as though he was getting ready to pounce.

Cole's body tensed. His thoughts were racing as fast as his heartbeat as he tried to decipher the wolf's intentions. Although he didn't have the feeling that the wolf wanted to attack him, he did sense that the wolf was prepared to fight if he felt threatened.

Then, without warning, the thick fur across the wolf's haunches puffed up, his body drew together and his head whipped around in a different direction. In less than an instant his entire body rotated, and he bounded out of Cole's sight. Cole still didn't move for several more seconds. A sense of relief flooded through him that the majestic animal had chosen not to have a confrontation. At the same time, the wolf's behavior surprised him.

Another noise caught his attention. He turned in the direction the wolf had looked before he had disappeared into the maze of the forest. The blood felt as if it had frozen in Cole's veins. An icy sweat erupted on his body. The trunks and swooping branches of the trees did not grant him with a clear view of the animal that lumbered through the woods several hundred yards away. Cole, however, did not want a clearer—or closer—look at the bear. His sweating hand clutched the shotgun, but he didn't have time to raise the gun up before the enormous grizzly moved out of his sights.

For a few more minutes, Cole remained completely still. His gaze moved frantically from one tree trunk to another, but the bear seemed to have disappeared as fast as he appeared. Cole's mind had the image of the bear memorized, however, and the memory made his knees want to buckle. This grizzly, Cole knew, was an exceptional specimen. The old boar was brown in color. Age had turned the tips of his heavy coat a silvery-white. He was walking on all fours, but Cole was sure if he rose up on his hind legs he would stand at least nine feet tall. There was a large hump on his back between his shoulder blades, and when he had glanced in Cole's direction, Cole could swear his eyes were a demonic shade of red.

Cole could hear the massive paws of the grizzly crunching down on the leaves and branches that coated the forest ground. The footsteps faded until there were no sounds other than an occasional chirping of a bird, or chattering of a squirrel. His shock over seeing the bear did not fade. He figured it was because of some minor miracle that the animal had not decided to attack him. Was this the same bear who had made the tracks around the cabin? he wondered. If it was the same bear—was he stalking them? Drawing in a deep breath, Cole forced himself to turn away from the area where he had seen the bear and made his way back to the campsite, glancing nervously over his shoulder. He would be worried about facing down any grizzly, but one the size of this old boar was a frightening thought.

He wondered if he should tell Dominique. Since he'd never mentioned the tracks at the cabin, he decided it would be best not to tell her about his encounter this morning either. He ran back to where she slept and found her in the same vulnerable position as when he left her. As he approached she stirred, and struggled to open her eyes. The way her long, ebony lashes fluttered against the soft outline of her cheekbones reminded Cole of the wings of a butterfly.

''Mornin','' he said, hoping his voice sounded normal. He leaned the shotgun against a tree, and stepped closer to her. His heartbeat had calmed a bit, but it still had not returned to a normal pace. Nor had the image of the bear been wiped out of his mind. But the longer he stared at Dominique, the less he thought about the grizzly. She had finally managed to open her eyes completely. The vibrant hue of her eyes never ceased to amaze him. She blinked several times, raised her azure eyes up to his face, and smiled in a contented manner that made Cole's heart pick up its frantic beat again. There were no thoughts of the grizzly clouding his vision now. He noticed she looked much better than she did last night. A sense of relief joined the other emotions he was starting to experience. Dominique's arms raised up in a long stretch. She still wore all her clothes—even her coat—to ward off the chill of the Yukon breeze, but Cole's mind imagined what each curve of her sensuous body looked like under the heavy layers of clothing. He drew a trembling breath and wondered if she would mind if he made love to her again.

"Good morning to you, Monsieur," she said in a teasing voice.

Cole's legs quivered under his weight. He loved that word . . . Monsieur. He watched as she pushed herself up into a sitting position, and instinctively raised her hand up to attempt to smooth down the tangled mass of her long hair. Abandoning the futile mission, she ran her tongue daintily along her parched lips. Cole knew he had no choice then but to make love to her. However, her next words were like a dousing of ice cold water.

"I'm as hungry as a bear. You know, we never did eat supper last night."

"Hell," he muttered under his breath. He noticed Dominique's contented expression change to worry and doubt. "Ah, don't pay me no never-mind," he said as he waved his arm through the air in an exasperated gesture. "It's just that eating was the last thing on my mind." Though a suggestive smile curled his lips he knew the mood was lost. As long as that grizzly was stalking this area, he could not allow his attention to be distracted, even if Dominique was a distraction that was hard to resist.

Dominique's tense expression relaxed as the meaning of his words penetrated her groggy senses. Her dark brows rose up, a hot flush colored her cheeks. The increasingly familiar longing raced through her being. She tilted her head back so she could look into his eyes. He was looking away, staring off into the trees as if he expected to see something of grave importance. Dominique's passionate mood evaporated. Her gaze followed his, but she saw nothing but the endless succession of Arctic spruce.

"Cole? Is there something out there?"

Her question snapped him out of his trance. He turned to glance down at her again. "There was a wolf," he said quickly. "He's gone now, but we probably should eat and get movin' before too long." He glanced over his shoulder again before he knelt down to retrieve his pack.

His sudden change of attitude caused a shiver to run through Dominique. She didn't like the idea of any wild animal being so close, but a wolf didn't seem nearly as terrifying as the bear tracks they'd seen on the first day. Not wanting to push Cole into a darker mood, Dominique decided to remain silent but she still planned to talk to him about her feelings before they reached Fort Yukon.

After a cold breakfast of biscuits and water, Cole broke camp, making small talk all the while. As his fear of the grizzly began to ease, his worries over their location increased. The detour they had been forced to make yesterday took them far from the trail he had planned to follow to the post.

By the time they stopped for the midday meal, Cole knew without a doubt they were hopelessly lost. Without the sun to guide him he had no idea in what direction they were headed. Every tree, and every rock looked the same. He was constantly on the lookout for any more signs of the bear, which seemed to leave him even more disoriented. The towering height of the spruce trees told him they had climbed high up the mountain slope, but Cole was sure that if he could catch a glimpse of the valley floor through the thick forest, he could get his bearings straight. Unless they headed down again, Cole had no way of knowing if they were moving in the right direction. He also knew he would have to tell Dominique, although his male pride dreaded this task.

"How much farther is Fort Yukon?" she asked as they gnawed on dried beef, shared a can of beans, and polished off the last of the biscuits. When they had left the cabin yesterday morning, she had wished they would never reach the post. Today, though, the small comforts of civilization were the most predominant thoughts in her mind.

Her question left Cole with no choice but to discuss their predicament. The hike from the sunken steamer to Fort Yukon should have taken no longer than three days if they had been able to stay with the river. Today was their third day out, and Cole sensed they were no closer to the post than they were on the first day. He set his tin plate down on the ground as he glanced around with a fervent hope that there would be something he hadn't noticed before—a landmark he'd recognize; the river, or better yet, the post at Fort Yukon. He glimpsed none of those things.

As she waited for Cole's reply, Dominique pulled off her hat, and ran her fingers through her tangled hair. They had not had a chance to wash the greasy mosquito repellent off and she felt grimy, sticky, and more miserable than she could ever remember. "Mon Dieu! What I won't give for a bath." She glanced at Cole as a soft rosy glow lit her face.

It was becoming a natural thing for their eyes to be held prisoner by one another. Dominique's innocent comment about a bath drew Cole's attention away from the seriousness of being lost as his mind filled with images of frolicking with her in a big, deep tub, or in the frothy waves along a tropical beach. Then his thoughts snapped back to reality and the towering trees seemed to close in around him. He vowed that if he ever got out of the Yukon, he would never come back.

The transformation in Cole's expression made Dominique's heart skip. In one glance his gray eyes had gone from fiery passion to silver cold as steel. She couldn't imagine what she had said to induce this change of mood.

"We could be goin' the wrong direction," he said. His thoughts could dwell indefinitely on his desire to be away from this terrible place, but wishing wouldn't sweep him away to the sea, or to the golden beaches he missed so desperately. Fleetingly, he wondered what it would be like to have Dominique at his side as he sailed toward a fiery red sunset in the Mediterranean or South Pacific.

"Are we lost then?" Dominique muttered in a rush of panic. "What do you think we should do?"

Her voice, and her expression, told Cole that she was putting all her faith in him. He only wished he was worthy of her trust. "I'm not going to lie to you." He glanced up toward the sky. Only a few patches of blue were visible between the jagged treetops. His gaze returned to her worried countenance. "I don't know where we are for sure, and I'm afraid our only hope is to head back down until we find the river again." He noticed the pout fade from her lips, and a twinkle light up her eyes again.

"Well, that's easy enough." She shrugged, chuckling. "Going down the mountain is surely easier than climbing up." Her smile faded when he began to shake his head.

"Have you forgotten about the mosquitos?" He realized she had forgotten as a look of horror covered her face. They had used up most of the repellent and, as long as the warm weather held out, the marshlands would still be infested by mosquitos.

"Do we have any other choices?" Dominique's skin crawled with the thought of those awful insects swarming around her again.

Cole glanced around at the seemingly endless forest. "We only have enough food for one more day." He noticed her gaze move to the shotgun. "There's plenty of game, but the smell of blood would attract bears and wolves." He shrugged, which made him appear nonchalant. "I know the river, but up here it all looks the same to me," he added.

A deep frown creased Dominique's brow. She tried to force a feeble smile. "We don't have a choice then, do we?"

Cole shook his head negatively. "I've been thinkin'." His face puckered into a thoughtful frown. "At night the mosquitos aren't near as bad as they are during the day. We could hike about halfway down the mountain this afternoon. We'll stop and wait until it cools off tonight. Then we'll make our way to the river."

"B-But it will be dark." An involuntary shudder shook her body. This wilderness was frightening enough when they could see where they were going. The thought of stumbling around when only blackness surrounded them was almost as terrible as encountering the mosquitos once more.

"It won't be so bad," Cole said in an effort to reassure her. "We'll make a torch of some sort. The fire will keep the animals away." He wished his bravery was more than just words. The idea of not being able to see if the grizzly was lurking in the trees was more than just a little unsettling. There was one consolation, though. The bear was probably too smart to put himself in the thick of the mosquitos, so he probably wouldn't follow them all the way down to the river.

Dominique placed her plate on the ground. She had had only one mouthful of the cold beans, but knew she couldn't swallow another bite. "At least we'll be able to wash when we reach the river," she said, "and then it won't be long until we get to Fort Yukon." Cole cast her a look of uncertainty and she turned away. He was her only source of strength; whatever doubts he had about their situation, she didn't want to know.

Cole tried to appear calm. He shrugged and rubbed his whiskered face. A bath and a shave would be nice, but right now he sure could use a bottle of whiskey, too. "If this weather holds out, and the river clears, Luther and the rest of the passengers from the Lady Susanah could beat us to Fort Yukon."

"How?" Dominique's mind attempted to envision women like Silver Belle and Lulu hiking over the rugged terrain she and Cole had walked in the past couple of days. The idea of them reaching the post ahead of them seemed impossible to her.

"Another steamer might come along and pick them up. But there's always the chance that won't happen." He gave a resentful-sounding laugh. "In this country, you can't count on nothin'."

Once again, Dominique was tempted to ask why he remained in the Yukon if he was so unhappy. She opened her mouth to question him on this subject, but he spoke before she had the opportunity.

"For your health's sake, you've got to eat something. We've still got a lot of walkin' ahead of us," Cole said as he looked at her discarded plate.

Dominique cast a disinterested glance at the food. She knew he was right, and they couldn't afford to waste what little food they had left. Unconsciously, she looked at his plate. Her gaze ascended, and met his unwavering stare. She could see her own distorted reflection in the depths of his gray eyes. The questions she had planned to ask fled from her mind. She could see the concern he felt, and she could almost feel his agony. Dominique had no way of knowing whether his pain was from their situation, or from something in his past that had left him stranded in this place he hated so much. She did know, however, that the most important thing was getting through this ordeal. There was more than their own survival at stake. A sense of guilt washed through Dominique. She had been so wrapped up with her own feelings that she had forgotten the main purpose of their trek was to seek help for the rest of the passengers and the crew of the wrecked steamer.

Cole picked up his plate when he noticed Dominique was forcing herself to eat again. Sitting there—choking down the cold beans, in her disheveled state—nearly broke Cole's heart. He hated himself for subjecting her to all this misery. He would never forgive himself if something happened to her because of his own selfish, lustful needs. The thought of what awaited her in Dawson City entered his mind. A sense of protectiveness invaded him as he recalled the wild, unsavory boomtown. He wondered if her intended husband could protect her from all the drunks, criminals, and hardships a town like Dawson City contained. Was it the gold that lured her there? Cole wondered. What was she really looking for by embarking on this insane journey?

He glanced at her out of the corner of his eye. She was dutifully forcing down the cold lunch he'd served up for her. He tried to conjure up the type of life she was headed for in Dawson City. As the wife of a miner in this hellish land, in less than a year she'd be a shell of the vibrant woman she was now. He recalled glimpsing women who accompanied their men to the boomtowns along the Yukon. Their dirty, haggard faces reflected a deep-seated sorrow, no doubt because of the hard life they were forced to endure. The Yukon offered none of the comforts a woman wanted, or needed. Only enough to satisfy the basic needs were transported to the almost unreachable towns and posts where gold fever reigned. The idea of Dominique living in one of the battered old tents that lined the street of Dawson City sickened him.

Again, he glanced at her. She seemed to be wrapped up in her own troubled thoughts, a frown creasing her brow. Her fork hung limply in her hand as she stared blankly at her plate. Dirt smudged the greasy repellent that coated her face. Dust covered her oversized clothes. Cole recalled how beautiful she'd been on the first day he had met her aboard the Lady Susanah. Already, the Yukon had taken its brutal toll on her. After a few months in Dawson City, Cole wondered if he would even be able to recognize her. But then, he would probably never see her again anyway.

He knew he would never be able to return to Dawson City; he could never chance seeing her after she was married to another man. The pain would be unbearable. He wanted only to remember her the way she was when he first met her—and the way she had been on the impassioned night they had spent in the cabin on the banks of the Yukon River. A fleeting thought passed through his mind, shocking him, as he recalled that night in the cabin. Without forethought or conscience he had made love to her over and over again. What if she had conceived his child? Cole took a shaky breath. The thought of having a child rarely occurred to him. But then, he rarely made love to a woman who didn't know how to protect herself. Dominique—he was sure—had not thought of this possibility either. If she was carrying his baby, everything—his plans, her plans—they would all be changed. This was one more thing Cole added to his growing list of concerns. When they reached Fort Yukon, they would discuss the prospect of her pregnancy. And, they would talk about all the other things he had been trying to avoid. But first, he had to get them down off this mountain in one piece, and alive.

Ten

"Here, let me help you," Cole said. He grasped Dominique's arm and assisted her over a protruding boulder. His grip did not ease until he was sure she was on steady ground again.

"Merci," Dominique mumbled. Obliquely she watched Cole. His behavior had changed so drastically since they had stopped for the midday meal that Dominique found herself wondering if he had eaten something that had affected his entire personality. Although he had been considerate of her ever since they had first begun the hike to Fort Yukon, for the past few hours he had been so concerned with her every move that Dominique was almost annoyed. She could hardly take a step without him wanting to help her. He kept asking her if she was tired, and if she wanted to rest. Was she hungry again? Was he walking too fast?

A short time after they started to descend

the mountain they came upon a narrow trickle of a stream. Cole's optimism was evident as they followed the shallow creekbed for he knew there was a good chance the creek would lead them straight to the river. They encountered mosquitos again along the stream, but so far, they had not been engulfed by the hordes they had faced yesterday.

"We'll stop here—" he said.

"I'm not tired," Dominique interrupted. There was an undertone of exasperation in her voice.

Cole's brows raised slightly at her reaction. From under the brim of his hat, he eyed her suspiciously. He knew he was acting foolishly, letting his imagination get the best of him, but he had never considered the possibility of impregnating a woman before now. He still hadn't decided how he would handle the situation if it should become more than just a possibility. Until he sorted through the mass of conflicting emotions the idea aroused, he found it difficult to act in a rational manner.

Motioning toward the widening creek, he said, "I'm not tired either. But the stream is flowing a lot heavier here. And," he swiped at a swarm of mosquitos as he added, "These pests are gettin' thicker. I don't want to go down any farther until nightfall."

For the past hour or so, Dominique had noticed the mosquitos were becoming a nuisance. She did not relish the idea of being completely engulfed by the blood-sucking insects again, either. With a defeated sigh, she looked around for a place to rest. She wished she could take off her clothes and plunge into the cold mountain stream. But the mosquitos that were buzzing around her face made this thought seem less desirable.

Cole noticed the longing look she cast in the direction of the creek. He wondered if they were thinking along the same lines again. "As soon as the sun starts to set, and the mosquitos thin out, we'll wash some of this trail dust off."

"Oh, that would be wonderful," Dominique said. She closed her eyes, dreamily thinking of how marvelous it would be to rid herself of these hot, sticky clothes. Her eyes flew open when another thought passed through her head—the image of being naked with Cole in the stream. Instinctively, her gaze sought him. A heated blush consumed her face when she realized he was watching her with eyes that shimmered like molten silver.

"How 'bout we rest," he said in a husky voice. "We'll save up our energy for later." His words held more meaning than they verbalized. Dominique, Cole could tell, deciphered all his unspoken insinuations. Her face glowed crimson.

The alders along the creek bed were overgrown and thick, but Cole managed to clear away a few branches and create a make-shift tent out of their bedrolls. After rubbing themselves down with the dwindling supply of repellent, they crawled under the shelter and stretched out in each other's arms. Under the blanket the temperature was almost stifling, but the secluded quarters—and the strong odor of the repellent—gave them peace from the mosquitos. Before long their energy was sapped by the heat and they fell into a drug-like sleep.

Hours later, Dominique's groggy mind told her to wake up, but her eyelids refused to obey. The heat of the day was gone, along with most of the sunlight. The chill that always seemed to accompany the Yukon nights was settling over the area. Dominique forced her eyes to open. She thought she'd heard something rustling through the brush nearby. But as she regained her senses, the night held only a permeating quiet. She listened for a few minutes longer. The noise, she was sure, that had interrupted her deep slumber was something heavy and big moving close by. Now, however, nothing greeted her ears other than the beckoning sound of the water running in the creek.

She dragged herself up to a sitting position. There was not one inch of her body that did not hurt. All the walking had left the muscles in her legs stiff and sore. Her feet hurt from the over-sized boots, and the rest of her hosted an assortment of aches and pains she knew she could do nothing to soothe. There was one thing she could do that would help, however. With a gentle shove, she pushed against Cole's chest and whispered his name against his ear.

Cole made a swipe at his ear with his hand. His sleepy mind envisioned the dreaded mosquitos flapping around his head again. The tickling sensation continued. He heard his name. His head cleared at once. His eyes opened without resistance. Through the faded light he glimpsed Dominique's impish grin. He reached out, embraced her and pulled her back down on top of him. She giggled, the sound like music to him. Instantly, her happy mood infected him.

"It's bath time!"

Cole felt the now-familiar sensation erupt in his loins. "It's goin' to be freezing cold," he warned in a taunting voice.

"I don't care." She tried to raise up. His hold imprisoned her against him. His intentions were making themselves clear. She could feel the pressure of his manhood hardening against her abdomen. She wondered if this was the way it was supposed to be between a man and a woman every time they were close to one another. Or was it like this only between special couples . . . like her and Cole.

Cole cleared his throat loudly. He knew how anxious she was to take a bath. There were things he was anxious to do, too. With a headful of lusty thoughts, Cole gently pushed Dominique up. The realization that it was almost dark surprised him. He hadn't planned to sleep this late. By this time, he had figured they would already be headed down the river. He knew he couldn't disappoint Dominique, however. After their dip in the creek, which he knew would not take long due to the temperature of the water, they would be on their way.

"Are you coming?" Dominique asked as she pulled away from him. Before he could stop her, she scurried out from under the blanket. She headed toward the creek, discarding her coat as she ran. She halted at the edge and turned to look back at Cole. He was standing beside the shelter, his expression unreadable in the dim light.

Cole stepped forward when she paused, impatiently, to wait for him. Watching her was like watching an excited little girl. He wondered if their children would look like her. Then he wondered why his thoughts kept dwelling on this subject.

"Are you taking everything off?" she inquired as he approached her.

The thought made Cole shiver. "Woman, you are going to catch your death if you take all your clothes off. But, then," he added thoughtfully, "if you don't take your clothes off it will be worse 'cause you'll have to wear 'em until they dry."

"And the nights are far too cold for that," she said in a teasing voice. She reached out and shoved his coat away from his shoulders. It seemed she was becoming an expert at disrobing him. His coat slipped to the ground without any further assistance. "That's all the help you'll get from me," she chided as she backed away and began to unbutton her own shirt. Oblivious to Cole's lack of activity, Dominique continued to undress herself. Modesty, or embarrassment, was not an issue tonight. The only thing on her mind was ridding herself of the horrible smell of the repellent, even if for a little while. When she had stripped the last of her clothes off, she turned toward Cole again. An indignant huff escaped her pouting mouth. "Do I have to do everything?" She stepped up to him, and grabbed the top button on his shirt.

Cole stood mute while she made short work of undoing his buttons. Could this be the same young woman who had cried when he took her maidenhood just days ago? he wondered. He remained unmoving while she did away with his shirt. The chilly night air penetrated his bare skin and an involuntary shiver racked his body. He found it incredible that Dominique would still think this was a good idea.

"We're going to end up with pneumonia," he warned. She answered him with another lyrical chuckle. His ears relished the sound of her happiness, and before long, her enthusiasm began to be contagious again. He allowed her to undo his belt and pants, then he leaned over, removed his boots, and disposed of his pants. Goosebumps broke out on the entire length of his body. He had the urge to let his teeth chatter together, but, he refused to let her outdo him. The cold, it appeared, was not affecting her in the least bit.

Once more, Dominique waited at the edge of the creek for Cole. As he reached her side, she stuck her foot out and submerged the tips of her toes in the water. A startled gasp flew from her mouth.

"I told you so," Cole taunted. His body shook visibly at the thought of stepping into that freezing stream. Dominique retorted by bending down, scooping up a handful of the icy water, and tossing it on Cole. The shock of her action, along with the numbing water, left him speechless for an instant. Then, his sanity returned. He roared like an indignant bull, and sprang toward Dominique. Her unabashed laughter turned into a gleeful squeal as Cole threw his arms around her waist. He pulled her up against him. "Okay, Madame," he said, gasping, "now, it's your turn."

"Mademoiselle," she corrected. "I won't be Madame until I'm mar—" her words cut off sharply. She felt Cole's embrace grow tense.

Cole did not release his tight hold on her. His mood was once again affected by circumstances he could not change. "Maybe it's time we had a talk . . ."

The unmistakable roar of a bear strangled Cole's words in his throat. He turned in the direction of the loud rumble. Briefly, he thought of the shotgun. The weapon was with his gear in the shelter under the alders. He cursed under his breath at his stupidity.

"Is it the grizzly?" Dominique asked in a panicked voice. She clung to Cole with a death-like grip. His reply was to signal for her to be quiet. Her blood felt as if it had just frozen in her veins. A devouring shiver claimed her body when Cole released her. She started to cry out to him—to beg him not to leave her alone. Rational thoughts kept her from making a sound as she realized he was retrieving his bone-handled knife from its sheath. Once he had the knife in his hand, he turned back towards her. Even in the near-darkness she could see the frantic gleam in his eyes.

"Get dressed," he whispered. Already, he was donning his clothes. Without taking time to button his shirt, or fasten all the buttons on his pants, Cole slipped into his boots. The entire time, every one of his senses were alerted to the sounds around them. He had been so unprepared for the grizzly's roar that he had no idea what direction the sound had come from. He tuned his ears to every chirp of the crickets, every rustle of the gentle breeze that was blowing through the shrubs along the creekbed. Nothing else joined the ordinary sounds of the night for several minutes.

Dominique placed herself at Cole's side as soon as she had thrown on her clothes. Now, the chill of the night air, combined with her terror, left her so cold she felt as if she was going to shiver until she broke into a million shards of ice. To keep her teeth from banging together was a desperate battle. She was even afraid to take a breath for fear of creating any noise that would draw the bear's attention.

When several minutes passed without anything happening to indicate the whereabouts of the grizzly, Cole decided to make a move. Retrieving the shotgun was his only thought. He clutched Dominique's arm. Her entire body jumped, and she emitted a frightened gasp. She did not resist when he began to lead her away from the creek. After each step, Cole would pause—and listen—and then inch forward again. Although their gear was only a hundred yards or so away from the creek, to Cole it felt like a mile. His anger at his own ignorance lent him courage. Never again—he vowed to himself—would he be caught unprepared. Fleetingly, he also vowed for the millionth time to get out of this damn Yukon Hades.

Dominique took her first full breath when they reached their gear, and she saw Cole grab the shotgun. He motioned for her to crawl back under the blanket. She hesitated to do as he commanded. The last thing she wanted was to be left here alone if he was planning on going out into the forest after the grizzly. She gave her head a negative shake. In the pale light from the moon that was starting to peek over the ridge, Dominique could make out Cole's tense expression. For an instant she was sure he was going to insist that she do as he wanted. Instead, he gave his head a quick nod, and extended his arm. Dominique glanced down to see him holding his knife out to her. With caution she grasped the end of the bone handle. When he released his hold on the weapon, she repositioned the handle so that it fit more comfortably in her palm. The smooth bone felt clammy in her hand. She wondered if it was Cole's sweating hand, or her own, that had dampened the handle.

The knife made her more confident as she waited for Cole to grab a handful of shotgun shells out of his pack. When he was at her side again, she turned to face him. The moonlight afforded Dominique a clear glimpse of his expression. In spite of the fear she felt, a sense of comfort washed over her when their eyes met. Theirs, she realized in that brief instant, truly was a special relationship. And it went far beyond the intimacy they had shared.

Cole studied Dominique's face. He wished the light allowed him to look more deeply into her blue eyes, desperate to know if he was only imagining the look of love he thought he glimpsed in her expression. Now, however, he did not have the luxury of time for these thoughts. The sound of the bear crashing through the brush along the creekbed drew his complete attention. He swung around to the source of the noise. The shotgun, loaded and poised against his shoulder, was aimed in the same direction. His arms felt weak, his knees quaked. To protect Dominique, though, he would not give into his fear.

Besides his determination to keep Dominique safe, Cole was also drawing upon his meager knowledge about Alaskan grizzlies. Their eyesight, he recalled, was poor. Even in broad daylight a grizzly's vision was limited. Darkness was a big asset for them, and so was the wind. Cole could feel a gentle breeze blowing against his sweat-drenched face. The wind was from seaward, which meant their scent would be hard for the old bear to detect. His confidence increased as he kept his gun leveled toward the creek. He did not have to wait long. Beside him, Cole heard Dominique gasp when the huge bear lumbered out from a heavy clump of alders. He steadied his gun, but refrained from pulling the trigger.

The grizzly took several steps, then paused. His head turned from side to side as he tried to decipher the scents that dominated the air. His front legs eased up, and his enormous body rose without effort until he was standing on his hind legs. Again, his head tilted back. A low, nasal bellow rang out from his mouth. He remained standing for a few more seconds. Then, almost gracefully, his front legs descended until he was once again on all fours. His hind quarters plopped down on the ground, and his massive front paw reached under the alders nearest to him. He scooped out a tangled vine and began to pick wild cranberries off the branch with his other paw. Almost daintily, he dropped the berries into his mouth one at a time.

Dominique had not made a move since the bear first emerged from the bushes. She still remained rooted to the same spot as she watched the bear's nonchalant actions. His size astounded her. The fact that he was oblivious to their presence, she found even more incredible. Cole had relaxed his rigid stance, although he had not moved. Her nerves, however, were like tight-wires. She was afraid the bear would be alerted to their whereabouts by the wild thrashing of her heartbeat, or the clanging of her shaky limbs.

When the bear was finished with his berries he tossed the barren branch on the ground. He grumbled as if he was annoyed at something, then slowly rose up onto his four legs again. His snout extended, his nose sniffed rapidly at the air again. Cole's stance, Dominique noticed, grew stiffer. Her wet, numb fingers tightened around the knife handle. She attempted to swallow the heavy lump in her throat. Instead, she felt as though she would choke. She held her breath again. If the grizzly did not leave soon, she feared she would collapse from lack of oxygen.

With another low rumble from deep in his chest, the grizzly swung around toward the creek. His large haunches almost appeared to waddle as he sauntered down to the edge of the water. He drank—in loud, slurping gulps—then he waded into the middle of the creek. The water reached past the shaggy hair that hung down from his sagging belly. He pushed through the water with no effort, seemingly unaware of the freezing temperature. Before long the splashing sounds he created began to fade into the distance as he made his way downstream.

It was not until the night was void of all sounds that Dominique allowed herself to take another breath. Her chest ached, and her entire body began to shake visibly. She was aware of Cole lowering his gun. He reached over and eased the knife out of her trembling hand.

"That old coot's blind outta one eye and can't see outta the other one," Cole said. He kept his voice low. Unconsciously, he glanced over his shoulder. His attention, and concern, returned to Dominique. In the pale light, she looked as white as a ghost. He shoved his knife into its sheath, then drew her into his arms. Guilt edged his emotions. Would she have been so afraid if he had warned her about the bear when he had first seen the tracks around the cabin yesterday, or glimpsed him in the forest this morning?

As he held her trembling body close, he decided he had done the right thing by sparing her a couple days of added worry over the bear. He heard her take several deep breaths, and before long, the violent shivers that shook

169

through her ceased to rack her slender form. She relaxed against him. He gently rubbed her back in a soothing motion, and the long strands of her hair entangled in his fingers. He smoothed them down, then overcome with a desperate sensation to bond her to him, he twisted the thick tendrils around his hand. He felt her arms tighten around his waist as if she, too, wanted them to be as close as was humanly possible.

While held in this tight embrace, Cole made a promise to himself: He would always protect this woman in any way possible. Even if it meant he would have to leave her.

Eleven

"Does that feel better?" Cole asked sympathetically.

Dominique nodded her head. She pulled her hand back and pressed it against her body. She was grateful the moonlight was not bright enough for him to be able to see the hot blush she could feel staining her cheeks.

"You could get an infection if you don't take care of those rope-burns," Cole warned. He rolled up the rest of the bandage material and shoved it back in his pack.

A shrug of her shoulders was Dominique's only reply. She had managed to tear open the freshly-healed skin on her right palm with her deadly grip on the knife while they'd watched the grizzly. The profuse bleeding had forced her to tell Cole what she'd done. The way he was making a fuss over her while he tended to her hand, however, made her feel foolish.

"Are you up to walking for a while?"

"My legs are fine," she retorted. To prove

her point, she pushed herself up from the ground in one bound. She watched Cole impatiently as he rose up to join her. "We'd best get a move on," she said, imitating his familiar expression.

A grin curved Cole's lips. He motioned for her to follow him. They had already missed out on several hours of traveling time. He halted when he noticed she had stopped abruptly.

"That's the way the bear went," she said in a voice that contrasted with her brave facade a few minutes ago.

"That's the way we have to go, too, if we want to get back to the river."

Dominique stumbled forward until she was at his side again. "I-I guess as long as it's dark we're safe."

Cole grunted a quick reply. If the grizzly picked up their scent it wouldn't matter whether it was dark or not. He was tempted to tell her he suspected the old bear of stalking them for the past few days, but decided against it. He hoped they would not encounter the grizzly again, and they should be at the river by morning. Then, he could figure out what their next course of action would be. Right now, there were plenty of other things to keep his mind occupied.

The light from the nearly-full moon was helpful, but traveling at night was still difficult over the uneven terrain. Rocks jutted out from the ground; dead branches, low-growing shrubs and weeds blanketed the landscape. The going was as slow as a turtle's pace. Cole wrapped strips of cloth around a spruce branch, and lit the materials with a match to use as a torch. But the material burned up more quickly than he thought it would, and they gained little ground before Cole was forced to abandon the idea.

"You could use some of my clothes for the torch," Dominique suggested. She noticed he cast her an annoyed glance. She gave an indignant huff. "I mean things I could do without—like these itchy longjohns." To prove her point, she scratched vigorously at her shoulder and collarbone area.

"You'll be wishin' you had all those clothes tomorrow," he retorted. He could tell by her expression of dread that Dominique didn't need him to remind her about the sharp lancets of the Arctic mosquitos.

"We'll just take it slow and easy," Cole said. He grabbed her arm, and escorted her over the rough tundra. Every rustle the breeze made through the trees, or even the faintest sound, brought them to a halt. The howling of the wolves no longer seemed so ominous when compared to the monstrous grizzly who lurked in this area.

Dominique could not wipe the image of the bear out of her mind. While he had tenderly cared for her hand, Cole told her the grizzly they'd observed at the creek was larger than most of his species. This knowledge did little to soothe her fear. She clung tightly to Cole's arm as she decided she was not going to let him more than one foot out of her reach.

Through the night Cole and Dominique did not make the progress he had hoped they would make. Hazy threads of grey streaked the eastern horizon as they topped a ridge at the edge of the foothills. A thin layer of fog had settled over the valley floor. From where they stood Cole could glimpse portions of the land beneath the sparse veil of fog. Above the fog the sky still clung to an opulent moon and several luminous stars. "Down in that valley is our river," Cole said. "But by the time we get there it will be mid-day." He glanced up at the sky. The approaching day would be another hot one. He looked down at Dominique. She was watching him. He saw nothing in her expression that hinted at her thoughts, but Cole could tell she was worn out from their long night of stumbling over rocks, and straining to listen for the grizzly. Beneath Dominique's lower lashes were dark purple smudges that were evident even though her face was covered with dust and grime.

"We'll push on a little farther until the sun is all the way up." He reached out and tugged on the brim of her hat, adding, "Then we'll find us a place to hole up for a few hours of rest before we tackle those pesky demons at the river again." Cole noticed her smile was a weak and forced effort. She nodded her head, drew in a deep breath, then motioned for him to lead the way. A rush of admiration shot through Cole. He had never known a woman with so much spirit. He told himself once more that he had to know more about her past, and her dreams for the future . . . everything there was to know about her.

Cole planned to talk to Dominique as soon as they stopped to rest. Now, he led the way down the slope. The early morning air held its usual chill. A slippery layer of frost coated the ground, making it even more treacherous to descend the rocky hillside. By the time they were to a level area at the base of the foothills, the sun was casting a golden shimmer over the landscape. The frost was reduced to no more than a few traces of moisture under the brush and around the rocks. A horde of mosquitos greeted them without ceremony or warning.

Since they had already rubbed themselves down with the smelly repellent when they'd begun their descent, Cole and Dominique did not let the attack stop their progress. As they forged through the swarm, Cole studied the area for a suitable place to build a temporary shelter. He couldn't believe their luck when he spotted what looked like a small cave or alcove peeking out from a stand of straggly pines a few hundred yards away from where they had climbed down the slope. He tapped Dominique's arm, then pointed toward the opening. Her head nodded an enthusiastic response. She didn't dare speak and risk a mouthful of mosquitos again.

When they approached the cave, Cole retrieved a long branch from the ground. He motioned for Dominique to wait for him while he went the rest of the way alone. With cautious steps he approached the cave. At the opening, he stuck the stick in as far as he could reach. A scurrying sound made him jump back. He took several quick steps backwards. There was another noise, then before Cole realized what was happening, something rushed out of the cave.

A startled cry rang out from Dominique when the black and white animal flashed past her. She did not realize what it was until the air filled with the distinct aroma of a skunk.

"Ah, hell!" Cole clamped his gloved hand over his nose and mouth. He had figured there was a good chance the cave was the home of a wild animal. A skunk was the least ferocious of their foes, but the odor the little devil produced was almost unbearable. Cole continued to back up until he was at Dominique's side. He turned toward her. She was imitating his gesture; her hand was held securely over the lower part of her face. Their startled eyes met for an instant.

Although there didn't seem to be anything humorous about this latest development, Dominique couldn't stop the chuckle that rose up in her throat when she looked at Cole. The shocked expression on his dirty counte-

176

nance was like that of a small boy who had just done something that would get him a whipping. Her amusement was contagious.

A chortle rang out from behind Cole's hand an instant after Dominique's laugh escaped. They allowed their hands to drop from their faces. Thanks to the skunk there were no longer any mosquitos in this area. After a few minutes of coughing, gagging, and adjusting to the strong, offensive smell, Cole realized the skunk did them a favor. He grabbed Dominique's hand, pulling her with him to the cave. She balked when he bent down and started to enter.

From where she stood, Dominique could see nothing more than a long, narrow black hole. She imagined its depths could conceal something much worse than a skunk. Cole, however, did not give her time to think. He pulled her in, forcing her to bend down to keep from banging her head on the low ceiling. Once she was inside, Dominique was immediately aware of a feeling of peace as her vision adjusted to the darkness. Although the interior of the cave contained a vague odor of skunk, it was definitely more bearable than the mosquitos. A cool, but sightly damp, atmosphere clung to the air. Dominique droped to her knees with a relieved sigh.

"We'll be able to get some decent rest in here, because that smell will keep the mosquitos away," Cole said with a satisfied grin. He blinked several times until the blackness no longer seemed so thick. The cave was not much more than a hole in the hillside; about eight feet deep, six feet wide, and about four feet high. Just right, Cole thought.

"What about the skunk?" Dominique asked, although she really didn't care anymore. The thought of stretching out her aching limbs filled her mind. She glanced longingly around the small cave.

Cole sensed her thoughts. "He won't be back for awhile." He laid the shotgun down beside him, and yanked open his pack. After he produced their bedrolls, he let Dominique roll them out, then made a suggestion he knew she wouldn't refuse. "I think it would be safe to rid ourselves of these hot, scratchy clothes while we're here." Dominique's face turned toward him. Even in the obscure light, Cole could see the twinkle in her gaze. Already, his body was thinking beyond this moment.

"Oh, Monsieur, merci," she gasped as she began to shed her clothes without a moment's hesitation. She kicked her boots off with ease. Discarding the rest of her outer garments was done in short order. She stopped when she was left with nothing but the itchy longjohns she had come to despise. She would be happy to never have to wear another pair of these uncomfortable woolen undergarments again, but she knew if she needed to wear them in the summer, she would undoubtedly need at least two pair in the winter. The thought of

178

staying in the Yukon Territory was becoming less and less desirable every minute. She leaned back, and stretched out on the mattress created by her bedroll. This cave was a heavenly refuge in a hellish land.

Cole watched in mute fascination while she hurried out of her clothes. A sense of disappointment filled him when she lay down without stripping off her red longjohns. "You'd best rid yourself of those things for a spell," he suggested, leaning over to tug on the material of her underwear. He sat back up and began to rid himself of his own clothes.

Dominique raised up on her elbows. Cole's bare chest was the first thing her gaze focused on. An ache worked its way through Dominique. She swallowed hard, almost embarrassed by the relentless throbbing that had developed in the depths of her womanly core. Her gaze moved slowly over Cole. He was kneeling at her side. The near-darkness in the cave outlined his sleek body, making his skin appear golden. Every inch of his muscled form seemed to summon her touch. His desire for her was evident when her gaze settled on his engorged manhood. She was not aware of anything else after that, except that she had never wanted anything more than she wanted Cole at this moment. A trembling breath whispered through her parted lips. This was the only invitation Cole needed.

He pushed her back on the bedroll easily and swiftly, then quickly pulled off her longjohns. She held out her arms to allow him to yank the sleeves away, then she eased her hips up so he could pull the bottoms down her legs. When he had tossed them away, he clasped her ankles and gently drew her legs apart. His fingers charted a sensuous trail up the sides of her legs—and his mouth kissed its way along her heated flesh—as he eased himself between her legs. This intimate position already seemed so natural to Cole it made him forget that he'd ever been with any other woman before her. He moaned with anticipation as his hardness pushed into her moist core. Her tight crevice engulfed him as they bonded into one.

His entry caused the deep throbbing inside of Dominique to expand. She wanted him so badly she thought she would explode. Her arms tightened around his taut body, her legs drew up, and her hands pushed down on his firm buttocks in an effort to quell her insatiable need.

Cole reveled in her actions, her desperate yearnings fueling his own passion. He drove into her urgently as her cry of ecstasy reached his ears. He made love to her like a man possessed by demons of desire—like he'd never made love to a woman before. The exhaustion and fear that had first accompanied them into this cave were gone—evaporated the instant they touched one another. Cole's energy was tireless, and Dominique's response was equal.

After what seemed like hours Cole realized

his passion and strength were spent. He plummeted into her harder, faster. She matched each of his movements. Their hot, damp bodies meshed together as they reached a powerful climax that left them both panting and gasping for air.

Dominique lay beneath Cole, dizzy, limp, and more satisfied that she thought was humanly possible. Deep, deep down, she knew there would be repercussions to suffer when they were forced to accept the responsibility for their swept-away passions. But now, she knew she couldn't let herself dwell on the heartbreak she would face in the future. Instead, she recalled his suggestion that they concentrate on the time they did have together.

When Cole felt capable of taking a full breath again, he rolled from Dominique. Their bodies felt reluctant to part, and in places their damp skin made little sucking noises when Cole pulled away. He positioned himself against Dominique's side, drawing her up against him so that their bodies curved into one another from top to bottom. The cool air in the cave penetrated his sweating pores, and the odor of skunk was joined by the musky scents of passion. Cole drew in a labored breath. He was forced to accept what he could no longer deny . . . he was in love with this woman.

"I-I-I lo—," the words that had only been in his thoughts an instant ago, somehow found their way to his dry mouth. He couldn't let them escape, though; at least, not yet.

Dominique's body shook visibly. She felt his embrace tighten. She waited for him to finish what she was sure he had started to say. Did she dare hope he was about to admit that he loved her? Her ears waited anxiously for those powerful words, but they didn't come. He was quiet as a tomb beside her, leaving Dominique's mind to run wild. She thought of Brigitte, and of the vow she had always made to be different than her mother. Cole Hawkins had made her forget all about that vow, although Dominique knew she could not lay the blame entirely on him. Her greatest worry now was that Cole would not allow himself to be in love with a woman he had been able to have so easily.

"What were you about to say?" she asked in a shaky whisper.

Cole forced down the urge to repeat the committing words. He coughed, then swallowed hard. "I want to know why you're here."

His question was a confusing as it was disappointing. "You-you asked me to accompany you to Fort Yu—"

"No," Cole cut in. "I mean, why did you come to the Yukon, and why did you agree to marry some man you've never met?" There! He'd finally asked the question that had tormented him since the first minute he had seen her on the deck of the Lady Susanah.

Asking the question, however, did not relieve his agony. He was forced to endure a long pause.

"It had to do mostly with my mother," Dominique said, finally. "I didn't want to end up like her."

Cole waited for her to explain. A silence engulfed them. He had to question her again. "You've lost me, woman. What does your mother have to do with—"

"Ever been to San Francisco's Barbary Coast?" Dominique interrupted.

"Yeah. But—"

"Well, that's where my mother resides. For now, anyway. I think she's lived in just about every red-light district in Paris, and New Orleans. But the city doesn't matter, because the brothels are all the same."

Her voice had assumed a hardness Cole had never heard in her accented tone before. He didn't move, nor could he make himself speak. Dominique's words were painting pictures in his mind that he didn't want to see. "Is that where you were raised?" he asked in a low voice.

"No, she enrolled me in private schools. I think it was her way of trying to make up for her own life. As a result, I got to see life from two very different perspectives. But, even with all that schooling, as the daughter of a truly dedicated whore, I learned my most valuable lesson from her." She tried to force back the sudden urge to cry. But as she continued to speak, her trembling voice bespoke her inner feelings. "I learned that I didn't want to follow in her footsteps."

Cole heard the way her voice cracked. He felt a shudder rack her slender form. He was already holding her as close as possible. He wished he could somehow absorb her pain as he listened to her speak.

"That's why, Monsieur, I am here."

As much as he tried, Cole still did not understand. "But just because your mother is a whore doesn't mean you don't have any other choices."

A snicker escaped from Dominique. "It certainly puts restrictions on a person when your mother has a reputation as wide-spread as the plague."

"But . . ." Cole struggled to sort through his confusion. "Why tell anyone about her? Surely, you could go someplace where nobody knows—"

"Yes, I have," Dominique interrupted again. She felt Cole draw in a heavy breath. His silence told her he was beginning to understand. Now, she wanted to know what he had started to say to her earlier but had not been able to finish. He did not give her a chance to ask her question, though.

"But, Dominique," he said in a tone edged with impatience. "There are other places that are a hell of a lot better than this."

"I thought this was a sure bet," she said, almost wistfully.

"A sure bet?" he repeated. "What do you mean?" He felt her shrug as though she was trying to analyze her own thoughts. She twisted around in his arms. Their faces were only inches apart. A sense of foreboding inched through Cole as he waited for her next words.

Dominique gazed at Cole's face. The darkness in the small cave granted her nothing more than the vaguest image of his features. She tried to imagine what she could not see; an undeniable look of love in his eyes. "Ever since I was old enough to know the difference between my life and the way most other little girls were raised, there have been two things I wanted more than anything else."

She paused. Cole's breath caught in his parched throat. A clammy sweat broke out on his brow.

"And what are those two things?" he asked, his voice raspy.

"I want to be respectable," she answered promptly.

Guilt edged into Cole's thoughts. "You are . . . and I was a blind fool to think you were like the rest of those women on the steamer."

Dominique shook her head slowly. "Marriage gives a woman respectability. That miner up there in Dawson City who wants a wife—no matter whose daughter she is—well, he's a sure bet."

"Ah, marriage," Cole said in a voice almost

too hoarse to be articulate. He grew cold, and his entire body trembled. "And, the second thing?"

"A home—a real home. You know, the kind of home where families gather for dinner every night, and where friends are welcomed after church on Sundays. A real, respectable home . . ." A sob escaped from her mouth, in spite of her determined effort not to cry.

Her words left Cole numb. He had spent the past fifteen years trying to escape from the confines of the two things she wanted most. Marriage to a woman like Dominique could be bearable, Cole thought. But then he tried to imagine the second thing she had mentioned—a home, a real home. Pain gripped his chest. He wondered if it was because his heart had just broken in two. There was nothing he could say in response to the things she had just revealed to him, so he kept quiet. He had learned two important things about her in the past few minutes, and now he knew two things about himself; he could never tell her how much he loved her, because he could never give her the home she so desperately wanted . . . and needed.

Twelve

Sometime during the long silence that followed Dominique's announcement, she drifted off to sleep. However, for Cole, sleep did not come so soon. Her words kept echoing through his mind. He couldn't imagine the shame she must have suffered because of her mother, and he could understand why she had felt the need to get as far away from her as possible. He thought of his own childhood. His upbringing in Ohio had been close to perfection, with loving parents and the type of home Dominique had described.

Cole's thoughts dwelled on the beautiful young woman who slept in his arms. He could hear her soft, steady breathing. Her hopes for her future taunted him. He clamped his eyes shut, and willed his mind to become a blank page. There was nothing to think about . . . nothing he could do to change the inevitable. At last, exhaustion took control of him.

A short time later, both Cole and Dominique

were jolted out of their restless slumber by a deafening roar from the entrance of the cave. Although she was not aware of it, a terrified scream tore from Dominique as her mind gained awareness. She knew the roar was coming from the old grizzly. Even before she was fully awake, she grabbed for Cole, but he was already reaching for his shotgun.

Everything happened so fast Dominique's groggy mind could hardly comprehend it. The massive bear was down on all fours, and his neck was extended so that just his head was inside the opening. The upper portion of his lip was curled up, revealing saber-like yellow teeth splotched with brown stains. These deadly teeth were the only things Dominique's spinning mind could focus on. Her natural instinct was to get as far away from the bear as possible, so she scooted back against the farthest wall of the cave. This only granted her an extra foot or two. She realized that in spite of the grizzly's excessive size, he could still squeeze into the cave if the urge claimed him. She was overcome in the small enclosure by a rank smell—primitive, wild—that overpowered the previous scents of skunk, dampness and passion.

Cole grabbed the butt of the gun at the same instant the bear grabbed the barrel. Dominique gasped in horror as the grizzly played a game of tug-of-war with Cole for the possession of the weapon. The muscles along Cole's shoulders strained as he exerted every ounce of his strength to gain ownership of the shotgun. Several deep growls rang out from the bear's throat. Then, it appeared he tried to intimidate Cole with a rumbling roar. Dominique was sure the entire hillside shook from the deafening sound. Although they lacked the ferocity of the bear's growls, animalistic noises also came from Cole while he fought to retain his grip on the gun.

Dominique realized she was making plenty of noise herself with all her screaming. Her head pounded from the sounds of her own fear. She clamped her mouth shut, and tried to calm herself enough so that she could concentrate on helping Cole. From the corner of her eye, she caught sight of the shiny buckle on his belt. Without thought or plan, she lunged forward and yanked the belt away from his discarded pants. His knife sheath hung from the belt. Dominique pulled the knife out, oblivious to the pain in her bandaged hand. She stared at the long, shiny blade for a second, uncertain of what she should do next. An agonized cry from Cole determined what she had to do.

The grizzly had grown bored with fighting over the gun. He took his other paw, and made a swipe at Cole. His long claws scraped along Cole's forearm, tearing open the skin like shredded paper. Dominique saw the bear's attack on Cole, and heard his painful response. She came forward, driven by determination to protect the man she loved. Cole still had not given up his tight hold on the butt of the gun, despite his bleeding arm. Dominique's attention leveled on her target; the only part of the bear she could reach without going out of the cave. She drew the knife up, then plunged the weapon down on the furred paw that clasped the barrel of the shotgun. The blade sliced through the tender flesh and the thin bone that ran directly above the bear's long claws. Surprised by this sudden infliction of pain, the grizzly released his hold on the barrel. He withdrew his paw for an instant . . . long enough for Cole to whip the shotgun's barrel forward, then snap it back in place so that it locked with the handle. His finger curled around the trigger.

By now the grizzly had enough time to overcome the shock and immediate pain that Dominique's attack had evoked. He made his anger evident with a rumbling roar that filled the tiny interior of the cave, and left its inhabitants quaking. The bear swung his paw out again, uncaring of his injury. The paw once again latched onto the gun barrel.

Dominique reacted without pause. She drew the knife down on the bear's paw, almost in the same area she had stabbed him before. At the same instant, the cave exploded with a flash of fire and a blast of dark smoke as the air filled with the scent of sulfur. A loud, hissing bellow rang out from the entrance. The grizzly backed away from the cave, snarling, whining, and pawing at his shoulder where the bullet had torn away a chunk of muscle.

Cole's hands shook so violently he was not sure if he could even shoot the second shell in the gun's chamber if it was needed. At this close range, he had expected the bear to be killed with one shot. But the grizzly's last grab at the gun barrel had thrown his aim haywire. Rising to his knees, Cole inched to the front of the cave. His head was spinning, and he found it hard to breathe the smoke-filled air. Terror raced through him as he forced himself to move forward. The sounds of the bear's loud bawling had faded away. He hoped—and prayed—this meant the grizzly was dead. It was unlikely, though. Cole knew he had hit the bear somewhere in the fatty part of his shoulder—the thickest area of the massive animal. Cole figured there was a possibility that the grizzly would bleed to death from his wound. But not this fast. Until then, the old coot would be even more vicious than before. This thought made Cole pause, and it took him more courage than he thought he possessed to ease himself out into the open.

Sunlight blinded his eyes, while fear paralyzed his body. For the fleeting second before his vision readjusted to the daylight, he imagined the giant paw of the grizzly ripping his head off his shoulders. Cole went no farther out of the cave than absolutely necessary. He scanned the area for the bear. Only the rugged terrain greeted him, but Cole still didn't take any chances. From where he stopped, he could see endless clumps of alders, pines, and off in the distance, the dense groves of cottonwoods. He knew the old grizzly could be hiding anywhere.

Cole pulled his head back into the meager safety of the cave and turned around. Dominique was crouched down at the extreme back of the cave. She reminded him of a frightened beaver he once saw caught in a trap along the edge of the river.

"I don't see him anywhere," Cole said gruffly. He crawled back to Dominique, resisting the urge to look back over his shoulder at the entrance. A cold chill whipped through him. He knew he would not have a moment's peace until he was sure the grizzly was dead.

"Did you kill him?" Dominique whispered. She still held the knife in her bandaged hand.

Cole's shoulders lifted with a shrug. "We'd best get ourselves dressed." He laid the shotgun down, and reached out for his knife. "Thanks for the help. That devil surely would have gotten the gun away from me if it hadn't been for you." She stared down at his outstretched hand. He noticed her eyes grow wide. She looked up at his face. Their eyes locked for a moment before his attention was drawn down to his arm. Spiralling shards of pain had just erupted in his hand and bolted up through his shoulder.

"Mon Dieu!" Dominique gasped. She leaned forward to get a closer look at his arm through the darkness of the cave. She could see enough to know that blood gushed from his wounds, and already, the front of his body was covered with blood.

Dominique crawled forward, grabbed the pack, and began to dig through its contents. The salve was their only form of medicine, but first, she knew, she had to stop his profuse bleeding.

"Tear up my shirt," Cole said. His voice shook slightly when he spoke. "We'll make a tourniquet to help stop this damn bleedin'." He drew in a quivering breath. When he focused on Dominique's face, he realized how badly shaken up she was. Even the near-darkness of the cave could not hide her ghostly pallor. He could hear her short, raspy breaths, which made Cole wonder if she was in shock. His worry over her condition gave him the strength he needed to cope with his own injuries. He scooted next to her in an effort to see her more clearly. Fleetingly, Cole wondered if her obvious worry might also have something to do with her other feelings for him. Could it be that she had been envisioning a future with him too? This thought fled from his mind as quickly as it appeared. He reminded himself there were too many other things to think about now—things that probably would determine whether either of them had a future at all—together or alone.

A dozen thoughts raged through Dominique's head, but she could only grasp one—

that Cole might die. This snapped her out of her shock. She grabbed his shirt, and began to tug on the hem. Finally, she was forced to use her teeth to start a rip in the heavy flannel material. With shaky fingers she pulled off a long thin strip. She looked over at Cole, who was sitting motionless, watching her. "Are you doing all right?" she asked in a quivering voice.

Cole did not move, nor did he answer. Although he did not feel as if he was hurt seriously, a light-headed feeling washed over him, leaving him weak. He glanced down when he felt Dominique tying the tourniquet around his upper arm. He stared down at the bleeding limb, feeling as if it belonged to somebody else. After the initial burst of pain, his arm had gone completely numb.

His subdued behavior added to Dominique's panic. She was terrified he would pass out from a loss of blood. Cole could not die, her mind and heart screamed—she would not allow it!

"Is that the right way to tie one of these?" she asked. Though she knew a tourniquet was used to help stop severe bleeding, she had never applied one before. A sense of relief invaded her when she noticed that her voice seemed to penetrate his trance-like state. He gave his head a vague nod. She grabbed for the water canteen in Cole's pack. To her dismay she discovered it was almost empty. She had planned to use some of the water to wash the blood away from Cole's wounds. Since she had no idea how long it would be before they reached the river, she decided to save what was left of the water for Cole to drink instead.

Cole drew in labored breath as he tried to focus on Dominique's movements. He was angry at himself for being hurt, and even more angry that he would somehow be more of a failure in Dominique's eyes. His mind was tormented by irrational thoughts, such as how he could prove to her what a capable and brave man he was if they were out on the high seas.

"Here, let me wipe some of that blood away," Dominique said. She used another strip of his shirt to carefully dab at the long shredded pieces of skin where the bear's claws tore into him. The urge to be sick to her stomach kept making her swallow heavily. To her relief, the blood seemed to be clotting, but in the dim light of the cave, she could not tell how deep or severe his wounds were. "We've got to go outside," she announced. "I have to be able to see what I'm doing."

"I need my pants," Cole mumbled, then added in a stronger voice, "And the gun."

For the first time since this nightmare began Dominique realized they had not had an opportunity to dress themselves. She did not relish the idea of taking the time to dress when Cole needed medical attention so badly, but being out in broad daylight without clothes was not appealing either. She scooted over to their pile of clothes and quickly dug out Cole's pants. "Let me help you," she said as she handed them to him. He grabbed them with his one good arm.

"Dress yourself," he ordered. His increasingly foul temperament kept his mind from dwelling on his injuries. With some degree of difficulty he finally managed to pull on his pants. The wool trousers felt funny against his skin without the longjohns he had worn almost constantly for the past couple of years. He turned his attention to reloading the gun. With only one hand, the process was awkward. But his determination won out, and soon the gun was ready.

Cole's dire mood added to Dominique's worries, yet she did not want to argue with him. She threw on her long baggy shirt—nothing else—then grabbed the salve and what was left of Cole's torn shirt. Without another word to Cole, she started to crawl out through the opening in the cave.

"Dominique—wait!" Cole hollered. Panic consumed him as he envisioned the injured bear lurking outside the cave entrance.

Turning back to glance over her shoulder, a strange feeling gripped Dominique. She couldn't miss the warning tone in Cole's voice, but she was already half out in the open before she was able to stop herself. The sunlight hit her squarely in the face when she swung back toward the opening. A blinding terror washed over her for the few seconds that it took her eyes to adjust to the light again.

Cole grabbed her with his one hand. He pulled her away from the opening. They both fell back on the cave floor. Dominique heard Cole moan painfully. She knew why he had reacted so harshly, and she hated herself for being so stupid. "I'm sorry, Cole!" she said, gasping. "I should have checked to see if the bear was out there." He did not reply. A weak cry escaped from her as she turned to look at him. He was cradling his arm and grimacing in agony.

"Take it slow this time," he whispered. With his good arm, he reached over and grabbed the gun again. He handed the loaded shotgun to Dominique as he added, "And be careful."

Dominique nodded, and took the weapon. She wondered if she should tell Cole that it would do her no good since she did not know how to shoot a gun. She decided to keep quiet. Clasping the gun tightly, she rolled over to her knees. Her heart thudded wildly in her chest as she crawled cautiously through the opening. Once again, her vision was blurred by the sunlight. She blinked rapidly, then focused on the closest grove of trees and rocks. She dared not even breathe as she inched farther out into the open. Her eyes darted from side to side, but her head barely moved. She did not want to make any more movements than necessary in case the grizzly was nearby. Once she was completely out of the cave, she slowly rose up to her feet. With the shotgun held firmly in her hands, she began to turn around.

The air, and everything around her, seemed unnaturally quiet. It was not long, though, before the buzzing sounds of the mosquitos filled her ears. The insects took full advantage of Dominique's uncovered legs. She made only a couple quick swipes through the air before she realized it was futile. Within seconds she could not even concentrate on looking around for the bear because of the hordes of mosquitos that had already discovered her bare skin. Pivoting quickly, she fell down on her knees and scooted back into the cave. Cole had been watching her from the entrance, and she almost plowed him over in her hasty effort to escape from the mosquitos.

"I didn't see the grizzly," she said breathlessly. She swung her arm through the air wildly. Most of the mosquitos, it seemed, had followed her back into the cave.

In spite of his pain, and everything else that was happening, Cole couldn't help but notice Dominique's appearance; her raven hair was hanging around her shoulders in wild profusion, creating a soft frame for her flushed face. But even more enticing was her attire; the loose-fitting shirt that covered barely enough of her to be decent. The feelings she aroused in Cole made him angry. He wondered how he could feel amorous when the cave was being invaded by mosquitos, he was bleeding to death, and somewhere outside there was a giant grizzly in a real foul mood.

"You'd best get yourself dressed," Cole ordered. His tone left no room for argument. He grabbed the dwindling supply of mosquito repellent and tossed it at her, then turned away. Silently, he cursed at himself, at this damn country, and anything else that happened to pop into his mind.

His bad temperament eased some of Dominique's worries for his health. She figured if he was capable of acting so hateful, he was still able to fight for his life. When her eyesight had once again adjusted to the dim light in the cave, she concentrated on pulling on the heavy layers of clothes as fast as possible. Once she was dressed, she scooped out only a fingertip full of the repellent and rubbed it on her face. For a moment, the pesky insects retreated. She turned toward Cole. It appeared that he was watching her again. She wished she could see his face more clearly. Mostly, she longed to be able to look into his eyes. She sensed—and hoped—she would see something in their gray depths that would make all this pain and hardship worthwhile.

Thirteen

"Does that feel comfortable?" Dominique asked as she finished tying the sling around Cole's neck. She met his intense gaze. She was sure the emotion she could see in his eyes could fill volumes. His gaze held hers for what seemed an eternity. Hope overpowered her fears. She sensed their love affair would not end at Fort Yukon, or even at Dawson City. The memory of Jack Scroggins passed through her mind. Surely, he would understand that true love could not be denied. She would just explain to Jack that she had fallen in love with Cole, and then she would pay back the money he had sent her. Well, she would have to figure out how she would pay him back, since she had no money of her own. But she would worry about those details later. Right now her only concern was caring for the man she loved.

"You did good," Cole said as he surveyed her work. She had cleaned his wounds with the water in the canteen after he had assured her that they would reach the river soon. Then, she had carefully applied the salve, and bandaged up his wounds without blinking an eye. The grizzly's marks had not been a pretty sight, either. The massive claws had ripped through Cole's skin tissue, the muscles and clean down to the bone, leaving his arm a gory mess. Cole gave Dominique a weak smile. She was staring down at his hand with a worried frown on her dirty face.

"That's a knife wound, isn't it?" she asked bluntly as she motioned to the cut that had left a deep gouge across the top of his hand.

Cole shrugged, attempting to appear nonchalant. "It couldn't be helped," he said. He'd hoped she wouldn't notice the wound on his hand was different from the ones on his arm. He knew she had accidentally cut him when she had lunged at the grizzly the second time.

A horrified expression flashed across her face. "It was an accident," Cole assured her. He forced another smile. Her worried expression began to relax into a look of regret.

Dominique reached out and gently touched Cole's whiskered cheek, then she said in a low voice, "Cole, I'm so sorry."

Cole attempted to make light of the incident. He failed. "No need to be sorry. It's not the first time a woman took a knife to me." A brisk chuckle escaped from him. Dominique did not join in his mirth. Her hand was touching the bottom tip of his old scar. He noticed her gaze flash to the side of his face. She pulled her hand back as if she had been burned. Her mouth opened, but nothing escaped.

"Maybe I'll tell you about it sometime," Cole said. He wondered what Dominique would think of him if he told her about Susanah Rowland. Cole already figured Dominique's present opinion of him could not be very high after all the mistakes he had made in the past few days. If she learned what had happened to him on the French Riviera she would probably denounce him as the most foolish man she'd ever met.

Dominique nodded her head, but she still could not find the right words to reply. In her mind's eye she saw Cole's handsome face being slashed open by the woman he had once loved. When she looked into his eyes, she could sense he was scarred inside, and his hidden wound was much worse than the one on the side of his face. Her heart ached with love for him, and she wished she could somehow make him forget the hurt that loving someone had once caused him.

Cole swiped at the ever-growing horde of mosquitos again. The afternoon heat was beginning to lure the insects across the expanse of the valley floor, and they had already used the last of the repellent. "We'd best get a move on before we're eaten alive," Cole said.

And before you ask me about my past, he thought.

Dominique swallowed the lump in her throat. There were a dozen questions raging through her mind, but none she had the courage to ask. If only he would talk to her now, then maybe she could understand him better. And maybe she could make him realize that she would never hurt him—not intentionally anyway. But now was not the time, she realized. They had to get to Fort Yukon as soon as possible—for Cole's sake, and also for the rest of the passengers. Dominique forced her thoughts to focus on the present. "I'll carry the gear," she said. She did not wait for him to reply as she hoisted the heavy pack up and draped the strap over her shoulder.

Cole didn't argue. He carried the shotgun in his good hand. If the grizzly hadn't bled to death by now, Cole was sure he would come looking for them again. The thought caused a chill to race through his body. Even with the gun, Cole feared he would not be much good against an injured bear crazed with pain.

"Wait," Cole said as Dominique began to head out. She turned, a worried expression on her face. Cole laid the shotgun against a rock, and began to undo his belt. "I want you to wear this," he said.

"No, I don't want it," she said quickly. She glanced at his hand—the hand she had sliced open with that very knife.

"You have to have a weapon," he retorted.

His voice lacked patience. He felt dizzy and the heat of the afternoon was making him feel sick to his stomach. He shoved the belt toward her.

"Why?" she asked, defensively.

Cole gave her an unwavering stare. "Just in case that bear shows up and—"

"You've got a gun," she interrupted. She refused to reach for the knife.

"If something happens to me, I want you to have this." He continued to hold the belt and knife out to her. Dominique shook her head from side to side, but he did not give her a chance to speak again. "I won't take no for an answer."

She looked down at the knife. She wanted to tell him that he was being ridiculous but instead, she reached out and took the belt in her shaking hands. It hung—and felt—awkward when she fastened it around her waist. She glanced up and met Cole's gaze. She wondered if he felt as she did . . . that everything they were experiencing together was creating a growing love, a bonding to one another that would last for all eternity no matter what else happened.

"Let's go," he said. Cole's thoughts were clouded by the throbbing pain in his arm, and his nagging feeling of defeat. He wanted to get Dominique to safety, and he did not want to think about anything else.

The trek to the river was uneventful with the exception of the horrible swarm of mosquitos. Dominique kept telling herself she would never be able to get used to this place, but then she would remind herself she had no choice. The pack she carried was heavy, and the strap cut painfully into her shoulder. Several times Cole tried to take the pack from her, but she adamantly refused. Although he appeared to be holding up better than she had expected, she knew he couldn't carry the burden on his injured shoulder, and she wanted nothing to interfere with the weapon he carried in his other hand. She hardly took a step without glancing back over her shoulder to look for the grizzly.

To Dominique's surprise, the river was not far from the cave. By late afternoon the muddy rivers of the Yukon were once again at their feet. She began to feel confident that they would make it back to civilization. Feeling rejuvenated, she turned to Cole. A bolt of fear shot through her when she noticed how pale he was. "You have to rest," she said in a worried voice. She quickly closed her mouth when a swarm of mosquitos rushed for her parted lips.

Cole tried to appear nonchalant, but he knew he had just about reached the end of his endurance. His legs were beginning to feel like elastic, his face felt flushed, and he knew his wounds had started to bleed again by the sticky wetness he could feel soaking through his shirt. The smell of his blood would attract more mosquitos, and worse, more dangerous predators, as nightfall began to close in around them. Packs of wolves, grizzlies—maybe even the same old bear Cole had already tangled with—would be lured here by the scent of easy prey.

"No, we've got to keep going," he said. His voice was raspy and shaky. He saw a look of alarm flash across Dominique's face, and he was sure he knew what she was thinking. She would left alone here in the wilderness if something happened to him. This thought renewed Cole's strength. He was determined not to give into the weakness that threatened to overtake him. Cole tried to concentrate on Dominique, and on the responsibility he had to protect her. Still, he knew he couldn't walk much farther.

"I'm worried about you," Dominique said in a voice that also trembled. His coloring continued to grow paler, and when she glanced down at his arm, she noticed his sling was streaked with red. "Mon Dieu!" she gasped, dropping the pack and rushing to his side. "You're bleeding bad!"

Cradling his arm against him, Cole glanced down and saw the reason for her panic. The sight of so much blood—his blood—made him feel even more queasy. "I'll be all right. We'd best keep going if we're going to make it to Fort Yukon by nightfall."

"You can't walk any farther," Dominique said forcefully.

Cole's eyes locked with hers. Even his reflection that was mirrored in her blue eyes looked ghostly white. He knew he had to admit defeat, but he still wasn't ready to give up completely. "We'll build a raft," he said impulsively before thinking this idea through. He knew there were some rapids between here and Fort Yukon. The bigger boats did not have any difficulty negotiating the rough water, but Cole had seen many rafts crashed to pieces in the swirling rapids in White Water Canyon.

Dominique swiped at a swarm of mosquitos absent-mindedly. She would never grow used to the terrible pests, but she was learning to cope with them. Before she spoke, she waved her hand in front of her face to clear the air of the insects for a second. "That's a good idea," she said enthusiastically. "How?"

If Cole hadn't been in so much pain, he would have laughed at her. She seemed so innocent, yet she was never afraid to meet life head on. He thought about her upbringing, wondering how, after all those years in private schools—and with her notorious mother's influence—she had still retained so much optimism. "Well, with some branches and—" he glanced at the pack she had dropped on the ground. "That rope in the bag," he added. He quickly clamped his mouth shut as the mosquitos swarmed around his face. He never thought he'd pray for rain, but right now he would give just about anything for a cloudburst. Only a few clouds floated through the sky, and they didn't appear too ominous.

Without wasting any more time, Dominique began to scour the area for fallen trees that could serve as raft material. She had seen plenty of rafts at St. Michael—some elaborately built craft and others that were constructed of skinny logs that were tied with rope—she figured that would be the type she and Cole would build. But, she didn't care what it looked like as long as it floated. She was confident she could steer the raft while Cole rested. With an apprehensive glance, she noticed he was grimacing painfully as he attempted to drag a log with his good arm. His sling was completely soaked through with blood now. Dominique dropped the branch she was dragging, and rushed to his side again. This time she would not take no for an answer. "Cole, you must rest." She grabbed his good arm, pleadingly, and stared directly into his eye.

Cole sighed with defeat. He knew he needed to save his strength for the river trip. He nodded and dropped the log he was holding. "I'll rest while you gather the logs," he said, breathlessly. A weak—and nervous—smile curved her lips. She glanced down at his bloody arm, her forced smile faded.

"I'm going to check your wounds and—"

"No," Cole interrupted forcefully. "I'll be all right once we reach Fort Yukon."

Dominique nodded, and backed away. She

didn't want to argue with him, and waste precious time. Getting him to the fort was the most important thing right now. She grabbed the log he had been carrying, and dragged it to the small pile they had already accumulated. Cole sat down and leaned against the trunk of the nearest tree. He rested his head and closed his eyes. Within seconds, he was engulfed by mosquitos. But, he didn't seem to notice. Panic ruled Dominique's actions as she rushed to gather more logs. When she had what she thought to be a pile of fairly good-sized logs, she grabbed the rope out of the pack. Common sense, and fear for Cole, ruled her actions as she began to line up the logs and tie them together with the rope.

Using all her strength, Dominique wove the rope around each log, then pulled it as tight as possible before knotting it. The knife Cole had insisted she take came in handy for cutting the rope. She kept remembering the wound on his hand, and the terrible guilt she felt for inflicting that wound. Then she would think about the scar on his face. He had said he would tell her about it someday, and she intended to hold him to his word.

As she worked on the raft, she kept a close eye on Cole. To her relief, she noticed that the blood was drying on the sling. His inactivity had obviously made the bleeding stop. He even appeared to be dozing, but every so often—without opening his eyes—he would take a wild swing at the hordes of mosquitos that swarmed around his face. Dominique worked at a fevered pace. She retied and re-checked the ropes, over and over again. Her greatest worry was that the ropes would come untied and the raft would fall apart. Cole would never be able to swim in his condition.

When, at last, Dominique felt she had secured the ropes as tight as she could, she approached Cole. She waved her gloved hand back and forth in front of his face to ward off the pesky mosquitos, then she shook him gently and called out his name.

Cole felt the breeze on his face. He heard the soft sound of her voice. For a moment, his eyes remained closed. In his mind, he envisioned himself on a white, sandy beach. A gentle breeze was blowing against his face. He could see his ship anchored off the beach. And wrapped in his arms was a woman, warm and willing. Dominique. His eyes flew open, and her face swam before his foggy eyes. But, she looked different than she did in his dream. In his musing, she had been wearing a thin cotton shift—the type the women wore in the hot climates of the South Pacific islands—and her silken skin had been slick with a light sheen of perspiration. He'd imagined her long slender legs stretched out in the sand, and her raven hair spilling out around her head. Her lips were moist and parted, eager for his kisses . . .

"Cole? Are you awake?"

Cole blinked, and stared at her. She was

wearing the heavy layers of clothes she had been wearing for the past several days. Her hair hung in a tangled dirty mass from under her floppy brimmed hat. Her face was shiny—greasy from the repellent—and her dry, swollen lips were pursed into a worried frown. For an instant, Cole grew angry. How unfair it seemed, he thought, that this beautiful girl should end up here, in this hell-hole.

"Cole?"

"Yeah," he finally answered. He cleared his throat and blinked again. He wished he could retreat into his dreamland forever, and take her with him. His gaze settled on the raft. A bolt of surprise shot through him. He looked back at Dominique. "You did good . . . again," he said with a tone of surprise, and admiration. With her help he rose to his feet. His knees felt shaky, but the light-headed feeling that had plagued him before was gone. Dominique continued to hold him tightly as if she was afraid he would fall down. Cole did not mind her nearness.

When they reached the raft, Cole leaned down and examined her work. He had seen men who were planning to float from St. Michael all the way to Dawson City build rafts that were more rickety than this one. Cole turned to Dominique. She was watching him with an anxious expression on her face. With his uninjured arm he reached out and pulled her close. "You're quite a woman," he said quietly. Their eyes met. He wanted to say

211

more . . . so much more . . . but he knew he couldn't allow himself to say too much.

"Do you think it will make it to Fort Yukon?" Dominique asked, motioning toward the raft. Although he held her to him, she was afraid to press against him too tightly for fear of hurting him. He nodded, and she noticed an odd expression flit across his face. As she continued to gaze into his eyes, she was sure she could read his mind. Someday soon, she hoped, he would be able to say what was written in his eyes.

Fourteen

By late afternoon Dominique and Cole were ready to push their vessel into the water. Cole had found two spruce branches he thought would work as paddles for steering, and after he had instructed Dominique on how to tie them to the sides of the raft, they were ready to shove off. Dominique held her breath as Cole climbed on board first. She studied the ropes, watching to see if any of them were loosening, or coming untied. When Cole motioned for her to join him she waded out to the raft, and carefully eased herself up. The logs rolled beneath her slightly. She grew tense until she realized they were not coming undone. Inching away from the edge, she drew in a trembling breath as she glanced at the river that awaited them. From here, it appeared to be smooth sailing. She exhaled hard, and began to relax slightly.

The raft accommodated its two passengers and their gear with little room to spare. The warm weather the past couple of days had helped to clear up some of the mud in the wide river, but there were areas where muddy tidal flats still devoured the water along the riverbanks. Using the branches as oars, Cole taught Dominique how to steer clear of the mud. Keeping close to the edge of the river, they stayed on a fairly straight course, only veering out toward the middle once in a while to avoid protruding rocks and the mud bogs. For most of the way the river was calm, which for the sake of the flimsy raft was fortunate.

As usual, the mosquitos were in constant attendance, so conversation was almost non-existent. Dominique felt that compared to the fear of falling off the raft—or worrying that the raft would fall apart—the presence of the pesky insects was minor. Cole's condition, she noticed with relief, did not seem to grow any worse. He would not allow her to see his wound, though, which caused her to worry that he might be bleeding again. Her only consolation was that he was certain they would be at the fort soon.

"Up ahead we're going to come across a stretch of rapids," Cole hollered. "You'd best find somethin' to hang onto. That's about all you can do." His voice broke through the soothing sounds of the running water and the constant buzzing of the insects. He tried to act nonchalant about the approaching danger, but he could tell Dominique had seen past his facade. Her eyes were wide with fear.

She glanced up at Cole. He gave her what he hoped would be a reassuring nod of his head. The gesture did little to boost her confidence. She stared down at the wobbly logs, wondering what she was supposed to hang onto. A sense of doom inched through her as she looked toward the approaching canyon walls. Dusk made the stone walls shimmer in golden hues. From here, the river still looked smooth and calm, but she sensed the water in the canyon wouldn't be so tranquil.

"There's only a couple of bad eddies." Cole yelled when he noticed her frightened expression. He gestured for her to sit opposite him. She crawled the short distance, and peered over the jagged logs. The murky water was growing swifter as they approached the mouth of the canyon, and her fear was growing apace. She looked back to Cole. His full attention was on the river. Dominique did not have any more time to worry, because in the next second, the raft took a sudden lurch upward. She cried out in surprise, and turned back to Cole. Using his good hand, he was attempting to steer the raft with the spruce branch.

The roar of the rapids was growing louder, and the raft was rocking up and down wildly with the fast running water. Cole raised up on his knees, still grasping the branch in his hand. On his face was a pained expression. Dominique glanced down at his arm. The sling was once again wet with fresh blood. She cried out, but the sound of her voice was lost to the deafening roar of the rapids.

Dominique attempted to crawl over to Cole, but she could she could not keep her balance. The raft was lunging up and down faster now. Water sprayed in her face, and the only thing she could do was grab for something to hang on to. Instinctively, she grabbed one of the ropes. To her horror, she felt the rope loosen when she pulled on it. She let go of the rope immediately, and looked around frantically for something else to grasp. Falling down on her stomach, she grabbed the edge of the raft, and hung on for her life.

The tiny raft began to turn in the swirling water. Everything became a blur to Dominique. She tried to see Cole, and tried to hang onto the raft, but she felt as if she was being tossed around like a rag doll. The water, the canyon walls—even the sky—merged together, until Dominique's head was spinning faster than the raft. She could not even scream, because every time she opened her mouth, the river water flooded her mouth. Her fingers groped for something stable to grab. Once again, she felt one of the ropes and entangled her fingers in it. She felt the rope loosen, and she thought she felt the logs beneath her move apart. The rocking of the raft made it impossible for her to tell if the logs were separating, or if it was only her imagination. She had no choice but to hang onto the ropes, because there was nothing else she could grab.

Turning her head to the side, she looked around. The water splashing in her eyes prevented her from seeing Cole clearly. But, she could tell he was still on the raft, and the knowledge gave her courage to keep hanging on.

Cole was sure he had never known such agony. He had no choice but take his arm out of the sling, so he could use both of his arms. The branch he was using for an oar was useless, and once he realized this, he tossed it into the rapids. He knew their only chance now was to hang on to the raft until they were clear of the rapids—that is, if the raft held together.

Dominique was not aware that the raft was coming undone until she felt the two logs underneath her come apart. For an instant she was too shocked to think coherently. When her mind began to function again, she realized her survival depended on clinging to at least one of the logs. She wrapped her arms around the log that was still beneath her, and held her breath as the rapids began to swirl the single log and its passenger through the roughest of the white water. Her mind went blank as the water rushed over her and stole away her breath.

An agonized cry escaped from Cole when he saw the raft fall apart. He reached for Dominique, but she disappeared into the foaming water. Common sense told him it would be useless to turn loose the log he was clinging to and dive in after her. He could only pray that she was not crushed against a rock before they were washed out of the rapids. Since the canyon was not very long, and they were almost to the end of the rapids, Cole was not ready to give up hope. Within seconds after they were torn apart, Cole's log began to slow down. He pushed himself up to a sitting position with his legs straddling the log and scanned the water for some sign of Dominique. He grew numb with fear, and a heartwrenching agony filled him when he looked back. Nothing but the last of the rapids was rushing out of the canyon walls. The calmer water on this side of the canyon was even more unsettling. If he didn't see her soon, Cole knew his worse fears would be realized . . . she had not survived the rapids, and must be tangled around the base of one of the large rocks that blanketed the river bottom.

His gaze began to blur, and his head started to spin. The panic that threatened to overpower him grew stronger. He kept remembering the last time he had seen her clinging to the log, then disappearing into the white swirling water. "No—please no," he said to himself. He began to curse this God-forsaken place with a vengeance, but his vicious assault was halted when he noticed something emerging from the canyon.

"Dominique," he hollered. Hope soared through his weakening body. He called out to

218

her again. She slowly rose up from the log. For a moment, she seemed confused. Cole could tell she was coughing and gasping for air, but the most important thing was that she was alive. He waited until she had caught her breath, then he yelled at her again. She glanced around. Her arm rose up and she waved at him, but she was too far away from him to make out her face. Cole tried to wave back at her, he didn't have the energy to make the small gesture. He glanced down at his injured arm. The bandages had been torn off in the rapids, and the claw marks were oozing blood. The blood ran down his hand and into the murky water of the river, where it slowly spread out into little puddles of red, and then disappeared. That was the last thing Cole remembered.

For a minute, Dominique was not sure what happened. She still felt breathless and dizzy. She remembered crashing through the rapids when an underwater whirlpool had sucked down her log. She thought she was drowning as the eddy whipped her around, but a miracle had occurred and the log had been flung out of the swirling pool. She clung to the log with a death-like grip as the log splashed down and continued to bounce through the rest of the rapids. Then, she had seen Cole. Nothing could compare to the joyous feeling she had experienced. She was silently thanking God for saving them when she saw Cole topple off his log. She screamed, and before she contemplated her actions, she dove into the water and began to swim towards him.

By the time she reached Cole, he was already sinking down under the water. Dominique inhaled sharply, then dove back under the water. Visibility was poor in the murky water, but she could see Cole's unconscious form slowly descending toward the bottom of the deep river. She grabbed blindly for him, clutching the collar of his coat. Strength she didn't know she possessed led her back to the surface. She dragged Cole with her as she paddled toward the shore. Twice, she almost lost her hold on him. But her determination never wavered. The shore seemed miles away, though it was only about a hundred feet. After what seemed like an eternity, Dominique felt the muddy slope beneath her feet. She fell down several times in the deep mud as she tried to pull Cole up the slippery bank. He was dead weight, but she would not give up.

When they were both completely out of the water, Dominique released her hold on his collar and let him fall face down on the ground. She fell down on her knees beside him and began to push down on the area between his shoulder blades. For a minute, he did not respond. Terror made her numb, but then the same sense of terror gave her the energy to continue. She spread her hands out on his back and pushed down. He coughed, then coughed again. Dominique cried out with relief. After he drew in several deep breaths, she rolled him over. His eyes were closed, but in a couple of seconds, his eyelids began to flutter. When he opened his eyes, his pupils were glazed, and he seemed disoriented.

"Cole? Can you hear me?" Dominique asked. She leaned down close to him, and stared into his eyes. He blinked several more times, then met her gaze. Inwardly, Dominique said another thank you to God. Her attention was drawn to Cole's arm. The ugly cuts were still bleeding, but it appeared the blood was beginning to clot. To Dominique's horror, the worse looking injury was the knife wound she had inflicted on Cole.

"You saved my life, woman," Cole whispered, breathlessly. He wished he had the energy to hug her, but right now, he barely had the strength to speak.

Dominique didn't have a chance to respond, because the sound of a gunshot close by caught her attention. Her eyes locked with Cole's. She could tell he had heard the shot, too. "Should I go and see who it is?" she said in a low voice. She was half-afraid that they would encounter more trouble, and Cole was in no shape to confront anyone who wasn't friendly.

Cole understood her hesitancy. But he also knew they needed help, and they had to take the chance that whoever was doing the shooting would be willing to help them get to Fort

Yukon. He nodded his head, then finding the last of his energy, he reached up and gently touched Dominique's cheek. He thought of telling her that he loved her, but even after all they had been through together, the words were still too hard to say. "Be careful," he said, instead.

Dominique nodded. She swallowed the heavy lump at the back of her throat. They had almost lost one another a few minutes ago; why couldn't he admit his true feelings? she wondered. She stood up slowly. The feel of his hand against her cheek lingered even after his hand slid away. A cool breeze flitted against her wet clothes, making her shiver visibly. The sound of horses drew her attention to the ridge above the river bank. She attempted to control her rampant fear. Before her panic had a chance to overpower her, the riders crested the ridge. They stopped, and stared down at them. Dominique's relief made her entire body shake as she looked up at the four Royal Canadian Mounted Policemen. They sat atop their horses in a regal manner, their red coats, tall black boots and plumed hats impeccable. Dominique was sure she had never seen a more welcome sight.

"Are you from Fort Yukon?" she called. After she spoke. everything began to happen in a rush. The Mounties were at their side, helping to bandage Cole's arm, wrapping Dominique in warm blankets, and giving them both cool, fresh water to drink out of their canteens.

"Looks like you tangled with the same grizzly we just shot," one of the Mounties said as he looked at Cole's wounds. "The old bear was close to bleedin' to death, but he was still a mean one."

Dominique exchanged glances with Cole. She saw the look of relief wash through his tired face. She was sure she wore a similar look. If the Mounties hadn't shown up when they did, she realized they probably would have had another encounter with the bear, since he was obviously so close by. Another shiver shook her body at the thought. She reminded herself that their ordeal was finally over. More importantly, once they reached Fort Yukon, Dominique was sure Cole would be ready to talk to her about their feelings for one another. Then, they could put all the bad things that had happened behind them, and they could make plans for their future.

"Are you up to traveling?" one of the Mounties asked Cole. He thought the man looked better than he had when they had first seen him, but he was still a bit pale.

Cole glanced at the horses. He nodded his head. Until this last river trip, he had preferred boats and ships to horses. Now, he was more than happy to ride on horseback for a spell. He looked at Dominique, and noticed that she was watching him again. A pang of guilt tore at him when he noticed how worried and tired she looked. He hated himself again for bringing her on this crazy journey, and he hated himself even more, for the pain he would still have to cause her before it was all over.

It was dark by the time the Mounties rode into Fort Yukon with their passengers. Cole's wounds were tended to again by the doctor at the fort. He was lucky, the doctor told him. The wounds were clean of infection, and should heal quickly and with little damage to the usefulness of his arm. Cole was grateful for this news, but all he really wanted to do was go to sleep. When he exited the doctor's cabin, though, he found Dominique waiting for him. He noticed that she still hadn't changed her wet clothes or cleaned up.

"You'd best get out of these clothes, and get yourself to bed," he said briskly. She glanced at his freshly bandaged arm and hand. He cursed silently at himself for talking so harshly to her. She obviously had been waiting out here the whole time he had been with the doctor. "The doctor says I'll live," he added in a gentler voice. Then, almost as an afterthought, he said, "And I have you to thank for saving my life on more than one occasion."

Dominique shrugged. All at once, she realized how tired she really was. "Cole? Tomorrow . . ." she hesitated, and glanced down at the ground.

"Tomorrow I have to help bring back the

passengers from the Lady Susanah," he said. A light shining from the window of the cabin they stood in front of gave him a clear view of her face when she looked back up at him. He could see an array of emotions in her weary face, and he knew what she wanted—and needed—to hear. Maybe, he told himself, it was time to end the agony for both of them. Maybe the time had come to tell her why he could never say those words.

"We've got sleeping quarters ready for you folks," a young Mountie said as he approached the couple. He tipped his hat toward Dominique, adding, "And I can show you where you can clean up before you retire."

Dominique glanced back at Cole. She thought he looked relieved to have the interruption. A sinking feeling washed through her as she wondered if they would ever have a chance to tell one another how they felt. "About tomorrow . . ." Dominique said, turning back to Cole. The thought of him leaving her here filled her with foreboding.

"I'll talk to you before I leave," Cole said. Unexpectedly, he reached out and grabbed her hand. His fingers tightened around hers almost desperately. She returned the gesture, and through the faded light they looked into one another's eyes.

Dominique knew—she just knew—if the Mountie had not been standing so close, Cole would admit that he loved her. She could see it in his eyes, and in the expression on his face. Maybe this was what he wanted to talk to her about tomorrow.

Fifteen

Dominique glanced around the small encampment. Fort Yukon was a mirror image of all the forts and trading posts that dotted the riverside. There were several roughly-strewn log cabins scattered along a single, muddy roadway. Heavy canvas tents out-numbered the buildings, mostly occupied by sourdoughs—the name given to the men who were rushing to the gold fields—who had stopped at the fort for supplies or because of health reasons that prevented them from pushing on to the upper Yukon territory. Dominique cringed at the bleakness of this tiny settlement, which was made worse by the cloudiness of the morning. She wondered if Dawson City would look the same. At least the colder temperature and the heavy cloud covering gave them a rest from the awful mosquitos for a while.

Dominique sat beside Cole outside the canvas tent where she had spent the night. It had been a restless one. During the past few days and nights, Cole's presence at her side while she slept had become a welcome habit. Last night, he had slept with several other men in a tent down the road. His absence left her feeling cold and lonely. Since they had reunited this morning, there had been a strain between them. "I never thought we would see this place," Dominique said in an attempt to make conversation.

Cole pretended to pout. "You mean, you doubted that I could get us here?"

She gave him a teasing smile. Cole openly stared at her. She looked more lovely than he had ever seen her. She'd finally had her much-awaited bath this morning. Now, her freshly-scrubbed skin was a rosy shade. A sprinkling of mosquito bites still dotted her complexion, but they were barely noticeable. She had pulled her long raven hair back and braided the thick tresses into one braid that hung past the middle of her back.

The proprietor of the trading post had provided them both with clean clothes, and Cole noticed that the pants and shirt Dominique wore fit her much better than the clothes she had worn previously. The jeans—obviously sized for a young boy—fit snugly across her hips and hugged her firm buttocks to perfection. A blue plaid flannel shirt and a lightweight canvas jacket topped her jeans, and brown cowboy boots completed her new outfit. To his annoyance, Cole couldn't keep his eyes off her. It was going to be harder than he had imagined to leave her.

"I think you're capable of doing anything you set out to do," she said. She noticed Cole's complexion pale slightly. He did not look in her direction.

"I'd best be getting down to the boat," he said in a hoarse voice. He cleared his throat loudly, then rose to his feet. He made no effort to leave. When he looked down at Dominique, their eyes locked. An awkward silence followed. Since they had arrived at the fort last night, neither of them had wanted to talk about his departure.

"Are you sure you're feeling up to it? Maybe you should wait until tomorrow."

Cole didn't reply, nor did his eyes leave her face. He was amazed she could still feel that he was a capable man after all the mistakes he'd made.

Without looking away from him, Dominique stood up. She had dreaded this moment all night. "I could go with you," she said in a weak, trembling voice.

Cole remained unmoving, continuing to stare at her. His mind was going in a dozen directions. He wanted to take her with him—desperately—but he knew he had to be logical this time. He had to think about the people who were waiting and counting on him to come to their rescue.

"No," he finally said. His head shook slowly from side to side. The look of disappointment on her face tore at his heart. It took all his willpower to keep from saying what he really wanted to say; *Yes, come with me now and stay with me forever. I'll prove to you that I'm worthy of your trust.* Instead, he forced himself to turn away.

Dominique felt as if the air she breathed had just been stolen from her. There was so much they still needed to talk about. But, for reasons she did not understand, they were unable to talk to one another. She stared at Cole as he carefully adjusted the sling around his bandaged arm. He was wearing blue jeans, instead of his usual wool trousers. His knife hung from his belt, and the navy pea coat hung over his shoulders. His head was hatless today. He had combed his wavy brown hair back away from his forehead; the longer strands in the back curled over his coat collar. He was clean-shaven, and the scar on the side of his face seemed more noticeable this morning, but it did not detract from his handsomeness. As Dominique looked at him, the sorrow that filled her was strangling. In spite of all the things she desperately wanted to tell him, she couldn't make herself say a word.

Cole glanced up, and noticed that she was still watching him. He wasn't surprised. Again—and against his better judgment—he looked into her eyes. The sad expression on his face bespoke his true feelings. He could not, however, put these feelings into words.

"How long will you be gone?" Dominique

asked as she gazed into his eyes. His agony was evident. Why couldn't he admit that they should not be apart—now or ever?

A shrug lifted Cole's shoulders. "Not long. But they'll take good care of you here." He had no doubt the Mounties would see to it that no one harmed her. And, he knew she was capable of taking care of herself, too. At times, he almost wished he possessed some of her strong spirit. She was, he realized, the first woman who could make him feel like a complete failure, and she did so innocent of intent.

Dominique swallowed hard. Her head nodded slowly. "C-Can we—I mean—when you come back," she drew in a deep breath, adding, "Can we talk then?"

Cole shrugged again, his throat tight. "W-What did you want to talk about?" He felt a hot flush on his cheeks. His question was foolish and unnecessary. They both knew what needed to be discussed.

"Dawson City," she said without hesitation. She noticed a strange expression cross his face and wondered—feared—what he was thinking.

Cole nodded slowly. "There's a lot to talk about." He gazed into her eyes, remembering the two things she said she wanted most in life . . . respectability and a home.

His odd behavior confused Dominique, but at the same time, gave her hope. "Yes, there are many things we should discuss." She couldn't look away, held prisoner by his eyes.

Why couldn't he tell her what he was feeling? Why did he look so strange? A sudden thought shattered Dominique's composure. "Mon Dieu!" she gasped, without thinking. "You will be back, won't you?"

Her question hit Cole like a blast of icy wind. Why would she ask him that question? He swallowed hard. "I'll be back." His voice sounded unnatural to his own ears. "Do you want to walk down to the dock with me?"

For a moment Dominique didn't answer. There was something frightening about his attitude, more terrifying than anything she had experienced here in the Yukon. She'd prefer to meet up with the old grizzly again, rather than face the possibility of never seeing Cole again. She tried to push the fear that he would not return to the back of her mind. She nodded and was surprised when Cole held out his good hand. She did not hesitate to place her hand in his and her fears fled, replaced by the comfort of his touch. He would be back! She was confident her heart wouldn't lie to her.

The walk to the river was far too short, and the boats that were waiting for Cole were too prompt. The two small freighters that were going downriver to pick up the stranded passengers and crew from the Lady Susanah were manned and waiting when Cole arrived. Also pulling out of the harbor was a large steamer that was headed back to St. Michael.

"I'd best get on board," he said, his voice

hoarse with emotion. He clutched Dominique's hand tightly.

Although it was causing her still-healing rope burns to sting, Dominique had no intention of pulling away. She needed to be as close to him as possible—for as long as possible. And, she desperately needed to tell him how she felt before he left. "Cole, there's something I must say—I have to say it." She spoke breathlessly as a blush reddened her cheeks. He purposely looked away from her.

"We'll talk when I return," he said. "We'll have more time then." He continued to look toward the boat knowing she wanted to tell him that she loved him. Although he loved her too, he knew there were things he had to work out before he could tell her how he felt.

"But I lo—" Her words were cut off by Cole's unexpected kiss. It was a brief kiss, but intense. Dominique's lips burned when he pulled away and her body trembled. Sorrow filled her heart. She didn't understand why he didn't want her to tell him she loved him. When he backed away, Dominique felt as if he had taken a part of her with him.

"I've got to go," he said quickly. He attempted to smile, but he couldn't pull it off. No more than a couple feet separated them and he longed to touch her again, to kiss her, to hear the words she wanted to say, and tell her he felt the same way. He felt like a tightly-wound spring that was about to snap.

Dominique tried to speak as she watched

him turn to leave. She couldn't make herself call out to him, couldn't even catch her breath. She felt a crushing weight in her heart. She watched him walk down the dock and climb onto the deck of the freighter. His footsteps seemed to drag, and Dominique was sure he was going to stop and turn around; a sense of foreboding joined her disappointment when he didn't look back.

Dominique saw him talking to a couple of the men on board the boat and moments later the boat pulled away from the dock. Cole turned in her direction, his expression was unclear at this distance. She wondered if his eyes still looked so sad. As the boat moved farther away Cole became no more than a dark blur on the deck. Dominique remained at the river's edge long after the boat had faded away in the distance.

She tried to figure out why Cole behaved so strangely, why he didn't want her to tell him she loved him. Maybe—she consoled herself by recalling his words—he just wanted to wait until he came back. Then, they would have time to explore their feelings and their future. She continued to gaze toward the river. The large steamer was moving slowly out of the harbor now, to the sound of the paddle-wheel slapping against the water. A raindrop plopped on the bridge of her nose. Memories of the day the Lady Susanah bogged down flooded her mind. That day seemed like a lifetime ago; it had been less than a week.

Since then, she had lived—and loved—what seemed like a lifetime, in Cole's arms.

For the first time in several days, Dominique thought about Jack Scroggins. Was he anxiously waiting for her in Dawson City at this very moment? Had he planned their wedding, and prepared a home for her to live in? Dominique shivered as a sprinkling of raindrops etched the surface of the muddy river water. Jack Scroggins was pushed from her mind and the image of a handsome, grey-eyed captain dominated her thoughts. She ached with a desperate yearning to be on the river with him now, to be close to him. But he would be back soon. Then they could say all the things they had not had a chance to say . . . and they would never have to be apart again.

Cole stood at the edge of the river and watched the troupe of bedraggled women load onto the freighter. Not all of them, however, were boarding the boat that would transport them to Dawson City. Nearly half of the women were loading onto the steamer that was headed back to St. Michael. From there they would board a ship that would take them down to San Francisco. These women had decided that whatever treasures the Yukon held, the price to claim them was too high.

At daybreak the freighter had reached the area where Cole had left his crew and passengers. Luther—and the rest of Cole's crew—had taken good care of the women, in spite of the adverse conditions. But then, Cole had never doubted Luther's ability to handle the situation. Several of the women were acutely ill, most likely with pneumonia. These women were among the ones returning to San Francisco so they could receive proper medical attention.

Cole returned his attention to the wreck of the Lady Susanah. The steamer was lying completely on its side, the receding mud, revealing the damage that had been done. Cole thought the riverboat looked like a broken and discarded toy, and he figured there wasn't much left to salvage from the wreck. By the end of the summer, sourdoughs that were floating down the river would take advantage of whatever wood was usable. The rains of autumn would wash away what was left, and then there would be no trace of what had once been the Lady Susanah. Cole realized that in spite of the financial loss, it was time he let go of everything that was a part of the past. Since he had met Dominique, not even Susanah's memory had taunted him. He no longer needed a shrine to remind him of the pain that woman had caused him all those years ago. Absently, he rubbed at his scar, and turned away from the wreck.

"You're bein' too hard on yourself," Luther said, glancing sideways at Cole. Cole didn't reply. Luther was unaffected by his silence.

"It's not just that you're feelin' like a failure 'cause you lost the Lady Susanah, is it?"

"I got lost, and I let a bear tear me up, and I almost got Dominique killed in the rapids. That, along with the fact that I have no money and no ship," Cole gave a sarcastic laugh, adding, "I suppose it all adds up to failure."

Luther shook his head, and gave a low whistle. "Guess you'd like for me to feel sorry for you. But it sounds like you've got enough self-pity, so you don't need none of mine."

Cole didn't respond, nor did he look at Luther. He had not slept last night; sleepless nights were a habit lately, it seemed. He pulled his raincoat tighter. His injured arm ached, his head pounded, and his heart was heavy. Luther's comments only fueled his anger.

"Well, I still think there's more to it," Luther added. The threatening look Cole cast in his direction did not intimidate him. "It's that little French girl, ain't it?"

"It's over," Cole retorted.

"She's waitin' at the fort for you, ain't she?"

"No," Cole said in a harsh voice. "She's waitin' for a man who can give her all the things I can't give her."

"What the hell does that mean?" Luther asked. He noticed Cole shrug as if he didn't care. His face told a different story. "Well, do you love her?" Luther's voice was demanding. Cole turned abruptly. Luther looked him

237

straight in the eye, shrugged, then continued, "So, you do love her. Does she love you?"

"What the hell is this third degree all about?" Cole shouted. He straightened his stance and glared at Luther through narrowed eyes.

Luther returned his blatant stare. "I don't intend to watch you moon around over this woman for the next ten years like you did for Susanah." The dark fury that reddened Cole's face made Luther cringe inwardly. He knew he had struck an exposed nerve.

"It's different this time," Cole said through gritted teeth. "Susanah led me to believe we would spend the rest of our lives together. I hardly even know Dominique."

"You just spent close to a week with her— alone. Appears to me that was plenty of time for you to get to know each other real well."

Cole shook his head angrily. "She wants marriage and a home." He let his good arm drop heavily against his thigh. "She'll get that when she marries that miner in Dawson City."

Luther huffed. "You and her already discussed all this?"

"She told me that's what she wants." Cole turned back toward the river. "I'm not the man to give it to her."

Luther stared at him. He could read Cole almost as well as he could read himself. Cole was right, it was different this time. He had been infatuated with Susanah Rowland; with her beauty, wealth and dangerous lifestyle.

But Luther had always doubted that it was true love. With Dominique Laval, Cole was learning what it meant to really be in love. Too bad Cole was being so damned stubborn. "Maybe you should give her the chance to decide for herself," Luther added.

"What the hell does that mean?" Cole did not look at Luther when he spoke.

"Did you tell her that you loved her, so she could make up her own mind about whether or not she still wanted to marry that miner up in Dawson?" Cole's angry snort told Luther what he wanted to know.

"Not that it's any of my business," Luther continued, "but I think you ought to talk to her about all this when you see her again."

Cole grunted and shook his head. He knew it was useless to talk to Luther about Dominique. It was useless to talk to Dominique when he got back to Fort Yukon, too. He had to accept reality; she wanted a home—he wanted to sail the high seas. She wanted respectability—his idea of decency was to never take a woman to his bed without first buying her a drink. Regardless of their different goals—even if by some miracle they could still be together—Cole knew he had nothing to offer her. This was eating him up, and driving him to the brink of madness. Just as Cole was about to tell Luther no amount of talking would make up for his failures, they were interrupted.

"You Captain Hawkins?" a voice called out

from behind Cole. He turned and glared at the man who spoke to him. As Cole sized him up, he could tell by the man's garb that he was a fellow sailor. Cole nodded, and tried to clear his mind of all his tormented thoughts. The man held out his hand to Cole.

"I'm Captain Lindsey." He shook Cole's hand, then repeated the gesture with Luther. "I guess you know my steamer is headed down to St. Michael," Captain Lindsey smiled at Cole. The gesture was not returned. His black beard had raindrops hanging from the straggly ends. "But I got me a little problem."

Cole's eyes narrowed slightly. He lifted one dark eyebrow in a questioning arch. "What's that?"

Captain Lindsey chuckled. "Well, when I was up in Dawson City I got myself into a poker game. Won me a hefty stake up on Bonanza Hill." He chuckled again when he noticed that both of the other men now gave him their full attention. Bonanza Hill held some of the richest veins of gold in the Yukon Territory. "Yeah—well—I got this obligation to take this steamer back to St. Michael 'cause it's owned by The Alaskan Freight Company. And I was thinkin'," Captain Lindsey paused and scratched at his thick beard.

Cole waited impatiently for the man to finish saying whatever it was he was trying to say. He glanced at Luther, noting that he also seemed rather annoyed with Captain Lindsey.

"We're headed to Dawson City," Cole said sharply.

"Yeah—well—I would like to be headed to Dawson City myself. With all the claim jumpin' going on up there, I need to get back up to my mine as soon as possible. And, if you would be willin' to take my steamer on down to St. Michael, I'd take charge of seeing to it that your passengers made it up to Dawson City." Captain Lindsey pulled out a small canvas bag, adding, "I'd make it worth your while."

Cole eyed the grimy bag for a moment. Captain Lindsey enticed him by opening the top of the bag. Gold nuggets the size of small rocks filled the bag. He looked at Luther. Their eyes met. "I need to talk to my First Mate," Cole said gruffly. He stepped away from Captain Lindsey, motioning for Luther to follow him.

"What do you think," Cole said in a low voice when they were off by themselves.

"I can't believe you're considerin' goin' back to St. Michael," Luther retorted. His voice was harsh, his meaning clear.

"She'd be better off," Cole said through gritted teeth.

"You have nothing to worry about then— you know—no obligations you might be responsible for in the future?"

Cole gave Luther a look that could turn fire to ice. The insinuation Luther made cut deep into Cole. Since this was not the first time the possibility had occurred to him, it was not hard to imagine having a child with Dominique. But her words taunted his memory . . . A real home where the family gathers after church on Sundays. He did not fit into that picture. "She'll be married as soon as she reaches Dawson City."

"You could live with havin' another man raising yo—" Luther's words were cut off.

"Yes, dammit!"

"Then I guess I have nothing else to say to you," Luther said. His voice held a note of disgust. He pulled his raincoat up around his face and fell silent. The rain continued to fall while Luther began to wonder when Cole had turned into such a heartless man.

Cole looked down at the muddy ground. Luther's attitude made him feel lower than a snake, but still it did not change his mind. "There's enough gold in that bag to put a down payment on a ship—a real ship—not some damn riverbarge." He felt a strange sensation clutch at his chest. Dominique's image haunted his thoughts. He tried, but could not make her go away.

Luther sighed heavily and shook his head. It was ironic that Cole would have the opportunity to fulfill his dream of having his own ship again at the expense of losing something equally precious. "I hope it's worth it," he said. He stared at Cole. Finally, Cole was forced to look up at him.

Though he was looking into Luther's eyes,

it was Dominique's image Cole saw. He remembered the way she looked when he had left her on the riverbank. He would never forget how she had trusted him; never forget the way she made him feel when they made love. And, although he had never thought it was possible, Dominique had finally made him forget about Susanah Rowland. Now, and forever, it would be Dominique he would think about when he thought of love . . . lost love.

Sixteen

Word of the women's successful rescue reached Fort Yukon the third day after Cole left. Dominique listened with excitement—and anticipation—as two sourdoughs who had drifted into the fort on a raft told everyone at the fort that the freighter transporting the passengers from the Lady Susanah was on its way. Their expected arrival was early the next day. Although she had worried for the past few days about Cole's attitude when he left, Dominique was positive they would have no more problems once they had a chance to talk.

After another restless night, Dominique hurried down to the riverbank to watch for Cole. The rain had ceased to fall, but the morning was still dark and gloomy. Dominique's displeasure with the Yukon Territory grew daily. The Mounties, and the other men at the fort, had told Dominique nothing to improve her opinion of this country. They had, in fact, told her things that only made her despise this place even more. If their account of the long, harsh winters was accurate, Dominique was sure she did not want to be here when winter set in.

Once she talked to Cole—and after she had figured out a way to pay back the money Jack Scroggins had given to her—she was sure she would be leaving the Klondike. Cole, she knew, hated it here more than she did. She had no idea where they would go, but it didn't really matter as long as they were together. They would be together forever—just as soon as the freighter pulled up to the dock at Fort Yukon.

Dominique heard the churning sound of the first boat long before it came into view. Tremors of excitement raced through her. She wondered if Cole was as eager to see her as she was to see him. A cold breeze blew across the river. Dominique felt the icy blast against her flushed face. She stood on her toes in an attempt to see the people on the deck of the freighter. The first person she recognized was Addie Mcfadden. Dominique waved, Addie waved back.

Once again, Dominique scanned the deck for Cole. She saw other familiar faces, but not Cole. He must be on the second freighter, she told herself. The wind whipped across the water again. This time Dominique shivered uncontrollably as a strange, uneasy feeling crept over her. She saw a man standing at the bow of the first freighter. His thick black beard was evident even from this distance. She recalled seeing Cole standing at the bow of the Lady Susanah. She strained to see the second freighter, where she was sure she would see Cole standing at the bow. Her stomach churned with anxiety. Soon she would be in his arms again.

The first boat pulled into the harbor. Dominique walked down to meet her traveling companions. Although it had been a week, it seemed like months since she'd last seen them. She was sure their time at the side of the river had not been nearly as exciting as her trek through the wilderness with Cole. Dominique smiled when she noticed that Addie was headed straight for her. They embraced as if they were old friends.

"Ah, civilization," Addie sighed as she looked up toward the ramshackle settlement called Fort Yukon. Her disappointment was clearly written on her weary face.

Dominique could imagine Addie's thoughts. Each passing second made the promise of the Yukon seem less promising. "Are you all right?"

A tired smile creased Addie's face as she nodded. "I'd sure like a bath."

Dominique understood Addie's sentiments. "There's a bath house in the back of the saloon." She rolled her eyes upward, adding, "Well, I don't know if a metal tub with a blanket around it for privacy deserves to be called a bath house."

"It'll do," Addie said. She noticed Dominique was staring toward the second boat that was approaching the dock. Addie knew who she was looking for. She also knew the girl was about to suffer a great disappointment. Anger shot through her, along with a pang of sympathy. Captain Hawkins had seemed like a decent enough man. But Addie had no doubt what had went on between him and Dominique when they were alone in the wilderness, and it sickened her to know that he had deserted her once he'd gotten what he wanted.

"He's not out there," Addie said. Her voice hinted of the anger she felt. Dominique turned toward her, confusion clouding her face.

"Who?" she asked innocently.

Addie stared at her. She realized Dominique never doubted the captain would return. Her fury toward the man abounded. She had not known Dominique long, but at this moment she felt an overpowering protectiveness toward her. "Once you meet your new husband in Dawson City, that worthless captain will be nothing more than a bad memory." Addie noticed a look of understanding start to dawn on Dominique's face.

"Cole's not—I mean—where . . ." her voice faded. Addie's expression told her everything she didn't want to hear. The cold wind seemed to cut clear through to her bones. The clouds grew darker, heavier—or maybe she just imagined that the world had become devoid of light.

"You'd better sit a spell," Addie said in a worried tone. "You don't look too good."

Dominique closed her eyes, trying to fight against the queasiness that claimed her. When she opened her eyes she forced herself to look at Addie. She hated herself for acting so foolish, but she could do nothing to stop the tears that flowed from her eyes. "Where is he?" she asked in a shaky voice.

Addie sighed. She let her arms drop heavily at her sides. "He went back to St. Michael."

"St. Michael?" The seaside port seemed like a million miles away. "Why?" Dominique asked, her voice was desperate. Inwardly, she prayed he had not had a choice, and that he still planned to return to her. But she sensed the reality was that she would never see him again.

Addie considered lying to the girl. She figured if she did, Dominique would spend the rest of her life waiting for the captain to come back to her. The truth would—Addie hoped— set Dominique free to carry on with her life. "He was offered gold by that man over there." Addie motioned toward Captain Lindsey, then added, "To take his riverboat down to St. Michael. Captain Hawkins didn't hesitate to jump at the offer."

"Will he be ba—"

"No," Addie cut in sharply. "He's planning to use the money to purchase a ship so he can

248

return to the Pacific Ocean." She knew this to be true, because she had overheard some of the captain's crew talking about his plans. The effect her words had on Dominique was more devastating than she had feared. The girl went pasty white, and Addie worried that she might pass out. She took Dominique's arm. "Let's find a place to sit," Addie insisted.

Dominique followed her, but she wasn't aware of anything that was going on around her. She felt as if the most vital part of her had just been taken away. Cole's promise to come back to her kept echoing through her mind. The future she had envisioned for them was a blank slate. All she had left was a shattered heart, and memories that would never allow her to love again. In a numb trance, she fell into the chair Addie had found at the front of the saloon.

"I'll go fetch you some water," Addie said. She hurried into the rough log building, uncaring that she was going into a saloon. When she had lived in Texas, she might have hesitated and looked for another establishment that would be more respectable for a woman to enter. In this country, she figured it didn't matter; a woman had to survive any way she could.

The second freighter pulled into the harbor. Dominique stood up, her heart thudding. Addie could have been wrong. Please let her be wrong, Dominique cried silently. She watched as the crew began to unload the few supplies that had been salvaged from the Lady Susanah.

"Drink this," Addie ordered when she returned. She gently pushed Dominique back down to the chair and handed her a glass of water. Intentionally blocking her view so that she could not stare at the steamer that had just pulled in, Addie knelt down and met Dominique's tear-filled eyes. Addie's heart ached for this lovely girl. She recalled when she had lost her husband. He had not left her by choice, though, and she knew he never would have left her if fate had been kinder. Now, Addie could only imagine how great Dominique's pain must be. *Her* man had purposely deserted her.

"Ah, home sweet home," Silver Belle said as she found her way to the front of the saloon. She glanced down at Dominique, then Addie. Her grimy face had a questioning look. "Is she sick?" she asked.

"Heartsick," Addie said. She patted Dominique's shoulder in a reassuring manner. Dominique's tears continued to flow, and she still stared at the river as if she thought her man would miraculously appear.

For a moment, Silver looked confused. She shrugged when she finally figured out what Addie was talking about. "Oh, yeah, the wonderful captain," she said in a deprecating tone. She leaned down close to Dominique, adding, "You're wastin' those tears. There ain't no man worth crying over, and especially one who used you the way he did."

"You leave her be. You've got no right sayin' something like that," Addie retorted. She stood up straight, towering over Silver. This was one woman Addie hadn't liked from the beginning of their journey, and she was in no mood to put up with her insensitivity. Anger flowed through her, but before she had a chance to give Silver a piece of her mind, Dominique interrupted them.

"What do you mean?" she demanded of Silver Belle. Her self-defense overpowered her sorrow for a moment. She rose up from the chair, and stood at Addie's side. "What do you mean—he used me?" she repeated in a stronger tone of voice. Angrily, she wiped at the tears that soaked her cheeks.

Silver was unaffected by the other women's attitudes. She shrugged again. "Well, it sure ain't no secret that the two of you spent all that time alone out there in the wilderness. And there ain't nobody who is gonna believe he took you along just so you'd cook for him."

"Shut up," Addie snapped. She wrapped her arm around Dominique's shoulder in a protective manner. Her gaze drilled into Silver.

"Well," Silver said, sighing, "truth is, the captain got what he wanted, and there ain't no use buyin' the cow when you can get the milk for free." She looked steadily at Dominique as she added, "From now on, you just make sure they always pay for what they get—whether it's with a weddin' ring, a cache of gold, or the same amount of heartache they caused you." Silver shook her forefinger at Dominique, adding, "Next time, you remember that!" She tossed her head back haughtily and stomped through the door of the saloon.

When Addie started after her, Dominique grabbed her arm. "No, let it be. She's right," she said. Her tears were gone now, and her voice was void of emotion. She thought of her mother again—of the legacy her mother had bequeathed her—and of how easy it had been for her to be tempted by the same desires as her mother was. She wondered if it would ever be possible to escape her mother's influence. Maybe it was something in their blood; something that caused them to forget about morality and righteousness whenever they were offered sins of the flesh. Cole certainly did not have to ask her twice, Dominique recalled. The first time he touched her she lay down in the mud for him like a dog in heat. The memory made her feel dirty and ashamed.

"She hasn't got the right to talk about anybody—that hussy!" Addie said, angrily. She glared at the saloon door.

Dominique shrugged. After her liaison with Cole, she knew she was no better. All her dreams: home, family, respectability . . . were they destroyed? She glanced at Addie, desperately needing to talk to someone about her pain. "I really thought Cole loved me," she said in a trembling voice. "He treated me like he loved me," she added in a pleading voice, her teary gaze raised to Addie's face.

Addie fought back her own urge to cry. This girl's pain invaded her. She wished she could tell her the things she wanted to hear—that the captain really did love her, that his leaving must have had something to do with how much he loved her. But, Addie did not lie. She would not start now. "Some men will do and say just about anything to get what they want from a woman," she said quietly.

Dominique thought about Addie's words. Although she was convinced that he did, Cole had never *said* he loved her. Maybe she had just wanted him to love her so badly, she had imagined he felt that way toward her . . . maybe all those loving emotions she had thought she had glimpsed in his gray eyes were nothing more than the guilt he felt for the way he was using her. She took a shuddering breath. "I'll always love him," she whispered.

"I'll always love my husband," Addie answered quietly. "But he's gone, and my life has to go on."

Addie's meaning was clear. Dominique knew she could not spend the rest of her life mourning something she had never really had. Addie's husband was dead, and Cole was dead to her. Her love for him, however, was not dead. Even if it was true that he had only been using her, she was sure she would love him forever. Now, however, she had no choice but to go on with her life. She straightened up and drew in a deep, cleansing breath. When she reached Dawson City, she decided, she would do her best to make up for the mistake she had made. She would marry Jack Scroggins, and be the most devoted and respectable wife possible. She never wanted Jack to find out about her mother, and she would not allow her mother's influence to sneak into her life again. And, she would make sure that her husband never learned about her foolish affair with Cole Hawkins, no matter what she had to do to keep it secret.

Seventeen

With its shores lined with boats, Dawson City was referred to as the 'darling' of the world, or the Paris of the North. But when Dominique stepped off the riverboat, and sank ankle-deep in the muddy street, the name she had for this place was far from endearing. The town, less than two years old, was built on a level section of swampland. Logs and stumps were tossed randomly throughout the black mud to serve as walkways.

The streets were not lined with gold, as the rumor held in other parts of the country. Rather, Dawson City's four-mile long main street was lined with crudely-built warehouses and numerous saloons. Every size tent imaginable dotted the hillside and cabins constructed of rough logs stood beside the tents. On every bare section of ground, construction was going on. The new buildings appeared to be of a sturdier build, and many of them were large structures that would house hotels and other big businesses.

The town boasted of having a population of 30,000 residents, and at times, it seemed like the entire population was crowded along the main street. The residents of the far-north settlement lived by the creed of the Yukon: "Do Unto Others As You Would Be Done By." Unlike most boom towns, Dawson City was not as rowdy and unsavory as its predecessors in California and Colorado. The Mounties kept a tight rein on the people who were allowed into the Yukon Territory. Undesirables and trouble-makers were given a "blue slip," which was the equivalent of a one-way ticket out of town.

"So this is paradise," Silver Belle said sarcastically. She gave a huff as she looked around at her bleak surroundings. "And I suppose those are our knights in shining armor," she added. Disgust was even more evident in her voice.

Dominique turned to where Silver pointed. A group of men were assembled at the side of the street. Their just-scrubbed appearance, and anxious expressions told Dominique they must be the men who had sent for them. It took all her control to keep from giving in to the urge to turn and run back to the steamer. She felt sick to her stomach, dizzy, and light-headed. For a moment, she was sure she would faint. Swallowing hard, then taking a deep breath, she told herself she had no choice but to go forth to meet her soon-to-be husband. Cole Hawkin's image taunted her with each step she took.

"Are you doin' all right?" Addie asked as she fell into step at Dominique's side. She noticed the girl had lost all her color, and she was sure she knew what—or who—she was thinking about again.

Dominique glanced at her. She nodded her head, but made no effort to speak. She was sure she would become ill if she was forced to open her mouth. The men's faces all seemed to become one large blur. Dominique tried not to focus on any one face. She was not ready to stare into another man's eyes; let him touch her, kiss her, or do anything else that Cole had done. Right now, she didn't even think she could make herself talk to another man.

The men moved toward the women in an awkward manner. Some carried gifts of flowers or packages wrapped in tissue. When Dominique was finally able to focus on their faces, she thought it ironic they all seemed to look alike. Nearly every one of them had a thick beard. They were dressed in new clothes, which were all similar since there was very little to choose from in the local stores. Even their wide-eyed expressions all seemed to be the same. To her surprise, though, they almost acted as if they were apprehensive about meeting the women.

As the group of women and men moved toward one another, the tension seemed to expand. Finally, face to face, they were forced to speak. There was a round of simple greetings, then an engulfing silence until one of the men took the initiative. "I'm figurin' one of you ladies is my mail-order bride." His gaze scanned the crowd.

Dominique felt another sickening knot twist in her stomach. She didn't think she could go through with this commitment. If Addie hadn't patted her arm in a reassuring manner at that moment, Dominique was sure she would have turned and run away.

"Mary Richards?" the man called out. His intense stare moved to each one of the women's faces. Another silence followed. The man's expression became a frown.

"She went back to California after we got bogged down in the mud," Silver Belle announced. "Ten of 'em went back, so I reckon there's ten of you who will be spendin' a few more lonely nights." She placed her hands on her ample hips, then tossed her blonde head haughtily. "Now which of you fellas is Maynard Hendricks?" Her eyes narrowed as she strutted forward. She stopped directly in front of the man who had just spoken. He looked down at her, then swallowed hard enough to make his protruding adam's apple quiver. He shook his head and looked back at the other men.

Silver followed his gaze. The men slowly began to separate, leaving a lone man in the center of the group. He gave Silver a weak smile. A dark red flush rose up in his thin face. He took a faltering step forward, and raised his hand in a lame wave. "I-I-I am M-M-Maynard Hendricks," he stammered. He did not move any closer. His gaze seemed glued to her face as if he was afraid to glimpse the voluptuous cleavage that swelled above the neckline of her low-cut dress, and was peeking out from her open raincoat.

Silver was not shy. She stepped up to Maynard and stared him straight in the eye. They were almost equal in height, but Silver appeared to out-weigh the man by several pounds, as he was skinny as a skeleton. She boldly looked him up and down. She took a step backwards, and once again let her gaze travel over all of him. Wire-framed glasses set on the bridge of his nose, and a long, wispy dark blonde beard framed his thin cheeks and chin. Shoulder-length hair in the same blonde shade was combed back from his high forehead.

"So, do you have a b-i-g," she paused. The silence was deafening. Silver smiled seductively before adding, "Gold mine?"

"File thirty-three produced a million-and-a-half so far," Maynard said in a breathy tone. In spite of the cold temperature, beads of sweat broke out on the tip of his nose and above his thin eyebrows.

Silver chuckled. She glanced over her shoulder at the other women and winked. "Well, girls," she said. "I guess I've found my man." She swung around and grabbed Maynard's arm. He gave a startled gasp. Another deep red blush flooded his face. "Show me your gold mine," she commanded.

Maynard stared at her for a moment, his eyes wide with what looked like terror. He glanced at the other men for reassurance. None was offered. Silver tugged on his arm, forcing Maynard to make a decision. His gaze lowered to her bosom, and he swallowed hard. He look up and gazed into her eyes. He swallowed again, then held out the crumpled flowers. Silver took them without hesitation, then allowed him to lead her away without further comment.

For a few minutes no one else moved. They all watched in disbelief and silence as the first mail-order bride was claimed by her unlikely groom. Soon, other men began to call out names. Many turned away—disappointed—because their prospective brides had been among the ones who had returned to California.

Addie squeezed Dominique's arm when a tall stout man with graying hair and a clean-shaved face requested her. Frank Doolin was his name, and Dominique thought he was a perfect match for Addie. It was evident when they first looked at one another that neither of them was disappointed. Dominique hugged Addie before she left with her intended groom.

"I hope you're as lucky as I seem to be," Addie whispered when they pulled apart.

Dominique nodded, then glanced at the dwindling group of men. A sinking feeling washed through her when she saw the men who were left; an assortment of bearded characters, and one other fairly nice looking man with a large mustache. But, she thought with a heavy heart, he was not nearly as handsome as Cole. Sorrow filled her, but anger quickly followed. She had to keep reminding herself that she would never see Cole again. She glanced back at the mustached man. He had just called out the name of his future wife. It was not Dominique.

"Promise you'll come visit?" Addie said. Her face was flushed with excitement as she spoke. A wide smile curved her mouth as she turned away to face Frank again. He handed her the small package he held, then extended his arm. Addie took the gift, and slipped her arm through his. She was gone before Dominique had a chance to promise her anything.

As she took a deep breath, Dominique returned her attention to the last couple of men. She noticed there were two other women besides herself waiting to be claimed by their future husbands. One man, an extremely short man with broad shoulders and a thick brown beard, was eyeing her speculatively. "Jack Scroggins?" she said tentatively. The man shook his head, and shrugged.

"Sarah Jean Walters?" he said in reply. A look of disappointment came to his face when Dominique shook her head. Even when Sarah Jean stepped forward, the man continued to stare at Dominique. Sarah Jean, a former dance hall girl from Seattle, cast her a look that could kill. Dominique looked away quickly.

The last man was not Jack Scroggins either. After he claimed the other woman, Dominique experienced a moment of panic. She was left alone, while everyone else hurried off to start their new lives. She turned around, thinking that surely Jack Scroggins would be close by. The bustling street was filled with men and, although many of them were looking her over, no one approached her and introduced himself as Jack Scroggins. Uninvited, Cole's image taunted her thoughts again. This was somehow his fault, Dominique determined. How could he do this to her? How could he leave her here all alone after he had pretended to love her so passionately?

"Miss?" a man's voice interrupted Dominique's tormented thoughts. She spun around, a mixture of emotions rushing through her. For a fleeting instant, she had prayed she would turn around and see Cole. When she glimpsed the elderly man who was speaking, her hopes were crushed. A part of her was afraid he wasn't her intended husband, another part was afraid he was. He smiled at her, but her conflicting thoughts continued to spin through her head.

"Jack Scroggins?" He shook his head from side to side. Dominique felt an instant of relief, then a moment of despair.

"No, miss," he said apologetically. The man nervously twisted a floppy-brimmed hat in his hands. "But I am a friend of his." He looked down at the ground for a second. When he looked up again, he stared directly into her eyes. "Jack couldn't come to meet you," he said.

Dominique forced a smile, then glanced away from from the man's penetrating stare. "I-Is he b-busy at his mine?" Her voice sounded shaky. Inwardly, she was a quivering mess.

"No, miss." The man leaned down in an attempt to look into her eyes again. Her gaze flitted from the ground to his face, then back to the ground again. "Jack's missin', been missin' for nearly two weeks now."

A startled gasp escaped from Dominique. She looked up at this man. His face was like worn old leather, but his hazel eyes seemed kind and understanding. There was something about him that was comforting. She thought of Cole, briefly, then forced her thoughts back to reality. "Mon Dieu! Jack is missing? What happened?"

The man shrugged, and continued to roll the brim of his hat into a tight wad. "He was workin' on a claim not far from his cabin. My claim is next to his. I seen him in the mornin', but I never saw him again." He shuffled his feet nervously, then added, "We thought maybe claim jumpers got him, but no trace of him has been found yet."

His words hit Dominique like a hammer. Ever since she had first met Cole, she had been dreading meeting Jack Scroggins. A tremendous sense of guilt overcame her, while at the same time, she realized the seriousness of her situation. She was in a strange place— far from anything, or anyone she knew. The money Jack Scroggins had sent to her was gone, and she had nothing of her own. Now, it appeared even Jack Scroggins was gone. She hated herself for not feeling more remorse about the man's fate, but she found it difficult to grieve for someone she had never met.

"He was sure lookin' forward to your comin'. That's all he talked about for weeks," the man said. When Dominique glanced up at him, he quickly added, "Oh, by the way, I'm Henry—Henry Farmer." He bowed his head slightly.

Dominique stared at him, uncertain of how to react. She sensed this man was someone she could trust, but then, she had thought she could trust Cole, too. "Thank you for coming here to meet me today, Monsieur Farmer," she said. She let her arms drop heavily at her sides as she glanced down the muddy street. Despair engulfed her, and wiped all thoughts from her mind.

Henry cast her a sheepish glance. He had come here for his own selfish reasons, and now he felt ashamed of himself. Jack Scroggins had been his friend, as well as his neighbor. Henry had spent days looking for him when he disappeared, and he feared for Jack's fate. But, he had come to meet Jack's mail-order bride with the hope that he could take

Jack's place. One look at Dominique, and Henry knew this was the foolish notion of an old man. This beautiful young woman would never want someone like him. It was even hard for Henry to imagine her with Jack Scroggins. Although Jack was in his mid-thirties, his manners were crude and rough. Henry glanced down at Dominique again. She was like a budding rose among sticker weeds. Henry couldn't help but wonder why she was here in Dawson City. If he didn't do anything else, Henry determined, he would protect this little gal from Dawson City's den of heathens. It was the least he could do for his friend Jack.

"I know Jack would have wanted to see to it that you were taken care of," Henry said. "And since me and Jack were friends, I-I wanted to help out if I could." Fleetingly, Henry was tempted to tell her that he wanted to fulfill Jack's obligations in every way. She looked up at him. He gazed into the bluest eyes he'd ever seen. He cleared his throat, nervously.

Dominique stared at him. She had no choice but to accept his offer. "I really find myself in a terrible mess, Monsieur," she answered honestly. She felt tears well up in her eyes, but she told herself they would not fall. "I don't know what I'll do. I have nothing left," she said in a rush of words. Her tears fell uninvited. She felt Henry's hand on her shoulder. His voice sounded far-away to her ears when he spoke.

"Don't cry, miss. Whatever you need, I'll see to it." He patted her shoulder in a comforting gesture. He thought of putting his arms around her, but he was afraid she'd recoil in disgust. Her hands were covering her face, but after a moment, she slowly put her hands down and gazed up at him. Even with her eyes swollen and red, and her face soaked with tears, he thought she was beautiful. How sad, he thought, that Jack Scroggins could not see what his hard-earned money had bought him.

"I would pay you back," Dominique said in a trembling voice. She glanced down the street again at the assortment of buildings and tents. "I'll get a job—I was a maid in San Francisco." The instant she said the words, she knew how foolish she must sound. There weren't too many homes or establishments in Dawson City that would require the services of a maid.

Henry didn't think anything of her idea. He was just grateful that she was no longer crying, and she was looking at him as though she was grateful to him, too. "Come on, Miss. Let's get you a decent dinner. Then we'll decide what to do next." Henry used his most business-like tone. Inwardly, he was as giddy as a schoolboy at the prospect of being in her company for a while longer.

Dominique didn't argue with him. The thought of a real dinner made her mouth water. She followed him eagerly to a restaurant called the Golden Griddle, oblivious to the curious stares they were getting from the people on the street. Most of the other women had either bought a new dress at the store at Fort Yukon, or else they wore one of the dresses they had managed to salvage from the Lady Susanah. Before they arrived at Dawson City, the women spent a great deal of time preparing themselves for their first meeting with their prospective grooms. Dominique, however, found that she preferred the jeans and flannel shirt she had obtained from the trading post. Although she had never worn pants before, she loved the freedom they gave her. And here in the Yukon, they seemed a sensible choice. She'd noticed men looking at her, but since she assumed they were disapproving of her unfeminine attire, she ignored them. If she knew they were staring because of the enticing way her jeans hugged her curves, she still would have ignored them.

Henry seated them at a table squarely in the center of the room. He glanced around, but was disappointed to see that there were only a few patrons in the restaurant at this mid-afternoon hour. He knew it wouldn't be long before everyone in Dawson noticed this beautiful girl, and when they did, he would be at her side. "Order anything," he said.

Dominique shrugged, and smiled. "You order for me. I'm so hungry I'm afraid I'd order one of everything." A man with a dirty white apron approached the table just as Dominique finished speaking. He glanced at Henry with a slight smirk on his face.

"We'll have one of everything," Henry said with a nod of his head. He smiled when Dominique gasped and began to shake her head from side to side. "Well, how about a great big steak with taters and gravy then?" Henry asked. The dreamy look on Dominique's face told Henry he had just won her approval. He nodded at the waiter, adding, "Make that two orders, and bring us some coffee."

"I'll pay you back, Monsieur," Dominique said again. She wasn't about to turn down a steak dinner, but she didn't want to be indebted to anyone.

Henry shook his graying head. "No, miss. I'm Jack's friend. It's the least I can do." He noticed a strange look flash across her face. He wanted to ask her what she was thinking, but he didn't want to chance offending her. To his relief, she began to speak to him without hesitation.

"I keep thinking about Jack. I mean—I didn't know him. But, I was prepared to marry him." A frown tugged at her lips. She shrugged and looked at Henry. "I don't know how I'm supposed to feel, or what I'm supposed to do now."

Henry's aging face creased with concern for this girl. He understood her anxieties, and he also knew she was in a desperate situation. Women in Dawson had few options. Those who were not married were forced to fend for themselves. With the exception of a few waitress jobs, the rest of the unattached women had no choice but to seek employment in the dancehalls and saloons. Paradise Alley—Dawson's red-light district—was a seedy area behind the saloons and dancehalls. The prostitutes who lived in the cribs of Paradise Alley conducted a thriving business. The thought of Dominique being forced to resort to any of these unsavory and degrading positions sickened Henry.

"As Jack's intended bride, I think you're entitled to everything that belonged to him. The Mounties have been keepin' the claim-jumpers off Jack's land for the past couple of weeks. 'Course they can't do it forever. If Jack don't show up, his claim will become public property." Henry rubbed at his chin in a thoughtful manner, then added, "Now, I don't see why you can't put claim to that land." His heartbeat raced at the idea of having her as a neighbor, and at his mercy for all her needs.

Dominique began thinking at a breakneck speed. She knew nothing about mining, but she could learn. Taking possession of Jack's mine would mean that she wouldn't have to go back to California. If it was a gold-producing mine, it might also mean that she would become rich and independent. She could go anywhere she wanted, then . . . she could even go in search of Cole Hawkins.

Eighteen

"I'm real sorry about Jack Scroggins," Addie said as she waited for Dominique to put the finishing stitches in her wedding gown. The dress, nothing fancy—a yellow silk with ruffles at the hem—was purchased at Dawson's one dress shop. The unexpected presence of a dress shop was a surprise to all the women who arrived in Dawson. The stores were still out-numbered by the saloons, but with all the new buildings going up it would not be long before there were more respectable establishments than pleasure palaces and cantinas.

"It was a shock," Dominique mumbled. She debated over whether or not to tell Addie about her decision to take possession of Jack's gold mine. A part of her felt guilty and selfish at the idea of taking advantage of his disappearance. At the same time, she was determined to find a way to get out of the Yukon. The money Jack's mine might produce could be the means she needed.

"Have you thought about what you'll do?" A frown tugged at Addie's lips when she looked in the mirror. She knew she wasn't a beautiful woman. At five-foot-eight, Addie was taller than most men. Her build was large, though not fat, and she had ordinary features. Addie felt her one good asset was that she was a hard-worker. Back in Texas, she had worked every bit as hard as her husband, and they had built a good life for themselves. Next to losing her husband of fourteen years, Addie's greatest sorrow was that they never had any children. When her husband had suffered a heart attack, she felt she could not stay in Texas and face an empty life without him. After selling the ranch, she went to California. While she was there, she had read about the request for mail-order brides in the Yukon.

Addie turned around slowly as she studied her dress in the mirror. She had no doubts she had made the right decision in coming here. Although she had known Frank Doolin for only a few days, she knew he was a good man, and a hard worker. Alone, he toiled in his mine on Rabbit Creek without complaint. Even now, on the morning of his wedding, he was working at his mine. He told Addie there was no use wasting the entire morning since they wouldn't be getting married until the afternoon.

Glancing at Dominique, Addie repeated her question. "What are your plans now?" She noticed a red blush color Dominique's cheeks.

Addie was answered by a nonchalant shrug of Dominique's shoulders, but she would not look at Addie. "Frank and I discussed this last night," Addie said in a firm voice.

"You discussed me?" Dominique asked. She glanced up, met Addie's gaze, then quickly looked away.

"Frank has two cabins on his place. One is real small, but it would be big enough for you." Addie stared directly at Dominique. She had come to know this girl well enough to sense there was something she wanted to tell her. "You've already made a decision, haven't you?"

Dominique nodded her head. Addie had become a good friend, and she hoped she would not lose her friendship when she told her what she was going to do. "I have decided to work Jack Scroggins' mine." She heard Addie's surprised gasp. The look on Addie's face was more than a little skeptical.

"How are you gonna work a gold mine?" Addie shook her head in disbelief. She'd gone out to Frank's mine yesterday and watched him work his claim. Frank had spent the day knee deep—and elbow deep—in mud and water. He had built what were called sluice boxes, long narrow troughs. One end of each sluice box was narrower than the other end so the boxes could be strung together. When Frank ran water through the boxes he created something similar to a running stream. He then shoveled dirt and rock into the sluices.

272

The water washed the rock and dirt away. The heavier metals, like gold, sank to the bottom, where riffles were built into the sluices to trap the gold. It was hard, dirty work; Frank had barely been able to keep up by himself. Addie could not even begin to imagine Dominique doing this sort of work.

Dominique put the last stitch in the hem of Addie's dress, then stood up. She glanced at the other woman. "I have to do it," she said in a quiet but determined voice. Fleetingly, she thought about the slums she had seen on the back street here in Dawson. The cribs—and the women she'd seen—were worse than any brothels or prostitutes she had ever known.

"No, you could come and stay with us," Addie insisted.

Dominique shook her head vigorously. "I can't take advantage of your kindness, and I have to make a living."

Addie sighed heavily. "It's money, isn't it? But Frank and I don't want you to pay us for staying at the cabin."

A poignant smile rested on Dominique's lips. She was growing more fond of Addie daily. "I have to support myself," she said. She reached out and took Addie's hand, adding, "I don't want to stay in Dawson City forever."

"Well," Addie's brows drew into a thoughtful line. "Maybe you could do chores for me and Frank. We could pay—"

"No," Dominique interrupted. She knew

Addie was serious with her offer, but she also knew Addie and Frank did not need to hire her to help out at their place. They certainly did not need a third person hanging around when they were honeymooners, either. She could see the worried—and hurt—expression on Addie's face, and she knew she had to try to explain. "I know you're trying to help, and I really do appreciate what you're doing," she said in an emotional voice. She noticed a look of relief filter into Addie's expression. "But I've always taken care of myself." She glanced at the floor, adding, "When I decided to come here, I thought maybe Jack Scroggins would take care of me. And then, I was foolish enough to think Cole—" Her words halted abruptly. She didn't want to admit how foolish she had been where Cole was concerned.

"There's nothing wrong with wantin' someone else to take care of you sometimes." Addie avoided talking about Cole Hawkins. It seemed to her that Dominique's grief over him was getting worse every day. If only Jack Scroggins had been here, then maybe she would be better able to cope with the pain of losing the captain. "So, why don't you come and stay with me and Frank—at least for a while?"

Dominique gave Addie a grateful smile. She gave her head a negative nod. "I want to make enough money so that I can leave here—before winter sets in."

"Frank and I can—"

"No, Addie," she cut in.

"Well, maybe you could get a job here in Dawson?"

Dominique chuckled, then said sarcastically, "Have you noticed how many options unmarried women have around here?" She met Addie's eyes. She knew they were both thinking along the same lines.

Addie huffed haughtily. "Women like us never have to consider doing anything that's not respectable. There's always other ways." Addie noticed Dominique's cheeks flame red again. Dominique turned away quickly and pretended to busy herself by putting away the sewing supplies.

"What me and Frank is offering is not charity, and it makes more sense than you thinkin' you're gonna work Jack's mine," Addie said. She saw Dominique's shoulders slump as if in defeat. When she finally turned around to face Addie, the look of sorrow in Dominique's blue eyes broke Addie's heart.

Dominique was thinking again about her mother, and about the rundown cribs in Paradise Alley. And she was thinking about Cole, and respectability. Fear ran rampant in her. Cole had taught her that she was capable of falling prey to her own desires, and she was terrified she would follow in her mother's footsteps. "I have to do this," she said. Her determination was apparent in her eyes, and on her face.

A defeated sigh escaped from Addie. She

knew when she was beaten, but what she didn't know was why this young woman was so afraid of accepting help. "Will Henry be there with you?" she asked in a resigned voice.

"He'll take me up there, and help me get settled." Dominique hoped her face didn't reflect her uncertainties. "But he has his own claim to work."

Addie gasped. "What about claim jumpers?" Her fears for Dominique showed clearly in her eyes. "When word gets around that there's a woman up there all alone, you're going to be in great danger."

"I'm not going to spread the word," Dominique answered defensively. "Henry informed the authorities that I would be taking possession of my fiance's mine. He asked the Mounties to check in on me when they're in the area. And Henry will come as often as possible." She could still see the skeptical look on Addie's face. Inwardly, she had plenty of her own doubts, but she would never admit them out loud.

"But how will you do it? Gold mining is hard work, Dominique. Will it be worth it?" Fleetingly, she recalled how she had helped her husband on their spread year after year. Under the burning Texas sun the hard ground had been as unyielding as iron, but she had worked in the fields until she was ready to drop. And she'd planted crops, fed cattle, delivered calves, and everything else she needed to do to make her life fruitful and worthwhile. Addie looked at Dominique. In her young face she could see the same fierce determination she had felt in Texas. She sensed no matter how hard it would be, Dominique would feel it was worth the cost.

Addie smiled. She held her hand out to Dominique. "Will you take time off from your gold mine once a week to come to Sunday dinner?"

Dominique clasped her hand around Addie's. "I'm going to be looking forward to Sundays." A strange sensation gripped her. She had thought she would be having Sunday dinners in her own home once she reached Dawson. She hoped she wasn't destined to spend the rest of her life chasing this elusive dream.

Addie glanced at the clock that sat on the bureau. For the past few days she had shared a room with Dominique at the Fairview Hotel, the newest and finest hotel in Dawson City. All of the mail-order brides had been put up at the hotel, courtesy of the town. The women's ordeal on the Yukon River was written up in all five of Dawson's newspapers. They were hailed as heroines for surviving, and even more so, for having the gumption to finish out the rest of the journey when they could have headed back to California with the others. "Look at the time?" Addie gasped. "I'm gonna be late for my own wedding!"

Dominique looked quickly in the mirror to check her own appearance. Frank Doolin had purchased both of the dresses the women wore today. Dominique's was a vibrant shade of blue silk, almost the exact shade of her eyes. It was a simple design, similar to Addie's, with a row of ruffles around the neckline, and several small rows of ruffles at the hem and around the short puffy sleeves. In her ebony hair, today worn in a ponytail, Dominique wore a long silk ribbon of the same blue shade. She eyed herself for a second longer. Her skin had finally healed from the wind and rain she had endured in the wilderness, and the painful mosquito bites had faded. Although she was not vain, Dominique knew her looks could be a great asset. Instead, they were a curse. She knew it was only her beauty that had attracted Cole, and look where it had gotten her.

"Let's go get you married," Dominique said in a tone that sounded almost too cheerful to her own ears. She hoped Addie wouldn't notice that she was forcing herself to act happy. The past few days had been more difficult than Dominique had imagined. One by one she had attended the weddings of her traveling companions. Even Silver's wedding had been a joyous event. Maynard Hendricks had spared no expense for his new bride. There had been scrumptious food, flowers, champagne, and music. Silver was radiant in a white brocaded gown that Maynard had arranged to be made for her before she had even arrived. Dominique sat, teary-eyed, watching Silver become the wife of one of the richest men in the Yukon. She tried not to feel jealous, but she couldn't help herself. It seemed unfair, especially knowing how Silver had lived before she came to Dawson. Dominique wondered if she was being punished for the way she had acted with Cole.

Dominique followed Addie down to the large meeting room in the Fairview Hotel. This had been the location for all the weddings so far. After Addie and Frank's wedding, only two more couples remained to be united in marriage. Both weddings were planned for the next day. Tomorrow, Dominique planned to go to Jack's mine.

"Well, I guess this is it," Addie said when they reached the meeting room. She smoothed down the gathers at the top of her skirt, then grabbed Dominique's hand and squeezed it tightly.

Dominique returned Addie's affectionate gesture. She glanced at Addie, noticing the blush on her face and the excited glint in her eyes. Dominique decided there must be some magic spell that was cast over all brides to make them appear more beautiful than they had ever looked. Addie was under that spell today.

Frank and the minister stood at the far end of the room. A large vase with bouquets of wild flowers stood on each side of the men. Frank wore a dark brown suit, which did not fit his large frame properly. He looked uncomfortable and anxious. But as soon as he glimpsed Addie standing in the doorway, his eyes lit up with a luminous twinkle. He held his hand out toward her. Without hesitation, she walked to him.

As she followed Addie, Dominique allowed herself a moment of fantasy. She imagined that she was walking up the aisle to meet her own groom. She envisioned herself in a setting far different from this room in the hotel. Her musing took her to a place where the sun shone brightly. Where she was didn't matter as long as it was not anyplace in the Yukon Territory. But whom she was walking toward was the most important thing of all. The end of the aisle became the foredeck of a ship. And in her dreams, the man who waited to claim her for all eternity was Cole Hawkins.

Nineteen

"I know this was my idea, but I don't feel right 'bout this, Missy."

Dominique rolled her eyes in an exasperated gesture. "I'll be fine, Henry," she said before a grin claimed her mouth. They had been in one another's company for over two weeks now. Dominique had become comfortable in his presence, and she already thought of him as a good friend. Lately, he had taken to calling her Missy, so Dominique knew he felt close to her, too. "Besides," she added, "you're only a short distance away if I need anything."

"A couple miles out here in the Yukon is a long way, Missy." Henry glanced around the cabin again. Since he had brought her up here, she'd worked harder than he had ever seen a woman work. Henry didn't recognize old Jack's cabin. The odor of the place was the most noticeable improvement. Down by the creek, Henry had started a bonfire, to which Dominique added an assortment of trash, spoiled food, and even bedding and clothes that were soiled beyond salvation.

Before they left Dawson, Henry had seen to it that she had almost everything she would need—except a man to protect her. She had firewood, food, and a rifle. Henry had bought her new linens, dishes and even a few frivolous things like a tablecloth and material for curtains. Henry figured Jack would be shocked if he could see the place. Dominique had argued with him about money at first, but he had convinced her that he was using gold he had helped Jack dig out of his mine, so now it was her money anyway. In the short time since he had met her, Henry had come to understand that she was proud and independent. He knew if he told her he had used his own money she never would have accepted his help.

Because of her determination to make her own way, Henry had finally given in to her insistence about working Jack's mine while he was at his own mine. For the past week he had been teaching her the basics of gold mining. After a few days at the creek, Henry thought for sure she would admit defeat, and be ready to head back into Dawson. Instead, he had discovered that hard work didn't offend her, and she didn't mind sloshing around in the mud. As much as he hated to admit it, Dominique was one woman who was capable of being a gold miner. Still, it just didn't seem right to leave a little gal like her out here on her own. "I think we should reconsider this," he said in a final plea.

"I'm not going back to town, Henry!" Her determination was apparent. She glanced around the one room cabin that was her home now. Since they had arrived here, she had scrubbed and cleaned until she thought her fingers would fall off. Jack Scroggins had not been a man who appreciated cleanliness. The rotten smell in the cabin was so strong Dominique thought she would gag before she was able to clean through all the filth. Even now, after all her effort, there was still a sour odor clinging to the wood surfaces of the furniture and rough log walls. She hoped after she'd given everything another thorough cleaning the smell would finally fade completely. A recurring sense of relief washed over her while she had been cleaning Jack Scroggins' cabin. She had discovered enough about the man to know she never would have been happy married to the likes of him. Of course, thanks to Cole Hawkins, she would never be happy with any other man anyway!

Henry dropped his arms at his sides in a defeated gesture. She was as hard-headed as she was pretty. Something told him he could talk until he was hoarse, and it wouldn't do him a bit of good. "Well," he sighed, "do you remember how to use the rifle?" She nodded her dark head vigorously. "Be careful with those sluice boxes. And you know not to leave the cabin after dark?" He noticed a patronizing expression flash across her face. Still, he couldn't resist adding, "And if any strangers should happen along—"

"I won't let them know I'm here alone," she said in an exasperated tone. She stepped forward and playfully pushed Henry toward the front door. "I'll be fine, Henry." He continued to shake his head, even as she shoved him out the door.

"What with wild animals, claim jumpers and all, it just don't seem right."

"The Mounties patrol this area on a regular basis," she reminded him.

"Still, if somethin' happened to you while I'm gone, I'd never forgive myself for suggestin' this."

Dominique looked up and met his worried gaze. Henry, she realized, was a very special man; he was sincere and caring. Unlike Cole Hawkins, a man like Henry wouldn't lie to a woman, or use her for his own selfish pleasures, then leave her without a second thought. Her aggravation with Henry fled. A soft smile curved her lips as she looked up at his weathered face. "I'll be fine, and—thanks, Henry. For everything."

Henry stared at her for a moment. The tone of her voice, and the tender expression on her face, made his heart pound like thunder. He had the strongest urge to kiss her. But he knew she would recoil in disgust if he tried something so foolish. Instead, he turned away from her, cleared his throat, then forced his mind to forget the nonsense he had just envisioned.

"I'll be headin' out then," he said in a resigned tone. He glanced up at the sky. It would be dark by the time he reached his own cabin. He looked back at Dominique. She, too, was gazing up at the clear blue sky. There was a faraway expression on her face, and a sadness in her eyes. He wondered if she was already feeling lonely and afraid. "Are you sure about this—" he began.

"Mon Dieu!" she retorted. "Yes, I am sure. And, you'd best get on the road. It's time you tended to your own work." Although she was looking at Henry, Cole's teasing smile flashed before her eyes. A second ago, she had been thinking about him again, and just now, she had used the same wording he always used. Would his memory ever go away? she wondered. Was he somewhere out on the ocean, looking up at this same sky, and thinking about her?

Henry noticed the strange expression filter across her face again. He longed to ask her what she was thinking about when her blue eyes took on such a melancholy look, and when her lower lip trembled slightly as if she was remembering a kiss from some long-lost lover. Whatever it was that claimed her thoughts, it was something very sad, and something that came to her mind frequently. Someday, Henry told himself, he would ask her about her past. Now, though, he knew he had to go.

Dominique followed Henry to his horse. She would never admit it to Henry, but she did have mixed emotions about being on her own here. She would be alone for the first time in her life—really alone—and completely dependent on her own resources. But she wanted, and needed, time to sort through her feelings about the way her life was turning out. There were many decisions for her to make, and out here there was no one to influence her—or tempt her. Paradise Alley passed through her mind. She grew cold in spite of the mild temperature of the July evening. Never would she be desperate enough to consider that horrible place as her only other choice . . . Never!

As she watched Henry climb up on his horse warmth replaced the chill that had just overtaken her. She had a feeling Henry had bought all her supplies with his own money—not money from Jack's mine as he had tried to tell her. Since she knew she needed all the things he had bought, she had finally given up arguing with him. But as soon as Jack's mine yielded enough gold, she planned to repay Henry for everything.

At his horse's side, Dominique tilted her head back to look up at Henry. His eyes, filled with kindness, gazed down at her. "Adieu, Monsieur Henry," she said, smiling. He nodded, remained unmoving for a moment, then turned his horse toward the narrow road.

Dominique did not wait for him to ride out of sight. She turned back to the cabin, and drew in a deep breath. From this angle the cabin appeared to be several inches shorter on one side. The roof was lopsided, and even the one window was built at a sloping angle. A flimsy-looking porch stood in front of the cabin, but like the rest of the structure, it was leaning to one side. The one favorable thing about the cabin was its location. Many of the other cabins Dominique had seen on the way up here were surrounded by nothing more than bench mines and mud. Jack's cabin was built in a small grove of spruce trees. Eldorado Creek ran nearby, and even the holes where Jack had dug in the hillside for gold did not destroy the beauty of the area.

Her delusion that all miners in the Klondike were millionaires was quickly shattered when she reached this mine Jack Scroggins had named No. 12 Eldorado. In the year since he had been working this claim, Henry told her, Jack had barely discovered enough gold to pay for his own living expenses, and her passage from San Francisco. Dominique did not let this disappointing news deter her from her plan to unearth enough gold from Jack's mine to repay Henry, and get herself out of the Yukon by winter.

Before she headed back to the cabin, Dominique glanced up toward the tree-covered slopes. Henry had told her it was believed that Jack had disappeared somewhere up in those hills. The thought sent a cold chill through her as she wondered once again what could have happened to him. Thinking about him made her feel strange. Although Jack had planned to bring her to this cabin when they were married, it seemed rather eerie to be here now. With the sun beginning to slip behind the distant mountaintops. Dominique felt even more uneasy being alone out in the open. Although she feared many things, her greatest worry was encountering another bear like the one she and Cole had tangled with.

With this thought, she started back up the small incline that led to the cabin. A noise nearby caused her heart to skip several beats. She turned toward the source of the noise, half expecting to see a monstrous grizzly with huge yellow teeth charging up from the creek. Instead, she glimpsed a large moose lumbering out of the willows down by the creek. She smiled and turned away. A lone wolf sang out mournfully. A cold chill traipsed down Dominique's spine. She hurried into the cabin, and bolted the door as soon as she was inside. Once she had lit the small kerosene lantern, she closed the hatch down over the window. A rope nailed to the bottom of the hatch, and another nail in the window frame, served as the lock when the rope was wound around the nail in the frame. This make-shift latch did little to make Dominique feel safe. A grizzly could rip the window—or even the door—apart with one swipe of its massive paws.

She grabbed the rifle Henry had given to her. For the past week they had gone down by the creek daily so that he could teach her how to shoot. Once, she had even hit an empty bottle he placed on a rock when she was target practicing. Henry told her not to hesitate to use the gun if she felt threatened by anybody or anything. The thought of aiming the gun at another human made Dominique nervous. But every time she recalled the fight she and Cole had had with the grizzly, she knew without a doubt that she could use the gun if someone she loved was threatened. Loved . . . yes, she still loved Cole . . . maybe even more now. And sometimes, she hated him equally as much for deserting her.

The weddings of her traveling companions had only intensified her feelings. She knew she was destined to see Cole again, if for nothing else but to tell him what a low-down snake he was for leading her to believe that he was coming back to her at Fort Yukon. The agony of never knowing why he had lied about returning to her—and worse, why he had made this decision, was slowly driving her insane. Someday, somewhere, she knew she would meet up with Cole Hawkins. She only wished Cole realized this, too.

She glanced around the cabin at the deepening shadows. For now, this was her home, but all of Jack's belongings still filled the cabin, and made her feel uncomfortable. Hanging on a wall by the stove was a small knife sheath. She thought of the larger one Cole wore at his hip, then she thought of the scar on the side of his face. He had said he'd tell her someday how he had gotten the wound. She thought of the new scar he would undoubtedly have on his hand. Cole, it seemed, now had another story to tell . . . one with another sad ending.

It didn't seem right to be here in Jack's cabin, and constantly be thinking about Cole. She felt even worse because she couldn't help but be grateful Jack wasn't there. The eerie feeling invaded her again. She forced her mind to clear these awful thoughts before she became so guilt-ridden she couldn't stay here without driving herself insane.

Outside the cabin a coyote yelped, joined seconds later by a whole chorus. Their high-pitched cries were different from the mournful howls of the wolf. Dominique clutched the gun tighter. She crossed the room, climbed onto the bed, and burrowed under the covers without bothering to undress; even her boots stayed on her feet tonight.

A long, sleepless night followed. She heard, or imagined she heard, hundreds of noises outside the cabin walls. By morning, she was a nervous wreck, seriously reconsidering her decision to stay out here alone. She told herself that in time she would not be so jumpy. After she had spent her first day wet and muddy from crawling around in the creek, she was even more disillusioned. Thoroughly exhausted, she slept without hearing a sound. The next day, she was so stiff and sore she could barely climb out of bed. Once she had forced herself to get out of bed, however, she discovered her first gold nugget in the bottom of the murky sluice box.

The nugget, only about a quarter of an inch in diameter, almost escaped her weary gaze. Covered in mud, the gold piece looked like any other rock. But as Dominique had started to rinse out the sluice box, she had seen a flash of yellow. A tremor of excitement shot through her as she reached her sore, reddened hand into the rocks and mud. Her hands shook when she lifted the nugget to examine it. An overpowering hope soared through her . . . she knew now that she would fulfill her goal to leave the Yukon—and see Cole Hawkins again!

Twenty

"She's a beauty," Luther said after giving a low whistle. A satisfied smile curved his lips as he ran his hand down the front of his new shirt. He felt good, and he figured he looked good too. For over two weeks now, he and Cole had been living like kings. Of course, after being in the Yukon for the past couple of years, San Francisco was like utopia.

"And she's all ours," Cole added, proudly. Like Luther, all of Cole's clothes were new and expensive, right down to his shiny boots. He even sported a new captain's hat, one that had a small brim and an anchor logo on the front. The black hat matched his new thigh-length jacket. Cole felt like a new man through and through. This morning at the hotel where they had been staying, he had soaked in a porcelain tub for an hour or longer. Luther had teased him about being as vain as a woman, but Cole ignored him and stayed in the tub. He felt as if he had finally cleansed himself of the past, and he felt ready to take on the future.

The gnawing guilt and lingering pain Dominique's memory always evoked still plagued him. Cole knew from experience these feelings would dim eventually. He consoled himself with his belief that she was better off without him, and he would not allow himself to think about anything else. But yesterday, in the hotel lobby, Cole had seen a young woman heavy with child, and the sight sent him into a frenzy. His legs had gone weak and rubbery, and his vision had clouded for a second. He told himself he was having a reaction from all the whiskey he had consumed the night before. Today, the woman's image still taunted him every so often. Uninvited, she passed through his mind again. But now, it was Dominique's face he imagined on the woman's body. He shook his head, and wiped away the beads of sweat from his brow.

Luther noticed Cole's flushed face. He was sure Cole's appearance was due to excitement about their new purchase. He held up a bottle of champagne. "Well, let's waste this bottle of sweet nectar and give this lady a name," he said, motioning toward the bow of the large ship. He had suggested several names to Cole, but they had not able to agree on one before the christening. Cole insisted that he had picked a perfect name out for their new ship, but refused to reveal it until they were ready to christen her.

With a deep sigh, Cole nodded in agreement. This freighter was by far the largest ship he had ever dreamt of owning. The gold nuggets Captain Lindsey had paid him for the trade in the Yukon had been worth much more than he had hoped. Providing that no unforeseen disasters claimed this vessel, Cole knew that he and Luther would make a generous living hauling merchandise along the Pacific coastlines. This merchant ship was equipped with the most modern conveniences, and a streamlined engine that would cut a fast course to the sunny beaches he missed so much.

"You do the honors," Luther said. Although Cole had made him an equal partner in this venture, Luther insisted that Cole retain his position as captain of the ship. With respect, Luther motioned towards the expensive bottle of champagne, then to the bow of the ship. Cole didn't hesitate to take the bottle. He strutted to the edge of the dock, with Luther close at his heels.

Under the towering arch of the ship's bow, Cole stopped. He tipped his head back and stared up at the wood timbers, which had just received a fresh coat of white paint. At the top of the bow, a beautifully carved mermaid adorned the front. Her long flowing hair cascaded down over her bare breasts, and her fish-like torso and tail curved down along the sharp edge of the bow. Her face was angelic yet, like the fabled mermaids who supposedly lured sailors to their deaths, she also had a sensuous quality carved into her intricate features. Although Cole wasn't sure why, he was reminded of Dominique every time he looked at this figurehead. Everything, it seemed, reminded him of her. He felt a feverish sweat break out on his face again.

Luther held his breath while he waited for Cole to swing the bottle against the bow. This was an important day for both of them, and he hoped no old ghosts would intrude on their celebration. He knew if Cole christened this ship the Lady Susanah, they would be doomed before they had a chance to get out of the harbor. He half-expected Cole to name this ship after Dominique, and he figured that name would be just as unlucky. He was unprepared for Cole's announcement.

Bringing the bottle down against the bow of the ship, Cole was sprayed with champagne and chips of broken glass. His laughter joined Luther's cheers. "I christen ye The Freedom Ship."

"The what?" Luther asked as he turned toward Cole. Between his neatly trimmed beard and mustache, his lips puckered with puzzlement. "Sounds like one of them slave ships or somethin'."

"Just the opposite, my friend. It means that this ship is our ticket to freedom—freedom from the past—forever!"

Luther stared at Cole. He could tell that Cole was determined to sound sincere—too determined. But the look in his eyes did not match his tone of voice. Luther sensed Cole was trying to run away from his true feelings, and he wondered how long he was planning to run before he was forced to face them again. "Are you sure about that, Cole?"

Cole's eyes narrowed, his chin squared. Out of habit, he rubbed absently at the scar on his face. He looked toward the ship without meeting Luther's eyes. "I've never been more sure about anything. Today is a new beginning—and once we set sail there will be no turning back."

Before Luther had a chance to reply, there was a commotion up on the wharf. He noticed a woman—obviously a harlot—yelling something about her luggage being stolen. Her screams had already drawn a small crowd. The woman shouted in English and then in French. Luther returned his attention to Cole, but Cole appeared to be concentrating solely on the woman. "There's plenty of people up there to help her," Luther said, impatiently. "Now about the name of this ship—"

Ignoring Luther's remark, Cole began to walk slowly up the long dock. His eyes never wavered from the woman. He continued to move toward her, although every instinct told him he should jump on board his ship and high-tail it out of here as fast as possible. As he grew closer to the woman, he had no doubt about her identity. Her eyes were a paler blue, her black hair graying, and even with all the garish make up, she still possessed the beauty that she had passed on to her daughter. Cole stopped when he was standing at the edge of the crowd, and stared at her. She was only about two yards away from him. She was still rambling on in French and English about her luggage. As he watched her animated description of the man who had stolen her bags, Cole began to feel a nagging sense of foreboding.

"Excuse me, Madame," he said, pushing his way to the front of the small crowd. She looked up at him, immediately falling silent. A coy smile curved her red lips, and her lashes batted flirtatiously over her eyes. "I-I couldn't help overhearing. Is there anything I can do?"

Brigitte let her gaze wander slowly up and down the handsome man who stood before her. "You could do plenty, Monsieur," she said, her voice dripping with innuendo. The reddened blush that colored his cheeks shocked her. He hardly seemed like the type of man who embarrassed easily.

"With y-your luggage—I m-mean," Cole stammered. Knowing that she must be Dominique's mother made her insinuation seem vulgar. He began to mentally compare the two women. Their physical resemblance to one another was their only similarity.

"The authorities have been called, Monsieur, but I could use a strong man to keep me company until my ship departs in an hour." She stepped closer to him, inhaling his fresh manly scent. "Are you the captain of the Excelsior?" she asked hopefully.

Her words hit Cole like a blast of cold wind. "Are-are you boarding the Excelsior?" he asked. Inwardly, he knew the answer, even before she nodded her dark head. "It's going to the Yukon," he said in a raspy voice.

She giggled. "I know. Can you believe it? Just a few weeks ago, I was telling my daughter how crazy she was to go up there. But now . . ." she gave him a seductive smile, then added, "I realize she had the right idea." She stepped closer, until their bodies were pressing against one another. Her gaze rose up to his scar, briefly, then she stared him straight in the eye.

Cole's eyes locked with hers for a fleeting second. He stepped back, almost stumbling, cleared his throat, and felt a hot blush soar through his face. A dozen thoughts were racing through his mind. He kept remembering when Dominique had told him about her reason for going to Dawson City—to escape from her mother's wide-spread reputation. "You can't—I mean—why would you want to go the that God-forsaken place?"

Brigitte shrugged, then grinned. "Rumor has it there's lots of money to be made there by a resourceful woman like myself. There's over a thousand men for every woman! And besides," she took a deep breath, which caused her voluptuous breasts to nearly explode over the top of her low-cut red dress.

Her smile widened when she noticed where Cole's attention had fallen. She straightened, so that her breasts were shoved out even further. Then she added, "My little girl has snagged herself a millionaire, but she needs her maman around too."

Her words made Cole's head pound. He wanted to shout that the last thing Dominique needed was to have her around. And the last thing he needed was to be reminded of Dominique and her new husband. His heart ached, the erratic heartbeat seemed to intensify the pain.

Brigitte stepped forward, and leaned into him again. "I'm Brigitte Laval. But Monsieur, you never did answer my question. Are you my captain?"

Cole forced Dominique's sweet image to the back of his mind. He stared down at this woman. He realized now—at close observation—that even under the makeup, she could not hold a candle to Dominique's natural beauty. He backed away again. Confusion filled him. He opened his mouth, prepared to tell this woman that she couldn't go to the Yukon—he wouldn't allow her to go. He clamped his mouth shut. Why should he interfere? Maybe by now, Dominique did need her mother. Who was he to say?

"No, Madame, I'm not the captain of the Excelsior. But I did just come from the Yukon. It ain't no place for a l-lady . . ." his words faded when he saw her surprised expression. He figured it had been a while since anybody had called her a lady. "You'd best forget about goin' up to Dawson—"

"How did you know that I was headed to Dawson City?" she interrupted. She stepped up to him again. He took several steps back.

"W-Well, I-I figured that was where you were goin'," he said quickly. He wondered if the heat in his face was making him blush red. "But, if that is where you're goin', then you should change your plans. Dawson is a real hell-hole."

"Mon Dieu!" Brigitte's hand rose to the side of her face. "Ma pauvre petite!" She looked up at the tall man, adding, "She really does need me then. Thank you for telling me this, Monsieur!"

Cole moaned inwardly. "No, you don't understand—" His words were drowned out by the hooting of a ship's horn.

"I must go, Monsieur," Brigitte shouted, "My ship is preparing to leave." She twirled around, then as she started to run down the dock, she called out over her shoulder, "Too bad you're not the captain of my ship, Monsieur. I think we could have made a few waves of our own!"

"What about your luggage?" he shouted in an attempt to detain her.

She halted, and turned back to him. Giggling, she shrugged, and said, "Luggage is like men, Monsieur . . . easily replaced." She giggled again, twirled on her heels, and rushed toward her ship without looking back again.

Cole started out after her, but after several long strides, he stopped himself. Instinctively, he turned around to where Luther stood. As they had many times through the years, their eyes met. But unlike times in the past, Cole could not decipher the strange look in Luther's eyes.

"You never change," Luther spat in a disgusted tone. He had not gotten a good look at the woman, or heard the exchange of words between her and Cole. But he figured he had seen enough to know what was going on.

Cole shook his head from side to side. "It's not what you think—"

"I ain't blind, Cole. That woman was a whore if I ever saw one." Luther didn't give Cole a chance to reply as he continued. "And she was French—dammit! How the hell do you expect to leave the past behind when you continue to chase after every French whore—"

"Dominique is not a whore," Cole spat through gritted teeth.

"Well, you treated her like one," Luther retorted. He glanced toward the Excelsior just as Brigitte boarded the ocean liner. It sickened him to think that Cole had gotten so desperate that he was now resorting to chasing down harlots in broad daylight.

Fury flooded through Cole, making him angrier at Luther than he had ever thought possible. He clenched his fists at his side, fighting the urge to punch his friend in the mouth. He didn't need anybody telling him how he'd treated Dominique. He condemned himself daily. Cole stared at Luther for a second longer, not trusting himself to speak.

Luther returned Cole's blatant stare. He could see the bolts of silver flashing through Cole's eyes and knew he had touched on a sore subject. He had no regrets about what he said, though, and he hoped it would spur Cole into facing up to his true feelings. Until then, Luther knew there would be no freedom on The Freedom Ship.

The Excelsior tooted its horn again. Cole was overcome by the urge to run its plank and drag Dominique's mother off the ship. Instead, he turned away and stalked back to his own ship. He knew Luther was following him, but he was keeping his distance. Cole took longer strides. He didn't want to argue with Luther, and in the mood he was in now, Cole knew that it would not take much to set him off again. He stomped up the long plank that led to The Freedom Ship. She had previously carried the name, The Maryland, because her former owner had hailed from that state. Cole's offer to to purchase the ship from the man had come at an opportune time; he had recently learned he was dying from tuberculosis. He wanted to spend his final days with a woman he had met here in San Francisco.

Cole stopped when he reached the foredeck of the large cargo ship. It was large enough to be converted into a luxury passenger liner but presently, she was used for transporting a variety of goods from Mexico and South America up the Pacific coastline. Cole planned to follow the same route and continue to haul the same types of goods. As Cole stood at the head of his ship, he let his gaze wander out to the far horizon. He tried to corral the thoughts that were running rampant in his head. It was useless. He turned to look at the Excelsior; Dominique's memory dominated his mind. He wondered how she would react when her mother showed up in Dawson. From the brief conversation they'd had on the dock, he already knew that Brigitte Laval planned to set herself up in business when she reached her destination. He knew this would destroy any chance Dominique had to escape.

"Ah, hell!" Cole spat. He swung around, and came face to face with Luther. They stared at one another for a moment. Luther no longer seemed angry. Instead, Cole could see confusion in his eyes—and worry. He owed Luther an explanation. But how could he explain something he didn't understand himself? "I'm going to get a drink," Cole said as he pushed past Luther.

"There's plenty of whiskey on board," Luther reminded him. They had both made sure the liquor supply was well-stocked. Cole didn't respond, and kept walking. "Are we still gonna push off this afternoon?" Luther shouted to his back. Their plan was to set sail for Colombia today. The crewmen were already prepared to sail as soon as Cole gave the word.

"I'll be back soon," Cole hollered without turning around. He needed to clear his thoughts before they left the port. And he couldn't do this as long as he was staring at the Excelsior, and thinking about Dominique. What he needed was a strong drink and a woman who would make him forget all about her—at least for a little while. Hadn't Dominique made him forget about Susanah Rowland?

With this thought in his confused mind, Cole headed straight for the red-light district along the Barbary Coast. He knew Luther had visited this part of town on a regular basis during the last two weeks. Cole had used the excuse that he was too busy with the purchase of the ship whenever Luther asked him to accompany him. Actually, Cole could not imagine himself with anyone other than Dominique. Now, he realized, this was just what he needed to get her out of his mind once and for all.

He entered the first establishment he came to. It was a small saloon with a lively clientele, even at this hour of the day. Cole scanned the saloon with one quick glance. It looked the same as all the other saloons in this area. His attention settled on a blonde dancehall girl who stood at the bar. She smiled when she noticed he was watching her. Dominique's image returned stronger than ever—it was almost as if she was standing right in front of him—looking up at him with those hypnotizing blue eyes. He blinked, and shook his head. Dominique was gone. Cole focused on the blonde again. A strange, uneasy sensation formed in the pit of his stomach and a foul taste coated his tongue. He stared at the saloon girl for a moment longer until her face became a blur. The feeling that he was going to be ill made him seek fresh air. He turned abruptly and stalked out of the saloon. The salty air, and the smell of fish that always dominated the seaside, made his stomach do flip-flops. He swallowed hard and began to walk quickly away from the saloon.

He didn't stop until he was back on his ship. Luther was standing on the quarter deck, but Cole didn't slow his steps. He did, however, holler at him as he stalked past. "Set our course for due south."

"Now?" Luther yelled back. An angry scowl was set on his whiskered face.

"Now!" Cole went straight down to his cabin. He shoved the door open with a brutal push, then kicked it shut behind him. His cabin was stocked with everything he'd need for this journey—including several bottles of expensive whiskey. He figured they were all he really needed. He was going to drink himself into oblivion. By then, The Freedom Ship would be headed down the California coast—

the exact opposite direction from the Excelsior. And, by then—maybe—he would be able to forget about Dominique and her mother . . . and his feelings of guilt . . . and most of all, maybe he could drink away the pain of another lost love.

Hours later—drunk—but not drunk enough to forget, Cole threw an empty whiskey bottle against the wall. It shattered, causing shards of glass to rain down to the floor. Cole cursed under his breath, and grabbed for another bottle. He latched onto an empty one, cursed loudly, then threw it in the same direction he had tossed the last bottle. A pile of broken glass was accumulating on the floor. A knock on the door interrupted Cole's next round of obscenities.

"Go away, Luther!" he growled.

The door flew open. Luther stepped into the cabin in spite of the orders he'd just been issued. Cole sat behind his desk. A dark scowl covered his face. Luther glanced at the broken bottles. A disgusted grunt rumbled from his mouth as he leveled a narrow-eyed stare back at Cole. "So, the past is gone for good, uh?"

"I don't want to talk to you," Cole mumbled. Clumsily, he turned his chair around so that he was facing away from Luther. His head was spinning. He realized he might be more intoxicated than he thought.

Luther came to stand beside him. He was

still angry, but he also knew Cole needed him now. He reached out and rested his hand on Cole's shoulder. Cole slouched down in the chair in a defeated manner. "Want to talk now?" Luther asked quietly.

Cole shrugged. He could feel Luther's hand on his shoulder. All his anger at his friend fled. They had always been able to talk about everything—except the two women that Cole had loved and lost. But when he had lost Susanah, he knew there was no way he could ever win her back. He would never know what might have happened with Dominique if he had gone back to Fort Yukon and proclaimed his love to her. Now he was afraid he was destined to spend the rest of his life wondering— and fantasizing about her.

"It ain't too late, Cole," Luther said in a firm voice. His fingers tightened slightly on the top of Cole's shoulder. He felt Cole tense beneath his touch.

"She's probably married by now," Cole mumbled.

"What if she ain't?" Luther felt Cole's body grow even more rigid. A long silence followed. Luther sensed Cole was thinking real hard about this possibility.

"We've got work to do," Cole finally said. Inwardly, his heart was pounding frantically in his chest. His mind was trying to combat the effect of the whiskey, while his thoughts were attempting to find a logical way for him to see her again. Luther solved the problem for him.

"We could sail up to Seattle, and pick up a load of supplies to haul on up to Dawson. It wouldn't be a wasted trip that way." Luther heard Cole draw in a deep breath. He still stared at the wall, and the whiskey was still ruling his thoughts, but Luther could tell he was concentrating on his proposal. "Now, don't get me wrong, Cole," Luther added, "I ain't sayin' I want to go back up there to that skunk-hole. But . . ." he sighed heavily, adding, "I don't like to see a friend sufferin'. And the way I see it, until you know for sure if she's married or not, or—" he hesitated before adding, "or if she's in trouble, then there ain't gonna be no leaving the past behind. I say, we just get up there and get it over with once and for all."

The pounding in Cole's chest increased, and his head kept spinning. Luther's words echoed through his mind. He kept thinking of the pregnant woman he'd seen at the hotel. He sensed—no he knew—he had left Dominique carrying his child. He knew this just as surely as he knew he loved her. And all of a sudden, it was no longer all right for Jack Scroggins to marry her and raise the child as his own. This thought enraged him. He jumped up from the chair, almost knocking Luther over.

Luther brought his fists up in preparation to fight. He had cold-cocked Cole on several other occasions when they had engaged in whiskey-induced battles. Of course, Cole had punched out Luther on a few such occasions, too.

Cole shook his spinning head, and attempted to focus his blurry vision on Luther. His rapid ascent from the chair left him dizzy. He shook his head again. When he realized Luther was ready to punch him, he began to get a grip on his senses. "I-I need that w-woman," he stammered, almost incoherently.

Luther let his arms drop down. He glared at Cole while he mulled over his statement. "You need her, or you love her?" he asked in an angry voice. Cole's face reddened, then went a ghastly shade of white. Luther thought for a second that he was going to get sick.

Swallowing hard, Cole fought for control. He returned Luther's unwavering stare. "I l-l-love her, damnit to hell!" Cole said through gritted teeth. There—he'd said it out loud. He hoped Luther was satisfied.

A smile broke out on Luther's face. He shook his head and sighed. "Painful, ain't it?" He chuckled, then added, "I'll tell the navigator to turn this tub around. We'll sail due north."

A heavy frown continued to tug on Cole's face as he listened to Luther's smug rejoinder. Inwardly, Cole was being pulled in two different directions. A part of him was rejoicing at the idea of seeing Dominique again . . . the rest of him was terrified to see her—and to face up to his feelings toward her. His fear was rapidly winning the tug-of-war. His head began to spin again, and his knees started to feel weak. "Want a drink?" Cole asked Luther in a shaky voice.

A snide chortle came from Luther as he turned to leave. "I'll save it for your wedding," he said as he exited from the cabin. His mirth increased as he thought about Cole's strange expression. Luther couldn't explain it, but he had a real strong feeling he would be attending Cole's wedding before too much longer.

Cole stared at the door after Luther disappeared. His head vibrated with Luther's parting words. Wedding? Cole didn't remember saying anything about a wedding. His legs began to shake violently. He plopped back down in his chair. Wasn't Luther ever satisfied? he wondered. He'd got him to admit that he loved Dominique, but marriage? Cole thought about the woman at the hotel again. The trembling sensation worked its way through his entire body. Love meant marriage—and a family—and a home . . . all the things he was running away from when he had left Dominique in the first place.

The ship began to turn at a sharp angle. Panic flooded through him. What was he getting himself into now? He tried to rise up from his chair but a blinding dizziness washed through his head. His legs refused to support him, and he fell back in the chair. The ship continued to turn as Cole's head continued to spin. "Ah, hell!" he grumbled.

He reminded himself that he was probably getting himself all worked up for nothing. He'd probably get up to Dawson City, and discover that she was happily married to her gold miner. Cole figured the last thing she would want to hear was that he loved her. By now, she probably hated him for deserting her at Fort Yukon. But there was her mother to consider too. If he could get to Dawson ahead of Brigitte Laval, he could at least warn Dominique. Maybe—Cole's drunken mind decided—she would be so grateful she would forget that he had deserted her at Fort Yukon.

So then, they would only have to concern themselves with the child—his child. And he'd be damned if he was going to let some half-witted sourdough raise his child up there in that hellhole. A sense of duty rose up in Cole's groggy thoughts. He'd claim the child, and take him out to sea with him, he decided. He envisioned himself standing on the foredeck with his son at his side. To his shock, he realized this was a picture he liked. Then, not to his surprise, he imagined Dominique standing at his other side. Now, the picture was truly complete. His head began to throb relentlessly. He dropped his head down on his desk and squeezed his eyes shut. There were just too many things to think about, and he wasn't ready to tackle them all. When he reached Dawson City, he would figure out what to do first.

The ship resumed a straight course, and the reality of what was happening settled down on Cole like a shroud; he was really returning to the Yukon. A sense of foreboding claimed the last of his coherent thoughts.

Twenty-one

Dominique hauled a bucket of water up from the well. She paused when the heavy bucket reached the top of the rock enclosure around the well, and took a deep breath. There was a cold breeze blowing, so thankfully, there were no mosquitos buzzing around her head this morning. Her gratitude did not last long, however, when she noticed that there was a thin layer of ice on the bucket. Even in the summertime the Yukon temperature dropped to freezing most nights. Dominique glanced up toward the dark spruce forest behind the cabins. The morning sun cast silvery shadows on their branches. For a few weeks the Yukon landscape had been a riot of colors, especially when the flaming fireweed had been at full bloom and painted the hillsides in brilliant orange and red hues. Now, even the greenery was beginning to turn various shades of brown as summer began to wind down.

Dominique forced her attention back to her chores. Today, she didn't feel like doing anything. Her arms hurt, her back ached—there was not one inch of her body that didn't feel as if it had been beaten. Addie had been right, mining was hard work, and Dominique knew she could not keep working at this pace. She turned loose of the bucket, and straightened up. A sharp pain shot through her abdomen. For the last few days, she had noticed this nagging pain more and more often.

Grabbing the edge of the well, Dominique waited until the pain had faded away. She hung her head down, and fought back the urge to give into another crying binge. She had been doing a lot of crying lately, too. Every time she was forced to accept reality, the tears would come. At first, she had denied the truth. But it had been over two months since she had been with Cole, and she knew without a doubt that she was carrying his baby. A feeling of terror gripped her. She took several deep breaths as she once again contemplated her unbelievable dilemma.

Jack's mine yielded very little gold. The few nuggets Dominique had uncovered in the past few weeks would not pay for her passage out of Dawson City. It was already late August; in another few weeks, winter would claim the Yukon Territory. Traveling would be impossible then. A building sense of panic claimed her. She was worried about staying out here at the mine all winter, but there was no way she was going to spend the winter in Dawson. She was sure no decent folks would hire her to work for them when her condition became noticeable, so that left her with no other options. The dirty cribs of Paradise Alley passed through her mind. She shook her head from side to side—no, she could never consider that an option.

The idea of having a baby out here all alone was still beyond her comprehension. Dominique could not even imagine it, but as far as she was concerned, she had no choice. She had come to the conclusion that she could manage if she had enough supplies to last until spring, since her baby should be born in late March if her calculations were correct. She told herself that women had babies alone all the time. She shivered—not from cold, from fear. She remembered once when she had been visiting her mother in New Orleans. One of the prostitutes had been careless and gotten herself pregnant. This was not uncommon in whorehouses—Dominique's existence was proof of that. But in this case, Dominique—thirteen at the time—had heard the woman's pain-racked screams go on for hours. Finally, the child had been born then, a short time later, the woman and the baby both died. Brigitte had told Dominique that they had both died because there hadn't been a doctor available to assist in the birth. She grew numb with fear when this memory once again passed through her mind.

With an angry swipe at her cheek to wipe away a teardrop, Dominique forced herself to think about something less morbid. Her thoughts, however, continued to dwell on the mess she had made of her life. Nothing had turned out as she had planned, and she blamed Cole just as much as she blamed herself. At times she loved him desperately, but most of the time she despised him passionately. She wondered if the possibility of impregnating her had ever crossed his mind, if that might had been the reason he had hightailed it out of the Yukon so fast.

Dominique pushed herself away from the well, and took a deep breath. Whenever she thought about Cole, which was almost constantly, her anger gave her strength. There were several things she was determined to do; she was going to raise her child completely differently than she had been raised. Somehow, she would provide this child with a home—a real home. She would be a good mother, too, in spite of the disgrace they would be forced to endure because the child was conceived out of wedlock. Her child would never feel unwanted or alone. And above all, this child would know who his father was. Dominique recalled asking her mother about her father when she was young. Brigitte had laughed, and told her that she could pick out any father she wanted. After that, Dominique had never mentioned him again, never even allowed herself to think about him again.

But her child would know without a doubt who its father was, and if she had anything to say about it, Cole would know of his child's existence, too. If it was the last thing she did, Dominique vowed to herself, someday she would track Cole down and introduce him to the child he had helped create. We're not through, Cole Hawkins, she vowed silently.

Her tears were gone now and for the moment, fury ruled her thoughts. She grabbed the water bucket and water sloshed over the sides as she lifted it from the well. She took one step with the heavy bucket before a stabbing pain racked her body, making her gasp and drop the bucket. The pain became more intense, until Dominique cried out and doubled over. She clutched her abdomen, and took several deep breaths. At last, the pain began to subside and she was able to straighten up. Her legs were shaking so badly she wasn't sure she could support herself. This pain, she was sure, was not normal. But since she knew nothing about the early stages of pregnancy, she was not ready to panic.

The spilt water ran in tiny rivulets at her feet, traveled a yard then soaked into the hard ground. There had not been any rain for over a week. The land, and even the creek, was drying up. Dominique stared at the disappearing water for a moment as she tried to understand what was happening to her. Maybe she just needed to rest. She glanced at the bucket lying on its side. Maybe she shouldn't carry heavy things anymore. But that would mean she couldn't work at the sluice boxes. She had to keep working the mine—no matter how bad she felt. Her knees continued to shake, and she realized the pain had not gone away completely, a strange sensation was working its way through her abdomen.

Fear overwhelmed her—fear for her own health, and for her unborn baby. She looked up toward the cabin. It seemed so far, yet it was only several hundred yards up the slope. Getting there, and to her bed, seemed the most important things at this moment. As Dominique started to move slowly up the slope, her fear increased. She had thought she would have seven more months to prepare for the pain of childbirth. The thought of a miscarriage here and now left her with no time to prepare or cope with her terror.

By the time she reached the cabin, Dominique had no doubt that she was losing this child. She grabbed for the door frame just as another cutting pain tore through her. She clutched the frame for support, and bit into her lower lip to keep from crying out. In the midst of the agonizing pain, she felt a sticky wetness flow down her legs. A terrified cry escaped her lips. She wondered if it was over, if her baby's life had ended in that brief gush of hot moisture.

Stumbling forward blindly, Dominique made it to her narrow cot and eased herself onto the mattress, feeling weak and dizzy. Since she believed the worst to be over, she decided she would get out of her wet jeans, and lie down for a while. She tugged off her pants, noticing the dark red blood that had soaked through clear down to her knees. A pang of sorrow shot through her breast, along with a deep sense of guilt. She couldn't help but wonder if this was the best thing that could happen under the circumstances.

Just as Dominique was pulling on her robe, another stabbing pain tore through her. Her hands clutched the quilt as she struggled to keep from screaming. The pain felt as if it was ripping her apart. She drew up her legs and curled into a tight ball until the pain subsided again. She knew she had truly lost her baby. Her robe, the bed—everything—was wet with blood, and she had felt something slide from her body right before the pain began to fade away.

For a while she was too shocked and too weak to move. Everything had happened so fast she was still reeling from the pain and the reality of what had just happened. She stayed in the same curled-up position until she was sure it was really over. She could tell she was still bleeding, but at least the pain was no more than a dull throb in the lower part of her abdomen. Dominique had no idea how long she stayed on the bed—her dizziness kept her in a state of confusion. And the loss of blood made her too shaky and ill to comprehend anything for a while.

Later in the day Dominique woke up from a restless sleep. She was disoriented and blinked and rubbed her eyes as she tried to focus on her surroundings. Everything seemed strange, and she could not remember where she was. Her body felt sweaty and sticky, the bed under her was wet. Finally, the memory of what had happened began to seep into her weary mind.

"Mon Dieu," she whispered as she clutched at her stomach. A deep sadness inched through her. Although she had been filled with uncertainty and shame when she realized she was going to have a baby, she had never once wanted for anything to happen to this child. The baby, after all, was all she had left of the love she had shared with Cole. Now, she had nothing but memories.

Dominique forced herself to sit up, feeling limp and shaky. The sight of all the blood made her sick to her stomach. She carefully eased her legs over the side of the bed and down to the floor with the intention of changing the bedding and cleaning herself up. It was several minutes before she felt strong enough to try to stand. She rose slowly on her wobbly legs. The room seemed to spin around her, and to her horror, she felt more blood run down her legs. She forced herself to remain standing, though, knowing that she had to cleanse herself and don protection for the bleeding before she could lay down again.

It was a slow, painful process, but Dominique finally managed to strip the bloody bedding, and replace it with clean sheets and blankets. She rolled the ruined bedding—with the remains of her baby—into a tight ball and decided she would bury it when she was feeling better. After she had cleaned herself up as best as she could, she wanted to do nothing more than climb back into the bed. She glanced outside before she bolted the door and was shocked to see that it was growing dark. The evening air held an icy chill, but she felt hot and feverish so she decided not to build a fire. All she wanted to do was lie down again. By tomorrow, she told herself, she would be fine.

Dominique crawled under the covers. They felt cool against her skin. She felt drained of all energy, and too tired to think. Tomorrow, she would get her life back on track . . . tomorrow she would decide what she was going to do now.

Henry banged on the door with more force. He knew Dominique was in the cabin, because the door was bolted from the inside. A sense of doom gripped him as he brought his closed fist down on the door again. He yelled out her name, then decided he would break the door down. Inwardly, he cursed himself for allowing her to stay out here alone. He should have insisted that she go back to town after the first week. She had been so determined to work the mine, though, and Henry had learned that Dominique could be one stubborn woman when she wanted to be. Now, he feared her stubbornness might have gotten her into trouble.

After taking several steps back, Henry aimed his shoulder toward the door. He charged forward, hitting the door with his full force. The construction of these mining shacks could not withstand much abuse, and Jack's cabin was no exception. The bolt on the door gave away with Henry's first shove. The door crashed against the inside wall, then bounced closed again. Henry pushed the door open again, this time holding it while he stepped into the room.

He knew at once something was seriously wrong. The cabin was filled with suffocating heat from the door and window being closed during the heat of the day. Henry wiped the beads of sweat on his brow. But when he glimpsed Dominique's small form lying under the covers, he went cold with fear. "Dominique, you all right?" he called softly. When she didn't respond, he called out to her again. Nothing. He forced back his fear and made himself walk over to the bed. When he looked down at her, Henry was sure she was dead. Lying there in the dim light, unmoving, she looked just like an angel. Then he noticed her lips part slightly as she drew in a labored breath. "My God!" he said as he realized she was alive, but deathly ill. He turned around and looked for a lantern. When he'd located one, he lit the wick and brought the lamp over to the bed so he could get a better look at her. Her cheeks were flushed with bright red streaks, which told him she was fighting a high fever. Henry couldn't recall anyone else coming down with any illness that caused a raging fever; he couldn't imagine what sickness could have gripped Dominique so quickly. He had been here only three days ago to check on her, and she hadn't said she was feeling poorly at the time.

Henry did know about fevers, though. He had been following the gold rush from California to Colorado, and now up here in the Yukon, for close to thirty years. In that time, he'd seen more than his share of sickness and death. Henry figured whatever had caused Dominique's fever could be treated the same as any other fever he'd ever encountered. He set the lantern down, and began rolling up the sleeves of his shirt. The guilt he felt for letting her stay here was only secondary to the other feelings he had for Dominique. He knew he was being a foolish old man, but Henry still harbored the hope that she would begin to see him as someone who would take care of her and provide her with a decent life. Maybe, Henry thought as he hurried to the well to get water, this would make her realize that she couldn't be alone anymore. Just maybe, after he nursed her back to health, she would see that she needed him.

Henry found the water bucket laying by the well. He wasted no time in getting back to the cabin with fresh water. All of his actions were done in haste. From the looks of Dominique she didn't have time to spare. Henry grabbed a washrag and began to wipe down her fevered face. She moved, and emitted a small moan. Henry was encouraged. Although she was unconscious, he was sure she was not so far gone that she couldn't wake up.

He continued to swab her face and neck with the cool rag. She moaned several more times. His next plan was to get some water into her since he knew she must be dehydrated. This was not an easy task. When he sat her up and began to dribble drops of water into her mouth, she began to cough and choke. Henry refused to stop, and before long, her eyelids began to flutter. "Come on, Missy, you can do it. Wake up now," he said. He laid her back down on the pillow and began to wipe her face again. She began tossing her head from side to side. Henry's hope soared. If he could get her to wake up, he was sure he could cure whatever ailed her.

Dominique was aware of someone's presence, but she couldn't make her eyes open. It was so much easier to stay in the dark. Unless, she had a reason to wake up . . . Her foggy mind began to draw a picture of a handsome sailor. His image grew so clear, she was sure he must be standing right in front of her. She could see him standing on the deck of his ship, smiling at her and reaching out his hand toward her. His gray eyes glistened with love and desire, and Dominique knew they were going to be together forever. She heard him call out her name again, and she answered him. "Cole, oh, Cole . . . I knew you'd come back."

Henry sat back and stared at Dominique. Her voice was raspy and barely articulate, but he did catch most of her words. They made no sense to him, however. "Dominique," he repeated.

"Cole," she whispered once more. She ran her tongue over her lips, and tried to force her eyes open.

"It's me, Henry." Henry leaned close to her and repeated her name. He heard her whisper the same thing over and over . . . Cole? Who was Cole? He saw her eyelids flutter several times and, at last, her eyes opened halfway. She looked confused, and didn't seem to focus on anything. Her eyelids began to flutter again. For a minute, Henry thought she was going to lose consciousness again. "Come on, Missy. Wake up now," he prodded.

The room was spinning, but Dominique forced her eyes to stay open. She couldn't remember where she was, but she knew she wasn't with Cole. Her eyes started to close— she wanted to see Cole again. She could feel someone shaking her, and calling her name. She fought against staying awake, but the man was relentless. Finally, Dominique let her eyes remain open. Her vision was misted, and her surroundings looked unfamiliar. She tried to focus on the face that was hovering over her. "Cole?" she whispered.

"Henry—it's Henry."

"H-Hen . . ." her voice faded. She remembered now, and with the memory came a terrible sense of loss and emptiness. She tried to move, but found that she had no strength.

"You just relax, Missy. You're fightin' a bad fever, probably influenza or somethin' similar, but I'm going to take care of you now." Henry wiped her brow with the washrag again. His actions were gentle and loving.

The weakness in her limbs left Dominique too drained to talk, but unfortunately, she could not stop thinking about the baby she had lost. She wondered if Henry knew, but then she became convinced that he thought she only had a fever, and she did not intend to tell him any differently.

Henry heated up a venison soup on the stove. He planned to get some of the broth down Dominique, and make his supper out of the rest. To his relief, she seemed somewhat better. Her fever was down, anyway, but she was still listless and unresponsive.

"Henry?" Dominique called out.

Her hoarse voice startled Henry. He dropped the spoon he was using to stir the soup with, and turned around. She still looked flushed, but seemed more alert. He rushed to her side, and sat down in the chair beside the bed. "What is it, Missy?"

Swallowing hard, she summoned up the energy to talk. "Th-thank you for coming."

Henry glanced down at the floor. He felt a blush soar through his face. He was fifty-three years old, but this little gal could still make him blush. "I'm just glad I happened along when I did," he said. The truth was he had not been able to stay away. Evidently, she had noticed that he was coming more and more frequently the last couple of weeks.

"I appreciate all that you've done," Dominique said in a hoarse voice. Henry had to lean down to hear her clearly.

Henry shrugged, and glanced at her. He quickly looked away before he made a fool of himself. "I've got some broth for you," he said.

"I-I have a favor to ask," Dominique said.

"Anything—anything at all," he said earnestly. She could ask him to walk off the cliff, and he would comply.

Dominique cleared her throat, and tried to figure out how she could ask Henry to go fetch Addie without hurting his feelings or arousing his suspicions. Although, she was sure she would have died if he hadn't showed up when he did, he could not tend to all her needs.

"What is it, Missy," Henry asked.

"I—I—it's just that I need—well—there are things that we women—"

Henry pulled back. He rose up to his feet abruptly, almost knocking over the chair he had been sitting in. "I think I know what you're trying to tell me."

Dominique cringed inwardly as she wondered how Henry could know. The odd look on his face made her wonder if he had figured out what was wrong with her. Panic shot through her, but his next words made her fear unnecessary.

"There's things—personal things—a woman needs," Henry said in a high-pitched voice. As bad as he wanted to be the one to nurse Dominique back to health, he also knew that she would be more comfortable with another woman here. Never having been married, Henry was reluctant to even think about the things she might be talking about. "I'll bet Addie Doolin would want to be here if she knew you were ailing."

"Yes," Dominique agreed. "Addie would want to be here." She knew if there was anyone she could trust it was Addie. And right now she needed a trusted friend more than she needed anything else. The pain she had experienced during the miscarriage was fleeting and eventually would disappear altogether. The agony she felt now, she was sure, would never leave her. She wanted to cry until she had no more tears left, and talk about the baby she had lost . . . and most of all, she wanted to talk about Cole and the feelings she had been trying to hide for the past couple of months. Until she could do all of this, Dominique knew she would never be healthy again—physically or mentally.

Twenty-two

"I don't think you're feelin' up to this," Addie said in a disapproving voice. She crossed her arms and glared at Dominique.

"I don't want anybody else to do it," Dominique said, determinedly. "Is everything ready out there?"

Addie nodded. The frown on her face deepened. "It's raining."

Dominique smiled. "It's been raining for a week, and according to everybody who has lived here in the Klondike for any length of time, it's going to rain for a long time to come. And then, it's going to snow for an even longer time."

Dropping her hands down in a defeated gesture, Addie knew her protests were in vain. Dominique was determined to bury her unborn child herself. Addie could understand her feelings, but she wished Dominique wouldn't go outside in the damp, cold weather. The infection she had contracted after the miscarriage almost killed her, and Addie didn't think she was ready to be tramping around in the mud. Obediently, though, she followed Dominique out the door.

The countryside surprised Dominique when she stepped outside. In the week she had been laid up, the last of the greenery had disappeared. The distant tundra was barren and brown, while the mountains behind the cabin were painted in shades of autumn reds and golds. Snow capped the mountaintops year-round, but now, even the foothills were topped in white. A cold north wind whistled across the land, and a light drizzle fell. Dominique shivered visibly.

"You can't afford to get chilled," Addie warned. "You're too weak already."

"I'm fine—thanks to you," Dominique said. She reached out and laid her hand on Addie's arm. "I don't know how I'll repay you, but I will. If you ever need—"

Addie raised up her hand, and interrupted. "Friends don't need to be repaid for helping each other." Her eyes met Dominique's for a moment. The past few days had made them close, but there were things they still could not share. Addie knew when the time was right, though, she would be needing Dominique's help too. For now, because of Dominique's recent loss, her happy news would have to wait.

Dominique knew Addie was right. Still, she felt Addie deserved a medal for all she had done for her. When Henry had went for her, she had dropped everything and left her new husband without a moment's hesitation. Dominique had dreaded telling her about the baby because it would confirm what had happened between her and Cole. Addie was so kind and understanding about everything, though, that she never once felt she was being condemned.

A blast of cold wind hit Dominique in the face, taking her breath away. She felt chilled clear through to her bones. It seemed like fitting weather for this glum task. She picked up the bundle that Addie had placed in a clean flour sack and proceeded to the back of the cabin. Earlier, Addie had dug a small hole under a spruce tree. In this hole, Dominique placed the sack and its contents. With Addie's help, they pushed mud into the hole, and in no time, the job was completed. Dominique stood beside the gravesite for a moment, head bowed, and her hands clasped together. She wasn't quite sure what she should ask of God under these circumstances, but she did say a prayer for the child she would never know. And then, as an afterthought, she said a prayer for Cole. She prayed that wherever he was, he would sometimes think about her, and remember the love they had once shared in the wild Yukon Territory.

"Come on, you're gettin' soaked through and through," Addie said. She grabbed Dominique's arm and tugged impatiently. Although she was worried about Dominique, she also had her own selfish reasons for wanting to get out of the foul weather. She didn't want to chance catching cold, either. To her joy, and disbelief, Addie was carrying Frank's child. After all the years she had been with her first husband, and believed herself to be barren. She didn't care to ponder over the past. If she was carrying Frank's child, she only wanted to rejoice in this miracle. When some time had passed, she planned to tell Dominique. She also planned to try to convince her once again to come to live with her and Frank. Surely now, Dominique would realize that she couldn't stay out here alone all winter.

"Frank's comin' today," Addie said as they shook the rain from their raincoats. They hung them from a hook on the porch and hurried back into the cabin. The temperature was dropping, and most likely, the rain would turn to snow before long. At this time of year the snow probably wouldn't stay on the ground at the lower altitudes, but it served as a reminder that winter was rapidly approaching.

"I want you to go home with him," Dominique said with a firm nod of her head. "I'll be fine now—thanks to you." She smiled wearily at Addie as she crossed the small room and climbed back into her bed. The brief excursion outside had left her feeling weak and shaky again. She found it unbelievable she could have gotten so ill from miscarrying at such an early stage in her pregnancy. But Addie was not surprised, and had even told her that she thought a miscarriage was sometimes worse on a woman than having a baby. A woman's body had time to prepare itself for childbirth, while a miscarriage was a complete shock to the body.

Addie handed Dominique a steaming cup of coffee. She noticed Dominique's pale complexion. "You can't be alone. I insist that you come home with me and Frank." Dominique started to shake her head, but Addie didn't give her a chance to speak. She placed her hands on her hips and leveled her gaze on Dominique. "I'm not askin', I'm tellin', and there's not gonna be any discussion about this subject. When Frank gets here, we'll all leave together."

Surprised by her bold show of authority, Dominique only stared at Addie in silence. She was slightly amused, yet at the same time touched at how much Addie seemed to care about her. Since she knew it would be some time before she would be able to work at the mine again, she decided there was no use fighting Addie right now. When she was stronger, she would come back to the 12 Eldorado and resume digging until she had enough gold to leave. "Well, it seems useless for me to argue with you—"

"It is," Addie interrupted. She paused, looked mildly surprised that Dominique had given in so easily, then began to smile. Abruptly, she changed the subject. "Isn't that Henry Farmer a nice man? I couldn't believe it when he told me that he'd never been married. What a waste." She leveled her gaze on Dominique, adding, "Don't you think it's a waste that a good man like Henry isn't married?"

A shrug lifted Dominique's shoulders. "I suppose he has his reasons." I'll never get married, either, she thought with a fleeting image of Cole Hawkins passing through her mind. All at once, the tears she had wanted to cry when she had dropped the flour sack into the ground—and the ones she hadn't finished crying when Cole had deserted her— and all the other tears she needed to release, came flooding out of her eyes. Sobs racked her frail body as Addie held her in her arms, letting her cry until there were no more tears left.

At last, too exhausted to cry anymore, or to think about the reasons for her outburst, Dominique fell into a mindless sleep. Hours later, the arrival of Frank Doolin woke her. She felt more drained of energy than before she had slept. But sheer determination made her get out of bed. Addie had already packed up the things she would need—actually, Addie had packed everything she could cram into the back of Frank's buckboard. It was apparent that she didn't think Dominique would ever be coming back here again.

"Are you ladies ready?" Frank asked, tipping his hat politely. He helped each of them up to the seat, then climbed on board beside his wife. Addie had told him that Dominique was suffering from an infection, but she hadn't elaborated on the cause and he didn't ask. It didn't matter to Frank either. In just the short time he had known his mail-order bride, Frank had fallen deeply in love with Addie. If she wanted to help this young woman, then Frank would do his share too.

Dominique was silent most of the way to the Doolins' place, although both Frank and Addie went overboard to include her in their conversations. She felt strange interfering in their new life together, but she knew she had no other option. It seemed that her options kept diminishing one by one.

During the brief month or so of summertime in the Yukon, the nights were more like twilight, not completely dark. But now, as August came to an end, the nights were beginning to grow darker again. Dominique had been told that for several months during the winter it would be like dusk for twenty-four hours a day. The thought of being greeted by a sunless sky day after day, was not something she welcomed. Each day that passed, however, made her more afraid that she would still be here when winter did arrive. With this fear imbedded in her, Dominique did everything Addie instructed her to do; she ate regularly, was in bed early, and did not over-exert herself. Before long, Dominique was in better health than she had ever been in her life.

For the past couple of weeks, Henry Farmer had been a regular visitor at the Doolins', and Addie had been on a campaign to make a match between him and Dominique. It took no effort with Henry, for he had admitted to Addie that he had been in love with Dominique almost since the first moment he had met her. Addie thought his belief that Dominique would think he was a foolish old man was utter nonsense. So, she was concentrating all her efforts on Dominique.

"You and Henry sure seem to get along good. It's almost like you've know each other forever," Addie commented as she waited for Dominique to button up the back of the dress she was trying on. They had arrived in Dawson earlier in the day. Frank and Henry had gone to buy mining supplies, while Addie had insisted Dominique come to the dress shop with her.

Dominique had agreed reluctantly. She had wanted to go with the men so she could purchase her own supplies for 12 Eldorado with the few, small gold nuggets she had managed to uncover before her miscarriage.

"I mean—he's a lot older than you," Addie said. "But that shouldn't make a difference to a woman if a man treats her good."

Dominique shrugged indifferently. She had had this conversation with Addie numerous times, and she knew what Addie was up to. Although she had told Addie that she had come to think of Henry as a very close friend, Addie continued to try to make their relationship into something more. "This dress is too big for you, Addie," she said when she had fastened the last button at the waistline. "See the way the waist is way too loose?" Dominique pointed out as she walked around to face the other woman.

A nervous chuckle escaped from Addie. "I'll be needin' it a little bigger."

"Why in the world would you—" The strange look on Addie's face halted Dominique's words in her mouth. Her eyes locked with Addie's for a moment. She sensed Addie had something to tell her, and she hoped it didn't have anything to do with Henry. There was nothing Addie could say that would change her mind about marrying him, or her determination to return to 12 Eldorado when they left Dawson City in a few days.

"Addie—about Frank—" she began. Addie shook her head from side to side. Dominique shrugged again, but before she could say another word, Addie began to speak.

"I have something to tell you, something that might be upsetting to you. But in spite of everything, I hope you'll still be happy for me."

Dominique continued to stare blankly at Addie. Since she was expecting Addie's announcement to somehow involve Henry, she was completely unprepared for her next words.

"I'm gonna have a baby, Dominique!" A radiant smile claimed Addie's face. She couldn't hide her joy any longer, and now that she was certain she was pregnant, she wanted to shout her news to the world. Still, she wanted to be sensitive to Dominique's feelings, so she quickly wiped the smile from her face, and added, "I've suspected it for a while now, and I realize this is really bad timing and all . . ."

"No!" Dominique interrupted. "I couldn't be happier for you and Frank," she said. This wasn't a lie, and she hated that Addie thought she was so selfish that she didn't want other people to have the things she was denied. "Mon Dieu," she gasped, "it's a miracle, isn't it?" She remembered Addie telling her how badly she had wanted to have children with her first husband. It also occurred to Dominique how hard it must have been for Addie to keep this exciting news to herself. Dominique felt a hot flush redden her cheeks. She leaned forward, and hugged Addie. She didn't want Addie to see the shame and guilt she was sure was written on her face. Before they pulled away from one another, Dominique promised herself that she would never inflict her own self-pity on others again.

"Thank you," Addie said as she stepped back. "I know it's been hard on you—what with losing your baby—and with the way you still feel about the captain." Addie noticed that Dominique's pallor went from a flushed shade of red to a deathly hue of white. They had not spoken of Cole since her miscarriage, and Addie had hoped her feelings for him had started to fade away. Dominique looked away from her, but not before Addie saw the look of unrequited love in her blue eyes. A deep sadness intruded on Addie's happiness.

"I'm the one who should be thanking you," Dominique said. She forced herself to look at Addie again. In the other woman's eyes she could see her own hazy reflection—just as she could see in Addie the type of woman she wanted to become. But first, she had to learn how to quit putting her own wants and needs first. "And I'm going to show you how much I appreciate what you've done for me—I promise you I will."

A tear burned in the corner of Addie's eye. She could see, and almost feel, Dominique's agony. "I don't want anything from you, Dominique. I only want you to be happy. That's why," Addie drew in a deep breath, then continued. "I'm not going to keep carryin' on about you and Henry." She saw the look of surprise flash across Dominique's face, followed instantly by an expression of relief. Guilt inched through Addie, along with a sense of obligation.

"I have something else to tell you," Addie said, sheepishly. She drew in another heavy breath.

Dominique had the feeling she didn't want

to hear what Addie was about to tell her. "I want to talk more about your baby," she said, changing the subject. Her face crunched up in a thoughtful expression. "Let's see—it must be due in late spring. Is that right?" Fleetingly, she recalled that her baby would have been due in early spring.

"Henry's plannin' to ask you to marry him tonight. That's why we came to Dawson today."

Dominique's mouth opened, but only silence followed as Addie's words sank into her spinning mind.

Addie sighed. "He's buying flowers right now." She rolled her eyes upward, thinking about her own part in this scheme. Actually, this entire plan had been her idea, which made her feel even more ashamed now. "Henry was gonna surprise you, but I realized just now, that what I've been doin' to both you and Henry has been real unfair."

Confused, Dominique continued to stare at Addie. "What you've been doing is being the best friend a girl could ever want."

Addie shook her head. "I've been interfering in somethin' that was none of my business, and don't argue with me," she said when she noticed Dominique's head start to shake from side to side. "I convinced poor old Henry that he should get up his courage to ask you to marry him, and I dragged both of you here to Dawson just for that purpose. And, I was thinkin' that you wouldn't be able to refuse if he did it all up just right. You know, with all the trimmings, and—" Addie threw her hand up the side of her head, adding, "I even told him to get down on one knee when he did the askin'." Addie leaned forward, and added in a breathy voice, "I am sorry."

"Why are you being so hard on yourself? You thought you were doing Henry a favor—and me too," Dominique said weakly.

Addie shrugged. "That was before . . . before I realized how much you still love Cole Hawkins." She looked into Dominique's eyes. "It's so plain, I can't believe I continued to ignore it. And—" Addie's voice cracked slightly, "knowin' this, I can't let you hurt Henry, or yourself." She reached out and laid her hand on Dominique's shoulder as she added, "I realize now that you need more time to heal—not just physically—but emotionally."

Dominique glanced down at the floor as she mulled over Addie's words. It was true that she needed more time to get over the loss of her baby, but she would never stop wanting Cole. Life hadn't stopped when he left, though, and Dominique knew she still had a lot more life ahead of her. But what kind of life? She couldn't intrude on Addie and Frank forever, and logically, she knew she couldn't stay at Jack's mine forever either. To get out of the Yukon it took money—lots of money. With the small amount of gold the 12 Eldorado had yielded so far, she would have to stay at the mine forever to have enough money to leave. Two days ago, The Excelsior had docked in the harbor with another load of passengers and supplies for the winter. When it departed for San Francisco in a week, it would be the last chance to leave Dawson by waterway before the ice began to make traveling in the Bering Sea too dangerous for the big ocean vessels. Dominique felt trapped, and more desperate than she had ever felt

"I really do appreciate what you tried to do, Addie." Dominique drew in a heavy sigh. She glanced up from the floor. Addie was almost old enough to be her mother, but she was without a doubt the closest friend Dominique had ever had. She wished she could do the things she knew would make Addie happy, but right now, she just had to get away. "I'm going for a walk down by the river to sort through my thoughts." She reached out and squeezed Addie's hand affectionately. "I'll see you later at the hotel. We'll celebrate your wonderful news."

Addie didn't answer, only nodding in reply. Her heart broke for Dominique as she watched her leave the dress shop. She, too, thought of Dominique as her best friend now, and she would do just about anything to see that she got the happiness she deserved. Maybe there still was a way, Addie told herself as she hurried to get her own clothes on so that she could go find Frank. She had something important to discuss with him.

* * *

Dominique wandered down to the dock.
The sight of the Excelsior anchored off the
shore sent her spirits even lower. She desperately wanted to be on board when it sailed in
a week, but there was no chance of that happening. Overhead, a clap of thunder shook
the sky and the chill wind cut through her
clothes. In other parts of the country summer
was just barely fading into early autumn. Here
in the Klondike, a person would miss summer
if they blinked.

With a weary sigh Dominique continued to
stare at the Excelsior. She wondered if Cole
was on a ship like this one. If he was, she
knew he would be docked at some sunny
southern port, or else careening through the
tropics where summer never ended. She shivered, and forced herself to turn away as a teardrop escaped her eye and started to roll down
her cheek. The wind whipped the tear away
before it was half-way down her face and she
angrily wiped at her eyes. She had shed
enough tears to last her a lifetime over that
man. Now, it was time to make another new
start.

She headed back to the main street. As she
walked, she kept glancing over at the rundown shacks that were called Paradise Alley.
An intense curiosity drew her to the end of
the narrow back street and she peered down
at the two uneven rows of shanties. Boards

were thrown across the street so that visitors and residents could cross the street without bogging down in the deep mud. Even now, at mid-day, this was a busy area.

When they had first arrived at the dress shop, Dominique had overheard two of the few respectable women in Dawson City whispering about the new batch of prostitutes and dancehall girls had been aboard the Excelsior. She had thought about her mother, and how foolish she had thought Dominique was to come all the way up here to find a husband. There were few words of advice that Brigitte had offered to Dominique that she thought were worth savoring. But her mother's opinion about this journey to the Yukon Territory was one she wished she had heeded.

An obviously drunk miner stumbled out of one of the cribs about midway down the street. He paused in the doorway and turned around. From where she stood, Dominique couldn't see the woman until the miner pulled her through the doorway and drew her up against him. Still, she could not see the woman clearly, because the couple engaged in a long, smoldering kiss. When they parted, Dominique's attention was drawn to the large bag the man pulled out from his coat pocket. She squinted her eyes in an effort to see the bag more clearly. What she saw her made her knees go weak. The bag was the kind used to hold gold dust, or nuggets. From the 12 Eldorado, she hadn't filled one of those bags even halfway full after nearly two months of hard work. This woman was receiving a bag that was nearly overflowing with gold after probably no more than an hour of—of . . . well, Dominique guessed what the woman had done might be considered work.

Fury flooded through Dominique as she thought about the unfairness in her life. The memory of the intimacy she had shared with Cole passed through her mind—the touch of his hands, his lips—everything about him. She tried to focus her waning attention on the couple again. For making a man feel like he was loved—even if for a short time—that woman was being paid more than Dominique could earn in six months. Fleetingly, a strange feeling washed through Dominique, and it was as unexpected as it was frightening. She was no longer feeling so furious, instead, she felt envious. Maybe . . . just maybe . . . she did have another option? As this unbelievable thought occurred to her, Dominique's gaze shifted to the woman's face. "Maman!" she gasped as she stared at her in a state of complete shock.

Dominique knew her mother had not seen her, but she did not take time to think about her next course of action. She swung around, and began to run as fast as she could from Paradise Alley—and from her mother. Why, or how, Brigitte had ended up here in the Yukon, she didn't want to know. She only knew that she had to escape from the sinful thoughts that had been consuming her, and she had to make sure her mother's influence never tainted her life again. But now that she knew her mother was here—of all places—this might not be possible!

Dominique didn't stop running until she reached her hotel. Without pausing, she hurried up to Addie and Frank's room. She banged on the door with her closed fist. There was no answer. She needed to talk to Addie, or to be with both Addie and Frank so she could be reminded of what her true goals were; respectability, a home and a family. Panic invaded her as she stood alone in the hotel hallway. What if she couldn't escape her legacy? What if it was bred into her so deeply the she had no other choice but to give into temptation and sin?

Her heart pounded frantically in her breast, and her fear grew apace. She was terrified that if she didn't find Addie soon, she would be lured back to Paradise Alley. Even now, she was vividly recalling the image of her mother's flushed face, the satisfied grin that rested on her kiss-swollen lips, and mostly, the heavy bag of gold she had earned for the brief liaison with the miner. Dominique's head was spinning, her mouth felt dry, her heartbeat kept racing out of control. She swung around in a state of growing panic.

"Missy! What's wrong?" Henry asked worriedly.

Dominique stared at him wordlessly. He

wore a new suit of clothes—one that fit his tall thin frame perfectly. His thinning gray hair was combed neatly back from his forehead, and he even wore shiny new boots on his feet. In his hand was a huge of bouquet of roses, on his aging face was a concerned frown.

"H-Henry," Dominique said in a breathless voice. "No-nothing's wrong." Her gaze moved from his face to the flowers, then back up to his face again. His frown eased away, and was replaced by a nervous smile.

"Are you looking for Frank and Addie?" he asked. He stepped closer, and peered down into her eyes.

Dominique tilted her head back and looked up at him. His hazel colored eyes held the same kindness she had glimpsed there the first time she had met him. She nodded her head slowly. There were half a dozen thoughts raging through her head at this moment, and nothing seemed to make sense.

Henry nodded his head, too, although he wasn't sure why. Her strange behavior made him feel even more awkward than he had already been feeling. He thought about all the preparation Addie had thought was necessary for this proposal, and he thought about what a foolish old man he was to think it would make a difference. But, to satisfy his equally foolish old mind, Henry decided to get this whole episode over with instead of prolonging his agony—and the rejection he was sure would come—any longer.

Falling down on one knee, Henry suddenly grabbed Dominique's hand in the manner that Addie had instructed him to do. "Missy? Dominique—I-I—know I'm just an old man, but I'm a decent type. I'll never hurt you, or desert you. My-my mine is yielding enough gold to provide a good home for you. And-and I guess what I'm tryin' to say is-is will you marry me?"

Dominique's mouth gaped open as she listened to Henry's raspy voice. Although Addie had already told her what he was planning, she was still shocked by the reality of his marriage proposal, and also with his sense of timing. Standing here in the hallway of the Nugget Hotel, they had several bystanders as witnesses. Dominique felt a hot blush soar through her body and flood into her face. Her embarrassment, however, was minor compared to all the other thoughts that were rushing through her mind. All the dreams she had envisioned seemed to be growing farther away from her grasp; Cole was gone, the child they had created was gone. Her plan to marry Jack Scroggins—the rich adventurer she had imagined—was gone too. Now that she had discovered her mother in Paradise Alley, she feared that her mother's influence was rapidly closing in around her. A numbing sensation inched through her when she recalled how—just moments ago—she had actually thought about how much easier it would be to earn money her mother's way than doing all the hard work she had been doing lately.

She continued to stare down at Henry as all these thoughts whirled in her brain. All she really wanted was to be respectable, and she did have one last chance, and she'd best take it! she told herself as her heart shattered into pieces. She looked deep into Henry's eyes; her own reflection looked back at her. The handsome, taunting face of Cole Hawkins swam before her teary gaze—briefly—before she made him go away—for good this time! "Yes, Henry, I will marry you," she said firmly, and without a shadow of a doubt.

Twenty-three

"One moment please," Dominique called out when she heard the knock on her door. She tied the sash of her robe around her waist. A guilty feeling still plagued her when she thought about how she had spent the last of her money. The gold nuggets from 12 Eldorado had bought her a few luxury items such as the pink silk robe she wore, and a couple of dresses—one of them she would wear when she married Henry tomorrow—and several other necessities she had not had since the riverboat had bogged down in the mud.

Before she opened the door, Dominique took a deep breath. She was sure her visitor would be Henry or Addie and Frank. Right now, she would rather not see any of them. Last night, after Dominique had told the Doolins about her impending marriage to Henry, Addie had announced that she and Frank had something to discuss with her today. Dominique couldn't imagine what they needed to talk to her about, but she sensed they might try to talk her out of marrying Henry. Addie was still concerned about Dominique's love for Cole, but Dominique knew she had made the right decision. The last thing she needed, however, was to have Frank and Addie remind her of the reasons she shouldn't marry Henry.

As Dominique turned the door knob, another thought entered her mind. What if her mother was on the other side of the door? That was unlikely, she reminded herself. Ever since she had spotted Brigitte down at Paradise Alley, Dominique had avoided that area, and at the time, it appeared that Brigitte was probably too busy to come looking for her. With as many people that were crowding into Dawson City these days, there was a good chance their paths would never cross.

"Miss Laval?"

Dominique nodded her head at the stranger who stood at her door. Since she knew this man was a hotel employee, and he was none of the people she had been expecting, she was stunned into silence.

"You have a visitor waiting for you down in the lobby," the man said. He nodded curtly, then turned to leave.

"Who is it?" she said absently.

The man stopped, and looked back at her. His gaze moved rapidly down the front of her robe, then back up to her face. A slight grin curved his lips. "They didn't say, Miss Laval."

The look in the man's eyes suggested something Dominique didn't care to acknowledge. She scooted behind the door. "Tell them I'll be right down." She started to close the door, but then one overpowering thought consumed Dominique's mind. "Is it a male visitor?" she called out to the man. His grin remained intact as he nodded his head. He made no further attempt to leave.

"Cole," she whispered. She slammed the door shut without further comment to the man. The expression he wore on his face motivated her to turn the lock. After that, nothing else she did was rational. Her heartbeat raced out of control, her entire body shook with excitement. "Cole!" she shouted to the room as she twirled around several times. Cole had come back for her. He would save her from a loveless marriage, and he would keep her from following in her mother's footsteps. And, he would take her away from this awful place forever.

She rushed to the armoire and grabbed the dress she had planned to wear for her wedding. The gown was pale blue satin with a low heart-shaped neckline, puffy sleeves that ended at her elbows, and a skirt that boasted yards and yards of material. This dress was completely unsuitable for anything but the most elegant occasions, but Dominique wanted to look her best when she saw Cole again. After she had managed to fasten the tiny pearl buttons that ran up the back, she rushed to the mirror. Her hair was in its usual bun at the nape of her neck. She yanked the pins out, letting the long tresses tumble down her back. With a brush she made several swipes, then she grabbed a handful of hair and pulled it up on one side. A tortoise-shell comb was lying on the bureau. Nature had painted the shell in shades of pale green, ivory, and misty blue. Dominique quickly slid the comb into the hair she had pulled up. When she released her hand, her hair fell softly from the comb behind her shoulder. On the other side, the thick tendrils cascaded against her cheek and down past her bosom.

Dominique stood back to appraise herself in the mirror. She thought Cole would approve. She had no idea how beautiful she really looked. Her healthy lifestyle for the past few weeks had given her a look of radiance. She was tanned, toned and slim; her pale complexion was flawless, her ebony hair shone like fine silk, and her eyes sparkled in the deepest hue of sapphire. Grabbing the pale blue shawl she had bought to go with the dress, Dominique quickly unlocked her door and hurried down to the lobby. Her thoughts were a jumble of memories of the brief time she had spent with Cole, and of the love they had shared. She wondered if she should tell him about the baby.

The lobby of the Nugget Hotel was not nearly as elegant as the one at the Fairview where Dominique had stayed when she had first arrived in Dawson City. But it had comfortable rooms at half the price of the Fairview. Dominique scanned the lobby area with a frantic sweep of her eyes. As with every establishment in Dawson, the place was overly crowded. Cole—she knew—would stand out even in a crowd. He was taller than many men, and his attire would be different than that of the usual sourdoughs who came to Dawson City. Dominique could not see anyone who even resembled the handsome captain. Her joy began to fade into panic. Did he grow tired of waiting for her and leave? She glanced toward the door. Maybe he stepped outside for a breath of fresh air. She reached up and touched the side of her face. A thin sheet of perspiration clung to her skin. Her dress felt as if it was sticking to her body. She told herself that it was extremely warm in here—Cole must be outside.

Without another glance around the room, she hurried toward the door. The moment she stepped outside, she knew it was unlikely Cole would be standing out here. A cold northern wind whistled along the street, and a light rain was falling. Shivering, Dominique pulled her thin shawl tighter around her shoulders. The wind whipped her long, loose hair around her face while she looked up and down both sides of the street. Her heartbeat continued to pound wildly, but now more from panic than from excitement.

" 'Cuse me, are ya Dominique Laval?"

Dominique swung around to the man who had just spoken. "Cole—" she cried. The smile that had lit up her face froze there. She stared at the stranger; a horrible-looking man wearing a filthy coat and a wide-brimmed hat that was stained with grease spots. A tangled mass of dirty reddish-brown hair stuck out from under his hat, and hung down to his shoulders. An unkempt brown beard covered most of his face, almost giving him the appearance of a wild animal.

"You is her—ain't ya?" He slapped his leg, and laughed. "Whewee! I never expected nothin' like you!" His gaze boldly moved up and down the entire length of her body. He slapped his leg again. "That there gold dust was well spent—yes siree."

"W-Who are y-you?" Dominique whispered. She swallowed the heavy lump in her throat. Her body grew numb. She knew who he was before he said another word.

"Why—Jack, Jack Scroggins—yore soon-ta-be husband." His grin widened into a broad smile. Several black holes in the interior of his mouth revealed missing teeth among the yellowed and chipped ones.

Dominique stared at him with wide eyes and a gaping mouth. Her gaze seemed to focus on his teeth; they reminded her of the grizzly bear's teeth. She tore her attention away from his grotesque mouth. His long, wild beard and mustache resembled the grizzly, too. Her frantic gaze moved up to meet his eyes. Gray—a darker shade of gray than Cole's silvery eyes—but unmistakably gray! She squeezed her eyes shut, and shook her head. She prayed this was all just a nightmare . . . a terrible, terrible nightmare. When she opened her eyes she would once again gaze into gray eyes—Cole's mesmerizing eyes. But when she opened her eyes reality was the same as the nightmare.

"This must be a shock ta ya, what with everybody thinkin' I was dead and all. But I was just up in them thar hills behind the cabin lookin' for another vein of gold. Found me a good 'un too." Jack chuckled. "I took myself over ta the assayers office first off when I reached town. They told me I had close ta twenty thousand dollars in gold, an' there's lots more where that came from too. And they told me where I'd find ya at, too. Told me ya was workin' the ole Eldorado." He leaned forward, smiling like a cheshire cat. "Ya was just waitin' fer me ta come back, weren't ya, sweetie?" He stepped back, and looked her over once more. A low whistle emitted from between his chapped lips.

The wind imitated his whistle. Dominique felt as if the wind had stolen away her breath. She wanted to deny who she was, but she couldn't speak. Her eyes would not move from his face. Gray eyes! He had gray eyes. If she was forced to marry this disgusting man she would spend the rest of her life looking into gray eyes that didn't belong to Cole. Marry . . .

him? "Mon Dieu!" she finally managed to gasp. What had she gotten herself into now?

Jack chuckled, then ran his tongue over his lips. "I love them thar French words." He wiped the back of his dirty hand across his wet mouth. "Yes siree, I'm abettin' you'll have even me speakin' them thar fancy words 'fore too long." He licked his lips again, then smacked them together hungrily.

A faint feeling came over Dominique. She almost wished she could pass out and try waking up again. Maybe then, she would discover that this really was just a terrible nightmare. "I-I need t-time to-to . . ." she needed to get away from here, and away from this awful man.

A vigorous nod made Jack's hat brim flop back and forth over his brow. "I reckon ya'd like a spell to prepare for our weddin'." He glanced down at himself, then scratched at his shaggy beard. Several crumbs of dirt or food were ejected from his beard. "Reckon I need ta clean up a mite too." He leaned forward, smiling broadly as he added, ' "Course, we could skip the weddin' and get right on ta the honeymoonin'."

Dominique recoiled in horror at the idea of being near this man, let alone being in bed with him. "Mon Dieu," she whispered once more. She noticed an unmistakable glint light up Jack's eyes. Her stomach tightened into a hard knot, and her entire body grew rigid. She stumbled back several more steps. The cold wind gripped her, but she barely noticed. "I have someone I must see, Monsieur," she called out. "I'll be back shortly." She spun around on her heels and began a rapid retreat, which was not all that fast because she had to be careful to stay on the boards and logs that lined the streets, or else she would fall into the mud. After she had gone a short distance, she mustered up the courage to glance back over her shoulder. Jack was still standing in front of the hotel, watching her with a lustful stare. When he noticed her looking back, he waved and winked in a suggestive manner.

Once again, a sense of panic consumed her. She turned away from Jack and continued to charge down the boardwalk as if she really had a destination in mind. Actually, she was running away, but she had no idea where she was going. It didn't matter, she told herself as long as it was far away from Jack Scroggins. At the end of the long street she stopped, and looked back toward the Nugget. Jack was no longer in sight. Maybe she had only imagined him, she thought in desperation. No, her luck did not run that way. She leaned back against the building where she had stopped, and drew in a deep breath. The wind began to chill her clean through, and her flimsy shawl offered no protection or warmth. Her satin dress felt like brittle ice against her skin.

What was she going to do? she wondered. She needed to find Addie and Frank, or even

Henry. But like a crazy woman, she had run away from the hotel and the people she needed the most. Now, Jack was there, and she was standing out here in the freezing cold, without the faintest idea of what she was going to do next. There was only one thing she was certain of; she could never even consider marrying Jack Scroggins. If he insisted that she fulfill her end of the mail-order agreement, she would simply repay him the money he had sent to her for her passage here. And, she would do just about anything to repay Jack's money. Although she would hate to do it after all they had already done for her, Dominique knew she would even ask Frank and Addie for the money. If they couldn't lend it to her, she would ask Henry. If Henry refused to help, which she figured could happen since he and Jack were friends, she would find another way to earn the money herself. There were new businesses opening up daily in Dawson; surely she could get a job somewhere.

The image of the huge bag of gold the miner had given her mother the other day passed through her mind. She tried to wipe the picture away. She couldn't. Trance-like she pushed herself away from the wall of the building, and began to move slowly along the boardwalk toward the back street that led to Paradise Alley. She told herself that she should turn around right now, and run back to the hotel before it was too late. There, she had friends who could help her, and she wouldn't have to resort to anything that she would regret for the rest of her life. But something stronger than she could control compelled her to keep going in the opposite direction.

Twenty-four

By the time Dominique reached the cribs in Paradise Alley, it was raining harder. She didn't notice the rain, or anything else around her. It was insane for her to come here like this, but she had a fevered hope that her mother would be able to help her with the money she owed Jack Scroggins. Then she wouldn't be further indebted to Frank and Addie, nor would she owe Henry money. Henry . . . just the thought of him made her feel bad. She knew he would feel obligated to bow out of the picture now that Jack was back. But, there was no need for him to, because she was determined not to let anything, or anyone, stop her from marrying him tomorrow. If they didn't get married, she might end up down here in Paradise Alley, or even worse, with Jack Scroggins.

As she made her way to the shanty where she had seen her mother yesterday, Dominique was grateful it was raining. The area was almost deserted, and the few men who were down here were rushing to get out of the rain. Unnoticed, Dominique hurried to the door of her mother's shack. All of the shacks were the same in this section of town, and a block of tents had been erected at the end of the street for the overflow customers. Scattered among the shanties and the tents was an assortment of garbage and discarded furniture. A sick feeling washed through Dominique when she realized that her mother had stooped as low as she could by coming here. Dominique knew why she had come, though, when the bag of gold returned to her thoughts.

After several knocks on the door without an answer, Dominique still hesitated to leave. She leaned forward to open the door but her hand froze on the knob. What if her mother was too busy to answer the door? It wouldn't be the first time Dominique had interrupted her mother while she was conducting business. She pounded on the door again. There was still no response. Finally, she took a deep breath and turned the door knob. The one room shanty was empty. Dominique stepped inside. She felt like an intruder. She had always felt this way about the places where her mother worked and lived. The interior of the shack was as dismal as the outside. There were only the bare basics; a bed, stove, table and two chairs. Dominique recalled some of the houses her mother had been employed by in the past. There had been a few elegant ones that had rich furnishings, thick carpets and the finest linens. Even in those places Dominique had thought that her mother was living a pitiful existence. Now, she couldn't help but feel a deep sense of sympathy for her.

Dominique backed out of the shanty and closed the door. For a moment, she just stood there letting the rain fall on her. She had learned something in the brief time she had glimpsed the inside of this shack. The lascivious thoughts, and the jealousy she had felt when she'd seen the man hand the bag of gold to her mother, were completely gone now. They were replaced by a renewed sense of determination to fulfill her original goals. She would somehow find a way to become the respectable woman she had always dreamt of being, and she hoped she would never again be tempted to fall into the trap that possessed her mother. Now—thinking about the way her mother was living and the way she would be forced to spend the rest of her life—Dominique realized the price Brigitte had paid for the bag of gold had been far too high.

As she hurried back to the Nugget, Dominique had many things to contemplate, but most of them centered around Jack Scroggins. She scanned the street in front of the hotel; luckily, she did not see him. The rain had cleared almost everyone off the street, but a few hardy souls still hurried along the boardwalks. Dominique did not feel too hardy right now. Her beautiful silk dress was completely drenched, and she was so chilled her teeth were chattering together. If she didn't catch her death of cold, she knew she'd be lucky.

Once she was inside the hotel lobby, she looked around again. Her purpose was not to find Jack, but rather to avoid him. Again, she sighed with relief. As she started for the stairway that led to her room on the second floor, a familiar voice called out to her.

"Dominique! Good Lord, where have you been?" Addie rushed to her side. The worried look on her face also held a hint of alarm. Water ran in rivulets from Dominique's hair and clothes. Addie recalled how sick Dominique had been recently, and she hoped her health would not suffer again. She glanced down at Dominique's shivering body, noticing that she was wearing the dress she had planned to be married in tomorrow. "You'll catch pneumonia running around outside without a raincoat or—"

"Addie, you're just not going to believe what has happened!" Dominique said. Impulsively, she threw herself forward and hugged the other woman with a squeezing embrace. When she backed away, she noticed she had left the front of Addie's flowered dress nearly as wet as her own. "I'm sorry about your dress, but Addie, something really terrible has happened."

The expression and tone of Dominique's voice infected Addie with a deep sense of dread. "What—what has happened?" she asked. Her mind was imagining something along the lines of a tragedy befalling Henry—Frank, she knew, was waiting up in their room. She had been searching for Dominique, because they had something very important to discuss with her today.

In a rush of words, Dominique began to tell Addie everything. "Jack Scroggins is back, and he's horrible—just horrible. And Henry will probably back out of the wedding when he finds out that Jack's not dead, and my mother is here, and—"

Addie held a hand up. "Wait just a dog-gone minute. This is a lot to digest all at once. Let's get you up to your room and out of those wet clothes. Then you can slow down and explain all of this to me in a way I can understand."

Dominique nodded her head as her teeth clanged together and a shiver shook her from the top of her head clear down to her toes. Addie grabbed her arm and they both hurried up the stairs. Dominique had left in such a rush earlier—when she had foolishly thought it was Cole down in the lobby—that she hadn't even locked the door to her room. Addie contemplated scolding her about this, but refrained.

"All right, now start from the beginning," Addie said as she began to unfasten the tiny pearl buttons at the back of Dominique's dress. The satin material was so wet she could barely work the buttons through the little button holes. This beautiful dress was ruined beyond salvation, Addie realized sadly.

Dominique drew in a trembling breath as she recalled the excitement she had felt when the hotel employee had come to tell her she had a visitor. "I was told there was someone waiting for me down in the lobby . . . a man." Dominique swallowed the hard lump in her throat. She stepped out of her soaked dress and grabbed for her robe as she went behind the dressing screen. As she slipped out of her wet garments, she continued. "I guess I just lost my mind for a moment there. I honestly thought it was Cole." Her voice cracked, and she felt tears well up in her eyes. She stopped talking, took a deep breath, and tried to force back the tears.

Addie sat down on the edge of the bed. She couldn't see Dominique's face behind the screen, but she didn't need to. The agony in her voice was enough to tell Addie the pain Dominique was feeling. A pang of guilt shot through her when she thought once again of how she had pushed Henry into asking Dominique to marry him. Dominique, Addie was sure, had only accepted because she had no other choices. Today, however, she would have another choice.

Stepping out from behind the dressing screen, Dominique finished tying the sash around her waist. She glanced at Addie. Their eyes locked. For a moment silence filled the room.

"Well, needless to say, it wasn't Cole," Dominique said as she walked to the bed. She sat down beside Addie. "It was Jack Scroggins, and oh, Addie, he's just awful." The unwelcome image of his grinning mouth and dirty beard flashed before her eyes again. A visible shiver shook her body.

"I thought he was dead," Addie said. She reached over and pulled a blanket up from the bed and draped it around Dominique's shoulders. Addie feared Dominique was going to get sick again, and she was just now getting back on her feet.

Dominique shook her head. "Well, he isn't, and he still thinks we're supposed to get married or—" she shivered again as she recalled him saying they could just move ahead to the honeymoon.

"Or what?" Addie asked in a worried voice. She pulled the blanket tighter around Dominique's trembling form. Addie noticed she had gone pasty white.

"It's too horrible to even imagine," Dominique said. Her voice was hoarse, and the expression on her pale face echoed the revulsion she felt inside. "I can't marry him—I just can't!"

"You won't have to marry anybody you don't want to," Addie said reassuringly. "Me and Frank have something to tell you. We had planned to tell you when we were all together, but under the circumstances I think Frank will understand." Addie reached into a pocket at the side of her skirt and pulled out an envelope. She held it out to Dominique.

Confusion joined Dominique's other jumbled thoughts. "What's that?"

"Well, take a look."

With shaking hands, Dominique reached out and took the envelope from Addie. She slowly opened the flap and peered inside. Still unsure of the contents, she pulled the piece of paper out. Her heart felt as if it had stopped beating for a moment, then it began to pound like a hammer. Her thoughts grew even more erratic. "A—a ticket?" she whispered as her gaze was drawn up to Addie's face.

A deep sigh of pleasure came from Addie as she nodded. The passage back to California had not come cheap—it cost nearly two thousand dollars to obtain that one ticket for the Excelsior's return journey to San Francisco. But Addie had no doubts the money had been spent wisely.

Dominique looked back down at the ticket in her hand as reality began to mingle with her disbelief. "Addie, I can't accept this. Mon Dieu! This cost you a fortune. I can't—"

"You can, and you will," Addie cut in. She crossed her arms in front of her, adding, "It's already done, and me and Frank won't take no for an answer."

"But—but what about Henry? A pang shot through Dominique's breast as she thought about the man she was supposed to marry less than twenty-four hours from now.

Addie hung her head and sighed heavily. "Henry will understand. Frank and me will even talk to him if you want. I know I've interfered enough already, but I can't deny it was my fault that you felt forced into marryin' him."

Dominique placed her hand over heart. She tried to imagine how hurt Henry would be, but at the same time, she felt a tremendous sense of relief. "Do you think Henry will be all right?"

Addie nodded her head. "He's a good man." She looked at Dominique, adding, "But he's not the right man for you." She smiled tenderly as she squeezed Dominique's hand in an affectionate gesture.

A smile started to curve Dominique's lips, but it was quickly replaced by a look of complete panic. "What about Jack Scroggins?"

Addie shrugged. "Well, you'll just have to tell him you've changed your mind, and that you're leaving in a couple of days for San Francisco."

"I don't think he'll go for that," Dominique said. "He paid for me to come up here, and I know he's going to hold me to my end of the bargain." Again, she shivered uncontrollably. "That's why," she added, "I went to look for my mother."

Confusion once again clouded Addie's face. She had never heard Dominique speak about her mother, or any other members of her family. "Your mother is here in Dawson City?" she asked, bewildered.

"Yes," Dominique said quietly. She hung her head, and tried to think of a tactful way to tell Addie the secret she had hoped to never reveal again. There was no way to disguise the truth, so the words began to spill out of Dominique's mouth; she talked about her childhood spent in distant private schools, and about her desperate fears that she would end up just like her mother. Dominique even told Addie about the frightening feelings that had invaded her when she had seen the miner hand over his heavy bag of gold to her mother back in Paradise Alley. Through all of this, Addie said nothing.

When at last Dominique was finished, Addie still did not comment for several more minutes. She was shocked and saddened by the story she had just heard, but she was amazed that Dominique could have grown into such a strong and caring woman in spite of her unusual childhood.

"I don't think you should leave Dawson without seein' her," Addie said. When she looked into Dominique's eyes, she saw a look of uncertainty. "She's here for a reason—"

"For the gold the miners pay her for an hour of—of her skills," Dominique spat in a cruel voice.

"And because you're here too," Addie interrupted. In spite of Dominique's feelings toward her mother's occupation, Addie sensed she still had deep, underlying feelings of love for her mother. "I'll go down to the cribs with you if you want me to," Addie added.

Addie's last statement reminded Dominique once again of the woman she wanted to strive to become. For Addie to offer to go down to Paradise Alley with her was even more special that the ticket Dominique held in her hand. "I couldn't ask that of you," Dominique said. A soft grin claimed her lips as she added, "But thank you for the offer."

A loud banging on the door interrupted the women's conversation.

"Sweetie? You in thar?" a voice bellowed out from the other side of the door.

"Mon Dieu! It's him—it's Jack," Dominique whispered. She clutched the blanket tighter around herself and stared at the door with wide, horrified eyes.

"I'll get rid of him," Addie said in a confident voice. "You get out of sight."

Dominique did not have to be told twice. She dropped the blanket and ran into the small washroom, shutting the door behind her and bolting the lock. Pressing her ear to the door, she strained to hear the conversation. To her dismay, she found she could not hear anything more than the inaudible mumble of voices.

Although she had Dominique's descriptions of Jack Scroggins—awful, horrible, terrible— Addie was still not prepared for the character who greeted her when she opened the door. Stunned into silence she could only stare at him until her shock began to ease away.

"Who in tarnation are ya? Where's my little sweetie?" Jack demanded as he stretched his neck out to peer into the room.

"Uh-uh she's t-takin' a-a bath," Addie stammered. Her gaze traveled down over the man. Her eyes were greeted with the same unruly sight Dominique had first seen. Except now, he had obviously been out in the rain recently, and he was dripping wet. A nauseating odor filled Addie's nostrils, like the smell of a wet dog.

Jack smiled, exposing his rotted teeth. "A bath, huh? Well, I'm her soon-ta-be husband, so I'll just wait fer her." He chuckled, adding "Or join her." He took a step toward the door, but was halted before he could push his way into the room.

Addie shoved the door almost all the way closed, leaving just enough of a crack so that she could still speak to Jack. With all her weight, she pressed against the inside of the door, just in case he decided to push his way in. Assuming her firmest voice, she said, "Now hold on there, Mister. I don't care who you are. You're not comin' here until Dominique is presentable for company."

"Well, just who in hell's tarnation are you?" Jack repeated. "Her mother?"

Impulsively, Addie spoke without thinking. "Why yes—yes I am. I'm her mother, her chaperone, and anything else she might be needin'," she added through gritted teeth. "Now, if you'll excuse me, I have to see to it that Dominique has everything she needs." She slammed the door shut, and shoved the lock into place with trembling hands. Leaning back against the door, Addie realized her entire body was shaking. To her relief, he didn't knock again. Lord! He was even worse than Dominique had described him. But she had a feeling Dominique had been right about one thing—he was the type of man who would insist that she marry him. Unless . . . they could somehow get her out of Dawson before he demanded that Dominique fulfill her part of their agreement.

Twenty-five

When she emerged from the bathroom, Dominique took one look at Addie's face and knew that they shared the same opinion about Jack Scroggins.

"He is awful," Addie said as they exchanged glances. She thought again how lucky she was to have a second chance at marriage, and with a wonderful man like Frank. It made her skin crawl to think that she could have ended up with someone like Jack Scroggins instead. Fleetingly, Addie thought of Silver Belle. Maynard Hendricks had nothing going for him other than the biggest claim in the Klondike, but compared to Jack Scroggins he was a Greek god. Addie had seen Silver Belle earlier today, wearing beautiful clothes and sporting a diamond ring as big as a tea cup. She looked like the million bucks her husband's gold mine had yielded, but it seemed unfair that someone like Silver should end up better off than a good woman like Dominique.

"What am I going to do?" Dominique asked in a high-pitched voice. "I can't—I won't marry him!"

"And I won't let you," Addie said, firmly. She knew Dominique—like all of them—had taken a chance when they had agreed to come here and marry men they had never met. But, that didn't mean they couldn't change their minds. "Get dressed," she ordered. Frank would know what they should do about this— at least, Addie hoped he would. And they would find Henry, too. He would help them. That is, if he wasn't too upset when Dominique told him she was breaking off their engagement and returning to San Francisco.

"Where are we going?" Dominique asked as she grabbed a pair of jeans and a flannel shirt. "I don't want to run into Jack."

An involuntary shiver bolted through Addie at the thought of seeing that disgusting man again. "We won't. We'll sneak down to me and Frank's room. Jack won't know to look for you there."

Dominique hastily buttoned her shirt. "But then what? I can't hide from him forever. And what if he insists that I either marry him or pay him back the money he sent to me to come here?"

Addie shrugged in an attempt to appear nonchalant. "We'll talk to Frank."

"I'm not borrowing more money from the two of you," Dominique insisted. "As it is, I don't know how long it will be before I'll be able to pay you back for the ticket and everything else you've done for me."

"I told you once before, friends don't need to be repaid for helpin' one another out," Addie insisted. She glanced at Dominique's attire. It bothered her that Dominique insisted on dressing like a man, that her style of clothes seemed similar to the ones Cole Hawkins wore, but Addie figured she had already interfered in the girl's life enough so she kept silent on this subject. "Bring along your coat—just in case."

Dominique didn't question Addie. She was learning that this was a waste of time. "I'm ready," Dominique said, clutching her wool peacoat against herself. As Addie opened the door and peeked out into the hallway, Dominique held her breath. Addie gave her the all-clear sign. Sneaking down the hall with Addie made Dominique feel like a criminal. She took her first real breath when Frank ushered them into their room.

"What's going on?" Frank asked as the two women rushed past him.

"Close the door quickly," Addie ordered. Frank gave her a strange look, but he complied with her command. "Jack Scroggins is back," Addie said in a rush of breathless words. "And Frank, he's disgusting!"

Frank stared at his wife wordlessly. He had never met the man who was supposed to be Dominique's mail-order groom. But since he knew Addie rarely said a bad word about anyone, he figured Jack Scroggins must be a real undesirable sort. "Did you tell Dominique about the ticket?" he asked.

"Yes, she's happy about that—and grateful to us, too. But what about Jack?" Addie implored. "Frank—you don't understand. He still expects Dominique to fulfill her agreement to marry him."

Frank was still unsure what the problem was. He shrugged. "Well, she'll just have to tell him that she's changed her mind." He glanced at Dominique. "Have you told Henry that you're leaving, yet?" Frank had never met Henry Farmer until he and Addie had been introduced to him by Dominique. He liked the man, and hated to see him get hurt. But in spite of Addie's match-making, Frank had never felt that Henry and Dominique belonged together. He was sure that if they did get married, eventually, they would both be very unhappy.

"I haven't had a chance to talk to him," Dominique replied. "I will, but first I want to thank you for everything, especially the ticket. Someday, I'll find a way to repay you."

Frank shook his head, and glanced down at the floor. "No need. Addie and me both feel that money went for a good cause. But, I do want you to talk to Henry as soon as possible. He needs to know that you've changed your mind about marryin' him tomorrow.'

Dominique nodded her head in agreement. She glanced at Addie as she thought about encountering Jack Scroggins again. Both women it seemed were thinking along the same lines.

"Could we ask Henry to come here—to our room—to talk with Dominique?" Addie asked Frank.

He stared at her, realizing finally just how worried the women were about this Scroggins fellow. "Did he say or do something to threaten either of you?" Frank asked in a calm voice. Inwardly, though, he was ready to go after the man if they told him anything he did not like.

"No," Addie admitted. "But—but, he's just so . . ." she looked at Dominique.

"So repulsive," Dominique added. A nervous sweat broke out on her brow. She wiped it away with a swipe of her hand. Her face still felt fevered, and the heavy knot was still settled in the pit of her stomach. Why couldn't something work out for her . . . just once? she wondered.

Addie returned her attention to Frank. "Actually, he's much worse than that, and we have to find a way to keep him away from Dominique until she can board the Excelsior in two days."

A stunned expression came to Frank's face. "He can't be that bad, Addie. And the least Dominique can do is to be honest with him too." Frank's face scrunched up thoughtfully as he realized that Dominique did have plenty of explaining to do in the next couple of days. She now had two engagements to break off before she left Dawson City. He looked at Dominique with a fatherly expression on his face. "The sooner you get it over with, the better you'll feel."

Mutely, Dominique stared at him. Deep down, she knew he was right. But the thought of being in Jack Scroggins' presence again made her feel queasy and weak-kneed. In reply, she gave her head a slight nod.

"She can't go alone, Frank." Addie was adamant. She stepped to Dominique's side in a determined stance.

Frank gave a defeated sigh. It was obvious Addie had made up her mind about this man; still, he wasn't about to let his pregnant wife face this stranger if he was as terrible as they both claimed. "Okay," he said, shaking his head. "I'll go with you." He glanced at Dominique, then directed his full attention on Addie. "You're gonna stay here and rest. There's somebody else to think of now." He pointed towards her stomach, making his meaning clear.

Since Frank's tone of voice left no room for discussion, Addie meekly agreed. Then she added with a soft smile, "Thank you, Frankie."

Frank's cheeks flushed with red. He cleared his throat loudly and looked back at Dominique. "Let's get this over with." From a coat hook by the door, he grabbed his raincoat.

A sense of panic filled Dominique again, but she gave her head a brave nod and followed Frank out the door. "Where do you think Henry might be?" Dominique asked as she hurried to keep up with Frank's long strides.

"He's over at Jimmy's Place," Frank answered. He knew this because Henry stopped by earlier to tell him that he was headed down to the general store called Jimmy's Place to buy Dominique a wedding gift. It was the biggest and the best store in Dawson. At Jimmy's Place, one could buy everything from exotic fruits to magazines. Like every other store in the Yukon Territory, however, the prices at Jimmy's were sky high. Tobacco sold $7.50 a pound, eggs for a dollar apiece, and a gallon of milk cost $30. For a hefty fifty bucks, you could purchase a bottle of whiskey, or a copy of Shakespeare.

"I feel terrible about Henry," Dominique said, almost to herself, but Frank heard.

"It'd be unfair to marry him if you're still in love with another man."

Surprise filled Dominique. She hadn't expected Addie to tell Frank about Cole Hawkins. She reminded herself, though, that couples who loved one another didn't keep secrets and they never deserted one another, either. As they exited the hotel, the icy wind whipped around them. It was growing colder with every passing minute, and the rain had begun to look more like sleet. Dominique wondered if it was going to turn into snow and delay her departure. The thought of being in

Dawson for one day—even one minute—longer filled her with despair.

At Jimmy's Place they hurried inside to escape from the foul weather. As usual, the place was bustling with activity. Dominique pushed her hood back from her head, and rubbed her hands together in an effort to warm them. Before she had a chance to look around for Henry, a crude, unwelcome voice reached her ears.

"Thar you is, Sweetie!" Jack hollered from across the store. He dropped the new pair of pants he was examining on the floor and hurried down the aisle. He planned to buy an entire suit of new clothes for his wedding to Dominique, but nothing was more important right now than finding out why his bride-to-be was running around with another man.

Dominique let out a startled cry, and tried to hide behind Frank. The sight of Jack rushing toward her filled her with horror. Luckily, Frank did not push her away. Rather, he seemed to realize why she felt the need to be protected.

Frank stared in disbelief at the man who was charging toward them. Addie and Dominique had not been accurate in their description of this man; he was actually much worse than the picture they had painted in Frank's mind. As Jack Scroggins stopped before them, Frank also recognized the expression on the other man's face . . . undeniably a look of pure jealousy.

"What ya doin' with another man?" Jack demanded of Dominique. He craned his neck so that the could see her as she continued to try to evade him behind the cover of the other man. He ignored Frank, keeping his gray eyes only on Dominique. "It jest ain't proper. Yore my woman!"

Frank kept his firm stance. He almost wished he had brought his gun along. Hopefully, he wouldn't need it, because he had left it in the room at the hotel. "I'm a friend of Dominique's," Frank said, then without mincing words he added, "She's got something to tell you." He stepped away from Dominique, leaving her exposed to Jack, but he didn't desert her completely. Frank stayed at her side, while he slid a comforting arm around her shoulders. "Go on, tell him," Frank said.

With wide, horror-filled eyes, Dominique stared up at Jack. His anger was obvious in the way his ragged beard shook while he gnashed his teeth like a wild animal. She swallowed hard, and opened her mouth. Words eluded her. She couldn't even remember what it was that she wanted to say to Jack. They were interrupted before she had a chance to sort through her turmoil.

"Frank, Dominique," Henry said as he sauntered up to them. The smile on his face quickly faded when he saw the other person who stood with them, "Jack?" he said hoarsely. Shock at seeing a man he thought was dead rendered him speechless for a moment. Even worse was that Henry found himself wishing Jack really was dead. This thought did not make him feel too proud of himself.

With a sharp nod of his head, Jack briefly acknowledged his neighbor. "I'll have ta talk with ya later, Henry. I'm a mite busy right now." His attention returned to Dominique. "I asked ya, who is this man?" he repeated.

"What's going on here?" Henry asked as he looked from one person to another. Although he had thought of Jack as a friend since they had been neighbors on Eldorado Creek, everything was different now.

Frank nodded his head at Dominique. "She has somethin' to say, and since you're both here, she might as well get it over with in one shot."

A choking sensation welled up in Dominique's throat. Her gaze moved up to Frank's face. Disbelief flooded through her. Did he actually expect her to say anything while Jack was looking at her as if he was ready to rip her throat out with his yellowed teeth? "I-I-I—" she couldn't seem to make the words form in her mind, or flow from her mouth.

"Mon Dieu, ma petite!"

Dominique, along with the trio of men, all turned to stare at the woman who had just entered the store.

"Maman?" Dominique muttered. She felt the last of her bravado drain out of her body. She was surrounded by the three people she wanted to avoid the most. Only Frank's arm around her shoulder, and the reassuring look on his face, kept her from falling into a defeated heap on the floor.

"Your mother?" Frank whispered to Dominique. For the past few years, he'd been living in Couer d'Alene, a French settlement in northern Idaho. He'd picked up a few French words. He couldn't recall Addie telling him Dominique's mother was here in Dawson, but he knew she had just called this woman "mother."

Brigitte sauntered up to the crowd. Her gaze scanned them all, but settled on the handsome man who had his arm around her daughter's shoulder in a possessive manner. He was older—probably fifty—Brigitte guessed. But she noticed that he was aging in a dignified and very attractive manner. She smiled at Dominique, then said, "What a lucky girl you are to have found such a handsome husband!"

For a moment, Dominique could do nothing more than stare at her mother. Brigitte was wearing a heavy wool cloak that covered her body completely. Thankfully, the embarrassment Dominique usually felt over her mother's skimpy attire was absent now. However, Brigitte's face was coated with garish makeup that boldly hinted at her profession.

Unaffected by Dominique's mute state, Brigitte held her hand out to Frank. "Bon jour, Monsieur. I'm Brigitte Laval, your mother-in-law."

Frank turned loose of Dominique. Shaking his head, he said, "I'm just a friend."

"I'm her fiance," Henry said. He reached out to shake Brigitte's extended hand, but his arm was pushed down.

"Ya are not," Jack spat. "I'm her man." He stepped forward, and shoved his face just inches away from Henry's startled countenance. "And jest what did ya do ta her while I was up thar slavin' away in them hills?"

Before Henry had a chance to defend himself, Dominique's senses returned. This whole scenario was ridiculous, she realized. "Wait a minute!" she said to Jack. "If it wasn't for Henry, and Frank and his wife, Addie, I'd probably be dead. They're my friends, and you have no right to accuse them of anything! And you have no right to put any claims on me either. I showed up to fulfill my end of our bargain, but you were hiding up thar in them thar hills!" Her voice was heavy with a French accent, but her imitation of Jack's poor grammar was clear. Dominique was surprised by her sudden outburst, but apparently she had surprised everyone else, too. They were staring at her with astonished expressions on their faces.

"Well—" Jack finally gasped. "I-I was lookin' fer gold. And you're indebted ta marry me." He shoved his hands down on his hips and glared at her. He noticed she did not back down, and leveled her bright blue gaze back at him.

"I am not going to marry you, Jack," she said without a waver in her voice.

Jack's jaw worked back and forth. The ends of his beard jiggled around his face. "Ya-ya owe me," he sputtered.

"How much? Brigitte said. She stepped to her daughter's side, and repeated, "How much does she owe you?"

Jack glared at the older woman. "I don't want the money—I jest want her." His narrowed gaze focused on Dominique again.

"Well, you can't have her," Frank chimed in. He straightened his stance, which was several inches taller than Jack's height. His cold expression echoed his words.

Henry stepped over to Frank's side. "If she says she's not gonna marry you, Jack, then she ain't gonna do it."

Jack's eyes darted from face to face. He was outnumbered—and outclassed. But he'd be damned if he'd be out the money he had paid for Dominique to come here. He looked at Brigitte. A smirk twisted his mouth. "She owes me twenty-five hundred dollars, an' if the money's not put right here in my hand— right now—then she's gonna have ta figure out a way ta pay me back." He held his dirty hand out towards Brigitte. The snide grin on his face remained intact.

Without so much of the blink of her eyes, Brigitte flipped her cloak back over her shoulder. Underneath, she wore a black satin dress, cut to a level of indecency, which revealed

387

nearly all but the tips of her voluptuous breasts. Ignoring Jack's gasp and leering stare, she produced a small black purse from the side pocket of her dress. She undid the velvet enclosure on the top of the purse, and pulled a wad of bills out. Luckily, she thought to herself, she had just come from the assayers office where she exchanged a huge bag of gold into currency. As she seductively licked her fingers, she glanced up at Jack. She gave a quick chortle when she noticed his drooling mouth working open and closed without a sound being issued out. Counting out a thick stack of bills, she then placed them in his limp hand. "There's your twenty-five hundred, Monsieur. Now, my daughter is free of her obligation to you."

Brigitte's performance kept everyone in silent awe for a few minutes as they all stared at her mounds of exposed bosom, and then at the money in Jack's hand. Finally, Dominique snapped out of her trance and raised her gaze up to her mother's face. She knew where the money had come from, but she was too grateful to care. "Thank you, Maman!" she cried as she threw her arms around her mother's neck.

Eagerly, Brigitte returned Dominique's embrace. In just a few days time, she had accomplished what she'd come to the Yukon Territory to do; she had wanted to make her own fortune with the Klondike gold, and she wanted to make sure Dominique was happy. The money she had already made was a small fortune, and as she returned Dominique's exuberant hug, she had no doubts she had just made her daughter very happy.

Jack tightened his hand around the wad of money, then glared at Henry and Frank. Their stances and expressions had not changed. Cursing inaudibly under his breath, Jack clutched the money in his fist and stalked past them all without looking back.

"This calls for a triple celebration, Missy," Henry said. A relieved sigh emitted from his mouth as he watched Jack stomp out of the front door of Jimmy's Place. He turned toward Dominique. "We have to celebrate Addie and Frank's good news, your mother's unexpected appearance, and our weddin'." Henry saw the smile fade from Dominique's lips. He felt a plummeting sensation bottom out in the core of his belly.

"I have to talk to you about the wedding, Henry," Dominique said in a flat tone of voice. His expression made her heart feel as if it was shattering. "In private," she added.

Henry's frantic gaze sought solace from Frank Doolin. He found none when Frank's gaze lowered to the floor. "Well then," Henry said, "how 'bout we go on over there?" He motioned toward the corner of the room where there were several tables with chairs. Here, customers at Jimmy's Place could sit a spell and have a cup of coffee while they were shopping.

Dominique nodded her head, then turned towards her mother and Frank. "I'll be back soon." Brigitte looked confused, but Frank gave Dominique an understanding smile.

Henry waited until Dominique was sitting down before he sat opposite her. He drew in a deep breath as he waited for her to speak. Her cheeks were flushed a deep fuchsia shade, and her lips were trembling slightly. Henry noticed that her hair was not in its usual bun or braid. He thought she was even more beautiful when she wore her hair loose like it was now. As he stared across the table at her, he wondered how he could ever have thought that an old man like himself would end up marrying a beautiful young girl like her. He could almost be her grandfather, but he had to face the fact that he was nothing more than a foolish dreamer.

"I know, Missy, and I understand," Henry said quietly. He reached across the table and gently squeezed her hand. "Can we still be friends?"

Dominique entwined her fingers with his. "Always," she whispered. She would tell him later that she was leaving Dawson City in a couple of days, but that news could wait. They sat there for a few moments longer, holding hands and looking at each other like two old friends. And, Dominique realized, they were like old friends. The Yukon made young people age in a hurry; it made poor men grow rich overnight, and new friends become like dear, old friends in a very short time because of the endless hardships shared. In spite of how much she looked forward to leaving the Yukon, Dominique knew she would leave here a wiser and better person because of the people she had met, and the lessons she had learned.

Twenty-six

Dominique stood on the deck of the large passenger ship, and watched the muddy shore—along with Dawson City—slowly fade out of sight. A sense of disbelief mingled with her excitement. Two days ago, she would have bet anyone a gold mine that she would never get out of Dawson City before winter. Now here she was on board the Excelsior, waving good-bye to the three most wonderful people she had ever known. Her mother was also standing with Frank, Addie and Henry. Dominique silently reprimanded herself for her lingering resentments toward her mother. If it wasn't for her mother's generosity, she would not be headed back to California today.

So much had happened to her in the brief time she had been here, Dominique couldn't imagine that anything would ever be the same in her life again. She planned to return to San Francisco and find herself a job. Being a maid no longer appealed to her, but Addie had suggested a career that did sound interesting. With her extensive schooling, Dominique was qualified to become a teacher. Becoming a teacher was appealing, especially since she figured she would probably never have any children of her own. Frank had told her they desperately needed teachers where he was from, in Idaho, and Dominique had promised Addie that she would visit them there someday. Frank and Addie planned to return to Couer d'Alene after their baby was born next spring. Frank owned a small acreage next to a lake, and he said it was the ideal place to raise a family. Dominique wondered if it might also be the ideal place for her to settle down.

Dominique could no longer see land. All around her was the seemingly endless expanse of the Bering Sea. She turned loose of the railing, and along with the other passengers who had been watching Dawson City disappear from view, she began to make her way back to her cabin. On this voyage, she only had to share a cabin with one other woman—a doctor's wife who was returning to California after a visit with her husband in Dawson. Mrs. Rafkin was not a real sociable type, which suited Dominique's mood just fine. She didn't want to spend the entire journey chit-chatting about her adventures in the Klondike. Rather, she preferred to spend the next couple of weeks recuperating from all the craziness of the past few months.

By the end of the first week, Dominique was beginning to feel as if she was capable of a full recovery. She had survived her usual bout of sea-sickness, and even thinking about Cole was not quite so painful anymore. Maybe—in time—she wouldn't even think about him anymore. As the large ship pulled into the harbor at St. Michael, however, Dominique couldn't help but remember the first time she had seen Cole Hawkins. As clearly as if it had only been yesterday, she could see him looking down at her; his dark brow raised in a suggestive arch, his gray eyes glistening with innuendo. The old, familiar pain shot through her breast, and worked into a slow, devouring ache as it inched its way through her entire body. She blinked her eyes to try to clear his vision out of her mind—it never seemed to work. He was always there, hovering somewhere in her thoughts.

Pulling her coat together in front to shield her from the brisk northern wind, Dominique tried to focus on the approaching town of St. Michael. Off in the distance, across Norton Sound, she could see the line of riverboats that waited at the mouth of the Yukon to float up to Dawson City. Many of them would not leave until spring, but some would attempt to make one more trip before the river froze up. In the bay where the Excelsior was docking, there were several other large ships. Dominique glanced at them, noticing that they all appeared to be freighters. One—the largest freighter among the fleet—had a huge figure-head adorning the bow. The beautifully carved mermaid head held Dominique's interest for a moment. Then, the captain of the Excelsior announcing that passengers would be board-ing for the next hour, drew her attention away from the figurehead. She decided to take this time to depart from the ship for a while. There wouldn't be another opportunity to set foot on land until they reached San Francisco.

Dominique joined the throng of passengers who shared her enthusiasm to take advantage of the time they had in St. Michael. She pulled the collar of her wool coat up around her ears to shield them from the chilling wind as she carefully crossed the wooden planks that led from the dock to the main street of the old Russian fort. She remembered that when she had been in St. Michael waiting to board the Lady Susanah, she had stopped for coffee at a cafe that was not too far from the dock.

With her head bowed down to avoid the cold wind, Dominique was intent on keeping to the boardwalk and not falling off into the deep mud. She wore the clothes she had become accustomed to during the past months; longjohns, jeans, flannel shirt, tall black boots, and a wool coat that reminded her of the one Cole wore. Her hair was pulled back into a tight bun, which was tucked into the collar of her coat to keep the long tresses from escaping and blowing wildly in the wind.

Dressed in this getup, and with her head buried deep in the collar of her coat, Dominique was unrecognizable.

"Are you sure it's fixed?"

Luther nodded his head. Cole's mood continued to grow more foul with each passing minute. Luther couldn't blame him too much, though. Just about everything that could delay their arrival in Dawson, had happened. When they had stopped in Seattle for a load of supplies, there had been a mix-up at the dock. Their cargo of winter supplies had accidentally been loaded on a ship that was headed south. Valuable time had been wasted while they had unloaded the south-bound ship, and reloaded the cargo onto The Freedom Ship. Cole had pushed on to St. Michael at a break-neck speed to make up for the time lost. By the time The Freedom Ship had docked at St. Michael, the engine was nearly worn out. More time had been spent making repairs. Cole's plan to beat Brigitte Laval to Dawson City had long ago been abandoned. His rage at this injustice, however, grew daily.

"We'll set sail immediately," he said as they hurried toward the dock. He ignored the people who were coming up from the harbor. The fact that the Excelsior had just anchored here on its return trip to San Francisco did not interest him in the least. Cole lengthened his strides. His thoughts were on the two things that had become his obsession—reaching Dawson and seeing Dominique again. Anything else that he encountered after he achieved these two goals, he figured he would tackle when they presented themselves.

Glancing up briefly, Cole stalked through the crowd of passengers from the Excelsior who were headed to the main street of St. Michael. A strange sensation suddenly came over him. He took several more long strides then his steps began to slow until he halted completely.

"What now?" Luther asked impatiently, turning to look back as he came to a stop several feet ahead of Cole. "Did you forget somethin'?" Cole stared at Luther for a second. On his face was an expression Luther could not read. "What is it?" Luther asked as an uneasy feeling gripped him. Cole looked as if he had just seen a ghost.

Cole turned abruptly and stared at the group of people who were walking away from him. Something—he didn't know what—had told him that all of his prayers had just been answered. His gaze searched the backs of the crowd. He saw nothing that would justify this overpowering feeling that he had. Still, something compelled him to call out her name . . . "Dominique?"

The wind whistled around her head, but despite the shrill howl of the wind, she heard her name. Instinctively, Dominique swung around. The rest of the passengers continued to pass her by, until she was left standing alone at the end of the long dock. She was sure her ears had imagined his voice, and her eyes must be seeing images that were not really there. But fervently—desperately—she prayed reality would not be so cruel. Her mouth opened in an effort to say his name, but she could not speak. She was afraid if she acknowledged him, he would disappear, and she would know it had all been another dream.

"Dominique, my God, I can't believe it's you," Cole said as he rushed to her. He pulled her into his arms—she offered no resistance. She said nothing when he held her tight, so he continued to cling to her. He was holding her, hugging her against him, saying words she thought she'd never hear again. And then she knew—it was not a dream this time. "I was coming to Dawson—I had to see you again," he said. "I was a fool to ever leave you, Dominique." She still said nothing. Cole leaned back, but he did not release her from his embrace. On her beautiful face he saw an expression of shock and disbelief. A sharp pang of guilt raced through him. He knew she had never doubted he would return to her when he had left her at Fort Yukon. Now, it appeared she doubted everything he said. He wondered if he would ever be able to win back her trust.

The emotions that somersaulted through Dominique left her numb with fear and excitement. His words—and his touch—were like a soothing ointment to the pain he had inflicted on her. "Cole," she finally whispered as she gazed, lovingly, into his eyes . . . the shimmering gray eyes that had haunted her with every waking moment.

A strangling fear claimed Cole as he looked deep into Dominique's eyes. He was afraid he would see that she no longer loved him. His fear began to fade as their eyes met. He knew she still cared—but still—there was something different about her, and it was this difference that kept him from feeling sure of her love.

"I just can't believe you're here," he said after a long pause. Briefly, he glanced toward the bay. "Were you on the Excelsior?"

Before she was able to speak Dominique had to swallow hard, and take a deep breath. "Yes . . . I-I'm going back to San Francisco."

Cole's hopes abounded. He had only one question to ask before his joy would be complete. "What about the miner in Dawson City?" He noticed an odd expression cross her flushed face.

The grotesque image of Jack Scroggins passed through Dominique's mind. "It didn't work out," she said with a nonchalant shrug. Cole's hands still held her by the arms. He seemed too far away. She wished he would pull her up against him again. She wondered if he could read her mind, because in the next instant, his arms encircled her again, and she was drawn up against his hard, warm body.

For a moment, she let herself be lost to the feeling of love and security his nearness always aroused in her. Then, she reminded herself that she could not ever be secure with him again. He could desert her at a moment's notice just like he had at Fort Yukon.

After a few seconds of reveling in his unbelievably good fortune, Cole pulled away from her again. "I want to show you something," he said. A smile curved his lips as he grabbed her hand and led her past Luther. Cole met Luther's gaze briefly. He saw Luther's expression of shock, but he also glimpsed the happiness Luther felt for him. There was no need for an exchange of words between the two men. Cole knew Luther would understand that his orders to set sail immediately were on hold for the time being.

Blindly, Dominique followed Cole to the end of the dock. A dozen thoughts crowded her mind, but only one made sense; Fate had taken her and Cole under its wing, and it had brought them together again. As Cole pulled her up the plank to the huge freighter with the mermaid figurehead, a sense of building excitement ballooned in Dominique. She glanced around the deck when Cole paused at the railing. Before he even made his next announcement she knew this ship belonged to him.

"This is The Freedom Ship, Dominique." Cole turned to face her as he added, "It's our ship—mine and Luther's." He took a deep breath before he added, "Once, I thought a ship like this was all I ever wanted or needed. But that was before I met you."

His tender words caressed Dominique's ears. She wanted him to keep saying those sweet things forever, but when his lips descended on hers unexpectedly, she knew there were sweeter things than words. When his mouth touched hers, his lips were cold from the icy temperature. In less than a heartbeat, his lips had heated to a fiery blaze. Dominique returned his kiss with abandonment. Her lips parted to make way for his imploring tongue, while her own tongue eagerly awaited the intrusion. Her body tingled with sensations only he could awaken, or satisfy. When she felt him pick her up into his strong arms, she was already lost to the passions associated only with him.

As he carried her to his cabin, Dominique was not aware of the crewmen who stared at them, or of the rain that had joined the cold wind, or of anything else other than being with Cole. She was not even vaguely aware of the interior of his cabin when he laid her down on his bunk and lowered himself down on her so that he could continue to kiss and caress her. All the old feelings returned and renewed themselves. It was as if no time had passed at all. But when Cole finally pulled away so they could catch their breath, Dominique also reined her raging emotions. The shock of seeing him was starting to make way for her common sense. She couldn't let herself fall prey to his kisses again.

"Cole—don't," she said in a breathy voice.

He stared down at her in confusion. "Don't do what?"

A shaky sigh rattled through Dominique's moist lips. "Don't do this to me again." A tear trickled from the corner of her eye and ran down to the pillow under her head.

Cole rose up and sat on the edge of the bunk. Inwardly, he fought with the tremendous guilt he had felt ever since he had deserted her at Fort Yukon. He was not much good at saying he was sorry. "I didn't go back because I thought you'd be better off with that miner you were supposed to marry up in Dawson." He was surprised by the sound of her laughter.

Dominique pushed herself up so that she was sitting next to Cole on the edge of the bed. If he only knew about Jack Scroggins, she thought to herself. Right now, though, Jack was the last person she wanted to discuss. "I guess you thought I'd be better off not knowing why you deserted me too?"

The coldness in her voice surprised Cole. The strange, empty look in her eyes was even more startling. Had her short time in the Yukon stolen away all of her innocence, along with her zest for life, Cole wondered, as a heavy sadness settled in his heart. "I had nothing to offer you," he said with a shrug

402

of his broad shoulders. "My riverboat was lost, and I had no money."

"You always thought it was just money I was after, didn't you?"

Cole shook his head as he looked into her piercing blue eyes. "No, I knew it was the home and the respectability, and everything else that goes along with those things." He hung his head, adding, "I knew you wanted all the things I could never give you."

Dominique stared at his sorrowful face. She saw his agony, and felt the futility of their situation. She did want all those things—with him. But it was obvious that he wanted something entirely different. She glanced around the small cabin. The few furnishings—a desk and chair, shelves, the bed and a large bureau— were all crafted of a rich, dark wood. The manly scent of tobacco hung in the air. Maps and pictures of sunny white beaches decorated the paneled walls. The sea was his mistress, and this cabin was Cole's home—the only home he would ever want or need.

Twenty-seven

Dominique rose up from Cole's bunk on shaky legs. Emotions she couldn't control stole away her energy. She had dreamt of being with him again, and now that her dream had come true, she realized the life she had envisioned with him would never be any more than fantasy. Tenderly, she reached out and touched his cheek with her fingertips. They touched the tip of his scar. Instinctively, she glanced down at his hand. There was a thin, dark purple line across the top of his hand—it was barely visible.

"It healed real nice," Cole said as he gazed up at her. He wanted to grab her, pull her back down on the bed, and make love to her until the sparkle was back in her blue eyes. He knew, however, that first they had to have that talk they had been putting off for far too long. "I never told you the story about how I got the other one, did I?"

Dominique shook her head. "There's a lot

you've never told me, Monsieur," she said quietly. Her hand caressed the side of his face. A tiny stubble of whiskers was just beginning to darken the lower part of his face, giving him an even more roguish appearance than usual. Dominique stared at him, hoping she could memorize every detail about him, so when she left him today she would always remember how he looked at this moment.

Cole's face warmed to her touch as she fondled the scar that had caused him so much pain for so long. "I told you we'd talk when I got back, and I know I'm a little late gettin' back." He forced a wan smile. He saw the anger flash in her eyes as he quickly added, "But I was comin' back. That's why I'm here in St. Michael. I was headed up to Dawson City to see you." His gaze lowered to her body. She was wearing a navy blue coat that hung past her hips and hid her stomach from view. Was she hiding something from him now? he wondered. Was that why she said it didn't work out between her and the gold miner she had planned to marry? Cole's heartbeat accelerated.

"You were really coming to see me?" Dominique's voice was hoarse. She felt the aggravating tears flood her vision. She blinked to clear them away, but several teardrops escaped and ran down the sides of her face.

"I guess I'd best start at the beginning," Cole said with a shrug of his shoulders. "I don't intend to make excuses for my actions.

I did wrong by you, Dominique, but I've gotta tell you why I ran away from you at Fort Yukon." His imploring gaze rose to meet her eyes and he saw a flicker of something besides anger in their blue depths. His heart pounded wildly in his chest.

Dominique's hand slid away from his cheek. She wanted to hear everything he had to say, but she was so afraid . . . afraid that he would tell her things that would make her love him more than she already loved him. When he was finished, she would still have to leave, because she would still be afraid that the story would always end the same way. Her gaze scanned the cabin again. Cole had everything he would ever need right here.

Whatever Cole thought he had glimpsed in her eyes was gone as quickly as it had appeared. A sense of panic claimed him. He reached up and clasped her wrists in a frantic gesture. "I guess it doesn't matter why I left you, does it?"

Dominique shrugged. She did care—too much—but she didn't want to get hurt again.

"Would it matter if I told you that I-I love you?" There, he'd finally said it. His throat felt dry; he swallowed hard and licked his parched lips. The choking sensation faded when he saw the expression that washed over Dominique's tear-stained face. His entire body began to tremble—the sparkle that illuminated her blue eyes was the answer to his prayers.

"Y-You do?" her raspy voice asked. Inwardly, she was numb. He had done it! He had told her he loved her, and everything— her mind, her body—everything was desperate to respond. Instead, she reminded herself that three little words did not change a thing. He said he loved her, but what did that mean? Mutely, she stared at him. A smile lifted the corners of his mouth. His gray eyes glistened with unspoken passions, and his love was written on his face like flashing lights. But, what did it all mean . . . marriage, a home, children to replace the one they'd already lost. All these questions raged through her mind as Cole gently pulled her down to his lap.

"I love you," he repeated when their faces were almost level, and he could gaze directly into her eyes. "I want you with me always."

"You do?" she asked again. Did that mean marriage? her mind taunted.

"We'll sail away from this hell-hole and never look back," he said, neglecting to tell her that first they had to take the load of supplied his ship carried up to Dawson City.

"We will?" It didn't sound like he was offering marriage, she told herself as her heartbeat thudded like thunder in her breast.

A deep laugh escaped from Cole at her response. "Have you ever been to the South Pacific?" She gave him a negative shake of her head. "Well, I'm gonna take you there." He envisioned the daydreams—and the night fantasies—he had been having about her for the past few months. "We'll lay on the white sand beach and make love over and over again as the warm waves lap against our naked bodies," he said out loud. He noticed a red blush paint the hollow of her cheeks. He chuckled again and drew her close in a tight hug. "Say you'll come with me, Dominique," he whispered into her ear. He heard, and felt, her draw in a ragged breath. He pulled back so he could see her face. Her turmoil tore at his heart. Had he caused her all this agony? he wondered.

Cole slid his hand down to the front of her coat, attempting to satisfy the nagging thoughts that he had carried with him since they had parted. She was as thin as he remembered, and if she was carrying his child, he knew she would be starting to show it by now. Relief eased his anxieties away. He never would have forgiven himself if she had been alone—and pregnant—in a terrible place like Dawson City. Now, he was glad to discover he could lay to rest some of the those guilty feelings. But at the same time, something else—like regret—plagued him. He'd almost grown to like the idea of being a father, if Dominique was the mother.

Once their eyes met, Dominique could not deny that her love for him was rekindled, and it was stronger than ever before. She wanted to believe everything he told her, and if he was lying to her, she didn't want to know. "I . . ." she hesitated to say the words that she had once been so eager to say. His worry was evident in his face. It mildly surprised her that he was afraid she would not return his love. "I love you, too," she said in barely more than a whisper. Her turmoil did not go away as she has always thought it would once she and Cole admitted their love to one another. Instead, she felt now as if this admission had just released a pandora's box of impending heartbreak.

A sense of total peace settled over Cole. He had not heard a woman say those words to him since Susanah—and she had been lying. The sound of a ship horn intruded into the silence of Cole's cabin. "Do you have something on board the Excelsior that you can't live without?" he asked. He noticed a fleeting expression of alarm flash across her face.

"Just a few clothes," she answered. "Nothing important." Panic gripped her; once the Excelsior left port, she could not change her mind about staying here with Cole.

"You won't need any of those heavy winter clothes once we get where we're going." He wanted to add that if it was up to him, she wouldn't ever need clothes again. "Then there's no need to leave here," he said, reaching out to unbutton the top button on her coat. She did nothing to stop him. In no time at all, he had unfastened all the buttons. He slid his hand into the warmth between her coat and her body. He felt her tremble, but he knew she wasn't cold. His hand instinctively sought one of her breasts. Immediately, he felt the tiny bud on the end harden against his palm. Her breathing grew heavy. His manhood swelled in his pants.

Dominique was vitally aware of her own growing passions, and she could not miss his intentions since she was sitting in his lap. The horn from the Excelsior hooted again. She was barely aware of anything other than the overpowering desires his touch was arousing in her. This time—this very minute—would determine the course the rest of her life would travel. She sighed deeply, tilted her head back, and lost herself to the feel of his hand fondling her breast.

The Excelsior sounded its final warning before pulling away from the wharf. Dominique did not hear the horn this time.

Cole wasted no time in pushing her coat away from her shoulders. She retaliated by undoing his coat with equal haste. As he unbuttoned her flannel shirt, she matched his actions. They both wore heavy wool longjohns underneath—both in red. More buttons ran down the front of their longjohns—obstacles that were rapidly conquered. Cole clasped both of her breasts in his hands. They fit his grip perfectly. His proficient fingertips taunted one protruding tip, while his lips sucked and his tongue lavished attention on the other one. She moaned, and slid her hands inside his unbuttoned longjohn top.

His skin was hot to her touch, and the muscles along the tops of his shoulders felt hard and strong. An anxious ache tightened her loins. She dug her fingers into his skin, and emitted a long, tortured sigh. He seemed to sense her agony, because in the next instant, he lifted her from his lap and placed her on the mattress.

Cole's actions now were impatient as he began to pull her tall boots off, then her pants, and at last the longjohns he knew she hated. When he had discarded the last of her clothes in a pile on a chair beside the bunk, he stood back and let his gaze move slowly over every inch of her body. Briefly, his attention focused on her flat belly. He had been so sure she would be carrying his child, but then, he reminded himself, he had been sure she would be married to the miner now, too.

Under his scrutiny, Dominique felt embarrassed and shy. His eyes seemed to set her body on fire everywhere they directed their gaze. She thought of pulling a blanket over herself, but to her relief, he began to tug off his own clothes with swift movements. It was her turn now to gaze at his body—a body that she was sure could not be equalled. His muscles rippled across his back and chest, his stomach firm, buttocks taut, and his long legs muscular and powerful. She couldn't help but glance at his bulging manhood . . . he was perfection from head to toe, she decided as the recurring ache spread through her entire body.

Once the bothersome clothes were gone,

Cole concentrated on Dominique again. He had felt her watching him; he didn't mind, especially since he could see the pleasure she was experiencing. Before they were through, he planned to take her far beyond any of the earthly pleasures she had ever known. When they had made love before, he had been plagued by his feelings of inadequacy about the wilderness. But now, he was in his own element—the captain of his own ship. He was proud, virile, and in love . . . a combination that gave him the power to make love to her as neither of them had ever imagined.

Cole reached down, and gently pushed her knees apart. She offered no resistance. He began to lower himself down to her when a light tapping on his door broke into the passionate aura of the room.

"Cole? Sorry to disturb you, Mate, but the crew's gettin' restless. Want me to give the orders to set sail for Dawson?"

A cold chill invaded Dominique when she heard Luther's voice. "Dawson!" she cried out as she bolted up. Her unexpected ascent nearly knocked Cole over. "I won't go back to Dawson!" She began to shake her head vigorously from side to side. Images of Jack Scroggins clouded her vision.

After he regained his balance, Cole stared at her in stunned silence for a minute before he spoke. "We have to go to Dawson City. We're carrying winter supplies up to them. Last winter, the residents nearly starved and

412

froze to death because they didn't have enough to last them 'til spring thaw."

"I won't go back there," Dominique insisted. "I'll have to return to the Excelsior."

Cole dropped his arms against his thighs, and glared at her. "Ah hell! The Excelsior is long gone. But if you'd be willin' to leave me so easily, then I don't know why you've stayed here this long." The minute the words were out of his mouth, Cole regretted saying them.

Hurt by his harsh words, and terrified about returning to Dawson, Dominique pushed herself up from the bunk. "I stayed because you did—you said—" Her words faltered. Her thoughts were on a rampage. He constantly said things that left her too confused to think straight.

"Because I said I love you, and because I did this," Cole said. Abruptly, he reached out and scooped the palm of his hand around the back of her neck. He drew her up against him, almost roughly, and brought his lips down on her mouth. His other hand clasped one of her firm buttocks and crushed their bodies together.

Dominique tried to resist him for a moment, but his kiss was too potent, and the feel of his rock-hard manhood pressing against her stomach made her too delirious with anticipation to fight him.

"Cole?" Luther's voice repeated from the other side of the closed door. "When are we plannin' on pulling out?"

Cole released his enslaving hold around Dominique's neck. He leaned back and gazed down at her. Her eyelids were half-closed over eyes glazed with passion. Her lips were slightly parted, swollen and moist. "I'll protect you from whatever or whoever it is that frightens you in Dawson. And we'll only be there long enough to unload, and then we'll hit the sea before the ice gets any thicker. You won't even have to leave the ship if you don't want to," he said in a hoarse voice. She didn't reply.

"Take over, Luther," Cole hollered toward the door. He heard Luther's footsteps fade away. Dominique was staring at the door with an odd look on her face. An icy shard shot through Cole, and left him covered in goose-bumps. What had happened in Dawson City that would evoke such an obvious sense of terror in her? He hoped he found out before they reached the town, so he would know how to protect her. Now, though, he had other things he wanted to do to her.

Resuming his intense kisses, Cole began to ease Dominique to the bunk once again. It took her several minutes to regain the same level of passion she had displayed before Luther had interrupted them, but to Cole's relief, she did begin to respond to his kisses with enthusiasm. Once he had her reclining on the bed again, she was kissing him without hesitation. He slid down between her thighs, and adjusted his hips so that the tip of his shaft was positioned and ready to enter her.

For a moment, Cole teased her, letting himself press into her, but not plunging deep. She writhed beneath him, moaned, and then raised her hips up in a desperate plea.

Cole couldn't continue to hold himself back. He plummeted down. Her surprised—and impassioned—gasp reached his ears. She wrapped her legs around his hips, making their movements match and their bodies and souls one.

The untamed feelings that claimed Dominique were nothing like she had felt when they had made love before. She thought she knew what to expect, but her own emotions, and his exuberance, made their love-making beyond anything she could have imagined. Every fiber of her body was alive with new sensations. It was almost like the first time, but so much better. She never wanted him to stop, and to her joy and relief, it appeared that it was his plan to prolong this ecstasy forever.

Twenty-eight

Cole smiled down at the woman in his arms. Her long black hair spilled across his bare chest and her cheek lay softly against his beating heart. A satisfied smile rested on her lips, and the tips of her long dark lashes curled up from the tops of her cheekbones. Cole knew she wasn't asleep, but she should be exhausted. A smile similar to the one she wore came to Cole's mouth. They had made love like an obsession all night long. The clock hanging above his desk said it was almost dawn. Cole knew he should get up and take over command of the ship. Luther could handle it, he told himself as he picked up a handful of Dominique's raven tresses. With the tips of her hair, he began to tickle under her nose. She wiped at her face without opening her eyes.

"Those damn Arctic mosquitos," Cole teased. Her eyes flew open. He chuckled. "Being out there in the wilderness with me wasn't all bad, was it?"

Her eyebrow drew into a thoughtful frown. She glanced down at the ugly scars on his arm. "I wouldn't care to encounter another grizzly, and those mosquitos are not something I'd want to encounter again either."

"What about the rest of it?" he asked slyly.

Dominique thought about the rest of it, and the baby they had created from the rest of it. They could have created another life already, she realized. The thought caused a strange ache in her abdomen. Her long pause drew Cole's attention.

"Was it that bad?" he asked indignantly.

Dominique forced the bad memories out of her mind. "No, Monsieur, *that* was never bad." She rolled over and placed her hand against his chest, then rested her chin on the top of her hand. She studied him in the glow of the kerosene lamp. Her love for him continued to grow, and so did her fear. Where could this all lead, and what if she conceived another baby? Cole's dream of making love on beaches of white sand was beautiful, but it was not real life. Dominique knew better than anyone that eventually, reality would catch up with them.

"What are you thinking about?" Cole asked her. He played with her long hair, entwining the silken strands between his fingers. Sometimes, he noticed a strange sadness overcome her. He wondered if she was still remembering when he had deserted her.

Dominique sighed heavily, and shrugged. So many thoughts were rushing through her head, but most were things she was not ready to discuss with him.

"Are you worried about encountering your mother when we reach Dawson?" he asked, drawing his own conclusion as to why she was so worried about going back there.

A shocked expression drew her mouth open. "How did you know my mother was in Dawson?" She raised herself up from his chest, and peered at his face. "Were you in Dawson?" she asked, her voice rising to a high pitch. How else would he know about her mother's arrival?

Cole saw the anger and speculation flare up in her expression. "No! If I was in Dawson, woman you would have been the first to know. You were the only reason I was returning in the first place." He reached up and pulled her back down against him. She did not try to get away, but she did not relax against him as she had been doing. Cole knew he'd best explain to her how he knew about Brigitte's presence in Dawson real fast before Dominique drew her own conclusions. "I ran into your mother in San Francisco," he said quietly. "She was gettin' set to board the Excelsior. I thought I'd be able to get up there ahead of her so that I could warn you, but I got delayed."

418

Dominique eyed him suspiciously. She wouldn't put up with his lying to her anymore. She sensed, though, that he was telling her the truth this time. "Her arrival was quite a shock," she said, easing herself up against his body again in a more casual manner. "But then, everything that happened in Dawson was just one big surprise after another."

Cole couldn't decipher her attitude. She seemed so sad, yet intensely angry. His guilt returned. If he hadn't deserted her at Fort Yukon, she might have been spared everything that had happened to her in Dawson. "Do you want to talk about any of it?" he asked.

Dominique gazed up at his handsome face. The light from the lamp cast a soft glow on his tanned skin. The scar on the side of his face was barely visible. She reached up and ran her fingertips along the slightly puffy skin of the scar. "She must have died a thousand deaths when she did this to you," she said quietly. "I know I did when I accidentally cut your hand."

A cold sensation invaded Cole. A fire ignited along the length of the scar. "It wasn't an accident," he said bitterly. Dominique's startled face blurred before his eyes. His thoughts traveled back in time to the night when Susanah had used his own sword to slice the side of his face.

"I was a young, impetuous sailor. And far too sure of myself." He gave a snide chortle.

"I thought I was invincible, and I thought I was in love." He paused for a moment. His hand stroked Dominique's silken hair in an absent manner. "Lady Susanah Rowland was a couple years older, and much more worldly than I would ever be. We met when she sailed from England to France on the ship where I was serving as First Mate. From the moment we looked at one another, we were prisoners to our excessive hunger for one another."

"Like us?" Dominique asked in a small, weak voice. She was no longer sure she wanted to hear this story. The image of Cole making love with another woman was not one she relished.

Cole shook his head. "Nothing like us. Susanah and I were like rutting animals. There was nothing else between us but the time we spent between the sheets. When we got back to the French Riviera, I thought I was crazy in love. Well, I was crazy all right." His jaw squared as he remembered what a fool he had been.

"Luther tried to warn me. He had her figured out almost from the start. Susanah knew he did, too. She never liked Luther—never wanted him around. She said he was like a thorn in my side, and I should find friends who would improve my social status." A crude grunt escaped from Cole's frowning mouth. "She started introducing me to her rich, blue-blooded acquaintances. I never fit in with any of them, but I did try because I thought I couldn't survive without that woman." He stopped stroking Dominique's hair and let his limp hand lay against her back.

"She kept me tied up in knots most of the time. I was either in her bed, or frettin' over keepin' up a proper image for her friends. She turned me into her puppet, and what she considered to be her perfect man. I wore only the clothes she picked out for me, ate fancy foods I'd never heard of, and talked like some dandy who didn't have his own mind. But, at the time, there was nothing I wouldn't do for that woman. Then, one day after we had made love for the third time in a row, Susanah bounded out of bed, patted me on the head like an obedient dog, and instructed me to stay out of sight for the remainder of the day. She said she had an old friend coming to visit—a prince or duke—some sort of royal bum." A quick, humorless chuckle escaped his mouth."

"By now I was starting to miss the sea, and I knew Luther was getting restless waiting for me to come to my senses. He was talking about hiring on with a merchant ship that was sailing to Spain, but I knew I couldn't go with him.

"Why not?" Dominique asked when he paused. He was painting her a picture she could not see clearly. This spineless man he spoke of was nothing like the man she knew now.

Cole gave a disgusted sigh. "Because . . . I

thought if I kept tryin' real hard I'd eventually be good enough for Susanah Rowland. And she told me someday—if I was good—she'd buy me my own ship. I honestly believed I could have it all; Lady Susanah Rowland, and my own ship." Cole felt Dominique's body stiffen. He tenderly rubbed her smooth back with his fingertips.

"On the night her *friend* came to visit," he went on sarcastically, "I went down to the wharf to say goodbye to Luther. The ship he had signed up with sailed the next morning. It was a helluva hard thing to do—sayin' goodbye. Me and Luther had already been together for several years by that time. Anyway, I cut short my visit with Luther 'cause I was anxious to get back to Susanah. She wasn't too anxious to see me, though."

Dominique's imagination was going wild. She tried to picture this stranger Cole spoke of—this man who let a woman rule his every move.

"When I got back to Susanah's villa she was busy entertaining in the only way she knew how." His voice assumed a patronizing tone that made his meaning crystal clear. "I guess I went pretty crazy—even worse than I was already. I called His Highness out of what I considered to be my bed for a duel. He refused. His clothes were laying next to the bed. I saw his saber on top of his clothes, and I picked it up without thinking. I drew the sword out and pinned him to the mattress—"

Dominique gasped. "Y-You ran the sword through him?"

"No—I just held the tip of the blade to his throat. Susanah thought I was going to do it. She jumped out of bed screaming at me—saying things like how I'd never be as good in bed as all her other lovers. She told me I'd better go back to Ohio because I wasn't man enough to keep a hot-blooded Frenchwoman like her satisfied. Then she told me how she would never buy me a ship because she hated everything associated with sailors. By now, I'm blind with anger, and I'm pushing the sword down harder on this bum in the bed. He's gagging and crying, begging me to stop. Blood is beginning to trickle down the sides of his throat onto the white pillow. I'm crazy enough to push that blade right through his throat . . ." He felt Dominique's whole body tremble. The memory left him sweaty and fevered.

"And that's when she cut your face?" Dominique asked. A sick feeling erupted in her stomach. She swallowed down the bitter taste in her mouth. Cole nodded his head, his expression distant, almost as if his mind had left his body and returned to that fateful night on the French Riviera.

"She was trying to pull me away from him. My own sword was hanging at my hip. I don't think she even thought twice about her actions. She was rantin' and ravin' about how I was nothing but a pretty adornment on her arm." He motioned toward the scar. His words halted abruptly.

Dominique shivered as a cold chill ravaged her body. "What did you do?"

Several seconds passed before Cole spoke again. "I was hurt, but I was sure the greatest injury was my broken heart. She had destroyed everything I thought I had achieved. I ran from her villa, and went straight to Luther. He doctored me up. By morning, I was sailing away from the Riviera and Lady Susanah Rowland forever. I carried more than one scar from that day forth." He fell silent. The permeating quiet engulfed the tiny cabin.

Dominique's own heart was breaking at the thought of the pain he had suffered. There were still things about his story that didn't make sense to her, though. "But, after all she said and did to you, why did you name your riverboat after her?"

Cole gave her a blank stare. He blinked as if he was trying to wipe away an undesirable image. "She said she hated anything to do with sailors. I thought it was a fitting tribute to name my sailing vessels in her honor. And I did other things in her honor too." Cole's voice hardened. He stopped rubbing Dominique's back. "After I left France, I tried real hard to become everything opposite of what she wanted me to be. And, to prove that I was man enough for any hot-blooded Frenchwoman, I made sure I bedded every one I came across. I've never had another complaint."

Dominique sat up abruptly. She turned away from him as she digested his words. His hand reached under her chin and turned her head so that she was forced to look into his eyes.

"That's not why I made love to you," he added. He gave a defeated-sounding sigh. "Maybe at first some of those old resentments were still in my head. But, then, I realized it was different with you. And I guess that's why I got so scared that I ran away."

His words continued to confuse her. Dominique's eyes closed for a moment as she tried to understand. "Were you scared of loving me because I was French?"

Cole shook his head. "No. It was all the other things."

"Other things?" she echoed, growing more confused each time he spoke.

"After Susanah, I vowed to myself that no woman would ever own me again, and if I ever did fall in love, it would be me who was the one to do all the providing." He shrugged, adding, "You want marriage, a home, and a family—all things I couldn't give you."

"Why did you decide to go back to Dawson then?" Her tone was flat, and betrayed the fear and pain she felt inside.

Cole let her hand drop from her chin. He looked away from her. Never before had he bared his soul to a woman like he was doing now. He felt drained of energy, and overwhelmed by the emotions he was feeling. His gaze returned to her face. Her eyes echoed her inner turmoil. He knew how badly she wanted to be respectable, and to have all the other things she had told him about. But he had only one thing to offer her. "I came back because I love you," he repeated.

They looked into one another's eyes for a time that seemed to extend into eternity. Dominique kept telling herself that his love was enough, that it was all she would ever need. The nagging feeling of emptiness tugged at her heart though . . . It was a feeling similar to the one she had experienced when she had lost their baby. She had no choice but to accept that loss, but she wondered if she could give up all the rest of her dreams in the name of love.

Twenty-nine

The next few days, Dominique felt as if she had become to Cole what he had said he had once been to Susanah Rowland. Dominique found, however, that she rather enjoyed being his love slave. The weather was foul, and sailing was becoming more treacherous in the Bering Sea with each passing day. It was a constant battle for the ship's navigator to dodge the enormous chunks of floating ice that dotted the sea. The constant tossing about of the ship and the high waves that splashed over the sides of the rails were terrifying to Dominique. She refused to leave Cole's cabin, because it was the one place where she felt even half-way safe. He left only when he felt it was absolutely necessary, and he came back to her whenever he wasn't needed up on deck. Inevitably, they would make love—sometimes for hours at a time. It amazed Dominique how this was an activity that never seemed to grow boring to either of them. And, it worried her that she could be so eager to initiate their loving whenever he was in her presence. On more than one occasion, Cole had come back to the cabin with a tray of food, but Dominique had enticed him to skip food in lieu of what she had to offer him instead. Her mother's footsteps always seemed to beat a path to Dominique's conscience.

"We'll be in Dawson by late afternoon," Cole said as he tucked his shirt into the waistband of his wool trousers. He glanced at the bed where Dominique still reclined. The rosy glow of their most recent love-making was evident on her face and on her body. When she noticed his gaze lowering to the mounds of her breasts, then going lower still, she grew modest and pulled the blanket up to her neck.

"I'm not leaving the ship," she stated firmly. Above the edge of the blanket, her chin stuck out in a stubborn tilt. She saw his questioning look, and hoped he would not continue to ask her why she didn't want to go on shore. Even though it was unlikely she would run into Jack Scroggins, it was not a chance she cared to take. She didn't really want to see her mother again either, since they had already said their parting sentiments when she had boarded the Excelsior a few days ago. Addie, however, would be a welcome sight. Dominique longed to tell her everything that had happened in the short time since she'd left Dawson. She knew Addie would be shocked to learn that she was back—and that she was with Cole. By now though, Addie and Frank would have left Dawson and would be back at their mine. To travel out to Eldorado Creek would take too long, and it would also increase her chances of encountering Jack. Dominique resigned herself to the fact that she would not see Addie on this trip.

"I'll take you to dinner at the Fairview, and buy you the biggest steak they serve," Cole said in a teasing tone of voice. "And we could stay the night there." A suggestive smile curved his lips. His gray eyes sparkled with silvery lights. "They have bathtubs big enough for two, and—"

"I know," Dominique cut in. "I've stayed at the Fairview," she added dryly. "You said I wouldn't have to leave the ship."

A frown drew Cole's brows together as he stared at her. Something bad—real bad—had happened to her while she had been in Dawson, and he was beginning to sense that it was something he should be made aware of. "Who are you afraid of, woman?" he bluntly asked. He saw her evasive look, and knew he was not going to receive an answer unless he continued to question her.

"This has something to do with your mother, doesn't it?"

Dominique's head shook negatively and her bottom lip trembled slightly.

"You're afraid she'll see you, and then everyone in Dawson will know she's your mother."

"I don't care what anyone in Dawson thinks, Dominique retorted. She sat up in the bed and cast Cole a defiant look. He could give her the third degree all day and she wouldn't tell him why she was afraid to go into town.

Cole continued to stare at her. Her refusal to talk to him was getting annoying. Then, something went off like a beacon in Cole's head. Maybe it wasn't her mother she was afraid of meeting again. "The miner," he said in a low voice. He saw her flinch. "That's it— the miner!"

Dominique attempted to hide her uneasiness. "Mon Dieu! You're acting like a crazy man. Why don't you just go unload this ship so that we can get out of this terrible place once and for all?" She forced a grin, one that she hoped looked seductive. "I'll keep the bed warm for you."

Her pretense aggravated Cole even more, but a gnawing fear ate away at him too. "Did he do something to you—something so horrible that you feel you can't tell even me?" The look of fake denial on her face told Cole more than he really wanted to know. He crossed the room in a couple of strides and sat down on the bed. He held her by her arms, and he looked deep into her eyes. There was something hidden there—and it was so embedded that it was hurting her even now. The fury he felt inside commanded his actions, even though he could see that her fear was because of him. "Ever since I left you, I have been living in hell worrying over what might have happened to you. If something did happen—if that miner hurt you—then I have to know."

His anger made his eyes grow darker, Dominique noticed. They were almost the same shade as Jack Scroggins' eyes at this moment. She tried to understand Cole's rage, but she could not conceive why he would react so violently. "Jack didn't hurt me, Cole. You're the one who hurt me." She saw his anger crumble into a look of agony. "I'm sorry," she added. "I didn't mean to say that—"

"It's true," he said. He let go of her and dropped his head. When he looked up at her again, he realized he was trying to blame someone else for the pain he had caused her. "I'm the one who should be sorry." He looked away from her briefly, then added, "I guess I can just be thankful that you didn't have to suffer any more than you did. I mean—" his eyes locked with hers again. "When I left you at Fort Yukon I had this crazy notion that you might be carryin' my baby. I don't know why I had this in my head, but I was really convinced of it until I saw you again at St. Michael. Thank God it wasn't so." Cole saw the color drain from her face. For an instant, he thought she was going to faint.

"Y-You thought I might be pregnant?" Dominique said, gasping. Did she really think she could love a man who would desert a

431

woman whom he thought was carrying his child? "And you still left me?" Her voice was so heavily accented she was barely understandable.

He knew he had said the worst thing possible, and he knew he could never retract his words. He could only try to make her understand. "I thought you wanted to marry the miner, and I-I figured he would probably give the child a good home." Wrong—the stunned look on her face told Cole he'd said the wrong thing again. He remembered Luther's reaction when he had said those same words. Why hadn't he remembered this before he blurted out this insensitive explanation a second time?

"Y-You what?" Dominique whispered as her mind went blank and her heart shattered. As she grasped control of her spinning thoughts again, her first thought was of Jack Scroggins. To think that Cole had deserted her, and their child, because he thought they would be better with someone like Jack Scroggins, was beyond her comprehension. It didn't matter to her that Cole had no idea what type of man Jack had turned out to be. All that Dominique could see was that Cole had run away even though he believed she was going to have his child.

Cole gave a helpless shrug. He hated himself right now, and he was sure by the expression on her face, Dominique was feeling the same way. "I thought I was doing the right thing," he said.

"The right thing by me and our baby? Or the right thing for you?" Her voice contained the contempt that flashed in her narrowed eyes.

He shrugged again. "I was wrong. I'm s-sorry." That was hard to say again, and he wished his admission had helped the situation, but it didn't.

"Sorry? Mon Dieu!" Dominique pushed the blanket away from her, and scooted past him. Naked, she stalked to the chair where her clothes had been stacked for the past few days. She grabbed her longjohns and began to pull them over her feet and up her legs. To be in this room with this man was unbearable.

Cole understood her anger. But it seemed she was carrying it to extremes. He rose up from the bed, and went over to her. She was hastily buttoning up her flannel shirt. "Don't you think you're over-reacting?" he said.

Dominique didn't reply. She was too angry to talk, and the last thing she wanted was for him to see her cry. She grabbed her tall boots and began to pull them on her feet. When she straightened up again, Cole grabbed her by the arms and turned her around so that she was forced to face him. She stared at his chest, refusing to meet his eyes, and wondering if he had a vacant hole where he was supposed to have a heart.

"Come on, woman," Cole said. He was beginning to grow aggravated with her attitude over this subject. He tried to raise her chin up with one of his hands. Stubbornly, she continued to fight against him, and refused to look up at him. "I said I was sorry, and I was prepared to come back here and try to make amends. That's the only reason I was comin' back to this hellhole. I could be floating down in the warm waters of the South Pacific by now. But hell no! I came back up here because of that nagging notion I had about you being pregnant with my child." He reflexively glanced down at her stomach, adding, "But that didn't happen, so why should we fight about something that never happened?"

"I thought you were coming back to warn me about my mother," she spat. She desperately wanted to cry, but she refused to give him the satisfaction of seeing how badly he was hurting her again.

Cole gave an exasperated grunt. "Well—that too. But, I was mainly comin' back to face up to my obligations." A fleeting image of the pregnant woman he'd seen in San Francisco passed through his mind. He remembered the way he'd felt when he thought about the possibility of Dominique being heavy with his child. Even now a strange yearning overcame him. He wondered if—after all the love-making they'd done in the past few days—there was a chance that she was pregnant with his child now.

"But you still thought I'd be better off married to Jack Scroggins?" Dominique's voice was incredulous. His selfish justifications and excuses only served as fuel for her fury. A brittle-sounding chortle escaped from her before she spoke again. "I'd be better off in a pine box," she added.

She shook her head to clear away the repulsive thought of being married to Jack as her attention returned to Cole's distorted opinions. "What if I was married to him? What would you have done then, Monsieur? Were you just going to sail back into Dawson and tell Jack Scroggins to hit the road? Did you really think you had that kind of power over my life?" Her rage expanded as her words gushed from her mouth. "You were only right about one thing, Monsieur. I never thought I'd be grateful that I lost our baby, but thank God there no longer is a child to be considered." She yanked her coat on over her shoulders, adding through gritted teeth, "I can't believe what you did, Cole, and right now, I don't think I can ever forgive you either."

Cole stared at her, wordlessly, as she turned and stalked out the door of his cabin. Her words still hung heavy in the air. Cole grasped for the meaning in what she had just said. A numbing sensation kept him rooted to the spot for several minutes. What had she meant when she said she had lost their baby? Cole clenched his fists at his sides. A raging fire swept through him, leaving his entire body fevered and his heart tinged with regret. He had known—had always known—that she had been pregnant when he left her at Fort Yukon. But now he also understood why she had seemed so empty and sorrowful when he had encountered her in St. Michael. How much had she suffered when she'd lost their baby, he wondered as a ragged pain shot through his chest. And what did she mean when she had mentioned the man she was supposed to marry? She said she'd be better off in a pine box . . . better off dead? Rage entangled with Cole's sorrow. Did Jack Scroggins have something to do with Dominique losing the child? he wondered. He had to know—and he had to somehow convince her to forgive him.

Cole grabbed his boots and tugged them on his feet. From the coat rack, he retrieved his coat and hat. He didn't take the time to put them on as he ran out of his cabin and down to the lower deck. His frantic gaze scanned the plank that led to the wharf. His crew was busy unloading the cargo from The Freedom Ship. Dominique was nowhere in sight.

Thirty

Dominique had no destination in mind when she ran away from Cole. The tears she had managed to control while she was with him were now running in torrid streams down her face. How could she have been foolish enough to stay with him in St. Michael? She had known then he was capable of deserting her. That alone should have been enough to keep her from falling prey to his silver tongue again. But, it was more than just his lying words that entrapped her. A rush of self-condemnation overwhelmed Dominique. She was truly her mother's progeny, she told herself. Why else would she rush back into Cole's arms—and his bed—so easily?

At the end of Dawson's long main street Dominique paused to catch her breath. She stared down the muddy street, now laden with patches of dirty snow. Wind whipped trash down the boardwalks. People hurried along the boards and logs with their heads covered and bent to protect themselves from the icy wind and the light snow that was falling. A sense of doom settled down around Dominique. She wondered if she was here to stay for good. Maybe she'd never escape from this horrible place again. She glanced back over her shoulder toward The Freedom Ship. Cole was not following her. Why did she hope so badly that he would be?

"Forget him," she cried to herself. She turned back toward Dawson. Where would she go? What would she do? She was in the same shape as she had been the first time she had stood at the end of this street; no money, no home, no Cole, no hope. And, she thought ironically, she might be pregnant again too. Everything might be exactly the same. A strange sense of déja vù passed through her. A sharp pain ripped through her abdomen to remind her of all that she had suffered. Panic made her start to run again. There was only one place she could go, she realized as she headed toward the back street.

The cribs of Paradise Alley seemed bleaker than Dominique remembered. Not even the cleansing white snow that was beginning to blanket the murky street and the roofs of the shanties could give this area a fresh appearance. Ignoring everything around her, Dominique rushed straight to the shack where she had first seen her mother with the miner. She didn't hesitate to bang loudly on the door with her closed fist. Inside, she heard noises—

obvious noises of a bed creaking and a man's aggravated grunt. Then footsteps padded across the room, and the door opened barely more than a crack. A strange woman with tousled red hair and flushed cheeks peered out at her.

A startled gasp rattled through Dominique. She quickly regained her composure once the shock of finding another woman here began to fade away. "I'm looking for Brigitte Laval. She used to live here."

The woman shrugged. "I think she's moved up in the world." She cast a discriminating glance up and down Dominique. A dark frown settled on her face. "I've gotta get back to business," she said briskly as she started to shut the door in Dominique's face.

"Wait—please," Dominique gasped as she grabbed for the door. "She's my mother, and I need to find her." She noticed the woman's expression soften as she stared at Dominique for a moment longer.

"I heard she was livin' at the Can Can," the woman said. She shoved the door shut in spite of the pressure of Dominique's hand.

"Merci," Dominique said, although the woman couldn't hear her. She stared at the closed door for only an instant as she digested the woman's words. The Can Can? She remembered seeing that dancehall on Dawson's main street. It was one of the new buildings that had been built during the short summer months, and one of many new saloons which now dominated the main street. Turning quickly, Dominique hurried back the way she had just come. The snow was not growing any heavier, but the cold wind made her shiver until she thought she would freeze to the spot.

As she headed toward the Can Can, Dominique tried to keep her thoughts clear of Cole Hawkins. This was not possible. She told herself she needed to concentrate on a way to forget about him, and she tried to accept the fact that she was going to be stuck here in Dawson for the entire winter. This thought caused her to shiver in a way that was even more chilling than the feel of the wind. Cole's image kept taunting her every time she tried to think of her other problems. She alternated between bouts of panic at the idea of suddenly running into him here on the street, and the strangling fear that she would never see him again.

Dominique wondered if he would just say "Ah, hell!" and sail away from Dawson City and never look back again. She halted and looked up and down the street again. Disappointment flooded through her, then anger intruded on her insistent longings for Cole. She should hate him, she reminded herself. She should—but she didn't.

Instead, she began to wonder if there was some basis to his irrational way of thinking. She recalled the story he had told her about Susanah Rowland, and the way the woman had affected his life. Maybe, Dominique told herself, he wasn't being entirely selfish when he had deserted her. Perhaps—in his distorted way of thinking about women—he really had believed that he was doing right by her. For an instant, she paused at the entrance of the Can Can. She glanced back down toward the wharf. Through the lightly falling snow she could see the distant outline of The Freedom Ship. Had she been unfair in judging him? She reminded herself again of how he had deserted her in spite of his certainty that she was carrying his baby. She turned abruptly and pushed open the saloon door. If Cole expected her to forgive him for that one, he would have to come on bended knee to ask for her forgiveness.

The interior of the Can Can was a complete contrast to the gloomy street outside. Bright lights glistened from crystal chandeliers, music at a fast tempo blared from a player piano, and even at this late afternoon hour, the place was filled with patrons. The stormy weather had brought many miners into town for the winter months, and most of these men had ample money to spend after their hard work in the gold mines during the Yukon summer. In awe, Dominique glanced around the large dancehall. She never would have imagined such an elegant establishment here in Dawson City. No wonder the woman who lived in her mother's old shanty had said that Brigitte had 'moved up in the world.' The Can Can was definitely an improvement over Paradise Alley.

As Dominique stumbled over to the bar, she drew little attention from the men in the saloon. Her wet hair was plastered against her head, her manly clothes dripped with melting snow, and her eyes were red-rimmed from crying. At the bar, she waved to catch the attention of a short, round-faced bartender. He sauntered over to her with a smirk on his face.

"Looking for a job?" he asked. His gaze scanned her in one quick swipe. "You'd better head on over to the cribs on the back street."

Dominique's anger flared. She drew herself up and stared directly into the man's leering face. "I'm here to see Brigitte Laval, and if I was looking for a job, this is the last place I'd look."

A more predominant smirk curved the bartender's lips. He raised his hand and pointed to something above Dominique's head. She turned to look. At the top of the stairs ran a balcony that housed several small rooms. Heavy red velvet curtains hung at the sides of each room for times when privacy was needed. But each of the rooms were fronted by railings so that its occupants could observe the activity in the main room below, too. Dominique remembered hearing about these 'gold king's boxes,' but she had never seen them before. In these boxes the heroes of the Klondike goldrush would entertain women with caviar and expensive champagne. Men who were known throughout the Yukon Territory—the ones who were written up in all the newspapers down in the States—were the proud occupants of the gold king boxes. These men had names like Big Alex, Swiftwater Bill, and Antone Stander; all millionaires several times over, they were the men who earned a box at the top of the stairs. Gold seekers who had not yet achieved this honor would look up at the reigning kings, and dream of the day when their gold mines would yield such immense wealth. Most of them would never earn this privilege.

In awe, Dominique stared up at the velvet lined boxes. At this early hour, several of the small rooms were still vacant. But the second one from the end had a dark haired woman whom Dominique recognized immediately as her mother. Dominique stepped forward. Her neck craned back so that she could watch her mother in action. Wearing a beautiful emerald green gown that to Dominique's amazement was almost decent. Brigitte was lifting a long-stemmed glass up into the air. A brilliant smile curved her red lips as she leaned toward the man she was toasting. Dominique's gaze moved with the glass, then settled on the face of the man.

A strangled cry hung up in Dominique's dry throat. The man—though wearing clean clothes, and with his brown beard cropped close to his face—was unmistakably Jack Scroggins! For a minute, Dominique could not look away. It didn't matter to her that his appearance was slightly more dignified, or that he occupied a king's box, which meant he was now one of the richest men in the Yukon Territory. He was still Jack Scroggins, and he was with her mother!

Twirling around, Dominique wasted no time in making for the door. The fear that either Jack or her mother would glance down and see her here in the Can Can ruled her rapid retreat. Once she was away from here—from them—she would figure out what she was going to do next.

As she charged out into the street, however, fate intervened again. The air was knocked out of Dominique's lungs when she collided full force with a man who was running towards the door from the opposite side. The man fell back when she struck him, but it wasn't until she saw him toppling off the edge of the boardwalk that she realized who he was. She saw his entire body—head and all—plop into the thick mud that was not yet frozen by the early snowfall.

"Cole!" she gasped when she was finally able to catch her breath. She leaned over the edge of the boardwalk as he slowly began to emerge from the mud. He looked like a black monster rising up from the bowels of hell, Dominique's shocked mind thought.

Gagging and coughing, Cole sat up and shook his head. Mud flew from him like roostertails. Instinctively, Dominique threw her hands over her eyes to shield them from the flying chunks of gooey murk. When she lowered her hands, she saw the whites of his wide eyes staring out at her through the mask of mud. Before she had time to think about how silly he looked sitting down there in the mud, he began to talk rapidly.

"I love you, woman!" he spat out from between lips dripping with mud. "I was wrong, and I'm sorry, and I'm gonna make it up to you somehow. And there ain't gonna be no more running away—by neither of us!" He gave his head a definite toss. Mud was sent into the air from the strands of his hair.

With a gaping mouth, Dominique stared down at him. He wasn't begging for her forgiveness on bended knee, but she figured this would have to do. She reached out and extended her hand. Without hesitation, his muddy hand gripped hers. She pulled on him, the mud sucked him back. Dominique felt herself tumbling forward. She screamed, but her voice was quickly swallowed up by the sound of the mud splashing around her head. Sputtering and spitting out mouthfuls of mud, she felt herself being pulled back up. For a moment after she was back on her feet, she was still too stunned to think straight. She felt fingertips gently wiping the mud away from her eyes. Through a muddy haze, she saw Cole's face.

"Are you hurt?" he asked. She shook her head. "Are you still mad?" he asked. She nodded vigorously. "But will you ever find it in your heart to forgive me?" His voice was almost pleading—and if it weren't for the taunting smile his muddy lips wore, Dominique would have hesitated to answer him. Instead, she shrugged her mud-laden shoulders and gave her head another quick nod. Cole's smile widened. His white teeth stood out starkly against his mud-caked face.

"Let's get the hell outta here before we get snowed in for the whole winter," he said as he reached out and scooped her up in his arms. It took all his efforts to pull his feet from the deep mud, especially with the added weight of Dominique in his arms. But he wasn't going to chance letting her get away from him again. As he sloshed along the boardwalk and down to the wharf, he wasn't aware of the odd sight they created, or of the thick trail of mud they left along the wharf. His only thought was to get away from Dawson City forever—and to spend forever with Dominique. When he stomped past Luther, Cole issued orders for them to set sail. He saw the stunned expression on Luther's face. Luther didn't utter a word, however. He just smiled and shook his head.

Once they were standing at the bow, Cole placed Dominique down on the deck. Covered in the Yukon mud, Cole thought she was just about the funniest looking sight he had ever seen. When she started to laugh though, he realized he must look pretty darn funny himself. His ears relished the sound of her laughter, and for an instant, he thought of kissing her. Her mud-drenched lips did not appear to be so inviting though.

"We'd best get ourselves cleaned up," Cole said when their laughter finally began to fade.

Dominique nodded her head in agreement. The sound of the horn that signaled that The Freedom Ship was about to pull out of the harbor rang out. She turned back toward Dawson City for one last time. "And we'd best have that talk, too," she said as she turned back to Cole. "That one about our future together." There was no longer any humor in her voice.

Cole drew in a deep sigh. He picked up her muddy hand, and looked into her eyes. "I won't promise you the type of home where folks come for dinner after church on Sunday." He glanced down at the deck, then added as he gazed into her eyes again. "This ship might be the only home I can provide for the time being. And when we're ready to settle down and raise a family, our home might end up being a shanty on some beach in the South Pacific or along the Caribbean." He clutched her hand tighter, wishing he could see her expression more clearly through the mud on her face. "But I can give you one of the things you want, Dominique. I can make you respectable, and I want us to be together forever." He fell down on one knee. His head tilted back so he could look up at her as he asked, "Will you marry me, Mademoiselle Laval?"

His tender words, and unexpected actions, left Dominique speechless for a moment. She stared down at his dirty face, while her love for him sent her senses reeling. If she accepted his proposal, she would have to forego her dream of living in a house like the ones she had always pictured. But he was offering her respectability, and he was offering himself to her forever . . . and forever was all she had ever really wanted from him. A smile claimed her lips. "Yes, Monsieur, I will marry you."

The Freedom Ship began to pull out of the Yukon Harbor as Cole rose up to his feet again. Mud or not, he knew he had to seal their impending marriage with a kiss. Off in the distance, a pink sunset began to break through the clouds. Clear sailing awaited them on the horizon.